Emily Beyda

The Body Double

Emily Beyda is a Los Angeles native who for the past three years has written the popular "Dear Glutton" advice column in *The Austin Chronicle*. A graduate of Texas State's MFA program, she currently resides back in Los Angeles. *The Body Double* is her first novel.

www.emilybeyda.com

The Body Double

THE BODY DOUBLE

Emily Beyda

ANCHOR BOOKS

A DIVISION OF PENGUIN RANDOM HOUSE LLC

NEW YORK

FIRST ANCHOR BOOKS EDITION, JUNE 2021

Copyright © 2020 by Emily Beyda

All rights reserved. Published in the United States by Anchor Books,
a division of Penguin Random House LLC, New York, and distributed in Canada
by Penguin Random House Canada Limited, Toronto. Originally published
in hardcover by Doubleday, a division of Penguin Random
House LLC, New York, in 2020.

Anchor Books and colophon are registered
trademarks of Penguin Random House LLC.

The Library of Congress has cataloged the Doubleday edition as follows:
Name: Beyda, Emily, author.
Title: The body double / Emily Beyda.
Description: First edition. | New York : Doubleday, 2020.
Identifiers: LCCN 2019948730
Subjects: LCSH: False personation—Fiction. | Motion picture
actors and actresses—Fiction. | Hollywood (Los Angeles, Calif.)—Fiction. |
GSAFD: Suspense fiction. | Thrillers (Fiction). | Thriller fiction. |
Psychological fiction. | Noir fiction. | Fiction.
Classification: LCC PS3602.E92 B63 2020 | DDC 813/.6—dc23
LC record available at https://lccn.loc.gov/2019948730

Anchor Books Trade Paperback ISBN: 978-1-9848-9743-5
eBook ISBN: 978-0-385-54528-0

Book design by Anna B. Knighton

www.anchorbooks.com

Printed in the United States of America
10 9 8 7 6 5 4 3 2 1

To my family. Who else?

The Body Double

1

*S*omeone speaks my name.

"Yes," I say, "right."

My hand, I notice, has stuck to the counter, where there is a slick of spilled soda, dark-colored, diet, I'm guessing—that's all anyone orders here. A large popcorn, sour gummy worms from the case under the counter, diet soda. The sodas are all off-brand. Mr. Pibb and Mello Yello. Big Fizz, Dr. Smooth. Moon Mist. The man in front of me has just ordered something, but I'm too tired to remember what it was. Everything swims fuzzy in the fluorescent lights of the lobby. Behind the man's head, I can see the faded velour nap of the curtains that hang on either side of the doorway, framing his face. At the painting class I'm taking at the community college, the instructor shows us how the old masters drape velvet and silk behind the profiles of their subjects, that noble swish of fabric a signifier of something my brain grasps toward but won't let me remember through the thick scum of no sleep and caffeine, sugar and sugar substitutes. My hands shake. I spit sweet.

We're on the third film of our triple feature, it's something close to three a.m., and still thinking about those sallow-eyed women whose images the teacher projected on the wall of the classroom—nameless, immortal, gazing past us into eternity—I feel my body pivot, working without me, so used to the motions after all these years of taking candy from the dusty case, scooping popcorn into the narrow mouth of the waxed paper bag, filling a big gulp with soda. I had thought, when I started this job, years ago now, that it would be a chance to be closer in some way to the world on the theater's screens, that smooth-surfaced place where everything is beautiful and poreless and clean. But it's stickier than I thought it would be. Messy. Even the cash my manager, Scott, pays me is soft and gritty from overuse, the pressure of too many hands. "Seven fifty," I say, and he, small, smooth-haired, limp-eyed, reaching forward to take his change back, brushes his fingers over my prone palm in a way that feels intentional. Too close. His sweat presses into my skin. I can feel it burrowing down through the lines of my palm, horrible. "Enjoy the show," I say. I smile wide. Even my teeth feel tired. I wipe my hand, once, twice, on the slick polyester of my uniform pants. The man disappears into the theater. Outside, I can sense the summer air pressing against the thin glass of the doors, straining to get in, the pressure around us immense, like water at the bottom of the ocean. I wipe down the counter. I wipe down the case with the candy in it. I think again of the girl in the painting, the weight of her averted gaze, that long-ago light, so thick and heavy around her that it almost seems damp.

The sun is starting to rise when the last customer leaves. Normally we lock up the theater together, Scott and I, standing in gathering warmth, the cracked asphalt cold under our feet. Across the street the windows of the shuttered pet store shine like soap bubbles on dirty water. I like to look at them, waiting for him, noticing the way the sun shifts pink across their surface. This morning I will not have the chance.

"Wait," says Scott as I start moving toward the door. "One second. I need to talk to you about something. There's someone who wants to speak with you before you go home. He's up in my office. Come on, it won't take long."

I'm tired. Too tired for whatever this is. I feel like something has crawled inside of me and died. Even now the light has begun worming its way in through the narrow window in the finished basement where I sleep. Between coming home and waking up I have, if I'm lucky, a good hour of solid semidarkness before the sunlight becomes impossible to escape, and now Scott has robbed me of even that. I consider my options. I could push past him and leave. Scott is a small guy, always wearing the same shirt, always trying to start conversations with the customers about obscure French films nobody has cared about for at least fifty years. Part of me feels sorry for him. Sorry enough to smile at him when I arrive at the theater, to put up with the ten minutes of requisite chat when he hands over my pay for the week, under the table, in cash. Neither of us wants anyone asking questions. In a way, we understand each other. Not sorry enough to want to listen to him talk, though, definitely not sorry enough to let him take me out for after-work drinks, even though he asks almost every week. Not sorry enough for whatever this is.

"Now?" I say. "You couldn't have mentioned this earlier?"

I feel a tingle of annoyance pass through me, and something deeper under that. The nauseating stirrings of alarm. *I trust Scott*, I tell myself. I should trust Scott. I've worked here for so long. There have been so many late nights, the two of us alone. I should trust him. I trust him, I do. But I don't want to go up to his office, that small space, impossible to escape without fighting. I'm afraid of what might be waiting for me there. He reaches past me to lock the door. I stand still, trying to ignore the nausea, the bright flash of fear that surges through me and wakes me up. Anyway, it's too late to object now. I tell myself to trust Scott. That everything will be fine. I stand with my hands in the pockets of my sweat shirt and look past him, trying to peer through the mirrored glass to the world beyond the theater. But he pulls down the security gate, blocking the light, and all I can see is my reflection, hunched and fragile, my face obscured by the shadow of my hood. My body looks abandoned. Like an empty pile of clothes.

"Okay," I say, "but I can't stay long. They're expecting me at home."

We both know this isn't true. He nods.

"Come on," says Scott. "Let's go."

The room Scott calls his office is the projection booth, hidden up a narrow staircase at the back of the theater. Its walls are painted a dirty shade of Pepto-Bismol pink, plastered with faded posters of the films Scott wishes he could run. The air is dense with the human smell of a small and constantly occupied space: dirty socks, fast food, something heavy and yeasty and alive, cut through with the sour tang of old weed. The lights are off, all except a gooseneck desk lamp, its shade turned up toward the low ceiling to cast a pale beam of light, throwing dramatic shadows across the room. Someone has been working hard to create an atmosphere. And it almost works. The dingy corners of the room are hidden, the grease smears on the walls obscured by darkness, the posters' tattered edges smoothed out by shadows, the bright walls dimmed to a pale pink. And there is a man sitting at Scott's desk. He is turned away from us, his back straight. If he has heard the door open, noticed us come into the room, he gives no sign.

"This is Max," Scott says.

I can feel Scott blocking the doorway behind me, shifting from foot to foot. Nervous.

"Hello," I say to Max.

His back seems to stiffen when he hears my voice. He must be holding himself incredibly tightly to silence the squeaky springs of that old chair. A sympathetic muscle twinge passes through my shoulders. He doesn't say anything back. There's a moment where he seems to be steeling himself, gathering his nerve, and then he turns, and for one instant I see his face light up with surprise. Joy. It is as though he recognizes me. Just as quickly as it came, the expression disappears. He carefully arranges his face into something critical, appraising. I can feel the weight of his gaze, considering me carefully. The way it moves up and down the lines of my body. What is it that he's looking for? I consider him from the corner of my eye, pretending to look at the posters, the old projector, anything else.

My eyes linger on a vintage lobby card for *Last Year at Marienbad* that Scott had scoured the internet for obsessively, a year before, when he briefly got ambitious and decided to put on a monthly classic cinema series. Nobody came. He gave up after two or three films, his enthusiasm lapsing, as his enthusiasms often did, leaving behind nothing more substantial than a few pieces of battered and expensive trash. The whole room is a shrine to his failures, the overpriced posters, the unnecessary equipment. There was a part of me that had wondered from the beginning where he got all the money from. But a bigger part of me knows better than to ask.

How does this stranger know Scott? Scott's friends are all old like he is, sagging quietly into middle age. This straight-backed stranger is young and handsome in an almost clinical way—his perfect suit, his hair combed flat, not a line out of place. It matters a great deal to him that he looks like he knows what he's doing. He is no friend of Scott's. Still, he says nothing. I look to Scott, but he avoids my eyes. I gather my courage and look down at the stranger instead, finally making eye contact, staring right into his face. In the half dark, the shapes his bones make under his skin are thrown into relief, forming something sharp and hard and real, the face of an animal, rather than a man. He is too still, too quiet. None of this is right. Slowly I start to edge away from him toward the door.

Behind me, I hear Scott clear his throat. His voice is anxious, eager to please. "Max came all the way from Los Angeles to see you," he says. "Tell her. She's perfect, isn't she? Just like I said."

Los Angeles. So far from here. I picture palm trees bobbing their shaggy cartoon heads, the beach. Some spark of curiosity starts to make itself known, a dull itch in the middle of my brain slowly throbbing itself into life, and I think of the way his face lit up when I first walked in, of the old movies I used to watch with my grandmother, before, where mousy brown-haired girls like me were swept off the streets of sad small towns like this one. Maybe it's real. Maybe I'm being discovered. Maybe this is how it happens—a stage name, a new life, an open door. An escape from all this. I'm perfect, Scott says. I've never been called perfect before.

But the stranger still doesn't speak. He looks over me, away from me, his eyes carefully scanning my face. I wait for him to say something, to tell me Scott's right, I am perfect. I'm the perfect girl he's been looking for.

"She's close," he says. "Not bad."

At last he smiles, a sharp-edged little thing that flits across his face as fast as that joy did, gone. *My name in lights*, I think. As if. Ridiculous.

"High praise," I say. "And close to what?"

I am trying not to sound upset. *Not bad* is nowhere close to perfect. I should have known that I was wrong, that this was just another one of Scott's stupid schemes. I should never have come up here. I'm tired. I want to go home. Neither of the men answers my question.

"I'm off the clock," I say. "Can I leave now?"

"No," says Scott, cajoling, "wait. Just a few minutes. Come on, we have . . . he has a proposition for you. Can you listen? I'll pay you overtime—just hear him out."

He moves closer to me, tries to grab my arm. I wrench it from his grasp. I hate it when he touches me. I hate it when anyone does. The stranger keeps still, smiling, and it all clicks into place. Not a star, not escape. Nothing like that. Scott has offered me up to this man, this stranger. A proposition. So this is how he has been getting all that money. I notice my body has shifted again, hands clenched into fists, one foot back in case I have to run. My body is taking precautions. This thought comforts me. I don't feel sorry for Scott anymore.

"A proposition?" I say. "So you're some kind of procurer now? I'm not a whore. I don't have to listen to this."

But part of me wants to. He's never offered me overtime before. This must be important. I must be worth something. *How much?* I think. I try to push the thought away, to tell myself I'm better than that, but I can feel it there, pressing, urgent, just below the surface. I think of all the things I could do with just a little money. The changes I could make. The bigger apartment, another semester of classes at the community college. Blackout curtains. A real bed frame.

"Come on," says Scott, pulling out a chair for me. He is working hard to make his voice sound gentle, or as close to gentleness as he can manage. "You know it's not like that. Don't you trust me? Will you sit? Sit."

If this is about money, fine. Money is something I understand. Maybe if it's enough money, I can allow myself to say yes. Nobody could blame me, if it was enough money. How much would it take for me to buy a plane ticket? To leave town? To put down a deposit on an apartment, somewhere far away from here? Five hundred dollars? A thousand? I feel my heartbeat slow. I sit. I'm closer to the man's eye level now, and his cold gaze settles onto mine. I flinch but don't look away. If I have something he wants, fine. He has something I want, too. I am looking at him just as he is looking at me, considering his face, his straight nose, sharp bones, cold green eyes. He frowns at my not flinching and then issues a little smile—another one, private, just for me. The two of us are conspirators. Together against Scott. Still, Scott is the one to speak.

"Max is looking for someone like you," he says. "Someone who looks like you, anyway. A few weeks ago, I was up late and I came across a post he had written. Or, I'm sorry, did you write it?"

Max still looks amused. He finally shifts forward in his chair, whose springs creak like screaming. I watch the tension leave his shoulders and shift through his body, moving somewhere hidden, lower down. He keeps looking straight into my eyes, not blinking. Like a crocodile. There is none of the nervousness of one person considering the presence and power of another. He looks at me the way you might look at a painting, dispassionately, appraisingly, your mind somewhere far away. Considering me for whatever it is my body has to offer.

"I fail to see how that information would be relevant," he says.

His voice is quieter than I expect, and I have to lean in close to hear, the arm of my chair pressing sharp against the soft side of my stomach. He smells warm and expensive, like soap and cigars, buttery shoe leather. For all this time, his eyes have stayed locked on mine, mine on his, a mysterious energy flowing between us. The men I know wear crumpled jeans, shirts stained with sweat under the armpits. Max is so careful, so purposefully dressed. *He really is handsome,* I think. There is something compelling about him, something fond and strange. And then finally Max's eyes snap away from mine. Part of me is relieved to have that pressure gone. But it is as though a light has gone out.

"Ah yes," says Scott, trying to sound nice. For a moment, I had forgotten he was still here. That it wasn't just the two of us, together alone in the world. "Of course," he says, "I don't want to pry."

Max sighs. He looks at me again. *We understand each other,* his look says. He seems almost apologetic for Scott, like he's being indiscreet. We would never act that way. We know things Scott never could. It almost makes me feel resentful, how he is acting as though he is letting me in on a secret without telling me a thing.

"It's not an issue of prying," he says, his voice measured and tight. "This is a complex and difficult situation. The people I work for, naturally, value discretion. I will give you the information I am able to give you. Nothing more. But nothing less than that, either, I promise. I'm not an unreasonable man. I understand that this is a sensitive situation for you as well."

"Well, I don't understand," I say. "I don't understand at all. Can one of you please tell me what's going on? If this is a porn thing, I'm leaving."

I think again of the money. I am no longer sure that this is true.

"No, no," says Scott. "No, nothing like that. Max is a sort of headhunter. People come to him with impossible positions they need filled, and he travels the country looking for candidates. He posts about it, does demographic research, all kinds of stuff. Finding the right people for difficult-to-staff positions. And he has a job for you."

A job. Again that quick fluttering, hope. A dangerous feeling. I push it down.

"I already have a job," I say. "I work here. I don't need another job."

"Yes," says Max gently, reaching forward to take my hands in his. I want to wriggle away from him, but his palms are soft, his grasp gentle. I find that I don't mind it as much as I normally would. "You do have a job. But this is something much more important. This is a calling."

His eyes are locked on mine again, liquid with sincerity. *A calling*, I think. *Religious*. Okay. Not porn.

He turns to Scott, smiling. "Scott," he says, "I'm afraid I'll have to ask you to step out. What we have to discuss is extremely sensitive. I'm sure you understand."

"Of course," says Scott, but he looks annoyed.

I can sense him in my peripheral vision, trying to catch my eye, get me back on his side, but I won't look away from Max. This is between us now. It's been between us all along. The thin door shuts with a quiet click. We sit together in the dark for a moment, listening to the silence as Scott stands outside, waiting to see if we'll start talking, and then, after a few beats, to the clap of his descending footsteps. We smile at each other. I imagine Scott pacing in the lobby, back and forth before the dimmed lights of the candy display, wondering what is happening above his head. Max seems to be waiting for something else. Another sign. I want to reassure him, but I don't know what he needs me to say. He folds and unfolds his hands. Are they shaking slightly, as mine are, or is it just a trick of the low light? He looks once, twice, at the door. He leans back in the chair. He looks away. He begins.

"Do you know of a woman named Rosanna Feld?"

His voice has a forced lightness. He has folded his hands back together and seems to be fighting to keep himself from fidgeting. His energy has shifted palpably, the tension returned to his frame. There is a new slipperiness to the way he sits, as though if I say the wrong thing he will leap up out of his chair and flee. For some reason, this question is more important than he can say. I wait to see if he will keep talking. He doesn't. He seems to be holding his breath.

"Yes," I say carefully. "I think so."

I remember her face on the shiny plastic display panels of the makeup section of the drugstore near our school, where I would go, cutting class, to wander up and down the aisles until the coast was clear and I could hide out back home. I remember her slick wide lips, her head tossed back in a perpetual silent laugh, her eyes too wide, too many rows of thick black fur-like lashes, the eyes themselves hidden and dimmed. I remember sliding a tube of the mascara she advertised out of the narrow slot where it waited, the next tube clicking into place, the slippery feeling of the plastic, tender against tender skin when I slipped it into my sleeve, the ache of acquisition. But what she was famous for, what she has become since, I am unable to guess. I know her only for that one frozen image of her face. I hope that this will be enough. Max is still waiting for me to speak.

"There was a time in my life when she was very important to me," I say.

I have said the right thing. Max's face smooths out. He sits still. He unclasps his tightly clenched hands.

"Good," he says quietly, almost to himself.

"So is that what this is about? Does she need an assistant or something?"

Not as good as a star, but still something. I can do that. I can be useful. I can assist.

"No," Max says. "It's a little more complex than that."

The mysterious weakness that was there before has fallen away. Somehow, I have given him whatever it was he wanted.

He pulls out a stack of papers from a briefcase that I hadn't noticed hidden beneath the desk. "Before we discuss the job, I need you to sign this," he says. "Don't worry, it's nothing serious. It just says that you can't disclose anything we say in this meeting. That everything I'm about to tell you stays between us."

This seems reasonable. I sign.

"Rosanna," Max says, "is looking for a double."

Rosanna leads a busy life, Max says. She does not want to do everything herself. She wants me to do some of the things she has to do for her. To take her place. He is businesslike as he ticks through a list of obligations, perks.

"We will lend you Rosanna's likeness," he says. "You're already close—the closest we've seen yet. We have been looking for some time. Ever since . . . well, we don't like to talk about it, we managed to keep it from the press, but you've already signed the NDA, so I'll tell you. If you mention this to anyone else, there will be severe consequences. For Rosanna. For me. Possibly for you as well."

"Don't worry," I say, "I won't tell anyone."

I notice that my voice is softer, lower than it was when I was speaking to Scott. I want to reassure this man. I want to make him like me. He rewards me with a beat of eye contact, a tight little smile. I have the strange urge to reach across the desk and squeeze his hand like he squeezed mine earlier, reassuring me. I want to touch him. To tell him everything will be all right.

"Besides," I say, "this is all so strange that no one would believe me anyway."

This gets another smile, a longer one. "You're right," he says. "They wouldn't."

"So why now?" I ask. "What's changed?"

He sighs, finally looks away. "This is the part you really can't tell anyone."

"Of course not," I say. "You can trust me. I promise."

"I know I can," he says, as if to himself. "I know."

He takes a deep breath. He begins.

"A while ago, Rosanna had a nervous breakdown. And everything changed. She's too sensitive, too fragile to live the kind of life she used to live. She has always had a hard time with some of the small demands of her life in Los Angeles. Social engagements, work—it's all hard for her. But now it has become impossible. She's afraid to even leave the house. And her brand is suffering: she's losing endorsement deals; the sales are dropping on her makeup line, her athletic gear. It's hard to sell an aspirational lifestyle when you're not being photographed, giving interviews, keeping your name in people's thoughts. I've waited, we've all waited, for her to recover. But she can't. Not without the help of someone like you. She needs someone to pick up the slack, to take care of the things she can't, make sure the money keeps coming in until she's back on her feet and out in the world again. And it's you. She needs you. You have Rosanna's face. The face Rosanna needs."

His voice goes thin here, so fragile it seems as though it will break. I don't know what to say, so I say nothing.

Max looks back to me again, his face wide open and vulnerable, eyes locked on mine. "Please say you'll help her," he says. "Please."

What else is there for me to do? To stay here, living in the buttermilk-smelling basement of my former foster mother's ranch house, paying her in cash, watching her get more and more annoyed with every day that passes? To keep working this pointless job, getting older and older and sadder and sadder until I transform into a female Scott? To keep visiting my mother's grave, spending every night at work or alone? When Max is holding a whole new world in front of my eyes, a world where I will be indispensable, valued. No, there is nothing for me here.

I nod. "Of course I will," I say.

A flash of relief, and then a protective shell seems to click over that vulnerable face. Max nods once, suddenly all business.

"Okay," he says. "Good. This is what I need you to do."

Max will get someone to pack up my things, drop them off at the Goodwill. I will tell my former foster mother that I am moving out, give her the cash Max will give me to cover my rent through the end of the month. She will not be sorry to see me go. I will take a leave of absence from the community college. I will claim a family emergency, a sick aunt. No one will care enough to check. After a while, they will forget that I was ever there at all.

"People drop out of college all the time," says Max. "And you're only taking one class this semester anyway. If you want to keep painting, learning about art, we can get you supplies in Los Angeles. A private tutor. Whatever you need."

I do not ask how he knows which classes I'm taking. I find it reassuring that he knows all this about me, that he has done his research. He knows who I am. And he wants me anyway.

"That won't be necessary," I say.

I want him to think me easy, amenable. He has showed me a

glimpse of a bright light, opened an aperture into the stifling confinement of my small life. I want to take his hand and let him lead me into the shining unknown.

Max will take me with him to Los Angeles, give me an apartment, pay my rent. The first year, they will pay me a hundred thousand dollars. The next year, if I do well, more. More and more in the years after that.

"And how much will Scott get," I ask, "as a finder's fee?"

A small smile cracks Max's face. "Five thousand."

I feel a smug little jolt of power. *We'll see who's smart,* I think. *We'll see who's in charge now.* "Can you make it ten?" I say. I gesture at the walls. "He could probably use a few more posters."

"For you," says Max, "anything."

The first contract will be for three years, extendable upon the agreement of both parties. They can fire me if they need to, but I cannot break the contract before then. The money will be collected in a Swiss account under a limited liability company Max has set up for me under a false name. Tax-free. Compound interest. I will have no expenses during my time on the job. They will provide me with food, housing, any little thing I want. I will be taken care of, cosseted like a privileged child. The money will be ready for me when I leave. When I leave, they will provide me with a visa to any country in the world, anywhere I want to go. Anywhere but here.

"You could buy an apartment in Paris!" Max says. "Look out your window at the Eiffel Tower. Or Florence, a villa outside the city where you'll eat pasta and spend your afternoons drawing under the olive trees. Think of it, the European countryside! A new life, totally on your own terms."

When my time as Rosanna ends, I will be asked to change my appearance to the point that I do not resemble her. She will own my old face as well as her own. My appearance will become her legal property. I will agree never to speak to anyone from my old life again, never to get back in touch with my distant family. I will let the few acquaintances I have here lapse.

Max must have seen me hesitate. "Will that be a problem?" he asks.

I think of my grandmother, long dead, of the scattering of cousins killed overseas or floated away to other lives in other towns, people I haven't seen in years. Of the friends I never had.

"No," I say. "I guess not."

I will never again return to this place. I will never again be called by my old name. In Los Angeles, I will be Rosanna. And when I leave, I can be anyone I want. I can pick a new name, a name without a past. Any name but my own.

Max puts the contract on the desk, turns back to the page with an empty space on it, waiting for my name. He comes around the desk, sits close beside me. I can feel the light pressure of his knee on my knee, his arm brushing mine. The warmth of him. I am surprised again that his touch does not disgust me, that I do not want to move away. He lets his hand linger as he gives me the pen, heavy and black and rimmed around the cap with gold. A beautiful object. Mine, if I want it. Max would give me anything I asked for now.

"Take all the time you need," he says. "But don't disappoint me. You know you are the only one who can do this. Rosanna needs you. I need you. Please."

I take the pen. I close my eyes. I think of my life here, of the dirty carpet in the basement, the hours of bad television, my stupid job. I think of my few almost friends, of the silent scraps of my family that remain out there somewhere, far from me. I picture myself three years from now, once all this is over, sipping champagne on a terrace somewhere, a sketchbook on my lap. A mysterious woman. A woman with a past. I slide the contract toward me. I look at Max. Max looks at me. I sign.

2

The plane is small, and I am the only one in it. They have taken away my phone, so I cannot tell how much time is passing. No one talks to me during the flight. I sit. I try to read the stack of gossip magazines someone has left tucked into the seat in front of me, all of them featuring articles about Rosanna, but the words swim. I drink the sweet champagne they bring me in tiny plastic cups, ignore the food. My old life already seems so far away. Last night I was sitting on the carpet of the empty basement, listening to my former foster mother watching TV upstairs, drinking the last of the beer from the mini fridge, thinking about calling someone, anyone really. Not telling them I was leaving, just grabbing drinks, being outside somewhere, with the people I cared about, secretly saying goodbye. But there was no one I wanted to call. I sat there and listened to the mutter of the television. I closed my eyes. I imagined my new life. *Soon,* I thought, *I will be on the other side of that screen.* And now I am here. I have never drunk champagne before. I have never been on a plane. I try to picture how the basement, the house, the theater, my whole town would look from up here. A fading speck of dirty earth. Nothing more significant than that.

I try to identify when we leave one state, enter another, where the borders are, the lines that separate one place from the next. But it is impossible to tell. Outside is mostly cloud anyway, a blank white screen I cannot see through, even when I strain my eyes trying to distinguish the vague shapes of the country passing below. I try to guess when we are over Arizona, where my father is presumably still in prison. It was a life sentence, but who knows? We haven't spoken in years. Now we will never speak again. I wonder if I will miss him. If I will regret this. *No*, I tell myself, *I won't*. Outside the window, the landscape slides by fast. I picture the shadow of the plane passing over it, darkening the mountains beneath, sliding over the land like some enormous deep-sea fish, leaving a rippling wake of light behind.

Los Angeles sneaks up on you. One minute you're above the vast splendid deserts of the south, and everything is gaping canyons, red earth, pink light, the landscape glowing as the plane passes silent overhead. Then dust seems to creep up over the mountains, turning them slowly gray. Everything flattens out. Becomes monotonous. Before you have time to prepare yourself for it, the city is below you, surrounding you, all you can see, endless miles of industrial sprawl, low buildings faded to the same undifferentiated shade of dirty white by decades of year-round sunshine, stretching out pure and uninterrupted to the horizon, skirting the broken-glass glimmer of the sea.

We land with a bump, the plane bouncing off the tarmac with a buoyancy that seems unnatural. I breathe into my abdomen, pushing away the familiar tightenings of an oncoming panic attack. *In, out,* counting the beats; *in, out, in again*. The plane comes to a standstill. *Breathe in*. Outside, the white concrete of the runway shimmers and twists in the dirty heat. *Breathe out*. Try not to feel the tightness of the walls around me, as plush as a coffin, slick and white. *In*. A black car, doors opening. *Out*. Max climbs from the back seat. I watch the way the wind gets its fingers in his hair, tugging at his coat, making the loose legs of his black suit rustle. Something about the shadow of him, dark against the bright bright of concrete and sun, makes my heart turn over in my throat. *I do not know this man,* I think. I do not know this man. *In,* I tell myself, *out. Breathe.*

The stewardess sticks her head around the room divider. "You're wanted outside," she says.

I make my way into the wind, waving from the steps of the plane like I'm someone important, a celebrity, a president's wife, like this is fun. I force myself to smile. Max squints up at me through the fading sunlight, his expression not changing, tense. Disappointed, I think. He is disappointed in me already, and we haven't even started yet.

"I'm here!" I say, falsely cheerful. "I made it."

I make my way down the steps to the idling car, my small bag slung heavy over my shoulder. *Now,* I think, *now he will break the awkward silence.* He will tell me he's glad I'm here, introduce me to the rest of our team. He will take my bag. His face will light up again, with that same excited softness from the theater, that same look of knowing, the two of us together working as one. This time I will understand what he means when he looks at me that way. But instead he nods, tight, swiveling his eyes around as if he is afraid, embarrassed to be seen with me, my rumpled shirt, my stretched-out jeans, his gaze sliding toward the sky, where clouds skitter like frightened sheep. A sign of rain, I would have said, in other places. I should have put on makeup. I should have done something about my hair. I shift my bag from one shoulder to another. Max waves me into the car.

"You did," he says. An afterthought: "Thank you. I'm glad."

The apartment they have found for me is far from the airport. As we drive the freeway rises and dips like a wave, so I can see the whole city spread out stucco-pale at my feet, interrupted here and there by startling rows of palm trees, their shredded leaves like the heads of strange creatures peeking over the rooftops. I feel so lonely I can barely breathe. I don't know what I had expected. Perhaps that Max would greet me at the airport with flowers and a team of personal assistants, everyone telling me how happy they were to see me, that

I had made the right choice, that I was exactly what Rosanna had been looking for. Perfect? I thought I would be special here, that Max at least would look at me and seem pleased. Now he sits with the driver in the front seat, far from me, silent. The radio is tuned to a classical station, and underneath everything there is a mutter of brass on brass, the discordant clash of horns like a storm. Inside me everything aches and pulls, my heart beating fast. I try to slow my breathing, close my eyes, but the effort just makes me feel sick. *I will not let myself regret this*, I think. *I won't.*

Arriving at the curb, Max thanks the driver with the same impersonal tone he used to thank me. He gets out before I do, leaving me alone to unbuckle myself and look up at the dirty cream facade of my new home. Out my window, across the street, lies the blurred twilight sprawl of the city beneath.

It's an old, Moorish-looking apartment building, like a prison out of the Arabian Nights, stucco scrolls and ornamental black iron balconies twisting from its blank face, narrow panels of stained glass blinking in the twilight like half-closed eyes. There is a turret studded with iron-barred windows, black mold growing thick and crusty across its surface. At the back, I swear I glimpse the edge of a golden dome, but for all its grandeur, it's small, maybe six to eight units, cowering between the neighboring mansions like a chastened pet. I thought that Rosanna would have picked something cleaner for me, newer—simple Scandinavian modernism, maybe, or a farmhouse-style loft. But maybe she is past the point of worrying about these things. Maybe someone else is already making these small choices for her, like I will soon.

Inside, the hallways are narrow and dim, green vines cloaking the windows, white walls, wood floors as dark and still as a frozen lake. As we pass the doorways, I listen to see if I can hear any sign of life from my new neighbors—music, maybe, or the smell of someone making dinner. But there is nothing but the sound of Max's shoes rhythmically clipping their way up the staircase behind me, echoing in the empty hallway.

I am surprised to find that the apartment itself is almost as cramped as my place back home, just one high-ceilinged room and a kitchenette, a door off to one side that Max points at, saying it leads to a closet and a bathroom. The furniture is heavy and expensive looking, but old, probably family heirlooms, or things Rosanna bought and no longer has an interest in. I feel a flash of disappointment pass through me, as quick and hot as shame. This must be her version of a storage locker, my borrowed body another thing too expensive to get rid of, too inconvenient to keep close. Every surface is coated with a sticky layer of dust that smears unpleasantly when I set down my bag. There is a futon, a coffee table, a small empty bookshelf, a single chair. This is not my new glamorous life, not the clean place behind the cameras that I dreamed of back home.

Out the kitchen window I discover a small overgrown courtyard, the wide leaves of birds-of-paradise, ornamental palm, reaching like pleading hands toward the pink sky. The fountain in the middle murmurs slowly, the surface of the water skimmed with green, a suggestion of mysterious movement beneath. The wind, perhaps, or fish, submerged and swimming, their fins flicking silent in the dark water. Out the front window lies the city, the rooftops of bigger houses, terra-cotta, gleaming bloody in the setting sun. The hillside is studded with them, houses from every architectural tradition: modernist boxes, French country houses with white shutters, Italian villas, a castle. So many dream houses, so many dreams. On the windowsill, there is a single footprint in bright white paint, left by somebody's cat. I run my fingers over it, hoping to feel the distinguishing bump of paw pad, to make some slight intimate contact, but the paint is old, the surface long since smoothed over, the cat presumably dead.

Behind me, I can hear Max puttering around, unpacking my bag, rearranging my things. I can see his reflection in the dark mirror of the glass, as dim and patient as a ghost. *I do not know this man,* I think, and yet here he is, pawing through my underpants as though there is no such thing as privacy. As though everything I own belongs to him. As though I belong to him, too.

"Right," he finally says, his voice clipped, professional. "You won't be needing any of this."

It's not until I see him shoving all my clothes back into the bag and taking it to the door, where he dumps it unceremoniously, that I understand what he means.

"But those are all my things," I say, "my clothes. I need them. Why did you have me bring them if I couldn't keep them? What am I supposed to wear?"

The injustice of this infuriates me. I am here on his summons. All this was his idea. I have left so much behind already, but the thought of losing this last small part of home—the smell of those clothes, of my laundry detergent, air freshener, movie theater popcorn, gas station incense—makes me want to cry. Max seems to sense this. I don't understand how, quite. I am good at hiding my feelings. I always have been. But he softens, coming to stand close beside me, the two of us aligned, looking out the window together toward those distant houses over the garden wall, one of them Rosanna's, I imagine, listening to the quiet murmur of the fountain below.

"We needed you to bring a bag, something. It looks strange getting on a plane without a bag. But you won't need any of your own clothes here. We'll be getting you a new wardrobe. Something more appropriate to your new position."

"I understand that," I say, trying to keep the frustration out of my voice, to remember that Max is above me, works more directly for my employer. "But why not tell me? I spent so much time packing, picking out the clothes I thought I might need. The ones I thought Rosanna would like."

"I'm glad you've prepared," he says. "I'm glad you're taking this seriously. But don't worry about your clothes. You won't need them anymore. You'll wear Rosanna's. She has so many. We picked out one of her favorite at-home outfits for you to wear tonight, and I'll be bringing more by soon."

He says this as if it's a kindness. He really thinks he's being nice to me. Homesickness claws at my throat. I think of my thrift-store clothing, the jeans I'm wearing, my shirt, oversize and gradient blue, showing the three zones of the ocean—sunlight, twilight, midnight. I used to be interested in the ocean. I used to be interested in a lot of things. And the contents of that small bag: an unread copy of *Tess of the D'Urbervilles*, a battered map of the stars. My one good dress, which is too short, probably, white lace. It almost looks like silk. I look nice in it. People have told me I look nice.

"Still," I say, "I can wear them around the apartment. Just privately. I can keep a few things of my own. For when I'm not working, I mean."

Max looks out the window, seeming to consider a house on the other side of the canyon. Is that where Rosanna lives? Is she there now, perched in a window, looking back at us? I hug my arms close. Night is falling. Soon everything around us will be dark, and from her house on the hillside Rosanna will be able to look right into my brightly lit bedroom window. I wonder if that's why Max wants me to change. So that she will like what she sees.

"I don't think that would be wise," Max says gently. "I hoped that I had conveyed this to you when we discussed the job, but this isn't regular work. You can't just clock in and out. If we're going to succeed, you'll have to learn to think like Rosanna even when you're not in public, not working. You'll have to internalize the way she thinks. And she would never wear any of your old clothes."

I am wounded at this, but he's right. I think again of the worn-out contents of my bag. Everything I own used to belong to someone else. How is this any different?

"Besides, it will make Rosanna so happy," he says. "She loves her clothes so much. It's a sad thing for her, being hidden away, unable to wear them in the world. She has such a wonderful style. Isn't it our responsibility, your responsibility, to honor that?"

"Even here?" I ask.

"Even here. It will be good to practice. We want them to feel as natural to you as your old clothes do. They belong to you now, too. I'll tell her how nice you look in them. And you will look nice, I know."

I think of Rosanna, wherever she is, wearing the same outfit day after day, too tired and confused to bother to change. Won't she like thinking of me in all her nice things, old things, carrying her memories around in my pockets? Won't she like picturing me the way she used to be, well-dressed, carefree, a citizen of a better world? That is, after all, why I'm here. To become the woman she used to be. Max is right. I owe her this much. A new life is beginning. A new life with new clothes.

"Okay," I say. "I'll wear them. I understand."

"Good. Here, a welcome gift." He leans over. There is a box beside the futon. He takes something out of it, clothes, folded, a gray cropped sweat shirt with matching pants. They are heavy in my arms, with none of the sheen of synthetic fibers. These are expensive clothes. These are mine. I try to feel pleased that he has brought me such nice things to wear. But they're not really mine, whatever he says. They belong to Rosanna. I can smell her on them, a faint whiff of expensive floral perfume. I feel a quick flash of disgust. I thought that in my new life I would never have to wear another person's clothes again. *But it's all part of the job*, I tell myself. Just a few years of this, and then I'll buy hundred-dollar dresses and wear them once. I'll throw whole closets away.

"Put them on," Max says, gesturing toward the closed bathroom door.

I do. My body feels numb, like I am wearing an extra layer of skin. I can barely feel the clothes, the way the fabric hangs heavy soft against my flesh. Max smiles when I leave the bathroom and try to hand him my old clothes, bunched into a messy pile, but he lifts his hands up in a gesture of renunciation and won't take them from me.

"Throw them away," he says. "I need to know that this is your choice. That you are deciding to be here. Committing to the project of Rosanna. Turning your back on that old self."

"Okay," I say. "I am. I will."

I am not exactly sure that this is true, but I know that I want him to think it is. Whatever parts of myself I keep are none of his business. I think of my squalid old life, of the money. This is worth it. It has to be. I take my old clothes and stuff them down into the bottom of the kitchen trash can, shoving them in deep so I won't be tempted to dig them back up and put them on. I tell myself they are no longer mine. They have nothing to do with me anymore.

"Thank you," says Max. "Well done." A pause. "You look nice," he says. "I knew you'd look nice in her clothes."

There are more things in the box. A pile of magazines with articles about Rosanna in them, which someone has helpfully bookmarked for me. The same ones from the plane, plus a few more, all of them back issues, months or years old, Rosanna's archive. At the bottom, there is a thick stack of flash cards covered in dense, sloping handwriting, full of the details of Rosanna's life—her friends, her acquaintances, her likes and dislikes. I flip through the deck, catching quick snatches of text: *rosemary*, one card reads; *Shalimar*, another.

"You'll need to memorize these," says Max. "I want you to know everything about her. Not know, even—more intuit. Feel. Everything that belonged to her is yours now. I want you to take all this inside you and make it your own. So that it seems natural. So no one will be able to tell but me. And Rosanna, of course. She'll know."

I am good at memorization, at pretending. This will not be a problem. I nod. Rosanna's clothes weigh heavy on my skin, sweet with perfume, a slight crushed cumin ghost of someone else's sweat. Max has taken my clothes, my books, my old life. Soon I will become another person. The person who wears these clothes. For now I want to hold something back, keep something for myself, a privacy that Max can't penetrate. I keep turning through the deck, pretending studiousness. The Rosanna I knew wore long silk dresses. She was everybody's girlfriend, stylish, carefree. There is some of that reflected here. But there are unexpected discoveries, too. A picture of the goldfish she keeps on her bedside table, his name on the back—Ron. *Little Women*, written on a card that asks about favorite childhood books, a book I'd loved back when my father was around to read it to me, before. Rosanna is closer to me than I thought. And I am closer to her. I can feel Max's hesitation. He's waiting for some signal from me, some sign to tell him that I'm ready, that I understand what he needs me to do. I do understand. I *am* ready. But I will not give him what he wants. Not this one small last thing. Finally he makes a noise, a little sound in the back of his throat like a hum. I want to turn to look at him. I don't. I turn over another card.

"See that?" he says.

His voice has changed. It's tender now. Cajoling. He is pretending to notice something in the garden outside, trying to draw my attention back to him. He must sense me moving away, escaping inside to some place beyond his reach. Despite myself, I look, following the line of his finger toward empty green, nothing. Then all of a sudden I see it. A flash of bright movement somewhere deep in the dense green tangle of leaves.

"Parrots," says Max. "There are flocks of them here in the hills. Their owners die or get sick of them or are careless and let them escape. Eventually they find each other. This courtyard is one of the places they like to nest. That's one of the reasons I . . . we . . . Rosanna and I chose this apartment. We wanted to give you something to look at during the long days of work to come."

I move back just a little, so I am standing closer to him, the edges of our bodies almost touching. Almost, but not quite. I can feel the prickle of electricity coming off his arm. I want very badly to reach toward him, to bring him closer to my own body. I am awash in a strangely powerful lonesomeness that makes me want to gather him up in my arms and hold on for ballast as I'm sucked away into this new life. Finally I speak, the words strange in my throat, my voice like my voice after I wake up from a long nap, disoriented in the afternoon sunlight, and after a long day of not speaking to anyone, answer the ringing phone.

"How can they survive out here alone?" I say. "Doesn't it get too cold for them? Where do they go when it rains?"

"They have one another," says Max.

He responds to my movement with his own, lifting his arm, running his fingers lightly above my back, rippling through the empty air, thrumming an alien sensation between pleasure and alarm into life somewhere deep inside.

"And it never rains in Los Angeles."

I know this can't be true. It rains everywhere. But right now, with Max beside me, and the purple sky, the fountain, the scent in the warm air of jasmine and orange, something bitter and rotten and sweet, I want so badly to believe him. On a branch in the courtyard, a lone bird fluffs its wings. And then as we stand there, watching, the air is full of fluttering. A cloud of birds circle and land, their wings flashing bright in the bushes, all colors, the air full of their sounds, until just as suddenly it isn't, and all that's left is their bodies deep in the branches, a quiet cooing click as they settle in for the night, shifting their tiny feet, gripping and ungripping their tiny claws. They are utterly foreign to this place. They are completely at home. Max stands close beside me. We watch the birds settle, the sun disappear behind the high rim of the golden dome. Night falls slowly over the courtyard. Together we watch the world outside go dark.

3

*H*ow long has Max been looking for me?

In the dark that first night, he holds me close like I am something precious. And then he's gone, out the door with barely a word, off on some mysterious errand. One day passes, another, and still he doesn't come back. I wait and wait and wait in the small room for three days, four—four mornings lying in bed staring at the ceiling; four sunsets watching the parrots, dumb creatures freer than I am, circle and scream; four days reading magazines and reviewing flash cards until my brain aches with trivial information, convinced that at any moment the car will pull up in front of the house and Max will emerge. But moment after moment passes and still he does not come. As I wait, I wonder. How long has he been looking? And why, now that I am finally here, is he making me wait?

I picture Max in the days before I came, traveling the country alone. I picture him at commuter airports and highway rest stops, sitting in pocket libraries and at small-town halls of records under the suspicious gaze of semiretired librarians. Was the post Scott had seen the only one or just one of many, replies pouring in, blurry footage, my image, the images of the others, captured by security cameras, scanned off old IDs, by Scott himself or men just like him, immortalizing the way we scowled down at the counter, our phony end-of-the-week smiles when they paid us, pretending not to notice when they let their hands linger over ours for too long, when they took a cut off the top. Taxes. I picture Max scouring yearbooks and school newspapers and microfiche, looking for someone who looks like me. Or like Rosanna. I have to remember that it is her face that has brought me here, not my own. There are others. Max had said so. How many other girls were there like me, a little less perfect, a little less right, but close, not as close, not the closest he had seen, but almost, almost good enough? How many girls are there waiting in the wings to replace me when inevitably they find out that I cannot be the person they want? I picture the other girls, girls in the thousands, a staggering number of girls, infinite copies of my own face, her face, apartment buildings full of them, streets, an army of girls, all of them almost Rosanna. There is no power in these numbers. I will be safe for as long as Max needs me. But how long will he need me for? Maybe that's why Max is staying away for so long. Maybe the other girls are here, too, in other apartments tucked throughout the hills. Maybe he is waiting for me to prove somehow that I belong.

At first being alone is nice. I try to settle into the emptiness of the room, the quiet apartment, having time to nap, to sit down, to do whatever it is I want to do. I cook elaborate dinners from the fully stocked fridge, take baths, take naps, lie on the couch all day reading the stacks of magazines. Boredom is an extravagance I have never before experienced, such a long stretch of time with nothing to worry about, no obligations to fulfill. But as the long empty days pile up, it becomes harder to relax. I become more and more nervous, thinking about Max, where he is now, about the invisible talents of all the other girls hidden away somewhere. Rosanna, the Rosanna I read about, is the ultimate performer, rifling through a jukebox of prepared anecdotes, relatable, charming. I am nothing like her. Her words fall heavy from my mouth as I repeat them, sounding totally phony, wrong, like a robot reading Shakespeare. I pinch the layer of fat on my stomach between two fingers, run my hands down my thighs until the skin goes taut and I can see the cellulite beneath. On the third day I stop cooking dinner. On the fourth I stop consuming anything but coffee and raw vegetables. I tell myself it is greedy to give my body more calories than it needs to survive. When I think of the perfect vision of Rosanna in the magazines, a horrible chill creeps over me, a nausea that seems to rise up from the very bottom of my soul. And I know there is no way I can pull this off.

On the fourth day, restless, I finally gather enough courage to take a walk. I know that Max could still come back at any moment, that the neighborhood outside is still as forbidding and unfamiliar as it always was, but surely a quick stroll up and down the hill, just once, won't hurt. The small room is becoming cramped with my smells, a staleness that I can guess at, rather than sense. All morning I have sat by the window with the sun on my face and practiced with the flash cards Max left. I know them all, or at least I am close. I can match the pictures of the executives, makeup artists, friends, to each of their names and the snippets of stories Rosanna likes to tell about them. I can see an icy blonde and think Marie, Rosanna's oldest friend, who grew up alongside her attending the best all-girls schools and commiserating about their equally famous and emotionally neglectful parents, sitting on the back patio of Les Deux drinking French 75s, the night she almost got arrested for letting a vial of cocaine drop from the front pocket of her Dior saddlebag in front of three mounted police on Melrose. I'll see a handsome man with a blunt-edged face and think Leo, remember contract negotiations, a long awkward lunch where we ate oysters and he was overly pushy about picking up the check, that lingering hug. I can picture Ron swimming in his tank, the bright flash of fins. I know it all by now. When Max comes back, *if* he comes back, I will show him how hard I am working, how I am piecing all the fragments he has left me into a mosaic, a fractured image of the woman I am here to impersonate. He will see how hard I've been working, how seriously I'm taking this job. Surely my hard work has earned me a little time outside?

I press the cards into a neat stack. I stand up. *Just ten minutes*, I think. For ten minutes, I will walk up the hill, let the sun shine warm on my upturned face. I scrawl "Out for a walk" on the back of a magazine subscription postcard. Just for fun, I try to match my handwriting to Rosanna's neatly sloping letters. I'm good at forging signatures—my mother's, my doctors', my teachers'. And now Rosanna's. It's not perfect, but it's close, sharing that same slanted narrowness, the letters leaning forward as if they're pushing against a strong wind. I prop the card up on the table where Max can't miss it. I'm feeling better now, full of the energy that comes with making a choice, and part of me almost hopes that Max comes while I'm gone so he can wait for me like I've waited for him. So I can give him a small taste of how terrible waiting feels.

I wish I had something to cover myself up with, sunglasses, at least, or a scarf I could wrap around my snarled hair. Max hasn't left me a hairbrush, and there's only so much damage control finger combing can do. But there is nothing I can use here, no way of concealing my face. I decide that's okay. There isn't any great mystery about a woman who maybe, if you squint hard, looks a little like another, famous woman, going for an afternoon walk in her slightly grimy designer sweats. I reach the door, put my hand on the knob, and remember that I have no shoes. Disappointment breaks inside me like an egg, and I try to reassure myself. Okay, no shoes. So I won't walk. Just take one of my magazines down to the courtyard, sit on the fountain and watch the birds. Isn't that why they picked this place? So I could have some slight distraction? I will go down into the courtyard and sit in the shadows of a bushy palm and watch the parrots return from their excursions into the surrounding hills. I reach out for the knob again and turn. But it doesn't move. My hand rotates around it, sliding over the cold slickness of the metal, the knob itself remaining maddeningly still. Locked. The door is locked.

A rush of nauseated fear and fury climbs up hot into my throat, pressing close into my lungs, choking me, filling my mouth with bitter spit. I close my eyes, breathe deep. I carefully search for some mechanism to open the door. I unslide the sliding bolt, click the knob back and forth in my hands, telling myself I will not panic, I will not allow myself that luxury, but my heart is speeding up and my breathing is shallow in the top of my chest. I am trapped here. Caged. I think of earthquakes, of fires, of Max forgetting to come back. The drop from the window is long, the building surrounded, moatlike, by a thick gravel belt. How could he do this to me? How could he leave me alone for so long? I picture the damage a fall could do to my body, my face, of movies where prisoners tie sheets together and clamber down vine-covered walls like the walls outside, running like I will run into the hills. But this isn't a movie. Someone will see the sheet rope, call the cops. The door, when I come back, will lock me out instead of in. If I leave that way, I will not be able to return. If I want to come back, there is no way out but the door. And the door is locked.

I pinch my eyes closed, force myself to breathe. One breath. Another. There has to be a rational explanation for all this, for why Max is staying away so long, for why the door is locked. I think of the money. How much must I have earned already? What's four days' worth of a hundred thousand dollars? A little more confinement is a small price to pay for absolute freedom in three years. More money, more freedom than I've ever had before. I just have to put up with a few more days in this room, making more money every day, getting paid to do nothing more than lounge around in my pajamas and read magazines, and then Max will come back. He has to. Then I will go out into the world, start living again, enacting Rosanna's life.

I make myself stop trying to force open the door. Soon the trying will turn to screaming and pounding and I will become my mother, just another crazy woman confronted by a locked door. I tell myself the door is locked because there is nowhere I need to go. I tell myself this is a good thing. I do not need the distraction of the outside world. I don't know how to approach it yet as Rosanna would, what she would look like going on a walk, how she would greet her neighbors. Surely that's why Max doesn't want me to leave. I am learning. I am here to learn. I open the window and lean my head out into the sunshine, force myself to take deep breaths. I tell myself that this is enough.

Max comes by with his arms full of garment bags. It has been almost a week since I saw him. I am not exactly sure how long. That was the first thing to go once I realized the door was locked. My solid sense of time collapsed, the days slipping over one another like waves, each becoming the next becoming the next, an endless liquid spill of hours. And now it's over. He's here. Sitting at the window with a stack of magazines, I see the car pull up to the curb, the door open. Max clambers out, lifting bag after bag from the trunk, artless, cumbersome. Anger passes through me, quick and electric, at the sight of him moving with such unconscious freedom through the open air. Does he have any idea what I've been through? Sitting here waiting for him, all alone? But I think of the other girls. I think of the money. I breathe. I stand up fast, dizzy from not eating, snatch my note off the table where it has been sitting for days and stick it into the gap between the wall and futon. How long has it been since I showered? I am suddenly aware of how I must smell, how the soft, heavy fabric of my sweat suit clings to my unshaven legs, how my hair is hopelessly tangled with dirt and sweat. There's no time to fix any of it. A key turns in the lock, and I hop back into the space in front of the window, where I pick up the magazine I was reading, trying to look focused, trying to look relaxed. Like I'm working so hard that I didn't even notice time passing while he was gone.

"Oh, hello, Max," I say as the door opens. "How nice of you to stop by!"

I try to keep my voice casual, soft, but it comes out sounding more sarcastic than I intended it to, and he smiles at me, a tight little thing. I wonder if he has just come from Rosanna's house. Did Rosanna ask about me? What did she say? I wonder if now, as Max looks at me, he is comparing my body to hers. I feel the softness of my upper arms and belly, the sweat smell of my clothes, the million invisible ways in which I am doomed to fail. I want to show Max all the things I have done, how hard I've been working without him, but he doesn't ask. Unceremoniously he drops the bags he is carrying onto the futon.

"A few things from Rosanna," he says.

"And how is she?" I ask.

"Well," says Max, "she's perfectly fine."

This can't be true. If it were, I wouldn't be here. But at least it means there's nothing wrong. She's approved of me. She has given Max her clothes. I am the best of all her identical girls.

Max zips open the bags, takes out water-loose swaths of heavy-looking fabrics in dark colors—olive, navy, maroon—plain shades and stripes. He moves with compact efficiency, not looking at me, not talking, body anxious and stiff. The air in the room changes, becomes heavy with her smell. It's warm, like Max's smell is warm, tuberose and musk and amber, the dank undertone of sweat, something intimate and human, evoking a body, a faint note of cigarettes. Does Rosanna smoke? I want to ask Max, but the way he is moving with such minute concentration—straightening each sleeve, brushing the wrinkles from the skirts, pulling on fabric until everything falls straight on the hanger—precludes conversation. I think of my best dress, how proud I was of it. It's embarrassing to remember it now, looking at all these fine things. I picture it, the dirty lace, the cheap sheen of the plastic fabric, the imprecise stitching at the hemline and neck. How could I ever have thought it was beautiful?

When all of Rosanna's clothes are on the rack, Max stands still in front of it, one hand on the sleeve of a long black coat I recognize from Rosanna's cover of *Vanity Fair*, where she wore it tied loose over black lace underpants, a leather bustier, her eyes heavy on the camera, as if she was making an accusation.

"Max," I say finally, "what do you want me to try on first?"

For a fraction of a second, he looks at me like he has no idea who I am, his eyes unfocused and wild, but the moment passes quickly and he smiles at me again, that same tight, professional smile. I wonder if I'm imagining things.

"Why don't you pick?" he says, his voice even. "I'm interested in seeing where your sartorial instincts lead, now that you've had a few days with the magazines."

I leaf through the rack and pick out a long white silk dress. I hold it up to my body. I recognize it from a red-carpet shoot Rosanna did with the blond woman from the flash cards, Marie, the two of them in coordinated shades of white, each a perfect mirror of the other, beautiful, elegant, impossibly slender. I could only dream of ever looking like that. But the fabric slips smooth and cold over the bare skin of my arms, and for a moment I believe I deserve to wear it. It is the loveliest thing I've ever seen.

"How about this?" I ask. "Fancy, right?"

I can't help but notice that Max still isn't looking at me, not really. Maybe there's another girl he liked better. Maybe it makes him angry to have to consider my less-than-perfect face. But Rosanna has chosen me. There's nothing he can do about it now.

"No," says Max. "Not that one. Although I admire your ambition. Let's start slow."

He takes a short striped dress from the rack, draping the shoulders over my shoulders, laying the arms flat along my arms. With the back of his hand, he smooths the fabric down into place so it clings tight to my body, his hand circling my waist. He still won't look me in the eyes.

"Try this on," he says, and turns away to give me some small measure of privacy.

The room is small. It has always been small, growing smaller over the past few days (weeks?) of loneliness, when it was just me, pacing back and forth across the worn beige pile of the carpet, waiting for something, anything, to happen. But I have never felt the smallness the way I feel it now. Max is so close that if I move my arms the wrong way, taking off my dress, I will touch him. Can he see the shape of my body, warped, wavering, reflected in the green glass of the window? I wonder if he will see me, dimly mirrored. I wonder what he will think when he does. But I don't want to go to the bathroom to change. This is my space now. I have the power here, not Max. Rosanna has chosen me, and even if he doesn't approve, he has to adjust. From now on, we will work together. I close my eyes. I take off my sweat suit, place it folded on the couch. The air of the room is cold on my bare skin. The air of the room is full of her. I pull her dress down over my eyes, the fabric falling heavy on my skin. Her smell, too, clings to me. I am almost afraid to breathe, like I will breathe it in and waste it, another small part of her gone, but I also want to breathe and breathe and breathe, swallow up as much of her as I can, so that her smell becomes my smell, her body mine. So Max will look at me again and know that she has made the right choice.

"Okay," I say, "I'm ready."

Max turns around. His gaze sifts over my body. I can see him noticing my hairy legs, the cracked nail polish on my toes, the line of the dress, how it hangs slightly crooked, too tight, uneven at my knees. How all of me, every inch, is wrong. He looks at me like he hates me. Like this is somehow my fault, when he's the one who picked the dress, brought the clothes. When he's the one who brought me here. If I'm not good enough, it's his mistake, not mine.

"Take it off," he says. An afterthought. "Please."

"But I—"

"Please take off her dress."

"But don't you—"

"Take it off, take it off *now*."

His voice stays low, tight, controlled, as clenched as his clenched fists. I keep my gaze locked on his, pull the dress up over my head, hand it to him. *If this is how you want it,* I think, *fine.* But he doesn't blink, doesn't even look down toward my body. I am nothing to him, not even a body, less than that. He snatches the dress from my hands. He unclenches his hands. He strokes the fabric slowly, smoothing out the wrinkles he has made.

"Shit," he says under his breath.

I stand with him in silence, so close I can smell the expensively medicinal scent of his cologne, bergamot and clove, the damp wool of his suit. It must be a cold day. I lift my hand and hold it just above the center of his back, an inch from his body, the same way he, his movements slowing and then coming to a stop, is holding his hand over Rosanna's dress. We stand there together for a long time, his cold scent in the air mingling with her warmth, the cold air of the room raising goose bumps on my bare skin.

Finally he turns.

"I have to go," he says. "I'm sorry. I made a mistake. I need to go back to the house for a while, to get the right clothes for you. Get dressed, I'll be back soon."

He's going back to argue with her, I'm sure of it. He's going to tell her how wrong I looked, wearing her clothes, how I am clumsy and filthy and hopelessly not right. I want to speak, but I can't make the words break through the hard knot of shame blocking my throat. Max slides past me, eyes down, apologetic, without another word. Outside, I can hear the wild parrots cackling, a noise like pinched laughter. I can feel my heart beat, slow and heavy, in the center of my chest. The door shuts with a terse finality. The click of a lock sliding into place.

I push down the quick rush of panic. I tell myself that this time it's different. That he's just going to her house, she lives right by me. Soon he'll be back with more clothes, a stern admonition not to undercut her authority. I tell myself I'm glad to be alone again. Or not alone—with Rosanna. I will practice even more, try even harder to prove myself worthy of her. When Max returns, he will see that she was right all along.

I stand close to Rosanna's clothes, running my fingers up and down the length of the fabrics, lifting them in my hands. They feel heavy and smooth, expensive. They have the substantial realness of real things, living things. I am almost afraid to touch them. I pick out a silk tunic whose light gray fabric slips through my fingers like water, leather leggings, a pair of leopard-print booties with red soles. I try not to think about how much each piece must have cost. Rosanna doesn't have to think about things like that. If I'm going to act like her, I have to learn to think like her. To forget how expensive her world is.

I try it now, imagining. I picture the Rosanna in the magazines, the casualness of her, the carefree grace. I want to dress like that.

I put the first clothes I picked to one side; they're too much, I'm trying too hard. Instead, I pick out dark-washed blue jeans, a white T-shirt, a heavy knit gray sweater, ballet flats, all thick and supple with the fineness of well-made objects. These are my clothes. I bought them with my own money. Money means nothing to me. I can do whatever I please with them. They are mine. They belong to me. Anything I want, I can own. Anything I look at, I can possess. I have nothing to worry about. Worry is a concept I do not understand. These are my things. These are the things I deserve. I can do whatever I want with them. I can do whatever I want.

Naked, I rifle through the bag of shapewear that hangs at the end of the rack, picking out a pair of control-top tights, an elastic corset, a push-up bra. I have hated my body for years. I know what to do. I slide the tights on over my thighs, wiggling when they stick, until they cover my body as tightly as a second skin. I suck in my gut, clip on the corset, push myself over the padding of the bra. When I put on the shirt, it floats over my newly defined waist, skimming against my skin at the nipples and hips like a bird landing on the surface of still water. In the tiny bathroom I stand close to the mirror, breathing through my nose so I won't fog it up. Up close, my face is an alien planet, the texture of my skin uneven, pitted like rained-on soil.

I will do better. I say it out loud to myself in the mirror. "You can do better," I say. "You will."

The girl in the mirror smiles back.

Max has left me with a case full of expensive cosmetics, the kind of stuff I used to wish I looked classy enough to be able to steal, all of it beautifully packaged and deeply pigmented and sweet smelling, baby powder, floral. Only rich women can afford to surround themselves with these powerful emblems of innocence. But when I start opening the packaging, I realize that every item bears the marks of Rosanna's use. I wonder why they haven't bought me all-new versions of the products she uses. Doesn't she have her own beauty line? Couldn't she afford to get me my own new kit, instead of sending me these castoffs? This decision smacks of Max's ignorance, I decide. Probably she gave him all her makeup, things she used to wear every day but is now too depressed to take out of the drawer, so he could go out and buy all-new versions. Clearly he misunderstood, thought she was giving them to me, like a mother giving her daughter the worn-down nubs of her old lipsticks to play dress up with. I tell myself this is an opportunity to learn even more about her. Little things, things Max wouldn't understand are worth knowing. Like how Rosanna is one of those women who press into the pigment from the top down, pushing hard into their pursed lips so that each stick ends up flat, a gesture that speaks to both nervousness and a kind of compensatory overconfidence. I picture her pulling a tube out of her purse, swiping it on with practiced insouciance. She is the kind of woman who puts on lipstick without a mirror. You can tell by looking at her, by the sharp, precise angles of her mouth in the photographs, by the way she laughs toward the camera, showing her lipstick-free teeth. I turn away and swipe the lipstick on, letting my wrist settle into the unfamiliar motion. It feels okay. But when I turn to look it's all wrong, crooked, and so I turn my back and try again, again, until I can do it in a moment and look over my shoulder at my perfect mouth, smiling Rosanna's smile, her mouth floating strange in the middle of my face.

I close my eyes and picture Rosanna, how it would look if she were looking back at me from that small dark mirror. I see the sharp tilt of her cheekbones, the tweezed neat perfection of her brows, her large eyes, fringed with dense, feathery eyelashes. I see the clean sheen of her skin, as milky and opaque as the flawless belly of a fish. I open my eyes and see my own face, red around the nose and at the corners of the eyes, pockmarked with acne scars. I look nervous, flawed, pinched. I look nothing like Rosanna. I will fix it. I can fix it. It's okay.

I close my eyes again and picture her moving toward me out of the darkness, close, close enough that I can see every detail of her, intimate, immense. Working quickly, remembering slicking quick layers of paint onto the porous surface of my sketchbook back home, the thirsty paper sucking up the color's shine, I smooth a layer of foundation on, the pockmarks on my cheeks and chin disappearing under a supple slick of liquid flesh. I watch myself disappear, becoming flat and smooth and bland. In the mirror my face floats, as pale and round as the moon. I draw on cheekbones, add a slight cleft to my chin, deepen my Cupid's bow. The lines make my face look like a skull, and I can feel the fragility of my own skeleton, the closeness of bones beneath my skin. I blend the sharp lines in with my fingers, softening them to shadow, faking real structure beneath real skin.

Night has fallen long ago. Outside the narrow bathroom window, I can see a sliver of purple sky. I step back from the mirror and turn off the light. I disappear. Rosanna's face swims into focus, like a deep-sea fish emerging from dark water. I can finally see what Max saw at the beginning. What Rosanna understands. Our correspondence. The way her face is hidden beneath my own, like an ancient fresco waiting to be dug up from the ash. I put my hands up to my face, her face, close enough that I can feel the warmth of my skin, the hair tickling my fingertips. I do not touch the surface, afraid it will smear. It is the strangest feeling. Part of me is terrified. I want to wipe my new face off, to leave the room, the apartment, all this, to take my old self back. I can be gone before Max returns, disappearing into this vast city, making a life of my own. I can still leave. I don't have to let myself disappear. Looking at Rosanna's face in the mirror, I know all this, and yet . . . and yet it is wonderful, too.

4

*E*very day is the same day. Every day I go deeper.

In childhood, my body had been a shelter, protecting the small sliver of my selfhood as the world around it shifted and shifted again, my mother and then my grandmother gone, my father disappeared. My little bit of self stayed safe, buried down deep where no one could touch it, as tender and thin-shelled as a quail egg. And then I was a teenager, and my body stopped protecting me. And now I am here, and it no longer belongs to me at all.

Things start disappearing. The name of my first grade teacher, the face of my best friend when I was small, what the lobby of the movie theater smelled like. The kind of messy little fragments of memory you don't even know you possess until you reach for one and find it missing. One morning I wake up and find that for a brief and panicked instant, I can't remember my own name. When it returns, it's with a flinch, a small violence, so separate and painful from my life in this room that I almost feel as though I do not want it back. Outside, the parrots shift in the branches of the trees, murmuring their morning song to one another, preparing to venture out into the world. Listening to them leaving has become painful, a reminder of the freedom I no longer have.

Still, the idea of encountering the outside world makes me more and more anxious. All those strangers, all that jostling and disruption and noise. I could stay here for a little longer, tucked inside my tiny room. Safe between these four walls, safe in the endless stretch of days and nights and days again, each day the same day as the day before it, time passing quick like a string of pearls sliding through limp fingers. It must be a month since I got here, more. I try to imagine how much money I've made so far, how much closer I am, even now, to my new self. My old life seems to recede further and further from me, a small island disappearing over the horizon.

I sit on the futon the way Rosanna sits, mouthing the words she says along with her. I wear her sweaters, her underwear. I draw her lipstick on in the mornings, all on my own, without a mirror. I mark the passage of time by the shifting patterns of light across the purple hills. Some days I read for hours, and it hardly seems to change. Some days, when I look up, it is dark. Inside, slowly, that small glint of self begins to dim. I'm disappearing completely, perfecting a skill I learned a long time ago. The only difference now is that I have someone else to disappear into. I will slip into the role of Rosanna like warm bathwater. I will find a new self, a better self to take the place of whatever it is I've lost.

Here are the things Rosanna says she likes: cashew milk, white-rimmed *Miltonia* orchids, the films of Terrence Malick, dry martinis at Musso & Frank. Here are the things she says she does not like: traffic, processed food, pears. Here is another thing she doesn't like: me. Days pass, days keep passing, and still Rosanna doesn't come. I know she isn't coming for me, won't, until I am so perfect that seeing me will be as natural as glimpsing herself in a darkened hallway mirror. Still, I sit by the window and wait. For what, I cannot tell.

· · ·

Max sits across from me on the futon, his body angled toward mine. I can feel him watching me, the warmth of it, the way he looks now, really looks, no longer afraid, his eyes resting comfortably on my fancy clothes, my clean, clear skin. I'm careful to wipe off my makeup around him, not ready yet for him to know how hard I'm trying. I want to seem effortless for him, like I'm just existing, my body naturally falling into aesthetically pleasing lines. I want him to see that Rosanna was right to pick me. I want him to go to her, after he leaves, and tell her how right she was.

"I like it when you wear your hair like that," he says, and I laugh.

"It's easier to have nice hair now that I finally have a hairbrush!"

Max laughs, too. "I'm sorry!" he says. "I already said I'm sorry. Rosanna doesn't always think of practical things like that. But it looks nice brushed out. You look nice."

He pushes one lock behind my ear. The light touch, his fingers lingering for a moment longer than they need to, gives me chills. "You have pretty ears," he says.

I roll my head away from him, clap my hands over them, pretending annoyance. In the interviews, Rosanna is a little possessive of her body, self-critical, self-effacing. She jokes to show she's comfortable.

"What a strange compliment," I say, turning the page, pretending to read. It works. He laughs.

"I think you mean thank you," he says.

Over the glossy frame of the magazine I can see he's smiling, looking tenderly at my face. I laugh back, mirroring him.

"Okay, sure, thank you!" I say. "You're still a weirdo for noticing, though."

He shakes his head. "I'm a noticer!" he says. "I'm good at seeing things other people don't. Like your ears. Which are, as I mentioned, very nice, as ears go."

He reaches back across the couch and keeps playing with my hair. I tilt my head toward him like a domesticated cat.

"Like with Rosanna? Do you notice things for her? Like you noticed me?"

His hand tightens around the hair he's stroking, and then falls still. "Yes," he says quietly. "Like that."

. . . .

When I am alone, I leaf through the interviews and try to assemble a timeline: what was going on when, what was she thinking, how did she feel? I try to sense her in my body, the tingle of her nerves raising the hair on the back of my neck, her excitement slicking my palms with sweat, like a Method actor preparing for a role. I sit on the couch with my eyes closed, answering the questions interviewers pose. At first I use her words. But after a while I feel my way toward new answers, other things she might say, if she was asked again, given a second chance. I try to let my tongue hang loose, to feel in the empty air for the words she would speak.

"What brings you the greatest joy?"
"My family. And lemon meringue pie!"

"What brings you the greatest joy?"
"My family, my fans, and a nice dry martini!"

"What brings you the greatest joy?"
"Solitude. What can I say, I love my alone time!"

"What brings you the greatest joy?"
"I haven't been happy in years!"

"What brings you the greatest joy?"
"Max."

He has begun bringing me boxes of loose photographs, Polaroids, printouts of paparazzi shots, strips of film and test shots for magazine covers, advertisements—every scrap of her he can find. I stick them on the wall, one image at first, and then a small cluster, and then the wall is covered with Rosanna and Rosanna and Rosanna. I stand close and let the shape of her burn into the folds of my brain, memorizing every image, the tilt of her head, the position of her hands, her glance passing just beyond the frame of the photograph to meet me, smiling, her gaze direct and unashamed. I force myself to stand so close to the wall that she's all I can see. When I step away, she is still there, watching. There is nowhere in the room I can stand without looking up to meet her eyes. Without her seeing me back.

In the mornings I do my makeup, spending hours in front of that tiny mirror. And in the afternoons, I put on her clothes, my clothes, ours. I take my time dressing. There are so many versions of her I can become. Lifestyle blog Rosanna, standing in her kitchen pretending to make a smoothie in a navy-striped marinière, slim-fit jeans, and boots, a gold bangle hanging light on her wrist. "Stars— They're Just Like Us!" Rosanna, coming out of a coffee shop with a chai latte and a soft leather bucket bag, white twill culottes, a chambray shirt the same light gray as the long gray mornings of the Los Angeles sky. Date night Rosanna, in those sultry silk shifts, crimson lipstick, lips tight, eyes cast upward at the man beside her. There are other iterations. Too many to count. Piles and piles of very fine things to dress the versions of Rosanna who would wear, for example, a peplum skirt, an A-line dress, a slinky black silk kimono with nothing underneath, a cream-colored jacket, a lace dress, gloves, a fisherman's sweater too fine to fish in. I have never seen the sea. I always look unconvincing, like an understudy, a child trying on her mother's clothes.

I spend a long time standing in front of the rack, imagining how she feels when she gets dressed. I touch one sleeve, straighten a hem. I bury my face in the fabric and breathe, searching for some small trace of her, some memory I can cling to and bring to life. I try hard not to remember doing the same thing with my mother's clothes— the heavy scent of her perfume, of her cigarettes; the nights when I would curl up into her fur coats and pretend that this was a place my father could not find me. But there is no warmth of life left in Rosanna's clothes, no sense of the woman who used to wear them. Even the heavy musk of her perfume is fading. Soon the clothes will smell like nothing. Worse, they will smell like me. The thought is disgusting, transforming the clothes into empty skins, horrible, dead things. I breathe once, twice, the air dense in my chest. I gently touch the sleeve of a white cotton dress with my fingertips. It is fabric. Just fabric. I close my hand and hold on tight.

When Max arrives every day toward evening, I have carefully hung all the clothes back on the rack. I don't want him to know how difficult her carelessness is for me to replicate. I am sitting on the couch with the stack of magazines, pretending to read, although really by now I have gone over each of the articles so many times that the words have lost their meaning, wearing the same soft white buttondown and black leggings I revert to every evening. I sit still and listen for the car, a series of sounds I have come to recognize and love, yes, like a pet dog, that's how bored I am, my heart jumping a little at the sound of the idling engine, the clunk of the door closing in the empty street, a wait, and then, bliss, the door unlocking, Max, here to save me from boredom, from the noisy fragments of my old self. In the kitchen, he unpacks my dinner, which is always the same, a series of small boxes of vegetables prepared in various ways— raw, steamed, roasted, dehydrated. Today it is food in dull neutral shades—mushrooms, brown rice, burdock root, lotus. I know the names of all these things now.

As he unpacks, he asks me questions. "What's your favorite food?" he'll say, or "Who do you love most in the world? Tell me about your dreams." He'll ask me to remember conversations I've read. "And how did you answer," maybe, "when she asked you what you were doing with your life?" or small details about my everyday activities: "What vitamins are you taking? What color lipstick do you prefer for everyday wear?"

"Dark chocolate," I say. "My father, probably. I had a strange dream about a glass mountain. Growing up, mostly, I think. It's a process. Vitamins E, A, K, collagen supplements, selenium. Some antioxidant pills. Coral blush, of course."

At the end of the recitation he smiles. "What have you been doing all day?" he always asks.

"Oh, you know," I say, my tone casual. "Reading. Dress up. Practicing. I missed you."

I don't look at him when I say this, afraid of the expression he will make. Max is a bad liar. But it's true, I missed him, miss him every day. I long to be close to him, even though I know that he's as responsible as Rosanna is for keeping me locked up in here, for the deadening monotony of my days.

"I would be flattered," he says. "But you don't have anyone else to miss."

I pretend to laugh. "True," I say.

But it isn't. I miss Rosanna.

In the first days I expected her every minute. I thought she would check in on me regularly, wanting to keep track of my progress, and I waited, expectant, for that first inspection, sure that I would please her. Of course she never came. I tell myself I am no longer waiting. That Max's approval is enough. Even so, l hold myself tense, in expectation. I am never quite myself, even when no one is watching. Because she could be coming, any minute. And I want her to be happy with what she sees. The exhaustion of this, of having to maintain two separate fictions at the same time—the Rosanna I cultivate for Max, and the Rosanna that exists only for Rosanna herself—makes me bleary. I am never not tired. But one day, I know, it will be worth it. Max will tell Rosanna that I am ready. And she will come to me. I will recognize her cautious footsteps on the stairs, her hesitation at the door. She'll be stunned when she sees me. She will stand in the doorway for a long time, looking. I will make the first move. I will reach for her, taking her hand very gently, so she won't be scared. "Hello," I will say, "I'm—" But no, I won't say my name, I'll greet her with her own. Ours. "Rosanna," I will say. "Hello." She will look at me with infinite humor, infinite kindness. She won't say my name back. She'll touch my face. We'll laugh. Our laughs will sound the same, like it is one person laughing. She will come into the room. She will sit on the couch, close beside me.

She will ask me what it feels like to be in her body, and I will tell her. I will tell her everything I know.

Max comes up with a set of exercises he wants me to do every morning. My bearing is better now, the attitudes of my body more precise, but there is still that softness, that imperfect sag. I'm glad he is doing something to help. He sits on the futon with his hands folded in his lap, watching me. The coffee table has been pushed to one side of the room, under the window, where I brush against its hard edge with my fingertips as I bend and stretch. I haven't moved this much in a long time. I am eating less than I used to eat. I am sleeping more. My muscles feel atrophied and soft, squirming like eels beneath my pale skin. A sharp cramp stabs my left side. I collapse on the mat, my hand on my stomach.

"Keep going," says Max. His voice is soft, encouraging.

"I can't."

I feel like my skin will rip open if I move, my insides wriggling onto the floor. Max pushes me with his foot.

"Come on," he says. "Keep going." His voice is still gentle, but it is a forced gentleness, a tightness he is trying to use to tamp down his frustration.

It's not fair, his frustration, but I want him to tell Rosanna that I'm doing a good job, that I'm ready to leave the apartment. So I push through the pain. I make my body move, pulling itself forward into another plank, every part of me screaming. I close my eyes and breathe hard. *I have nothing to do with my body,* I think. It can't bother me. It isn't my problem. It isn't even my body anymore. I finish the set. I collapse into a heap on the floor.

"Very good!" Max says. "You're doing so well."

I am supposed to do one set of exercises on my own, another when Max visits in the afternoon. One morning, tired and sore, I skip my set. When Max comes over, he doesn't say a word to me, just sits down on the couch and nods for me to start. I complete one set. My form is perfect. I congratulate myself; not tired out from my morning exercises, I do a better job. I'll have to skip my set more often. I pull myself out of the last plank and smile at him, perfect, pristine.

"Again," he says. His voice is clipped and hard.

I stand for the first movement, pulling myself into warrior pose, my arms above my head, palms pressed together, sweaty, starting to slip, and it's a little harder this time, a little less precise, but I do it.

"Again."

The third time is harder. My body feels heavy. My muscles are starting to burn.

"Again."

I am filled with a deep and profound loathing for the dead weight of my body, the useless flab of it, the space it takes up. Even the smallest movement is torture. I keep moving, I push myself through, each pose turning into a feint, a symbolic gesture toward that pose more than the pose itself. I ache. I hate him. I hate everything that's happening to me.

"Again," says Max.

I can't. My body feels like a deflated balloon.

"Please," I say, "can we stop now?"

"You skipped your set this morning," Max says, his voice implacably calm. "We have to make up for lost time."

I am moving slower now, trying hard to breathe. My muscles ache and shake and strain. Halfway through, I start to cry, the tears running silently down my face. Max just sits there, calmly watching. I hope he will mistake them for sweat. He reaches forward and softly brushes away the hair plastered to my forehead.

"Keep going," he says tenderly. "Just once more. For me."

At the end, I collapse on the mat, dry heaving. Max leans down from the futon to scratch the small of my back.

"I knew you could do it," he says. "I'm proud of you."

He pulls me up, letting me lean my whole body weight against him, and takes me to the bathroom, where he draws me a warm bath with Epsom salts and lavender oil. The running water covers up the sound of my vomiting, but the smell lingers, sour, in the small, humid room.

. . .

When Max leaves, I check the apartment for cameras. I pull up the rug. I leaf through the books. I take down every picture of Rosanna and inspect the wall behind it for pinholes. I remove the pillows from their cases, squeeze through the stuffing inch by inch feeling for microphone lumps. I examine the hinges of the cabinets, the folds of the curtains, carefully scoop the dirt from the potted plant languishing on the windowsill. I find nothing. I tell myself this is because there is nothing to find.

Still, he keeps noticing things. He notices when I don't make my bed first thing in the morning, and so when I wake up, I pull the sheets tight into hospital corners, tuck the lumpy mattress of the futon back in on itself. Rosanna, he says, likes to keep things neat, so now, so do I. Every morning I am supposed to eat one of three meals selected from my food diary, green juice, a handful of goji berries and almonds soaked in water, or a small bowl of brown rice with sweet potato and miso paste. I must write down exactly what I've consumed, when, and how much. Max notices discrepancies down to the ounce and will bring less food at dinner. He's never cruel about these small corrections, but there is an insistence on perfection, on precision, that gradually seeps into my performance. I am more and more careful, more and more aware of my new role. The better I get at acting like Rosanna, the sweeter Max is to me. He brings me little gifts, things he knows Rosanna likes: a blue-cloth-covered book of poems, bouquets of lilacs, matcha-glazed éclairs from her favorite bakery in Koreatown, expensive-smelling bundles of incense, little gold bracelets studded with her birthstone. He tells me I'm as pretty as the things he buys. He touches me more now, I have noticed. He comes closer to me, the closer I am to getting it right.

I try hard to leave my old life behind. If I dream of myself, when I wake up I lie with my eyes closed, running through my memorized Rosanna lists or trying to conjure a perfect replica of one of her pictures, until I can no longer remember what I dreamed of. It seems important not to waste mental space on anything that doesn't belong to her. Every thought is one thought closer to perfection. To being good enough to leave this room.

It's morning, and I am practicing my makeup. It is early, still far too early for me to expect a visit from Max. But suddenly through the thin wall of the bathroom, I hear a click as a key turns in the lock. The front door squeaks as it opens, and then there is a long silence as whoever opened it looks around and doesn't find me. Rosanna? It must be her. She must have heard I'm ready. She's here now. It's time. I look at the imperfect replica of her face I have created, overcome with guilt. I do not want her to see me like this, this sad imitation, and I move to wipe it away. But then I stop myself. I look at my beautiful face in the mirror. It is my face, with Rosanna's written over it. Rosanna's and my own. Her spit on my lips, flakes of her dead skin over my living flesh. Even now she is burrowing into me, taking me over, her host. The thought fills me with a strange paralyzing joy. I want to laugh, to scream. Instead, I wait for her to find me, sitting on the edge of the bathtub with my hands neatly folded in my lap.

Max walks in without knocking, my privacy a lie we tell each other. And then, seeing me, he stops. For a moment, he thinks it's her. I can tell by the way he looks at me, that mixture of terror and awe. Perhaps he has just come from Rosanna's house, telling her about my progress, and now here she is again, in two places at once. A miracle. The look on his face wipes clean the anger I feel at seeing him, not Rosanna, standing in the doorway. I press down the amusement that bubbles up inside me. If he didn't look so panicked, I would laugh. He stands still for a long time, looking and looking at my strange new face, although what he expects to find, I cannot say. Finally he speaks. "Rosanna," he says, softer than anything, in a voice that is almost a whisper. In the quiet of the small room, I can feel his breath against my ear. He says her name like it has power. An incantation. He says it again, just once, even softer: "Rosanna." I sit perfectly still and look up at him, my eyes finally meeting his. We are locked together, the two of us alone in the world.

And then a loud noise outside as a truck passes up the narrow street, and the birds in the courtyard scatter in a panicked cloud, calling to one another with shrill cries, flapping. Had any of them learned to talk in their domesticated lives? Or were they too far gone, their human voices lost to wildness? Would one of them call out my name?

Max moves close to me. For a breath, he just stands there, looking. And then he sticks his thumb into his mouth and runs it down my fake cheekbone, smearing the new lines of my new face, running it, warm, wet, past the soft plane of my cheeks and down onto my chin, then up to my lips, where he rests for a long beat, as though he is quieting me, his thumb pressing hard against my teeth. In the mirror behind his shoulder, I can see my ruined face. I can feel the sticky traces of spit and filth and smeared foundation cooling hard against my skin. I look beautiful. I look like her.

"Almost," says Max.

I wake to the light switching on. Max is standing at the foot of my bed with his back to the dark window, as sharp and unexpected as a night terror.

"Less sleep!" he says. "Sleep is good for the skin."

"Good morning!" I say, trying to keep my voice even, as though his presence is the most natural thing in the world. "What's all this?"

"We have to damage your skin," says Max. "Rosanna, of course, is older than you. Her skin doesn't look like your skin. I've noticed that there was something missing from our regimen, something that's not quite right. Maybe it's your skin. Maybe this will help."

His voice is incongruously cheerful, the inspirational chirp of a camp counselor, a motivational speaker trying to convince me to live his truth. It is a shock to see him in the morning. I wonder if this is what daytime Max is like, if he, too, has a hidden version of himself. Maybe this is the Max Rosanna knows. Groggy, I get out of bed, and he folds the sheets, stows the comforter, pushes the futon back into a couch, sits beside me in the dark. Together we watch the sunrise, the white walls turning gray, then pink, in the growing light. He makes me coffee the way Rosanna likes it, the way I like it now, too—strong, with agave, a little steamed almond milk. We sit so close beside each other that I can hear the tiny motions of his body, his breath. We don't speak. When the room has grown light and it is too late for me to get back to sleep, he leaves. I know I won't see him for the rest of the day.

I am on a low protein diet, then low carb, then macrobiotic, miso soup for breakfast and a fridge full of celery, flavorless prepared meals in little plastic trays. Max makes me smoke cigarettes and drink diet soda instead of water. Then for days on end I consume only water with lemon and cayenne and maple syrup, and become so weak I can barely stand. In the mornings in the mirror I can see that it's working. There are new circles under my eyes, and my face looks almost gray, the skin thinner, clinging closer to the bone. Little wrinkles like parentheses appear on the sides of my lips from smiling. I listen to the departure of the parrots. I stand in front of the door and rest my hand on the slick wood, listening. I am close, closer to perfection than ever before. Soon the door will open and I'll walk through the hills in the sunshine, in my new skin, the city spread supplicant at my feet.

One morning when I wake up, there is a tanning bed in the living room, turned diagonally to fit in the small space, as sleekly compact as a coffin. Max stands beside it, looking down. I wonder how he managed to maneuver this enormous object up the stairs and into my room. Did he do it on his own? Has someone else been here? The air feels different somehow, disturbed, my head thick and cottony with too much sleep or something else. I can't remember falling asleep the night before, can't remember any of my dreams. Did Max put something in my dandelion root tea? The taste is so bitter it would be easy to disguise another, deeper bitterness within it. I sit up, smiling brightly at him, pushing the hair from my eyes. I say nothing, waiting.

"Good morning, sleepy!" he says.

He crosses toward the kitchen, where there is a cup of coffee waiting for me on the counter. He turns the handle toward me when he hands it over, protecting me from the heat of the cup. A small tenderness, and a new one. I wonder what it means. He takes a pair of bright blue tanning goggles, domed, with little pinhole eyes, out of his jacket pocket. I put them on. The world looks submerged.

"Take off your clothes," he says. "There's a bottle of lotion on the table. Put as much of it on as you can."

I get out of bed, walk behind him so I'm not in his line of sight. I want him to know that I'm still in control of my body. That I'm agreeing with his instructions, not letting him tell me what to do. I take off my top first, then my pants, folding them and placing them on the pillow beside me. For a moment I hesitate, and then take off my underpants, too, rolling them into a neat little ball and hiding them under my pajamas, shy for no reason; after all, he's seen them, he bought them for me. I slick my body with the thick white lotion, which has a cloying chemical smell, heavy with artificial flowers, like the air freshener they use in malls. For a moment I wait, standing there naked, expecting him to turn around and see the results of our hours of work, what the artifact of my body has become beneath the protection of Rosanna's clothes. But Max stays still. I lower myself into the bed, the chill of it making me flinch, and pull the lid shut. The tight space makes me nervous. Tight spaces always have. But Rosanna isn't claustrophobic.

"Okay," I say, "I'm ready."

I clamp shut my eyes and pretend.

I can hear Max moving outside, the switch flip on with a hum. The narrow space I'm in turns blue, as if I'm floating in water I can breathe. One breath. Another. I am feeling less anxious now. More like Rosanna. I lie there in the light for what feels like a long time, listening to the quiet noises of the machine, the sound of Max moving around outside. It's strange to be so close to him without being able to see his face. To feel unwatched, for once.

"Max?" I say. "Tell me about her."

We haven't talked about Rosanna much since that first day, not the real Rosanna, the person who exists outside all those photographs, magazines. Rosanna, her private self. I almost don't want to know what he thinks about her. Some strange feeling of propriety, like there should be some part of Rosanna I allow her to keep for herself, just as she doesn't want to know about me. Maybe we're better for each other in the abstract. But now, in this small light-filled space, I want her to feel real. To remind me why all this work is worth it. In here, I don't have to look at Max's face as he speaks. I don't have to watch him trying not to notice the imperfections in mine. In here, he can tell me the truth. Outside, there is a light sound that I think might be his hand resting on the lid. A long pause before he speaks.

"You know," he says. "You know so many things about her."

"I don't," I say, "not really. I don't know her the way you know her. I don't know anything beyond the facts. Not the way you do. You know what she's really like."

Another silence. I can sense the weight of his palm.

"It's a pointless question," he finally says. "What is anyone like? What are you like?"

The light of the bed pulses soft against my closed eyes. I think for a moment about how he wants me to answer. I understand that there is no part of him that actually wants to know.

"I don't know anymore," I say finally. "Maybe I used to. But I've forgotten."

"No," he says, "you never knew."

He drums his fingers on the lid of the bed, a quiet tapping like rain on a roof. It hasn't rained once since I got to Los Angeles. I wonder if it ever does. The sound calms me. I never liked small spaces. I do not like them now. *Rosanna is not claustrophobic*, I tell myself once more. And so for now neither am I.

"No one ever knows," says Max. "You think you know yourself, but you don't. We tell ourselves stories about what we're like. We assemble a set of anecdotes to show the people around us that we're thoughtful, say, or clumsy, or have a good sense of humor. But it's all fiction. The only true thing is just beyond your reach, the version of you held inside the people who decide to know you. That's the best any of us can hope for. That someone decides we're worth knowing. That they will tell our story. That they will help us decide who we are."

"Like you did for Rosanna," I say.

And heavy in my mouth is the thing I can't say, can't even whisper into the hard top of the bed. *Like you will never do for me.*

"Yes," says Max.

The tapping stops.

My skin begins to blister from days and days in the fake sun. When I'm in the bed, Max reads to me, books that were Rosanna's favorites from childhood, about little women and little princes and little houses on prairies and grasslands and in woods, everyone cozy, everyone safe. I grow to like the small space of the bed, the tenderness that comes when I am tucked away inside. Rosanna isn't afraid of small spaces. And now neither am I. Afterward, Max cuts a hunk from the aloe plant he leaves on the windowsill. He spreads the thick cold gel onto the parts of my back that I can't reach, as gentle and impersonal as a nurse. I always thank him, wanting him to think me nice. He never says anything back. But sometimes he rests his hand between my shoulder blades a moment longer than he needs to, the skin aching like it's on fire where he touches but still, still. I hate when he lets go.

5

"Close," says Max. "You're doing so well. Better than anyone could have hoped."

He gently holds my face between his hands and tilts it from one side to the other, looking at me with tenderness. I have been getting better and better at my Rosanna makeup, practicing every day, making adjustments as Max suggests them. He sees her now when he looks at me. Or something like her at least—a shadow, a mirroring, a closeness that is impossible to deny. I have learned to dress like Rosanna. I sit like she sits. I smile like she smiles. My face, in the mornings, when I put on her makeup in the wavery bathroom mirror, is no longer entirely my own. I avoid the window when it gets dark, afraid to catch a glimpse of something not quite myself. I don't feel like myself anymore. I don't even feel like a person anymore. I feel like I've been hollowed out from the inside, incredibly fragile, a china cup filled dark with tea. I live in the spaces between myself and her, a hungry ghost floating between two worlds. I can feel her emerging from me, a moth discarding its stiff cocoon, climbing damp and pale into the liquid light of the moon. The sensation is painful but not entirely unpleasant, a kind of pushing against, a cracking. I am getting closer every day.

But Max wants more.

"It's time for surgery," he says.

With one finger he traces my jaw, the crooked line of my nose. I try not to flinch. He looks right through me as he speaks, through my careful contouring, down to the imperfect slope of my bones, the betrayal of my body inside the body we are working so hard together to create.

"We've gone as far as we can with makeup. It's a risky step, I know, but I trust you. I know now that you're right. You're perfect. I can't believe we've made it this far without it, but you're almost there. Almost. We are so, so close. But we won't be finished until we make a few changes. Nothing drastic, very tasteful, very natural. Just like Rosanna would do."

"Surgery?" I say.

"Yes," says Max.

I feel a chill pass through me, nausea. I can wipe off makeup. I can buy new clothes. But once the surgery is over, I will no longer possess even the tiny fragments of my old self that remain, the narrowness at the corners of my eyes, the way my nose crinkles when I smile like my mother's nose used to. Already I am forgetting so much. Soon everything that used to belong to me will be gone.

"Okay," I say. "Just fillers, though, right? Some Botox?"

"No," says Max, "more than that. Nothing major, but we will have to operate. I found a doctor, someone Rosanna consulted with, of course she never had any work done, but she trusts him. He'll come here to look at you before we do anything."

"And then I'll go to a clinic somewhere?"

A bright flash of hope. If I can't get out of surgery, at least I'll get out of the apartment. The sun, the feeling of fresh air on my face—all this will be worth the pain of the operation, the loss of my face.

"No," says Max, "we'll do it here. Much more discreet. Rosanna doesn't want people talking."

I stiffen, and he grabs my arm, keeping me from getting up and moving farther from him.

"It's nothing to be afraid of," he says, "I promise. It will all be worth it in the end. I go to Rosanna's house every day and tell her about you. How well you're doing. You're making her so happy. And me," he adds when he sees that I am still pulling away. "You're making me happy, too. Don't disappoint us now."

I think of Rosanna, greedy for her old self. I want to give her what she wants. I know I've made a promise. But I feel something inside me shudder and catch. I don't want to be touched that way, by a stranger who will split open my skin, reach inside me and shift me around. I am going too far, further than I had allowed myself to imagine. When it's done, I will be gone. And I am no longer sure I want to know what will come to take my place. When I speak, I try to keep my voice matter-of-fact, calm. I don't want to know how he'll look at me when I say no.

"Of course I'm willing," I say. "It isn't that. I would, will, do anything for her, for you. You know that. Rosanna must. But is this really what she wants? She hates needles, doctors. Most doctors. Anything this, well, unnatural. There must be another way."

A silence. He moves his hand up to my jaw. I remember Rosanna's interviews, talking about homeopathy, ayahuasca, plant medicine. She wouldn't approve of what Max is doing. He knows this as well as I do. Has he told her? Does she know?

"Rosanna doesn't approve of Western medicine," I say, talking quickly now, trying to get all the words out before he can interrupt. "We should try something else: a healer, some shift in energy? It isn't my face. My face is perfect, or almost perfect, you said it yourself, and I'm so close to her I can feel it. She's here in me already. I can make myself perfect, Max, please, I'm working so hard. I don't need anyone else's help."

I can hear my voice tightening up, a note of panic enter the last sentence. I am betraying myself, showing that I am not the easy, languid girl he needs me to be. Nothing like her, still. Even after all this time. My panic betrays my lie.

Max drops his hands, his face going blank. When I had pictured my future self, after all this was over, she had my old face. While I'm here, I can wear Rosanna like a mask, but after, after, when the money sits heavy in that secret account and I am far away from here, it is some improved version of my old self that I picture on that balcony, smiling into that sunset, far away. My old self, but better, with more elegance, more money, interesting stories I wasn't able to tell. I imagined myself in a garden somewhere, an American heiress, beautiful now, but with my own beauty, a beauty I had learned for myself. If I let them take that from me, what will be left? A blank space. A tight-skinned mess of scars. No small thing to call my own. I reach forward and grab Max's hand. I try to make him look me in the eyes.

"I'm doing such a good job," I say, "I'm working so hard. You said it yourself. I'm doing all I can. Please, Max, don't make me do this."

He shakes my hand off with a quick little shiver, like flinging away a dead leaf stuck to his skin. He doesn't look at me. He looks out past me, toward the hills, toward the house I imagine is Rosanna's house, bloodred in the setting sun, and his face is wiped so clean that he looks like a child. Totally vulnerable. Abandoned. And I am the one who has done this to him. I am the one who has let him down. I try to breathe, to reason my way through. This is just one more small thing. My body is nothing. My body is no longer my own. But the loss grows in my belly until I am sick with it, kicking like an unborn child. Whatever small fragment of my old self remains is screaming to survive. If I do this, there will be no turning back. There will be nothing left for me to revert to, once all this is over. The woman on the balcony will no longer be a person I recognize. She will be a stranger, with a stranger's face. I have made my promises. It is probably already too late. But still. Still. I can't.

"Please," I say, "I can't. I'm so sorry, Max, but I can't do it. Please don't make me. I'll wear makeup, I'll do whatever you want, just don't cut me open. Not yet. Not until all this is over. No one will be able to tell the difference, I promise. I promise, Max. Tell her, convince her for me."

Max stands slowly. He wipes his hands on his suit jacket, as if he has been touching something rotten. His eyes, bouncing from wall to wall, are glazed, and his voice, when he finally speaks, is free of emotion. Carefully ironed out. Flat.

"Okay," he says, "I'm going to consider this a lapse. You're not thinking clearly. You're not in a rational enough mood to discuss this with me. I'll come back when you're ready. When I'm ready. And if you really want to give up now, well—"

At this he stops, makes a futile little sweeping motion in the air. Well, what? Well, nothing. If I give up now, we have failed her. And I have failed them both. I close my eyes for a moment, breathe. I will get a new face. A better face. A face that Max or anyone could love. Maybe I can say yes. Dream of a new life. A new and better self. Maybe, after, we can re-create my old smile, the invisible markers of my past. I open my eyes to ask. But the door has already slipped shut behind him.

In the morning when I wake up, I do my exercises, sure that Max will be back at any moment, maybe with Rosanna, ready to talk. I want to show them both that I'm serious. That I'm working hard. I'm ready. I run wind sprints back and forth across the worn rug. I do my makeup, wiping it off and starting over again and again until it's flawless. I am too nervous to read. I sit on the couch waiting for Max and Rosanna for at least a full hour, trying my best not to move. I want them to find me perfect. I do my planks, I tan, I make espresso in a metal pot on the small stove. In the afternoon, I run more wind sprints. I go to the kitchen and take inventory. I have half a head of celery, three slightly floppy carrots, two small jars of chia seeds and flax, and a packet of dried seaweed.

I remember an article where Rosanna discussed how to cook with chia seeds. She stands beside me in the kitchen, her voice an encouraging chirp. "It feels so indulgent, but it's great for you! They're hydrating, super high in vitamins, fiber, and all kinds of good stuff. Definitely one of my go-to healthy snacks!"

I measure out a tablespoon of seeds and leave them to soak until they swell with liquid, a sticky mass of black-and-gray goop. It is one of the most unpleasant things I have ever forced down my throat, viscous, slimy, tasteless. I drink it with a series of short and painful gulps, and smile like she smiles in the pictures. I see her there beside me, smiling back.

"So simple, and so good!" I say to the empty room.

The sky goes dark and I give up on Rosanna. Still, I wait for Max. Still, he doesn't come.

I run out of food on the third day and decide to try the door. Maybe Max isn't planning on coming back at all. Maybe he's abandoning me here, like an unruly animal left on the side of the highway. Before I leave, I go through Rosanna's handbags. There are wallets in some of them, gift certificates, memberships, passes, unactivated platinum cards. Crumpled handfuls of cash in the pockets of the coats, softened by her sweat. I put all the money I can find in a small leather clutch and dress myself in Rosanna's most ordinary-looking clothes. Maybe I can find her house somehow. Go to her directly, plead my case.

I stand behind the door for a long time, getting my nerve up. I know I am already close to the edge. If Max discovers I have left without his permission, even for a minute, even just to get food, fully intending to come back, this will all be over for me. My contract will be terminated. I will be sent somewhere far away. I will never meet Rosanna. I will never see Max again. I rest my hand on the wood, feeling it warm and grow slick beneath my palm, weighing the two paths in my head. I think of Rosanna, how disappointed she will be, having to start over, find someone new. How angry she will be at Max for failing her. How angry she will be at me for letting her down. I think of how much progress I have already made, of my future self, my beautiful self; how I will get another face after this that belongs to me alone, not Rosanna's face, but a new face, a dream face, even more beautiful, more perfect than Rosanna could ever be, because it will be constructed from the purity of thought. *It's worth it*, I tell myself, *it has to be*. This is a test. Max is testing me. And if I open the door, which I am sure is unlocked this time, I will fail. If I want to stay, I will have to prove my consistency to him. I will have to wait. I take one breath, another. I picture Rosanna's smiling face, her standing in front of me, my mirror. I let my hand fall from the door.

I take the money out of the clutch and redistribute it throughout the apartment, hidden underneath the small refrigerator, stuffed into the pillowcases, rolled up and tucked deep into a jar of kosher salt. Just in case. I know what Max is capable of now, the depths of his neglect. After that, there is only black coffee and water until the sun sets. I should stay still, conserve my energy, but it seems important that I still do my exercises, although every movement makes my body feel like it's about to break into a million tiny pieces. I get through a set. I move slowly. My makeup is slightly less than perfect. I have to force myself to wipe it off and start again. I am so tired. But I am still here. When Rosanna comes back, I want her to see my devotion. I picture the way her face will light up, seeing me, seeing her, that horrible blank sadness gone. At night, I crumble half of a chicken bouillon cube I discovered tucked away in the back of the pantry into a cup of hot water, a trick from my foster care days to keep the hunger pangs at bay. It works. I sleep.

It is four days until I see Max again. Four times the parrots fly noisily out of the courtyard in the morning. Four times they return at night. It is sort of a relief that I can still do this, that there is still a way for me to hold on to and calculate time, keep it from slipping past me in an undifferentiated stream. So I count. I wait. I wait.

On the fourth day, my patience is rewarded. Max comes alone, carrying a gold takeout bag. It is noon, and I am sitting on the couch in my close to perfect makeup, hands folded in my lap. I have not consumed a single bite of solid food for almost two days now. I am shaking, I think from the coffee. When I hear the door open, I don't turn my head. I am determined not to move, not even to breathe too loudly. *Everything is normal,* I think. *Everything is fine.* Max goes into the kitchen and unpacks the bag, placing tiny dishes on a wooden tray. There is wild mushroom soup, lobster ceviche, crispy Brussels sprouts and black cod, spicy tuna hand rolls. A tiny red box with a little round cake and a scoop of melting ice cream tucked inside like a ring. All Rosanna's favorites. She must have picked them out just for me. A way of saying sorry for everything she's put me through. From the corner of my eye, I watch him, my mouth watering. I want everything so badly. He brings the tray in, sets it on the table. I do not move until he tells me to.

"Here," he says, an embarrassed tenderness in his voice. "Eat. I thought you might want something special. I got this just for you. Your favorite. All your favorite things."

We, I think. I force myself to eat slowly, as if he never left, as if I'm not hungry at all. This is just another meal. Everything is fine. I am in control, and I want him to see that. I even leave a few scraps behind, although I want so badly to reach in my fingers and wipe the bowls clean, lick out every last sticky dab of sauce. It is almost too much. I feel sick, afraid I will vomit the overrich meal back up, betray the frailty of my body. When I finish, he clears away the plates and, as he passes, lightly strokes the back of my head.

"I'm sorry," I say, not looking at him.

I look out toward the window where the sun is shining bright, almost too bright to look at directly, thinking of the distance to the street. I can hear cars passing, life going on outside, without me. Without Rosanna. And I know what I have to do.

"Max, I'm so sorry," I say.

"Good," he says.

"I'll do it," I say.

A silence. He says nothing, just keeps stroking my hair, his eyes wandering vague around the dirty corners of the room. *It's too late*, I think. *He's here to tell me the bad news. It's over. Rosanna has lost her faith in me.*

"Please," I say, "I know I was wrong. I know it's what she wants now. I'll do anything she wants me to do. I trust you, Max. I'll do anything you say."

Max puts his arms around my shoulders and squeezes me lightly, paternally, giving my back a little pat. In his arms, I can feel how fragile my body is, even after just a few days of deprivation. My bones seem to float loose. I picture them floating in the bloody quiet inside. I picture the doctor, slipping his fingers beneath my skin, as easy as dipping a bucket into the cold dark water of a well, rearranging me until I am perfect. Building my body like carving a statue, pulling beauty from a flawed stone.

"I'm sorry, too," Max says.

I want so badly to believe him.

A doctor comes to the house in street clothes. He is the first person I have seen in months—two months, maybe, close to three. My orders are clear. I will not speak to him. Even if asked a question, I will not say a word. But he won't ask me any questions; he knows the rules, too. We have paid him a tremendous amount of money. He will forget what he has seen. Max has told him there are certain threats against Rosanna's life, that she needs me for protection. I wonder what is more true. That as the doctor thinks, she needs protection from some outside threat, that my body is a blind, a duck decoy? Or what Max has told me, that I am her mirror, her charm, absorbing all harm. That she needs protecting from herself. What does she picture when she pictures me? What needs of hers do I fulfill? Soon, I think, I will know. When I have her face, I will know what she knows. I will be completely trusted then. They will tell me what I need to do.

I cannot speak, but I can look, and even looking is overwhelming. The doctor's presence in my small room feels like an unbearable violation. He is older than Max, with a reassuringly placid air, his forehead as smooth and glossy as a frozen lake. Everything about him is icy white and still—his hair, his skin, his suit. He nods politely when he sees me, letting his eyes slide slick over my body with professional detachment.

"Please," he says, "remove your clothes."

I look to Max, who nods, his face tight. This makes him feel uncomfortable, too. Somehow I find this reassuring. I keep my eyes on him, pretending the doctor isn't here, concentrating on our common goal. I take off my clothes. This time, Max doesn't look away. Neither does the doctor. I look at them, but they don't look back.

Even Max doesn't meet my eyes. To him, right now, I am an imperfect object, nothing more. They walk around me in tight circles, discussing.

"You're right," the doctor says. "The resemblance is uncanny. Where did your team manage to find her?"

"Oh," says Max, "we have our ways."

The doctor nods. "And a mute," he says. "Extraordinary. Not the strangest thing I've seen in my line of work, though. Not the strangest by far."

Max finally catches my eye, gives me a conspiratorial little smile. "Not strange," he says. "Lucky."

The doctor has a pen, and he uses it to make little marks all over my body, dotted lines like borders on a map. I'm glad that he uses a pen. It spares me the indignity of his fingers.

"We could taper her jaw," says the doctor. "Shave a little bit of bone off here and here."

He marks the lines on my face, making the same shapes I do every morning with my contouring makeup. I can feel the marker catch and snag on my loose skin.

"Nothing drastic," the doctor says. "Maybe narrow the bridge of her nose a little, shave off this slight bump."

He makes two lines. Here, and here. I stand as still as I can, look past them.

"The cheekbones are a little flat," says Max, "and I think her breasts are too large. Uneven."

"Good eye," says the doctor. "Both are easy to fix. A little Botox wouldn't be a bad idea. Best to get these things started when they're still young. Preventative measures, you know."

I cannot eat for six hours before the surgery. But it feels like my stomach has shrunk in Max's absence, growing small and hard, and I find that I do not mind. I drink sweet things, water, tea. Max sits up with me for all six hours. He reads to me as much as I want him to, books that Rosanna has lent me. My favorite is a folktale I make him read three times over. A girl guides herself out of a dark wood by the firelight of a magic skull, burning her enemies to ashes with the bright glare of its gaze. At the end of the story, the girl returns safely to a faraway city. She weaves beautiful cloth with her flame-scarred hands. She tells no one what happened to her, how she got her scars. Max sits close beside the bed and strokes my own hand, gentle. I do not move away or flinch. He is the one to hold the mask over my face as the doctor watches. He holds my hand. He tells me to breathe in and count down from ten. I don't feel drowsy at all. *It's not working*, I think.

I wake up in the dark in a stranger's body. My face feels puffy and swollen. My breasts are tender, hollow, as though I have been nursing some infernal being who has sucked me dry. My body lists like a sinking ship, woozy with anesthesia and a helpless emptiness, sick with longing and hunger and loss. I ache. I can't breathe through my nose; the nostrils are stopped up thick with cotton wads. Blood drains down my throat when I tilt my head. My mouth feels impossibly dry, my lips cracked like they cracked in winter, back when I lived through winters, before. Someone (Max?) has propped me up on a stack of pillows, left a carafe of water and a small bowl of something that looks like porridge on the bedside table. The room is dark. I am alone. And then I see them. Sitting on the windowsill, their heavy heads drooping like the heads of sleeping animals, a narrow planter full of white *Miltonia* orchids. Rosanna's favorite flower. Rosanna has been here while I slept. Maybe she's still here now, on her way out the door, making her way silently down the hall.

I have to see her. I drag myself out of bed, my legs shaking like the legs of a baby deer, that precious, that vulnerable, new. I feel I am in a quiet house in the eye of a storm, the air around me heavy and still in the few long moments before the sky breaks open and the wind sucks down the walls. I sway. I stumble. I right myself and walk to the door, turning the knob like I'm in a dream, sleepwalking. As in a dream, it opens. I say it out loud to myself to be sure.

"The door is unlocked."

In the quiet, my whisper cracks the air like a whip. My jaw

aches. I find myself standing in the open mouth of the doorway like a woman on the ledge of a skyscraper, preparing herself to leap. My body is heavy and strange, with new aches all over, pumped full of fluid. I watch the world outside swim into existence through my drug-fuzzed gaze. I step over the threshold, toward the pull of Rosanna, the night.

The street outside is empty but for the dead palm fronds that litter the road, the streetlights extinguished, everything dark. I feel the wind cutting through my tight layer of bandages, the light, painful pressure of air on my new bruised skin. Santa Ana, Max had said before, when the wind blew all night and gave me strange dreams. The air crackles with a fierce electricity that makes the fine hairs on my arm stand on end, the silk of my thin nightgown spark with static. I feel alive with it, dangerous. I am something strange and raw and new, newborn. I am something that has never been before, in this world or any other. I cross the street to an empty lot where the ground drops away to nothing, the city spread out below. There are houses on either side of me, clinging to the cliff like great birds poised before flight, perched, like I am, on the edge of everything. I stand on the curb and look down over the city, the darkness spilling out from the foot of the mountain like the hem of a black dress, darkness for miles, and then light again, sparkling to the vague shapes of the islands in the far darkness of the sea. I look to the bruised purple sky for stars. I feel the bruised tenderness of my stranger's body. I scream and I scream and I scream into the wind until my new face cracks with strain.

6

For days, I am in bed, my face so swollen I feel newborn, puffy-cheeked and tender, my chin in a sling, a plastic nose protector taped to my face so my fragile bridge won't shift as I sleep. I sleep a lot. I spend most of the day dipping in and out of consciousness, floating between two states distinguished from each other only by the relative brightness of their fuzzy light. I sleep. I wake up to take my pills. I sleep again. I feel adrift, unmoored in my new body. The painkillers make me woozy, brain floating loose in my skull. The time between dreaming and waking blurs so that I am no longer sure what is imagined and what is real. The fabric of reality begins to fray, growing matted and fuzzy at the edges.

Max stays near. In the mornings, he sits in a chair close to my bedside, speaking to me with quiet tenderness when I wake, bringing me tiny glasses of sharp ginger ale, liquefied vegetable soups. I sip painfully through a straw as he sits close and reads to me, more folktales, fragments that seem like extensions of a dream, small girls blooming from flowers, a woman becoming a spider, a house with the crouching legs of a bird. He is there in the twilight, holding my hand. At night he sleeps curled up on the carpet beside me, his suit jacket pulled over his body like a blanket. Time keeps slipping by, faster and faster, gaining momentum, days folding over and in on themselves like taffy stretched on a machine, an endless, numbing, sugar-sweet stretch of time. Everything is one long dark afternoon. I sleep and sleep. I stay still. Slowly my face begins to grow back together. With Max beside me, I become whole again.

One morning I wake up and the pills are gone. I reach out my hand to take them, but the table is empty except for a glass of water holding a single rose, its pink petals wadded up grotesquely, like a clump of flesh. Gradually I return to myself. My body feels empty, my legs too weak to stand. Carefully I pull myself up on my pillows. I look around the room, noticing the gray sky outside, the light coming in the color of pearl. I wiggle my fingers against the smooth blanket, stretch my feet into points, looking for familiarities. *Yes,* I think, *this is right, this is all right.* This is how it feels to be a person, alive. Coming back to my body, this body, is like visiting the house you grew up in, years later, when your family is long gone and the rooms where you slept are occupied by strangers. Everything is still here. But it no longer belongs to me.

The door clicks soft as Max comes in. He smiles when he sees me sitting up. "Sleeping beauty," he says.

"Max, where are my pills?"

I am still sensible enough to smooth my voice out, make my statement a question, not an accusation. I don't want him to know how badly I need the help. How strange this body still is to me.

"No more pills," he says.

"It hurts," I say. "I hurt."

I am tender and raw, like an animal, dying, like meat. The thought of my face, red and peeling beneath the bandages, the fluid-bloated bruises padding my nose, my cheeks, disgusts me. I look up at all those pictures, at Rosanna's perfect faces gazing down. I close my eyes and try to picture my mother, the way her face was like Rosanna's face, loving, distant. I thought she was the most glamorous person in the world. But the edges of her image seem fuzzy now. Eroded. I am no longer certain that I am correctly picturing her heavy eyes, the long elegance of her fingers. Was the scar to the right of her mouth or the left? Slowly she is disappearing from my memories. She has disappeared now from my face. I do not know what will be left for me, now she is gone.

"No more pills," says Max. He carefully takes my face between his hand, turns my gaze to meet his own. "It's not good for you to get used to taking so many. You don't need them anymore. Your body is starting to heal. And I need you to focus. I want to be careful of you. Soon you will be ready for the next step."

The next step. The next. It's impossible to imagine that this isn't the last thing I need to do. How am I not done working yet? Max hands me a cup of coffee. My face is so stiff I can't drink from the cup directly. Instead, I am forced to take tiny sips through the stirrer, like a hummingbird at a feeder, the liquid plastic cooled and stale.

"Will Rosanna come to see me?" I ask.

Surely this is what he means. Now I am ready. Now I have proved myself irrevocably, my willingness, my devotion to her. Won't she want to come look into her mirror? It seems impossible that any person, no matter how far she had disappeared into herself, would be so incurious.

For a moment Max looks away, back up at the wall where Rosanna looms. Infinite, perfect, larger than life.

"Soon," he says. "When you're ready, you'll know. But not today, today isn't the right time."

I nod, blinking away any sign of the tears I can feel gathering tight behind my cheekbones. Max smiles. Finally he looks away from the wall.

"You know," he says softly, leaning in close now, whispering, "she did come see you. The night of the surgery. I told her not to, she's still fragile, and it was the first time she's left the house in ages, but she was so worried about you, she had to check in. Didn't you notice? She asked me to pick up her favorite flowers for you. She wanted you to have something alive."

The orchids. On the windowsill, in the gray light, I can see them ducking their heavy blooming heads, as if ashamed of the ostentation of their own beauty. I knew it. I knew she had come for me.

"Have you been watering them?" I ask. "I hope you haven't been watering them too much. Ice cubes, Rosanna says."

Max smiles.

"They're yours to take care of," he says. "Not mine. And that's not all. I have another gift for you from Rosanna."

He takes a cardboard box from beneath the bed, opening the lid so I can see what's inside. It's full of footage. All kinds—DVDs, minidisks, thumb drives, tapes small enough to nestle in the palm of my hand—each of them neatly labeled with Rosanna's handwriting, careful and pristine, that delicate forward slant. I recognize it from the flash cards. *Rosanna Beach*, says one; another *Shopping*, another *January. Wedding. Horseback. Haircut. Karaoke.*

"Rosanna picked these out for you. We've been assembling this archive for months. Waiting for you to arrive. Now you're here. And you're ready."

He takes a tablet from the bottom of the box and places it on my lap. He plugs it into an enormous machine that he takes from underneath the box, connecting them with an intestinal tangle of cables before connecting it all to a second, larger screen. He pulls my hands on top of the screen, takes them in his, the screen sputtering to life beneath our fingers.

"The magazines are one thing. Anyone could read those. But this archive is precious. In this box is everything you'll ever need to know about Rosanna. Things she doesn't even know about herself. So you can see why we had to wait, why we had to be sure that you were as committed to Rosanna as I was. That her secrets would be safe with you."

He leans forward when he speaks, closer and closer until his face hovers inches from mine. His breath presses soft against my skin.

"I know you'll understand how important all this is," he says. "Now you have her face."

He's right. I can feel Rosanna inside me now, closer than ever, and outside, too, pressed against the surface of my skin. I want to look in the mirror to see what he sees. But I know I can't. I won't look until my face has fully healed. I don't want to know myself as less than perfect. I don't even want to speak. I want to give myself the gift of silence, this perfect moment of alignment with Rosanna. This moment in which Max looks at me, at the scar-flawed, swollen, bandaged surface of my skin, and finds me beautiful.

"I can't wait for you to meet her," he says.

I smile.

Lowering himself to the floor, he fiddles with the wiring, lifting the monitor so it's perched precariously, vulturelike, on the flimsy coffee table. In the instant before he presses play, the room is so small and quiet that I feel I can hear the blood pumping through his veins, his heartbeat racing to meet mine. The room seems warmer when he's in it. I run my fingers through his hair. The wooziness from pain pills has given me access to new liberties with him, and I pretend now that I still feel it. That I need him to support me. We sit in the darkness, close together. Together we watch Rosanna.

She is walking the red carpet. Her hair is sculpted into an elaborate updo, the loose ends falling down crimped, glossed stiff with gel. She is wearing a long silvery gown with a gap in the middle, the bodice dipping in on either side to reveal her impossibly flat, tanned stomach. "Rosanna!" they shout, the crowds pressing up against the barriers in an urgent black mass. "Rosanna!" Past the thin screen of bandage, I can feel Max looking at me, his gaze sticky with longing.

Another clip, her hair down, straight, hanging to her waist. She wears a pink lace dress that flows around her as she walks, the fine layers of fabric catching the air like an undersea plant, undulating as the tide comes in. She smiles wide, white teeth glinting in the flashing light.

Another. Here her hair is short, skating the shoulders of her long white dress, tight through the bottom, where it flares out like a mermaid's tail. She puts one hand on her hip, tilts her head, flirts. I can hear the questions the reporters shout. "Who are you wearing?" they ask. "Are you here with anyone?" "Smile!" says one, and then again: "Rosanna, look over here, give us a smile!" Rosanna smiles, tilts her face toward the sound, a flower unfolding in the light. She does not say a word. I tilt my face like that toward Max, soaking in his warmth.

Rosanna in gold heels and diamonds. Rosanna in leather and lace. Rosanna looking like she had fallen out of a 1940s propaganda film, like she was on her way to a garden party at the embassy, like she had come down from the moon. Rosanna in silk. Rosanna in pearls. The same flowing walk and studied smile. Rosanna, Rosanna, Rosanna. Once you get past the glamour, there is something surprising about the cramped smallness of it all, the way she seems to have spent her life walking down the same narrow red pathway, hemmed in on both sides by her adoring public, the same dense black crowds aching with want, trying to touch her, calling her name.

Max tells me what to notice. "Those earrings," he says, "were lent to her, and after the show she got drunk and left them in the back of her limo!"

He looks to me quickly, afraid I'll get the wrong idea. "Of course, that kind of thing isn't typical of her.

"See the way she pauses, just for a moment, in front of the *Vogue* reporter? She doesn't actually say anything, making them want to talk to her even more. Masterful. She got the cover that year.

"Watch how she stops on the staircase there, with just one leg lifted. She's posing, but in the photographs it will look like she's in motion, makes for a more dynamic composition. The more exciting a shot is, the more likely it is to be prominently featured in the magazines. She was a master of manipulation, nothing got past her.

"Notice how she's always smiling? Just a little. Not a full smile, that would look too affected, just a slight turn at the corners of her lips, like she has a secret. It makes her look appealing, like even when she's right in front of you, she's just out of reach. That's how I want you to look."

I try to mold my bandaged lips into that same slight shape, but I can feel the fabric catch and pull at my scars, and I wince.

"I'll work on it," I say. My voice sounds strange, harsh and unpracticed, like one of the parrots attempting to talk.

Together we watch her walk until sunset, when the clatter of the birds returning jolts Max from his concentration. He stands up and begins gathering disks back into the box.

"Aren't you going to stay?" I ask.

The idea of a night alone is daunting. I'm used to his presence in the room now, the quiet pressure of his breath in the air.

"I don't think so," he says. "It's going to be hard enough for you to sleep anyway. I'll just distract you. And I need to check in on Rosanna."

"At least leave me something to watch," I say. "I'm sick of reading. And I can work on making my way through the footage without you, there's so much of it. Might as well have something to do if I'm going to be up all night anyway."

"No," Max says, "I've worked very hard on curating these, presenting them in a particular order. Letting you access them any way you wanted to without me would be . . ."—he pauses here, steadying the heavy box on his hip, groping in the air for a word—"destabilizing."

With that, he leaves. The birds settle into the courtyard; the room darkens, goes silent. In the dark, the pain spreads through my body like a poison. There is no escaping it. Sleep is impossible. Even staying still, lying down, is overwhelming. The pain gathers and pools like an itch beneath the skin, building until it becomes impossible for me to remain in bed. Instead, I spend hours walking back and forth across the room. Imitating Rosanna.

The first tape the next morning is a dinner party. Before he puts it in, Max runs his fingers lightly along the broken edge of my jaw, feeling for strength. The hurt of his touch disappears into the larger oceanic hurt, the heart of this strange prison I am trapped in, which feels like it will go on forever. Max has brought me juice to sip through a crimped straw, and I watch, jealous, as Rosanna sits at the head of the table and tears meat off a small bird. The camera is angled up from below, with patches of color at the top of the frame that could be the undersides of flower petals. Only the bottom of her face is in frame, and I can see her mouth wide, laughing. I let myself look over at Max. He was watching me as we watched those first tapes, looking to see how I would react, making sure I was as charmed by her as he was. But now he is staring straight at the screen, his body tight. I watch Rosanna's mouth open and shut, the flash of those clean white teeth.

Another clip. Rosanna is in the bedroom, sitting at a mirrored vanity. Her face is pale and creased with sleep. She looks washed out without makeup. It's as if she's naked, she is that vulnerable, that bare. She brushes her hair out in long smooth strokes.

"So, master, what are you making me do today?" she says, joking, not joking, not looking up from the mirror.

The camera and whoever's holding it aren't reflected. I lean forward, straining to see beyond the frame, but there is nothing there to see. Is it Max who stands there, helpful, silent, her friendly ghost? Rosanna puts down the brush, tests the bounce of her hair with the flat of her palm.

"It's too boring," she says, and in her best Garbo impression: "I vant to be alone."

She finally looks up at the person filming, grinning until she sees the camera in their hand. Her face goes dark, the hand holding the brush frozen in the air. The screen turns black before she can open her mouth. Max fiddles, tense, with the next tape, but as he puts it in, the screen abruptly goes black.

"Shit," says Max. "It's the cable, it's been giving me problems. I have another one in the car—sit tight, don't touch anything, I'll be right back."

I stay still, my hands folded in my lap, as he walks to the door. But then there's an unexpected sound—the harsh, familiar click of the lock. A burst of resentment passes through me, as quick and sharp as a stabbing knife. Even now, even now that I have Rosanna's face, I still don't have her freedom. Max treats me like I'm becoming Rosanna as she is now, fragile, overwhelmed by fear. But I don't want to be that Rosanna. I want to be the Rosanna from the magazines, the tapes, bright and shining, afraid of nothing. Boldly herself, encountering the world. Who is Max to tell that woman what she can and can't touch, what she can and can't know about herself? Who is he to tell us anything at all? Rosanna made the tapes for me. Max might have his order, his curation, might want to keep my experience of my new self under his control, but he isn't in charge here. Rosanna is.

Quick as a striking snake, my hand jolts out and grabs blindly at the box of tapes. Rosanna has compiled this archive for me. I want to learn everything she wants me to know. And there's so much to learn; *Rosanna Riding*, one says. *Dancing*, another, *Met Gala*. Excitement leaps liquid up my spine. This is more like it.

The cover of one disk says *L.A. House*, and I pick it up. This seems like a good place to start. I've seen her homes only in little snippets—the kitchen, the hallway, one wall in the bedroom. Surely the first thing to do in attempting to understand someone is to see the way they live, the objects they surround themselves with, especially since Rosanna spends so much time these days cooped up within those walls. Watching will give me a better idea of who she is when she's alone. I will be an archaeologist, scraping dust off the bones of her old life, examining her kitchen, her bedroom, her den, as if they are the hidden chambers of a sacred tomb.

A key turns in the lock.

Rosanna, I think. This has all been a test. She has come to me.

Quickly I shove the thin disk down into the crack between the mattress and the futon frame. *What am I doing?* I think, but it's too late now, I'm acting on instinct, too used to hiding after spending so long in the dark, and as the door opens the disk is hidden and I have shuffled the row of tapes in front of me into a chaotic pile, hoping that if Max is with her, he won't notice the missing footage in the disorder. Rosanna will notice. But she'll understand.

I snatch a magazine from the bedside table and lie down where the disk is hidden, leaning forward as though I'm paying close attention to her autumn makeup tips, and when the door opens and I see that it isn't Rosanna, was never Rosanna, was never going to be, I am disciplined enough not to let even the slightest flicker of disappointment pass across my bandaged face. My hands do not shake. I hold them steady as I imagine Rosanna, leaning forward toward me from my mirror, pulling the skin of her left eye tight as she sweeps a cat eye on.

"Hi, Max!" I say. "Back so soon? Guess you missed me."

I try to stand, the box of tapes sliding from my lap, my legs shifting to cover the space where I had shoved the disk, although rationally I know there is no way the gap it creates would be large enough for him to see. Now that I know it was Max at the door, I don't feel bad about hiding the tape. I will watch it on my own, secretly. I will gather all the information I can. If he wants to keep secrets about Rosanna, fine. I can keep secrets, too.

"What are you doing?" asks Max. He crosses the room quickly, kneeling by the chaos at my feet. "Why were you touching the footage?"

There's a wounded tone to his voice. He wants me to feel remorseful, like I've betrayed some kind of trust. He's getting agitated, examining the label of every tape as he puts it back. I hop up, casual, trying to ignore the swimming feeling in my head as I sit down close beside him. Does he really distrust me so much?

"I just wanted to hold them," I say. "I wanted to feel close to her. I'm sorry I made such a mess, though. Here, let me help you!"

I pick up a big pile of tapes and disks and drop them into the box, chattering as I crawl around the room, my head pounding, gathering up messy stacks of footage and piling it at his feet, like a tribute, like piling wood on a pyre. He has slowed down, isn't looking so closely at the tapes. He is losing track, listening to me. It's working. I sit down close beside him and stroke his arm.

Beside me, Max sits still. "You really shouldn't have touched them," he says.

"Not without you," I say. "I know."

Sitting still, trying not to breathe, I start to notice all the things I've trained myself not to notice: the filth of the room; the tightness of the bandages pressing up against my mouth, my nose. I think of Rosanna's house, all that empty, unused space. How deeply unjust it all feels. She should have me with her. She should keep me close. Rage builds inside me, glowing like a hot coal, but I keep stroking his arm, keep talking, quiet and sweet.

"Maxie, I'm sorry. I didn't mean to make you nervous. It won't happen again."

This is something Rosanna does. Everyone has a sweet little nickname with her. I know them from the cards. I think she does it for two reasons: to show familiarity and bond with the person she's addressing, and to establish her dominance over them. They are her pet, her project. I have never called Max anything but Max before. The name feels clunky on my tongue. But he seems to like it. He smiles. He leans close, holds my chin in his hand. His grip is gentle, but the pressure of his fingers on my raw skin still hurts. He looks deep into my eyes. I keep smiling. *Breathe,* I remind myself, *breathe.* Everything is normal. I picture Rosanna's face from an interview she gave about handling the pressures of her growing wellness empire, how she tilted her head back to catch the light. I picture her face floating down to cover my own, a living mask, protection. I smile, the bandages scratching painful against my jaw.

Finally Max lets go. He shakes his head at me, pretending annoyance. But his eyes are bright. "You're getting a little *too* good at this," he says. "That's exactly how Rosanna would have reacted. You're sticking your nose where it doesn't belong, and when you get caught you try to flirt your way out of it. Classic Rosanna."

My face goes hot. I might be blushing, but I'm so numb with fillers that it's hard to tell if what I'm feeling is the heat of emotion or the afterburn of pain. Either way, Max can't see it. And if he can't see it, it's like it never happened at all.

"Anyway," he says, "it's time to remove your bandages. None of this matters if the operation didn't work. And it's been long enough. I want to see you."

"I'm ready," I say. "I want to see me, too."

Max takes a slim pair of silver scissors from the pocket of his coat and lays them on the table beside a little bottle of rubbing alcohol, some gauze. His hands are shaking, just slightly. I can feel the vibrations agitating my swollen skin. He makes three cuts, two on either side of my jaw, one beneath my chin, the thin edge of the scissors nestling close. His gaze is clinical, taking in each part of me at once, a tight focus on the bridge of my nose, my lips. The bandages are soaked in blood and sweat. They cling. When he pulls them off, I can feel my skin coming, too. But I do not flinch. And then all at once, the bandages are gone. I close my eyes. I'm afraid of how he'll look at me. Max runs the tips of his fingers gently along the jawline of my new face. I can feel them snagging on the places the doctor has stitched up, lightening, gentle against my skin, a new-earned tenderness. Outside, I can hear the wind picking up. I imagine the feeling of it, the heat, the raw bitter urgency of air. I want to go out, to let the air blow sharp on my face. I want the outside light to cut me clean.

I open my eyes. Max looks at me. He doesn't say anything. He doesn't have to. He looks at me now like I'm brand-new. I take his hand in mine. He lifts my hand to trace the contours of my face, and I can feel it, throbbing, her skin, her lips, her soft little nose. The sweet tuck of her chin. Max looks at me and I look right back, and everything in me lights up. I am so happy. I am almost happier than I can stand.

7

When Max comes back the next day, I am ready, propped up in bed with my stack of magazines. I am aching and slick with ointments, vitamin E oil, aloe, sweet-smelling creams in tiny, perfect jars. All of it is almost too much, the pain mixing with the floral smell of everything on my face making me feel permanently nauseated. My head hurts too much to read, and so instead I try to concentrate on the images of Rosanna on the red carpet I find in the back pages of the magazines, comparing them to the tapes. I gently rub one finger along the edge of my healing jaw. The pain keeps me focused. Rosanna is always the winner in the "Who Wore It Best?" celebrity face-offs. Is she really always so triumphant? Or does Max not want to give me the chance to think of her as anything less than perfect? Will her small failures be revealed to me, now that I've proved my loyalty in such an irreversible way?

Max sits down on the edge of the futon, another cup of coffee in his hand. No plastic straw this time. My jaw is unbound. Theoretically, I should be able to drink normally, calibrate the opening of my new mouth. I try. My cheeks ache and stretch, the liquid burns my tongue. I smile at Max.

"Thank you," I say.

He nods, seeming distracted. "I've been thinking about last night," he says. "My selections. I think I may have started you off on the wrong foot with all those private moments. Maybe it was too much all at once. For now let's stick to persona work. More will come later. There's much more to come."

"I understand," I say, although I don't, I want to know more, know everything there is to know about her, want to know it now. I slip my fingers in over my newly full lips, reassured by the press of warm skin. A child's gesture, I think, suddenly ashamed. Max inserts the first disk.

"For me it's all about balance."

It is a shock to hear her public voice. Rosanna's performing voice, her voice for outsiders, is nothing like the private voice she uses at home. It is lower than I expected it to be, a little throaty. Glamorous as she is, there is something cozy about her. I must have heard it before at some point in the past, and the sensation is strange, remembering and not remembering, a slippery feeling like trying to catch a glimpse of some distant and tremendous monument, an iceberg hidden just out of view. Max leans toward the screen as if it is a source of warmth in a cold room. I remind myself to look at Rosanna, not his rapt face. She continues.

"And that's what makes these bars so great. They're the best of both worlds. Like, when I'm at home, I try to eat clean, have my green shakes, miso soup for breakfast, the good stuff Elsa, my brilliant nutritionist, is always trying to steer me toward. But I'm a Cali girl, so you know I love my In-N-Out! And those trashy spicy tuna rolls with gobs of mayo on them—it's horrible, I'm addicted to those things. But you gotta indulge yourself occasionally, am I right, ladies? Life is for living!"

The crowd applauds. Max hits pause, rewinds.

"Ladies? Life is for living!" Rosanna says.

"That's what makes her so amazing," says Max. "Those aren't just words. She was always so full of life. There was nothing on earth that scared her before the breakdown. I wish you could have known her then."

He hits play before I can respond.

Another talk show. Rosanna wears sleek leather pants, crossing her legs with casual elegance, folding into herself. Her hands float as she speaks, tracing invisible lines in the studio air.

"The most important thing is that you don't forget to have fun! Meditate, hike, but remember to dance, too. I love to put on some Beyoncé and just move! Eat cake for breakfast once in a while. You have to find the happy medium between kale and chaos."

This is her laugh line, and she pauses, looking out archly at the audience, that head tilt again, one eyebrow raised, and they obligingly laugh. They love everything she does. I can feel it through the screen as surely as she must, sitting on that stage. She gives the camera a wry look, as if to hold herself above the commercialized new age facetiousness she's peddling. It's almost as if she's looking right at me, like it's a signal. Look how smart we are, it says, smarter than this, but some things just have to be done. I lift my eyebrow the way she does, tilt my head. My hands open and move as hers move, through the air, floating on the same currents, making the same waves.

Max hits pause again and looks over at me. I feel suddenly aware of my imperfections, how broken my tender, swollen new face is still, yellowing like a bruised plum under his eyes. I give him the same small smile Rosanna gives the cameras. Offering something to him, holding something back. I pull back the blanket. I stand, feeling her power flooding through my body. I walk over to the kitchenette the way I practiced the night before, stalking back and forth across the worn wooden floor, copying Rosanna's small, graceful movements, the way she slips through space, the way her hips, my hips, swing, the careful slightness of her. It was a wonder the neighbors hadn't complained. Maybe there are no neighbors. The only evidence I have of the existence of other people is the occasional bark of dogs being walked on the street outside, the faint hum of engines in the morning as drivers descend from their hillside homes to the long streets of the city below, a light glimpsed in the window of a neighboring house. But inside my building, everything is still. The only sounds are the sounds I make, the chatter of the parrots. Once I thought I heard a baby crying and pressed myself up against the thin far wall, trying to absorb the sound of life, any life, going on without me. But there was nothing. I was wrong.

I walk my Rosanna walk over to the sink and back, pouring myself a glass of water from the carafe in the fridge, moving so smoothly its surface stays flat, the meniscus's arc unbroken, the same small smile on my face, a smile meant for no one in particular, the public smile of red carpets and talk show couches, a smile directed toward a kind and giving audience who already loved me as much as they could, who didn't need me to explain myself. I don't offer to get Max a glass. Rosanna never offers anyone anything in the footage I've watched, and I don't know how she, how I, would do it. Max looks almost frightened. I sit down beside him and touch his leg with the side of one hand, tracing his kneecap's soft sliding bone.

"Okay," he says, shifting his leg away from me, "I understand. We'll try the private tapes again."

He leans forward and hits eject.

Rosanna chops carrots with a sharp, expensive-looking knife. There is a small symbol engraved on the side of the blade, and it seems to shimmer in and out of being as the light shifts with the practiced motions of her arm. She is singing to herself under her breath. She thinks she is alone. She scrapes the carrots into a blue bowl and turns, smiling, a smile I haven't seen before, her face lit up and vulnerable. When she sees the camera, it disappears.

"Oh, you!" she says. "Stop! Don't I get enough of that nonsense already?" Her voice is light, like she's joking, but the corners of her mouth stay tight.

It's the same as the tapes from yesterday, just a little too private. Invasive, somehow. Wrong. I can feel the tautness in Max's legs, how his whole body is tilted just slightly toward mine. My bruises pulse. I turn toward him, tilt my head, give him that same small smile. I look right into his eyes.

"Don't I get enough of that nonsense already?" I say, Rosanna's voice pouring flawless from my throat. It's all a game. A game I am getting better and better at playing.

Max smiles. Leans forward. Slips in another disk. I lean close to his silent body in the dark.

. . .

For weeks, we sit together in my small dark room and watch Rosanna. As the nights pass, we move closer and closer until our bodies almost touch—almost, but not quite. If I move toward Max, he says nothing to stop me. He never moves closer to me. My face slowly begins to heal. When I catch a sideways glimpse of my reflection in the shadowy mirror of the window, it is almost as though I see Rosanna looking back at me, beautiful. I feel a tenderness toward myself that is like nothing I have ever known. I rub my ointments on my scars every night before I go to bed. I can no longer tell where I am numb.

Every night we stay up late, drinking Diet Coke and smoking cigarettes, binge watching Rosanna's life like it's reality TV. Slowly Max starts staying over again, with no medical excuse this time. When he is there, I sleep through the night. Something about his presence, another breathing body in that silent room, comforts me. In the mornings I hang my hand down over the edge of the bed, my fingertips brushing his shoulder, hunched under the crumpled blanket of his suit, his face smoothed calm by sleep, soft, open, like the face of a child. When he starts to stir, I clamp my eyes shut so I can listen to him moving around the kitchen. I like to have him wake me up, sitting on the edge of the mattress, coffee in hand, to talk with him a little before I do my exercises. I like to watch him taking care of me.

We move from topic to topic: business meetings (the camera up high over one end of the boardroom table; "it's not acceptable," Rosanna says, a blond man, her agent, subservient, nodding back), lunches with friends (Marie, her best friend, most often, and a few times martinis with a suavely handsome man whom I recognize from the cards as a professional acquaintance; she calls him Leo and smiles up at him from under her eyelashes), interviews (on talk shows, red carpets, backstage, the same few faces over and over, as familiar as old friends). The moments I like best are Rosanna at home by herself, having conversations with people offscreen, watching television, brushing her hair. Making salads alone in her enormous kitchen, talking on the phone. Max likes everything the same, all of it Rosanna, a proof of our dedication to her work. I don't ask Max any more questions. I take the footage as it comes.

We watch until we get hungry. Really, Max gets hungry, and he tells me when it's time for me to eat. One meal a day is almost too much. I'm used to so much less, am sleek, efficient, slimmed down. I drink chia seeds and water until I stop flinching as they slide viscous down my throat. I have found I cannot trust the feelings in my body. I listen to Max when he tells me what I should consume. I don't know what my body needs. It doesn't belong to me anymore. Sometimes I make us lunch, standing at the open counter of our tiny kitchenette, watching Rosanna prep the same meals on talk shows or in her own much larger kitchen, my body in sync with hers, trying to move so smoothly that if Max looks at me it will be as though the screen is a mirror. But he never looks, his eyes focused on the screen. I stare hard at Rosanna's smiling face. I chop hard with my own sharp knife. Max leaves me and returns with Rosanna's favorite dishes from Rosanna's favorite restaurants, full sets of cutlery and glassware and plates. I watch Rosanna eating oysters, the way that she twirls spaghetti in a soup spoon, how, when someone makes a joke, she puts down her fork, laughs, picks it up again. I practice ordering. "A carafe," I say, or "No anchovies." Rosanna has a voice she uses to speak to waiters—friendly, neutral, flat. Max watches me as I watch Rosanna watching shows, syncing up the images so we see the same moments of the same sitcoms at the same time. I laugh with her, paint my toenails, swear under my breath when we smear the polish. Sometimes I angle my body so I can't see her. But I can always feel her, the two of us together in one smooth sweep, synchronized swimmers moving silent through dark water. My body has taken on a new gravity, a thrillingly substantial weight. For the first time in a long time, I feel that I am present in the world.

"What was it like growing up in a show business family?" the interviewer asks Rosanna, Max asks me, their voices clumsily layered. It isn't like that when Rosanna and I speak. When we speak, we sound the same. One voice, not two. We pause, and I turn away from her toward an imaginary camera, smiling.

"Well, Dad was a real character. I remember one time when I decided to put on a circus for my parents' friends during one of their famous dinner parties. It was going to be the greatest show on earth. I wanted to show them that I was a real professional. I got my nanny to help us assemble a costume. I was a ballet dancer for the first act, then a lion, when I would pull my tutu up around my face."

Another glance to the audience, small smile. Picture me, isn't that charming?

"I crept downstairs ready to show off. I came onto my makeshift stage and started doing a magic trick I had been practicing all week. I was so proud of myself! But one of the guests, I think it must have been my aunt Clementine, she took these things so seriously, yelled that she could see what I was doing. Performing was important to them. It was important that I got things right."

The interviewer, a middle-aged woman with a blond swoop of thinning hair laughs. "She really called you out!"

Rosanna laughs, too. I lean my head back as she leans hers, put my hand on Max's knee the way she touches the interviewer. I try not to notice that he flinches.

"She did! And I of course was shattered. I thought I was so smooth."

"No," says Max, pausing the tape, "not like that. That last bit needs to be more of a private aside, like you're thinking out loud."

Hand on the knee again. "I thought I was so smooth!"

"Almost. 'She really called you out!'"

"She did! And I of course was shattered. I thought I was so smooth."

I want to look to Max for approval. I don't. I look straight out toward where the camera would be, into Rosanna's eyes. I want to know what she knows. I want to feel what she feels. I keep talking, my sore jaw smiling wide. My arms are exhausted, but my hands, like her hands, float effortlessly through the air.

"So Daddy leaps up from the table and starts directing. He tells me my blocking's all wrong! He puts me up on a chair, says, 'Action!'

and I go through the whole act without a hitch, to thunderous applause, of course. I was so pleased with myself! I thought I was a star."

"There should be a little anger leaking, though. You're trying to make it sound like a funny story. But it's not funny to you."

"I go through the whole act without a hitch, to thunderous applause, of course. I was so pleased with myself. I thought I was a star."

"Clementine wasn't really your aunt. Your father was with her when your mother died. A few months later, they were married. You were sent away to school."

"I started doing a magic trick, and one of the guests, I think it must have been my aunt Clementine, yelled that she could see what I was doing."

"She really called you out!"

"She did! And I of course was shattered."

Max nods once. "Better."

There is one scene Max gets stuck on. It opens with Rosanna sitting in her living room on her milk-white sofa, her body language telegraphing exhaustion. When she speaks, her voice is tense. It is one of the few times in all that footage that she allows herself to get angry.

"You're making this into a bigger deal than it has to be," I say, says Rosanna, turning the page of our book. I try to look over the pacing man's shoulder, but she is obscured by his body, which is in turn obscured by the angle of the camera. All I can see are her hands, turning the pages with a violent flick of the wrist.

"Oh, so it's not a big deal?" the man says with Max. Their voices sound so similar it's as if one person is speaking. *That's right,* I think, *that's just what I should sound like.* I answer, trying to sync my voice exactly with hers, pitching down my tone slightly until it purrs in my throat, a radiator hum.

"It's not a big deal! A few months. Three at most. You can fly out and see me anytime you like. I have to work. Three months is nothing."

The man's body shifts, just a little, and I catch a glimpse of Rosanna's face. It's totally neutral. She seems profoundly uninterested in this conversation, her mind somewhere far away. She turns, I turn, another page, looking. The man sits down, disappearing from the frame. Rosanna's eyes stay on the page.

"Rosanna," he says, "it's always a few months with you. A few months in Paris, a few in New York, you're always disappearing. How long has it been since we slept under the same roof for more than a week?"

"It's not like you're sleeping alone," we say, turning a page, our face neutral, our voice flat. Pause. Rewind.

"Again," says Max. "Less angry, more sad."

"It's not like you're sleeping alone."

And then on the same tape, the next scene, a brief snatch of empty darkness. Rosanna lies still in bed, her hair pushed across her face, disheveled with sleep. She stirs when she hears him coming.

"I'm sorry," she says. This is her private voice, soft and low in her chest, the words planted deep. I think I understand why Max keeps returning to this moment. It is my only chance to know this part of her.

"I'm sorry about before. I'll be nice. You know how nice I can be when I want to. Don't leave. I love you. I love you so much."

She keeps her eyes closed. Her skin is pale and glossed with sweat. She looks like she is dying. I lie down on the futon and shut my eyes. Max brushes his cold hand across my forehead.

"Don't leave. I love you. I love you so much," I say.

"Again," says Max.

He pauses the tape, rewinds. Rosanna and I speak as one.

"Don't leave. I love you. I love you so much."

Pause. Rewind. Play.

"I love you. I love you so much."

Rewind.
"I love you so much."
Rewind.
"I love you so much."
Rewind.
"I love you so much."
Max sits beside me, silent, in the dark.

8

*W*e are sitting on the couch watching videos when someone knocks on the door. Rosanna is in front of a live audience, laughing, so at first I do not register the sound as coming from my side of our shared reality. It blends in with the applause, the shouts of the crowd. But then it comes again. Three deliberate knocks. My brain skitters to a halt, turns over a few times, a hollow knocking against the inside of my own skull. And then I realize what it means. Rosanna wouldn't have to knock. There is someone here who shouldn't be. A stranger. For a moment, I am not sure whether or not I want to be discovered. There's this long instant where I don't look at Max and he doesn't look at me and I shrink back against the cushions and think about what it would be like to fling the door open, announce myself to whatever has come knocking. But no, not now. It's too late for any of that. I force my body to move. If there's one thing I know, it's how to hide. Leaping up, I turn the television off and lie flat on the ground to avoid anyone's seeing me through the window. I grab Max's hand, try to pull him down with me, to wiggle my body under the narrow space of the futon's frame, but he laughs, *laughs!* Like this is nothing. Like our door is an ordinary door in an ordinary building full of ordinary people. Like we live in the sort of place where neighbors drop by for visits. Like any of this is normal.

He laughs at me for following the rules of the reality he has created for me. Hatred passes through me, sharp and hot.

"So nervous," he says. "I promise it isn't the feds!"

He knew this was coming. He has invited someone into my space without asking, without so much as giving me a warning.

"I can't do this," I say. I whisper, trying to pull him down to the floor with me. "I don't care who it is, tell them to go away. I'm sick. I'm not ready, Max, I can't."

He crouches beside me, gathering me up in his arms, gently guiding me to my feet. "Yes, you can," he says. "You can, and you have to."

For months it has felt as though the world outside has quietly come to an end, the two of us the only survivors, alone together in this tiny apartment. Of course I know this isn't true. There are signs of life everywhere: passing cars, barking dogs, people walking in the street. The world keeps going on without us, however improbable that seems. Max has spoken about the things that will happen when I venture out, how I will start small, lunches with Max in Rosanna's favorite restaurants, long walks on the beach. Plans are being made; a scaffolding is in place. I thought my life outside this room would begin gradually. I thought there would be preparation, long hours of practicing, rules. But here it is, my new life starting. An ordinary day. A knock on the door.

Max walks past me. He opens the door. And then there is a woman, first in the hallway and then in the room, our room, mine, striding over the threshold without pausing, like it's nothing, like there's no barrier there, no border to cross. The door is just another door to her. She stops and kisses Max, once, twice, lingering a little too long, and she's beautiful, taller than me, impossibly slim, her red hair shining in soft waves around her milk-white heart-shaped face. I hate her. I hate her being here. I want to move toward her, push her out the door, and lock it behind her, keeping Max inside, here, with me. Instead, I move closer to Max, hiding my still flawed self, my cellulite, my scars, behind his familiar bulk.

"So good to see you!" the woman says, moving forward, and I shrink back from her body, farther toward the wall. All I can do is look at her. She is so loud, chatting, unpacking her cases with a zipping tear of Velcro noise, clicking her heels across the floor, rupturing the quiet. The air is suddenly full of her smell, the strong punch of soap and deodorant and perfume, mint from the gum she is chewing, the animal presence of an unfamiliar body, so unafraid of taking up space that the world seems to contract around her. In this way, she is more like Rosanna than I am, moving so casually, unpacking two pairs of scissors, a comb, a brush, draping a sheet over the wooden chair that stands by the window, laying out a towel for her bottles, shampoo, conditioner, pomade, gel, opening the window and leaning out for a moment, looking up and down the street. The way she angles her body out into space suggests a casual relationship to the outside world. The fresh air is not precious to her. I hate her more and more.

"And you, Holly," says Max. "Thank you for coming. It's been too long."

"Whose fault is that?" says the woman, laughing, putting one hand on his arm. "I kid, Max, I kid. I know how busy we both are. And you look good! Although those edges aren't mine. Are you stepping out on me?"

A light laugh, she touches his arm again. I want to swat her hand away.

"Never!" he says. "I'm a one-woman man."

It's weird to hear him talking this way, so flirtatious, unserious, relaxed. She laughs again.

"Sure," she says. "Like I haven't heard that one before."

I notice that she still hasn't looked at me. What has he told her? Has she been warned?

"Anyway," she says, "I'm sorry to have kept you waiting! Traffic can be murder on this side of town. Beachwood on a Friday afternoon, all those tourists jumping out of their cars in the middle of the street to take pictures of the Hollywood Sign—my god, Max, what were you thinking? It's a good thing I like you."

Holly finally cranes her neck around him to look at me. "So this must be my mysterious client!" she says. "Don't worry, Max told me discretion is paramount. I'm here to help. This haircut isn't going in my portfolio. Although look at those snarls, hon—you'd make a great before and after."

I put one hand up to check, gently patting the side of my head. She's right, it's a mess, full of split ends, matted with sweat. I haven't been taking care of myself. I haven't remembered to. My hair seems almost incidental in the face of so much dramatic physical change. I attempt a smile, but my fingers stick in the thick knots and I am filled with a powerful shame.

"Okay," I say. "Thank you."

It has been so long since I've been in the presence of another person that I've forgotten how to behave. Surely there is a script here, words I'm supposed to say, motions I'm supposed to go through, but my mind feels fuzzy, my thoughts a disoriented blur. All I can think is that something is not right. That her presence is an intrusion, a violation, like the doctor sliding his fingers under my skin. A reminder that my body is not my own. I keep my widest smile plastered on my face. I am dimly aware that I must look crazy, but I can't stop, can't stop smiling. It's the only thing I remember how to do.

She is closer to me now, and I inch my way up the couch toward Max, who laughs meanly.

"Where are you going?" he says, grabbing my arm and making me stand up beside him. I try to subtly pull him back with me into the small safe space of the kitchen where we can stand close together and hide, his body protecting me from her. This woman means me harm, I am sure of it.

"It's okay," he says. "Holly is a friend."

"I know," I say. "It's just . . ." I find I am unable to continue.

Holly comes close again, smiles at me encouragingly. "It's nice to meet you," she says, speaking slowly, as though she suspects I might not be able to understand her, "I'm Holly. What's your name, sweetheart?"

I realize that I have no idea what to tell her. Does Max want me to use my old name or my new one? I can't say Rosanna, that's not my name, but I can't say my old name, either. The contract was very specific about that. Still, as I think of it, as my lips try to move into its old familiar shapes, I realize that the feeling of it has totally changed. The syllables of my old name weigh heavy on my tongue, as numbing and slick as ice. It no longer feels like it belongs to me. I find that I cannot say it. I can't say anything at all.

"I . . . ," I say, "I'm—"

"This is Rosanna," says Max.

My name in his mouth is a shock. I can feel the warmth of it spreading through my whole body, bringing me back into myself.

"Rosanna," I agree.

Her eyes widen. "Oh," she says, "of course you are. I almost didn't recognize you under all those snarls. Well, that explains a lot. I thought you looked familiar. I'm a fan, of course, but we don't need to talk about it. I understand the need for discretion. I'm an old friend of Max's, I have many celebrity clients."

I force myself to stick out my hand for her to shake. Rosanna is good with strangers. Max smiles. Her touch, as she reaches out to take my hand, is surprisingly gentle. Hesitant. She is the first person I have touched in months, apart from Max, who doesn't count. He doesn't really feel like a separate person anymore. Her hands are so soft. It's kind of repulsive how soft they are, like slick slabs of butter. I have to make myself hold on until her grip loosens, make myself stay still and not try to wipe her off on the fabric of my sweat pants. It's all too much. Everything is more than I can bear. But Holly doesn't seem to notice.

"I have to say," she says, "you look fantastic! Have you lost weight? I'd heard you were undergoing some . . ."—she pauses to gesture vaguely in the air—"changes. And what has become of that beautiful hair?"

She reaches past Max to touch it, running her fingers across the scalp. I try not to flinch. I force myself not to move away from her, to look straight into her eyes and smile. I am determined to look normal. Welcoming. Like I'm not scared of her. My tongue is stiff in my mouth, pressed up hard against the smooth back of my teeth. I can feel her waiting for me to speak. She gives me another helpful little smile.

"I just," I say, trying to figure out what's expected of me, what I am supposed to do, "I'm not sure."

I look to Max again, but he just smiles and smiles, his face stiff with falsely casual rigor. His eyes are hard against me. I know that he is sure I will make a mistake. I want to hit him. He's supposed to be taking care of me. It's his fault if I'm not ready, his fault if I don't know what to do. My heart is beating so hard I feel like it's going to burst out of my chest and flop down bloody onto the carpet. Max stays silent. Holly is waiting.

"I don't know what happened," I say. "I'm sorry. It's been a difficult time."

Everything in me wells up. Holly stares, still holding a fistful of my hair in her hand. It can't have been much time since she spoke, a few seconds, maybe, but it feels like forever.

"Are you okay?" she says.

Her voice is more gentle than I have any right to expect, I, this bedraggled stranger, tearing up in a dirty apartment. *She's trying*, I think. At least one of us is trying. I cannot speak. I nod. She removes her hand from my hair.

"Oh," I say, "yes, sorry, just . . ."

Max is silent. I can feel the burning fixity of his gaze.

"Long day," I say. "Forgive me."

"Hey," she says, "it's fine. We've all been there. I understand."

I do not let myself look away from her. I breathe. Holly is in our space now. It's my job to make her feel welcome. To show her she's less important than me. I take a deep breath and reach out to hold Max's hand, pressing my nails hard into the soft skin of his palm. I want to hurt him, just a little. To make him aware of my capacity to hurt. If Max asks, I will say I was nervous. I didn't mean to hurt him. Of course not.

"So nice of you to come," I say.

My voice comes out right this time, modulated with Rosanna's low warmth. I can feel her words slide into my mouth, something inside me clicking into place. I take a deep breath. I let go of Max's hand. I'm not afraid anymore.

"It's been so long since anyone decent looked at my hair," I say. "Thank you so much for taking the time."

I am regaining my footing, my charm. My voice grows steadier. Rosanna's easiness flows into me like water, new blood in my veins.

In the bathroom, Holly sits me down on the floor next to the tub and runs the water, testing it on the inside of her wrist, waiting until it's the perfect temperature before she tilts my head back and pours warm water down my forehead, gently massaging my scalp with some sweet-smelling shampoo, the sounds she makes disappearing into the murmur of water on water. Her hands are so gentle, but it hurts, it's too much, the touch, the closeness of her. When I was small, my mother used to wash my hair this way, cupping my forehead with her palm so the water didn't run into my eyes. It was the only time she really touched me with anything like gentleness. It was important to her that my hair was properly washed, pretty. That I looked neat, despite everything. That people would know, when they looked at me, that she was a good mother. Holly sits in the same pose, moving with the same gentleness, the same soft hands and soft warm water. I close my eyes tight to hold back the feeling that wells up, but it doesn't work. I start to cry, not making a sound, the tears mingling indistinguishably with the water running through Holly's palms. *A baptism*, I think. If Holly notices, she is too polite to say.

We don't talk when she's done, don't let our eyes meet in the mirror in the long silence as she combs and cuts my hair.

"Much better," she says when she's done. "See how pretty you are now?"

I can hear my mother's voice in her mouth.

Afterward I sit on the floor, a towel still wrapped around my shoulders. Through the thin door I can hear Holly and Max speaking in hushed tones. I listen, closing my eyes, feeling their voices drift toward me through the wood.

"Is she okay?" asks Holly.

There is a long pause in which Max doesn't say anything.

Holly continues, "I don't want to pry. And I mean, it's obvious that she hasn't been out in a while. We all know that. But is she okay now? What happened? She seems so strange, poor thing."

There is an excited, gossipy edge to her voice. This is big news. I am big news. I wonder how long I've been gone for, and correct myself—Rosanna, it's Rosanna who's been gone. I have been here all along. I couldn't leave if I wanted to. I don't have anywhere to go. I close my eyes and rest my head against the cold porcelain lip of the bathtub.

"She's fine," says Max. Another pause. "The past year has been tough. Well, you know it's been tough for a while. But she's out of treatment now and happy to be back in Los Angeles. Thank you again for coming over. Rosanna's house is under construction, and her useless contactor has had the water shut off for a week now. Her assistant was kind enough to let us use her place, although I know the space is less than ideal. I can't tell you how much we appreciate your discretion in this matter."

"Of course," says Holly, "of course. And I'm glad she's getting better, but she doesn't seem fine. Neither do you, Max."

He sighs. His voice with her is different from the way it sounds when he talks to me. Less controlled. He is allowing himself to sound annoyed, confused, vulnerable. Emotions I'm not supposed to hear him feel.

"Well," he says, "as you can see, I've sort of had my hands full. But I can't tell you how good it is to see you. Now, don't tell anyone about Rosanna. I'll call you soon, I promise."

"Please," says Holly, "save it. I don't care about calling or not calling. This isn't a jealousy thing. It's just that I don't see you around anymore, not at all. Nobody sees you. You've disappeared as much as she has. I know your job's important to you—really, I do; no one understands that better than me—but this is too much. You can't let her problems become your responsibility. I know you think it's none of my business, but whose business is it, Max, if not mine?"

I expect him to defend me. His problems are my problems, Rosanna's. A calling, he said. But there is only silence. Max says nothing in response. I swear I can hear the movement of bodies. Are they closer to each other now? Is he moving toward her? Do they touch? I press myself against the door, listening. I cannot stand it. I cannot stand him telling her secrets, letting her think that they are close, closer than he and I are, when both of us know that could never be true. And then I hear her gathering her things. I hear the door click closed behind her, the turning tumblers in the lock. I want to throw the door open, confront him, sitting there with his head in his hands, thinking about the mysteries of his old life, whatever it is he thinks he has lost. It's nothing compared to what I've given up for him. He knows nothing about what true loss is. Nothing about me.

And then the bathroom door opens. Max is there, looking down at me, smiling in a way I haven't seen him smile before, his face wide open. Happy, I think. I guess I haven't really seen him happy before.

"Hey you," he says, "I wanna see your new look."

The sight of him there in the doorway, acting all friendly now that Holly's gone, turns my stomach. I don't want him to touch me. I can still feel the pressure of Holly's hands. She knows things about him I will never know. And neither of them knows a thing about me. It is my body, not his. Whatever Max might think, this is Rosanna's body and mine. I swat his reaching hand away, my fingertips making brief, sharp contact with his skin. I hope it hurts.

"Didn't Holly do a good job?" he says. "You clean up nice."

I don't like the way he says her name. I didn't like the way he talked to her out there, manipulating her. Like he tries to manipulate me. I think of the softness of her hands, her gentleness in cradling my skull, protecting my neck from the cold tub with a folded towel. Max will destroy her. For her, it is probably already too late. She believes him, his fake loneliness, his dedication to his own made-up cause.

"I heard you talking," I say. "I don't think you should see her anymore."

I expect him to laugh, but his face closes off. Sadness. It's like saying no to a child. He is so sure that this world, my world, was made for him. "Somebody's jealous!" he says.

I feel embarrassed somehow, like someone is watching and can see how bad we are at pretending to be what, friends? Max keeps smiling that painful little smile.

"Don't be absurd. As if I had anything to be jealous of. As if I could be jealous of you of all people, Maxie."

I keep my voice light, too. Playful. But I hope that he can hear the disdain in it, for his fake hurt, his fake loss. I stand up. I stand close to him, so close he can smell my shampoo, the same one Rosanna uses, rose sweet with a faint bitter tint of herbs. I am using her soap. I am wearing her perfume. I eat the same things she eats. If he closes his eyes, it is as if she is right there in front of him, so close he can almost touch her, if he dared to. Maybe with his eyes open, too, now. Maybe when he looks at me she is right there, staring out from behind my eyes.

"Don't be sorry," I say. "I'd be jealous of me, too. But it's time, isn't it?"

He shakes his head once, no.

"Yes," I say. "Yes. If you thought I was ready for Holly, then I'm ready. It's time for me to go outside."

He is looking straight into my eyes. He is looking at Rosanna, Rosanna's hair tumbling down around my new face, the gloss and bounce of it enveloping me like a protective curtain. It feels perfect. Holly did a good job.

"I know it's hard for you," I say, "I know. But she's seen me now. I know she said she'd be discreet, but she'll mention it to someone, just one person, Max, and it'll spread like wildfire. They'll hear that I'm back. I'm in Los Angeles, locked up in some crappy apartment. People will talk. Our only option now is to get out in front of it. I have to go somewhere public, be seen. We need to go somewhere I can be in control. Reclaim the narrative. I look like her. I have her face, her hair, her name. I'm ready, Max."

I brush my new smooth hair out of my eyes and step toward him, entering his space, and he moves away from me into the living room.

I think he will leave, but he just stands there silent, not turning on the lights, his back to the door. When he speaks, his voice is soft, hesitant.

"We'll have to practice," he says.

"We've been practicing," I say.

He looks away for a moment. He nods. When he speaks again, his voice is clipped, businesslike, all traces of hesitation gone.

"Tomorrow would be best. Let's get that hair photographed before you wash it again, yes?" He gestures at the futon. "Here, sit down. I'll be the waiter, you order."

I've watched so many hours of Rosanna at lunch. Of course I know what to do.

"A salad, please," I say. My waiter voice is perfect.

"Come on," says Max. "You're joking, right?"

I roll my eyes.

"A Diet Coke," I say. "No ice, and a Caesar salad with no anchovies. Thanks so much!"

I smile her distance-establishing smile, friendly but minimal, not too warm.

"Good," says Max, "again."

"Can I please have a Caesar salad? No anchovies, thanks! And a Diet Coke, no ice."

"Again," he says, and I sigh.

"Come on, Max, this is basic, can't we do something else?"

A tight frown crinkles his brow.

"This is important," he says. "It's a small thing, but it's important, and we have to practice. If you can't take it seriously, maybe you're not ready after all."

"I'm ready!" I say. "I'm ready. CaesarsaladnoanchoviesDietCokenoicethanks!"

I don't even pause for breath.

"Okay," says Max, perfectly calm. "Again."

We run through the sequence over and over until my words stop sounding like words, don't feel tied to any meaning at all. Finally Max is satisfied.

"There's one more thing," he says. "You know there will be people waiting for you. Photographers. You know from the tapes that they'll be yelling questions, but I don't know if you're prepared for how ruthless some of them can be. They might be soft on you, since it's been a while, but on the other hand, that's when an image of you looking upset would be the most valuable. You can sell a lot more magazines with tragedy than joy, that's for sure. So don't say anything. Not a word. I don't want them to trip you up. Besides, the more you say, the less money we can get for your first interview. We have to build as much mystery as we can so that your story will be desirable. The less you say, the happier Rosanna will be."

So there will be pictures. There will be images of me that will make their way into magazines, that Max will make sure get to Rosanna, so she will finally see me, see how convincing I am. All across America, maybe the world, people will sit and sift through those glossy pages, slump bathed in the blue light of their computers paging through gossip websites, reading about Rosanna and looking at me. Maybe someone from my old life will see me. They will look at Rosanna, so glamorous, so self-assured, so perfectly composed, and they will never, ever know the secret she is, we are, keeping from them.

"You can trust me," I say. "I won't say a word. Not even a sound."

9

The next morning when the car comes to drop off Max it stays, idling at the curb. I wonder if the neighbors will notice; the street is narrow and it seems suspicious, the same car parked out front all day. I swear I can feel the engine vibrating all the way up where we are. Suddenly my situation seems a lot more precarious than it did before. Maybe it's just nerves making me worry. *This was your idea*, I remind myself. Your stroke of brilliance. Last night, in the contained space of the bathroom, it did feel right. But now the interruption of our routine is unbearable. Max has forgotten to bring me my coffee, and the light streaming in the window cuts sharp as a knife. Everything outside feels brighter than I remember it being. He seems nervous, too, insistent on picking out my outfit for me, switching shirts and jackets, spending a solid ten minutes making me try on a series of identical gold bangles. Nothing is quite right. Maybe it will never be quite right again, the comfortable order of our little world disrupted. There seems to be a filmy skin in front of everything, keeping me apart, cut off from the world. I wonder if Max can see it, too.

At the door, I hesitate. In the apartment I am safe. Nobody can find me. Nobody Max doesn't invite in.

"Are we sure this is a good idea?" I say. "Because if you're not certain I'm ready, maybe we should wait."

"We're sure," says Max. "And you're right, we can't afford to wait any longer. Holly will have already started telling people about you, how oddly you behaved. We have to get out there ourselves, get ahead of the narrative, show everyone you're back, and better now."

He sounds frustrated, forcing a false comfort into his voice like he's reassuring an unreasonable child. After all, I can sense him thinking I asked for this.

"We'll leave soon," I say. "But maybe I need more time. A few days. Maybe I need to practice, just a little more."

I've thought so much about leaving my room. It's all I wanted. But now I realize that in my absence the outside world has grown without me, become larger, more frightening. I have no home there anymore. I'm not ready to carry Rosanna with me out into the sunlight, that clear and bright and shining world. I am afraid I will fail. I will fail her, and this will all be for nothing.

Max seems to sense my nervousness. He speaks more softly now, reaching out to put his hand on my arm.

"You're ready," he says, "I know you are. And it's a small thing, just a few hours. We're starting slow. We'll go to the restaurant, just me and you. You'll order the things we've practiced ordering, smile for the photogs, that's it. No big deal. We'll chat, we'll have lunch. You won't have to talk to anyone but me."

I remember how tense I felt yesterday, how overwhelming Holly's presence had been. The outside world will be far worse than that. So many things outside my control. But Max won't let me say no. He takes my arm and pulls me over the threshold into the silent hallway. I keep my eyes closed, letting him lead me. I am afraid that seeing the hallway will remind me too much of my late-night walk after the surgery, that something will snap inside me and I will begin to scream.

"You can do this," says Max. "I know you can."

Walking out into the open air is like getting slapped in the face. It's colder than I thought it was supposed to get in Los Angeles. Through my window everything always looks sunny and still, the world a perfect framed box, everything breathless, neatly contained. Out here, the wind kicks loose leaves up the street. The sky over the city is clear and cold, as blue as the water at the bottom of a pool. What month is it? I can't make my mouth form the words to ask. My tongue lies heavy as a slab of meat, and I stand there, frozen, in the open door. Max pulls at my arm, hurrying me. All this is happening too fast. He is asking for the impossible. He is asking me to fail publicly, humiliatingly. He wants to ruin me. I want to push past him and run, run up into the hills, away from here, leaving him behind. No one has seen me as Rosanna yet. I can gain back my old weight, break my new nose, dig up my old clothes from whatever landfill they're buried in. It's not too late for me to uncover some fragmentary version of myself. But the light makes me squint, helpless. The air feels thinner somehow than it does in the small coziness of my room. Outside smells like car exhaust, like dust, like nothing at all. Outside smells like Max, his body close as he pulls me through the doorway, and then there we are, together, in the world. He whispers in my ear as we walk down the gravel pathway.

"You look beautiful," he says. "You're doing so well."

The inside of the car is quiet. There is a driver in the front seat, maybe the same one from my first day, maybe someone different. I cannot see his face, just the back of his head, the soft fuzz on the neck there, a few red spots, the flush along the edges of his ears, a rash. Driving is the most surreal feeling. I try to figure out how long it has been since I was in this car, that strange first day, impossibly long ago. I should have been paying closer attention, marking time. I should have tracked the color of the leaves in the courtyard, the daily arrival of the birds, the quality of the room's light. But it is always the same, endlessly sunny and green, green. Every day the same day, an anonymous smear of perfect weather like the spilled slur of a dropped watercolor box. It is too late now to ask what has happened while I was busy not noticing. The motion of the car, the soft blurred noises of the air conditioner and Max's breath beside me, lull me into a feeling of surreal calm. The world around me feels strangely irrelevant, like a story someone else is telling.

My neighborhood unspools as we drive down the hill, turning

and banking, slowing at corners, the smooth movement of the car like the heavy strokes of a swimmer cutting through deep water. The streets open their arms, widening to accommodate the increasing flow of traffic, of other people in other cars, hunched over the wheel or texting at stop signs, all of them alone. I peer through the tinted glass trying to categorize every expression on every face, looking for some emotion I can recognize. One woman sings along to the radio, bopping her head from side to side. I am jealous of her freedom. She doesn't even consider that there might be someone watching. She is so unselfconsciously assured of her own perfect right to be herself, to be unobserved, alone. Then again, she is wrong.

I recognize the building we pull up in front of, the low striped awning, the gold frame painted on the windows, set dressing designed to make it look like a café in some small town in France, everything about it fake, pretend. It's one of Rosanna's favorite restaurants. Out front there is a group of men in black, pressing themselves back against the edges of the sidewalk, some of them standing in the street, waiting for something. Waiting for me. The thought lands heavy in my stomach. I watch them shifting, clumping together, pulling apart, a random pulse like the movement of insects. How long have they been here waiting? How did they know I would come? In the videos, there is always a crowd of them, parting like water as she moves through, security in front of her, haloed by flashbulbs, a force so large that it feels inhuman. But there are only a few men here, standing, smoking, all with the same harried look in their eyes. And I am just one woman, with a thousand imperfections that even Max's fastidious eye has missed, my skin tight from the shower's hard water, a small run starting in the toe of one stocking. I am just one woman, as good as alone, sitting in a stranger's car. Max hands me a pair of heavy framed sunglasses, and I slip them on, grateful. I need something to protect me from the directness of their gaze, the pressure of their attention on my brand-new face. The driver unbuckles his seat belt, and I realize he is coming around to open my door for me.

"Wait," I say, "just a minute. Just give me one minute to breathe."

"Okay," says Max, "be quick." And I breathe just like I said I would—*out, in*—fixing my lipstick with the compact in my purse—*out*. I smooth down my hair, fix my hem. It is only a few seconds of contact. I can do this. I am ready. I am as ready as I'll ever be. Without waiting for the driver, I open my own door.

The light filters in, blue, blunted at the edges, like I'm watching it on film, the noise of the street outside rushing into the quiet. I try not to teeter on my too-high heels. I try to remember her smile.

"Rosanna!" they shout. "Rosanna!"

Their voices come at once, a chorus, and then they splinter off, each of them lifting their camera, smiling the same stiff smile, shouting questions at me like we know each other.

"Looking good, Rosanna!"

And

"We missed you, Rosanna!"

And

"Who are you wearing?"

And

"Where have you been?"

"Rosanna, where have you been?"

Even the traffic seems to fall silent, the street holding its breath. I give them a little wave and glance behind me. Max is waiting in the shadow of the car. I see him like they must be seeing him, deferential, mild. My employee. Out here, Max belongs to me. I feel my new power flash through me, a rush of heat like blushing. Is this what being Rosanna feels like? I toss my new hair and smile my new smile. I say nothing. The crowd of men parts with the force of us, just like I imagined, a miracle. And then we are inside, the strange quiet of the busy restaurant. No one even glances up. There are so many people, so many bodies in this room, with their smells and heartbeats and secrets and pasts. I try not to think about the infinite little worlds all these strangers must carry around inside them, so many of them featuring my face. I stand tall in my high heels. I smile my Rosanna smile.

"Why isn't anyone looking?" I whisper to Max.

"It's L.A.," he says. "This is how we do things. Everyone's acting like they're too big a deal to care that you're here. But believe me, as soon as our backs are turned, the phones will come out. Your name will be all over the news tomorrow. The reappearance of the mysterious Rosanna Feld, as beautiful as ever."

Beautiful, I think. *He called me beautiful.* Then no, I realize. He's not talking about me. He's talking about Rosanna. He's picturing her face, beautiful as ever, beautifully alone in the silent dark.

"Oh, Maxie," I say, "please, you're too much."

The hostess leads us toward the back of the room, up a slight skip of stairs to a red leather booth. There is a brass plaque on the wall with my name on it. As I slide in, I lay my hand flat on the cold surface of the dark wood, tracing the tiny indents of the letters with my fingers, those familiar shapes, the familiar prickle of my own name cold against my skin. I can see that Max was right. Across the room, people are studiously not looking at us, whispering to one another, typing away under the table. Soon everyone will know that I am here. I think of Rosanna, alone in her house, looking at pictures of herself at lunch, and try not to shiver. My performance feels more real and more uncanny out here than it did in the apartment—unnatural, somehow. Strange.

"So nice to have you back with us, Ms. Feld," the waiter says.

I had been so distracted with all the strangers that I hadn't noticed him approach. I smile up at him, an instinct, bathing him in her warmth. *She's here with me,* I think. She's here in my reactions, my instincts. She's here keeping me safe.

"It's great to be back!" I say, smiling up at him.

"Always good to see you, Alan," says Max. "I'll have a panino, please, with prosciutto and mozzarella."

Alan looks to me.

"A Diet Coke, please," I say, "no ice. And of course one of your wonderful Caesar salads. Thank you, Alan!"

He smiles back at me, and makes a quick little note on his pad. "Coming right up!" he says.

I have perfectly executed my waiter voice, light, casual, with a slight uptick at the end of every phrase. I am gaining confidence, gathering strength. Maybe everything will be all right after all. I look at Max to see if he has noticed, but he won't look back. His face is blank and neutral. He has taken a calendar out of his jacket pocket and is pretending to point something out to me. I lean close to see what it is.

"No anchovies!" he whispers.

He speaks low enough that anyone listening in won't be able to make out his words. His voice is pleasant, helpful sounding, innocuous, the voice of someone hired to walk me through the intricacies of my day. My stomach drops. He's right.

"How could you forget?" he says. "We've been over this a million times. You've seen so many restaurant tapes. What were you thinking? You forgot to tell them no anchovies. Rosanna is—you're very particular about that."

I can see him catch himself as he says it. His voice goes even lower. He's looking past me now, gazing out into the restaurant with an inane smile. But his eyes are hard, the corners of his mouth drawn tight.

"You better hope they remember, or you'll have to send it back when it comes, and that's a bad look, and they'll notice if you don't, and if they notice that, they'll start noticing other things and this will all be for nothing. Jesus, I thought you were better than this. I thought you'd be better by now."

Alan walks past our table, close, and Max lets go of my hand. I raise it up again, out of his reach, stroking the plaque with my name on it. I feel it again, that same familiar tingle. Rosanna is with me. She'll tell me what to do. As I think this, a rush of confidence passes through me. A strange otherworldly warmth. I made a mistake. So what? I made a mistake, people like me make mistakes all the time. We never have to fix them. That's what people like Max are for. This is his job. I pull a compact from Rosanna's purse and pretend to adjust my lipstick as I whisper so no one can see my mouth.

"You have to tell him," I say.

He looks at my reflection in the mirror, his eyes still hard. "Are you crazy?" he says in that light, helpful tone, smiling wide.

"I'm not crazy," I say, "and I don't make mistakes. Not out here.

Not in front of other people. You do. You didn't remember to tell
him about the anchovies. You need to tell him you were wrong. It's
the only way we can make this convincing. Out here, Max, you work
for me." I snap the mirror closed. Rosanna winks out of being. I give
Max a bright smile.

Max looks at me for a long time. I can see how angry he is, can
tell that he wants to slap me, to shake me, to scream. But he can't.
He knows I'm right. Under the table, I wrap my fingers around his
wrist. I pretend to be looking for something in my purse. Finally
looking away from me, he waves Alan down.

"Yes?" says Alan. "Anything else I can get you?"

"Could you remind the kitchen that Rosanna doesn't like anchovies in her salad?"

I look up, noticing, and place my hand on his arm. "You're sweet
to think of it," I say. "But Alan's the last real waiter in Los Angeles, a true professional. None of this actor/singer/dancer business.
He takes his work very seriously. I'm sure he remembered my usual
order!"

Alan smiles. "Well, you're very memorable, Ms. Feld."

"Thank you, Alan," I say. "You're too kind."

I feel Rosanna's name pulse, sending a burst of energy down my
spine.

"Christ," I say, turning to Max, maintaining my normal volume,
"what a day. I would kill for a cigarette." I lower my voice so only
Max can hear me. "That was good," I say. "Right?"

Max smiles back. "You were right. It was perfect. Exactly
what Rosanna would have said. And how did you know about the
cigarettes?"

"I've seen the way she disappears from the table sometimes, for
longer than it takes someone to use the bathroom. And you can
never really get the smell out of her clothes. I know all about her
sneaky little habits. You can't just give me the good parts, Max. I
signed up for Rosanna, the whole thing."

Max turns to me, his face open, something like wonder written
on it.

"So, what about that cigarette?" I say.

"You really want one?"

I nod. I do. "You know I always have a smoke when you do something stupid."

"Incredible," he says. "Go through the kitchen. There's a door that'll spit you out into the alleyway."

I check the front pocket of my purse. It's all inside, a cigarette case, a little red lighter, a slim blue pack of gum.

"I wish you wouldn't smoke," Max says, almost loud enough for the people seated close to us to hear. "You know how bad it is for you."

I smile my warmest, most public Rosanna smile. "Oh, Maxie, you're no fun. One cigarette a day won't kill me. I deserve a few guilty pleasures!" I put my hand on his arm, giving him an affectionate little squeeze.

"You deserve everything in the world," says Max.

And the way that he looks at me, I know he's right.

Max comes to the apartment with a stack of magazines as thick as a phone book. I'm leaning against the counter drinking lukewarm coffee and craning my neck to look out the window when I hear the car pull up. It's been almost a week since we had lunch together, and I haven't seen Max since. I have done the usual things I do while waiting for him, exercised and read and eaten piles of raw vegetables standing over the sink, but I haven't been bored. I feel animated with a strange excitement. I know he's coming soon, bringing word from Rosanna. I can feel the nearness of him like a low murmur inside me. The birds shift and clamor in the courtyard. I know he must be halfway up the stairs by now, but I don't move. I remember how good it felt in the restaurant to have him listen to me, accept my way of doing things. I want him to know I can handle myself here, too. That I am doing fine on my own. Normally I can't hide my eagerness to see him when he's been gone for more than a few hours. I get so bored, so desperate for a glimpse of life outside my own head. I don't feel that way anymore. I can feel the whole world opening up around me, as silent and slow as a blooming flower.

"Hi," says Max.

"Hi," I say back.

I turn the page. I know what he has in his arms, but I can't bring myself to look. That's why he waited a few days. He was waiting for the magazines to come out so Rosanna could see how I did. I can't tell from his body language whether I did well or not, if they're calling me beautiful, welcoming me back, or saying all those horrible things he warned me about. If Rosanna is angry or pleased.

"Well," he finally says, "they're in."

There's a copy of one of the thin supermarket celebrity weeklies on the top of the stack, and he hands it to me. I am shaking a little, and the pages make a loud thwapping sound, like the crunch of dead leaves.

"Page fourteen," he says.

There's a Post-it marking the correct spot. I turn to it, and there's Rosanna. Walking into the restaurant, smiling, the sun shining bright on her face. Just like any of the magazines I read every day, the magazine that's wedged under my arm as I read this one. Only it isn't Rosanna. It's me. Even knowing this, for a moment I do not recognize myself. There is Rosanna, the slim-waisted grace of her, her smile, those eyes obscured by large sunglasses. But it isn't her at all. Intellectually I know this. I can remember walking that sidewalk, smiling that smile. I remember, or I think I remember, passing through that crowd of strangers, all of them calling my—her—name. But I can no longer be certain. I feel like I am sliding out of my body, the way that when riding a roller coaster, you sometimes feel jolted out of yourself, lagging somewhere behind, stuck in a loop or upside down, both there and not there all at once, divorced from the immediate sensations of your existence. I know it's me there on the page, that I am the one smiling, so self-assured, my hair lifted by a friendly wind, Max glowering behind me like my shadow. But it doesn't look like me. It looks like Rosanna. There is the small half grin she uses to charm strangers, the listing sway of her hips. Her hands are floating in the air in front of her like two white birds, her back straight, head tilted to one side. She looks like she always looks in paparazzi photos, beautiful, carefree. I have never looked that way. I have never felt that way. I run my fingers over the slippery barrier of their paper, pressing hard, as though I can break through to that perfect, glossy world. I want to feel the same easiness in my body that she carries in hers, there on the page. But I don't. I just feel like me, trapped in my heavy body. Weighed down by my flaws.

"What a nice picture," I say. "They really did a good job." I try to fill my voice with awe to hide how unsettled I am.

"That's my girl!" says Max.

He moves closer to me with this weird, awkward jolt. It is strange to have him being the one to touch me. I have always been the one to ask, to reach for him and be denied. Does he move toward me now because I've done so well? Because I look like that, like her, because I've taken on some small part of her power to bring the things she needs to herself without lifting a finger. For a moment I keep my body stiff, uncertain of what I should do. *I haven't earned this*, I think. The closeness, the touch. But still, it feels nice. If he's pleased with me, she must be pleased, too. She must know I'm doing well.

"Rosanna Steps Out!" the headline reads.

"Read to me," says Max. His arm is still draped around my shoulders. I am trying hard to act like all this is normal.

" 'Rosanna Feld was seen yesterday grabbing lunch in Los Feliz, security in tow.' Are you this alleged security?" I ask, trying to puncture the tension in my belly with a bad joke. "I better hope nobody tries to assassinate me."

"Very funny," says Max. "Keep reading."

" 'The star's team refused to comment on her time away from the Hollywood scene, saying that rumors about her secret pregnancy and brush with a notorious New York City sex cult are nonsense. Here's hoping she's back for good!' "

There she is, with her camera smile. There I am. I remember the bright faces of contestants on the television makeover shows I used to watch on those long afternoons home faking sick with my mom, looking in the mirror after their transformation. "Wow," they would always say, "I can't believe that's me."

"Wow," I say, "I can't believe that's me!"

Max lets me go. "Right," he says. "Of course it is."

His whole manner has changed. He looks the way I am used to him looking—kind, professional, a little stiff. Somehow this is a relief.

"Should we look at the rest?" I ask.

"Sure," he says, and then, seeming to catch himself: "Yes, of course. How exciting!"

But his voice sounds flat. He's not very good at pretending. I find this comforting. With Max, I will always be able to see what's coming next.

I pull another magazine from the pile. Max seems to assemble himself as I watch, standing up straighter, smiling. This is good news, after all. He should be happy for me. For us.

"Good choice," he says. "Go on."

" 'Reclusive heiress Rosanna Feld came out of hiding for a meal at Hollywood hot spot Doppia, where she was often seen with friends, fans, and fiancés in happier times. We're glad to see her out on the town and back on her feet. Feel better soon, Rosanna!' "

"What suck-ups," says Max, grinning, swept up again in the excitement of our success, "gunning for that first interview. Like Rosanna cares what they think. And *fiancés*, plural? There was only one, and that didn't last long. I do like the phrase *reclusive heiress*, though. Has a certain Gothic ring to it. Another."

" 'Hollywood Heartbreak: Still mourning the loss of her long-time partner, a grief-stricken Rosanna Feld braved the crowds at a restaurant they used to frequent in happier times, before their split and Rosanna's subsequent disappearance. Hollywood insiders are calling it a hopeful sign that the starlet is finally starting to recover from the devastation of what may have been a miscarriage as well as a breakup. Let's hope we'll be seeing more of her signature Euro Chic style on the town soon!' "

Max has nothing to say about that one.

We keep going through the stack, magazine after magazine, story after story. Each one has a slightly different theory, a slightly different angle of approach. Some talk about Rosanna like she's an eccentric loner holed up in the hills or a calculating businesswoman manipulating the laws of supply and demand by withholding herself from the public eye. Some speak about her as if she's a diva too good for us all or an emotionally fragile sweetheart who's just taking time for herself. The theories they offer about her disappearance don't seem plausible to me, and Max of course isn't saying anything. Maybe what he told me is true. Or maybe she's just bored by it all, caring for her mental health, on the mend in her mansion in the hills, tucked away watching her new life begin. It becomes less and less strange to look at the images, but still, I mostly keep my eyes focused on the captions. Looking directly into Rosanna's, my own, face, gives me an uneasy feeling.

"And what does Rosanna think about all this?"

What I really want to ask is what she thinks about me now that she's been forced to acknowledge the reality of my existence. I wonder how she feels now, wherever she is, looking at those pictures of me. Us, I guess. Watching me take my first steps into her world.

Max flips through another magazine, studiously casual. "Oh, you know how these tabloids are," he says. "It's all nonsense. She's experienced enough not to take any of it personally."

He knows this isn't what I mean. My heart sinks. She didn't like me, then. If she liked me, he would have said.

"Of course," I say. "A true professional."

I don't let my smile shift. I keep my voice calm.

"Like you," Max says.

"Yeah," I say, "like me."

10

The first thing is to go to the old places, the beautiful places that she, I, haunted before I came, where we were photographed dancing, drinking, buying clothes, eating lunch, kissing strangers.

"You get to go back," says Max, "live her life again, making the right choices this time. It's what everyone wants, isn't it?"

"I guess," I say.

It's not what I want. It's dangerous, thinking about what I'd change in my previous life. There are too many turning points to pick one moment and say, *There—there is where it all went wrong.* I imagine Rosanna feels the same.

"Anyway," says Max, "it's what's good for Rosanna. She was alone the first time. But now she has me, watching out for you in a way I could never watch out for her, orchestrating everything carefully so you don't do anything she shouldn't. It's perfect. A balanced and logical system. What I'm offering you is something Rosanna never had. Deliberation. Control. I'm going to help you take her life back for her."

We'll make people love her again. We'll remind them of her. And maybe she'll see it and be ready to come back into the world. I'll smooth down the ground before her, make her landing soft. When she returns, it will be to a better, brighter world. All thanks to me. I will take the darkness from her, draw the poison from her blood like a leech. But not yet. Now we are taking things slowly. It is important to take things slowly, Max says, to artificially create the rhythms of ordinary life, building a new reality one day at a time.

"And after that?" I ask.

"After that, maybe she'll get to go somewhere new. You will."

I am Rosanna's reincarnation. My footsteps will cover up her old tracks, obscuring them, keeping her hidden while she still wants to hide.

"But part of this is up to you," Max says, "a big part. You have to learn to sense her needs. I can't tell you everything, especially when we're out in the world together. You have to internalize every part of her personality so you know the things she wants to do but can't do on her own. So you develop an instinct for how she wants you to live her life."

I nod, as if I'm considering this for the first time. As if understanding Rosanna in this intimate way, getting under her skin, wasn't my goal all along. Let Max think this is his idea. That he has control here, too.

I begin meditating for large chunks of the day, trying to feel my way toward Rosanna's energetic hum. I want to be her avatar, her haunting, her projection. I try not to think of her as a person separate from me, as myself as separate from her. Watching the tapes becomes an exercise akin to looking at old yearbooks, seeing that smooth young face, glowing, hopeful, both you and not you, looking out from a past so blurred by distance that it's almost as though you imagined it. Not that I have any yearbooks. Not that there are any pictures of me where I look like that—beautiful, hopeful. I mostly skipped school on picture days, or hid in the bathroom until it was too late and the photographer had gone home. I changed schools so much that it seemed pointless to create a permanent record of anything, to act as though some kind of continuity existed, could exist, for me. Like the ground was ever steady beneath my feet. It was my way of feeling invisible, and in my invisibility, safe. But I can imagine what it would feel like, and this is it, this strange sensation of lateral movement, of both changing and not changing, holding on to a version of yourself that stopped existing a long time ago. Rosanna, wherever she is, aging in the darkness, nervous and alone, is nothing like the self-assured young woman on the tapes, the woman the public knows her to be. But I am. I am emerging into the world, clear-skinned and beautiful, wearing her old clothes, her old face. I am more like Rosanna than Rosanna is, now.

In the mornings I dress to leave the house, and so the next time the car idles at the curb and Max stands in the doorway of the apartment instead of coming inside and tells me we're going to lunch again, I am ready, made-up, dressed; my purse, Rosanna's purse, packed with her lipstick, cigarettes, half-empty wallet; and I stand up from my cross-legged pose, calm, like this is nothing unusual, and walk past him with a smile. *She wants a martini today*, I think, *red meat*. I crave gin, the salty tang of green olives stuffed with little slivers of pickled pimiento. I never liked olives before. Carrying Rosanna is like a strange pregnancy, bringing an onslaught of urgent new needs, cravings I never would have come up with myself.

"Today," I say, "Rosanna wants a martini for lunch. Somewhere pretty, with white tablecloths."

"Right," says Max. "The Chateau it is."

He takes my arm and leads me out the door. The air outside feels sharp against my skin, but I don't flinch, I welcome the feeling now. I love it. With Max beside me, Rosanna within, everywhere feels like home.

We drive to an old hotel in the hills where fountains drip in silent courtyards and climbing vines choke the wavy glass windows. There's a no-phone rule in the dining room, so I can relax my public smile and spend a slim half hour hunched conspiratorially with Max in the back booth, making bets as to who will pretend not to look at us next.

"Over there," I say, discreetly angling my chin toward a studiously underdressed couple in expensively minimal athletic gear. "They're definitely noticing."

"Well done!" says Max.

He picks out less obvious gawkers: the preppy family in matching navy blue and white outfits; a smooth-faced older man in a perfectly cut gray suit.

By the time we leave, a crowd of paparazzi stands outside, waiting to capture me climbing into the waiting car. A few of their faces seem familiar, maybe from the other day, the other lunch. It's sort of comforting, like going to a party where you don't know a soul and being surprised by an old acquaintance, a neighbor's daughter, someone you were distantly friendly with at school. I take this as a good sign. They are coming back for more. I give one of the familiar ones a conspiratorial little wave. When we get back to the apartment, the photo's already up online. Max shows it to me on his phone: "Rosanna Gets Flirty with the Paps," the headline says.

"Don't do that again," says Max. "It's too desperate. Not a good look."

I won't.

The next time we leave, it is to drive together down the hill to an outdoor market in what looks like it might be downtown. The streets are filled with a crush of strangers smiling into the air at nothing in particular, baskets and babies in their arms, their tranquillity unaffected by the cars rushing past, so close, the smell of gasoline and burned rubber giving the hot air an acerbic edge I can feel pressing against my teeth. I look for the Hollywood Sign in the hills above us. I haven't seen it yet. As is true of many things, part of me is wondering whether it even exists.

Max and I smile back at all the strangers. We eat raspberries out of the carton, rifle through rainbow stacks of leafy vegetables whose names I don't know. He buys me a bouquet of lilacs that scratch my arms, a small jar of buckwheat honey. I don't want any of it, but it feels good to be out in the world together, free. Someone takes a picture of us on their cell phone. In it, I am looking up at Max and smiling. "Rosanna's Forbidden Romance?" the headline says.

Max sighs. "You can't look at me like that."

"Whatever," I say. "It's like you said. They just need something to write about. People look at each other. It's not a big deal."

But my heart speeds up a little. Now Max is the one to hold the magazine close to his face, to press his fingers down hard on the glossy image, as if that would be enough to erase it. He says he will find me a new companion. It looks strange, he says, the two of us spending so much time alone. But days pass, weeks, and he doesn't find anyone else for me. I tell myself it is because he doesn't want to.

Max has a present for me. I am in my apartment. The light outside is the same light it always is: a clear, flat, seasonless gray. I am sitting on the couch with my magazines, not reading. I don't read anymore. I remember. I know every word of every article, the specific details of Rosanna's weight-loss tips, fashion tips, makeup tips, tips for interior design.

"Close your eyes," he says.

I don't want a present—the room is overcrowded already with the photographs, clothing, magazines. I feel hemmed in by objects. Is this how Rosanna feels? But Max has been so nice, so considerate about getting me out of the house every day, taking me beautiful places. So I mirror the expression on his face. I am expectant. I am pleased. I close my eyes. He places something small and smooth in my hand.

"Open your eyes," says Max. "Open your hands."

I do. I look into my palm. A phone. He is still looking down at me.

"Thank you," I say, neutral, pleased. "That's nice. Is it Rosanna's?"

It's an older model, a little worse for wear, the edges battered, one corner of the screen cracked like a spider web, both more and less than I expected somehow. I think about my mother's phone, which I had been so impressed by when I was little. If I was good, if I promised not to show Dad, she let me play games on it. A black-

and-white pixelated screen where a snake chased its own tail, getting longer and longer until it grew too long to sustain itself and the screen went blank. But I don't want to think about that old phone, that old life. I don't want to think about the people I might call, the possibility of a secret life it represents. I don't want to think about how Max is handing me the key to a door I am no longer sure I want to unlock.

"Thank you," I say.

He's still looking at me expectantly, smiling wide, eyebrows raised. Clearly this is important to him in a way I don't yet understand. I try doing what Rosanna would do, making a joke. "Aren't you afraid I'll run up a bill making personal calls?" I say. "Drunk-dial my old boyfriends? Order a hundred pizzas sent to your house?"

"You can't," he says. "You don't have anyone to call."

He's still smiling. But it's not a joke. His face has snapped shut, a cruel heat coming into his eyes. He wants to remind me that I am not, that I have never been loved. As if I could forget. *I could say the same thing about you,* I think. We look away from each other, mutually embarrassed. Max clears his throat. His voice, when it emerges, is businesslike, flattened out.

"I've logged into Rosanna's account on both this phone and mine, so all the texts you'll receive will also go to me. All other functionality has been suspended. There is no internet browser, just an email application. I'll read the message, and we'll decide together how you should respond. If I'm not in the room with you, I'll need you to send me your responses before you reply. Read receipts are on, so I'll see when you open your texts. You need to open and read all texts within five minutes, respond in ten, no matter how late it is. Keep the phone charged, the volume on. It's important that you don't keep anyone important waiting. If you do not respond, there will be consequences."

I don't care. I don't care about his limits. The important thing is that I have some way of getting in touch with the outside world. There is always a way around these things. I can call the police, remove the SIM card. The door is open now. Now it is my choice not to walk through. I sit up a little straighter. I look Max in the eyes.

"Now that you've been going out in public," he says, "people have started asking questions. I'll make sure you don't have to talk to anyone who isn't important, but there are a few relationships I need you to prioritize. If you receive a message, it means that person has your new number, and if they have your new number it's because I think it's essential that you participate in a conversation. Pay attention, Rosanna. I need you to remember this."

"I know," I say. "I will."

He doesn't notice that he has called me her name. Inside me something feels like it's clicking into place. Power. A quiet hum.

"Here," says Max, moving away from me.

He comes back with three boxes, phone-book-size binders filled with printouts of what seems like every conversation Rosanna has had in the past two years. I flip through a book from the box at random. Some of the texts are blacked out, so there are odd gaps, chunks of conversations missing, inked-over time stamps and contact names. It feels like I am reading letters sent from the front lines of an incredibly pointless war.

"Has Rosanna agreed to this?" I ask. "Is she okay with me reading all her texts?

"Rosanna's privacy is important," says Max. "But I want you to understand what she sounds like. I want you to know her voice."

Together we read through pages and pages of Rosanna's old conversations—texts, mostly, but a few phone calls that someone has transcribed, capturing every awkward pause, every sigh, the way that Rosanna often seems to be talking herself toward rationalizing the decisions of the people around her.

"It's good," she'll say. "I mean, it's totally fine. I really feel loved. But also singled out, you know? And honestly, he had to lie to me to make this happen."

Max is in the listening role.

"You're so right," he says.

His name has been redacted from the top of the printed screen.

. . .

We sit on the floor together and pass pages back and forth. It starts out serious, with Max carefully pointing out the different ways Rosanna uses language. He has me guess what she's feeling so I can learn her cues, the way she uses a lot of commas when she's excited ("so basically she emails me, and, I don't want to make a big deal of it, but, it's kind of a big deal"), how she never puts a period at the end of anything unless she's mad ("fine." "sure." worst of all, the dreaded "k."), her surprising enthusiasm for semicolons ("lol; well I gotta go over to George's house and tell him about the other dude I'm seeing sooo"). I like her. I don't know why this surprises me, but I do. Rosanna on the phone is different than I expected her to be, different than she is on-screen. Here she feels real. Full of life, effusive sometimes ("honestly I just feel so blessed to have you in my life" shows up a few times, a verbal tic or insincerely copied and pasted?), but also deadpan ("send videos, I beg you"), sarcastic ("It's raining in Los Angeles, so everyone's driving about ten miles an hour and I'm pretty sure we're all gonna die"), shifting moods as she moves from conversation to conversation as lightly as a butterfly. She is quick with a comeback or a snappy response ("God, she has no idea how to even be a person, are we gonna have to Kaspar Hauser a bitch?"). With every piece of information I learn, I feel more and more complete. I feel the version of Rosanna I carry around inside myself slowly coming into focus.

There's one subset of texts I find particularly interesting. In them, Rosanna sends messages, usually late at night, usually one at a time, to men whose names are blacked out on the screen. "Hi," she says, "I was just thinking about you."

Or "Heyyyy," she says, "you up?"

Sometime she just sends an emoji. They respond with pictures of themselves, shirtless, a protective black line drawn thick over their eyes, everything else exposed. They flirt back, calling her gorgeous, asking her what she's wearing. When they ask her to come over, though, she doesn't respond. Max moves quickly through these conversations, but as we read them power tingles in my fingertips. The power of Rosanna's silences.

The day passes fast, the sky outside going pink, then dark, the pages in our hands getting harder and harder to read. Max doesn't switch on the light, and neither do I. Soon it is so dark I cannot see a thing. In the dark room, the light of the phone seems substantial, like a ghostly presence, another living body between Max and me.

"Okay," he finally says. "Okay, I think you're ready."

He takes my phone back from me, makes some adjustments. A name pops up on the screen. Marie. I remember her picture from that photo shoot, Rosanna's best and oldest friend. She is beautiful. I think of the way she must look now, hunched over, waiting, lit blue with the screen's light. I wonder what she and Rosanna talk about when they're together. Does she know? Is she in on our little conspiracy, helping Rosanna hide out? I open the message.

"Hey," it says, "I've heard you're back. Is it true?"

I look at Max and speak in Rosanna's voice. "I'm back!" I say. "Thank goodness; so excited to see you, honestly, you can't imagine the quality of conversation I've had to put up with, save me!"

Max nods, rewards me with a small smile. I type.

"Ask her to go on a hike with you," he says. "She'll want to see you face-to-face. It's better if you make the offer."

"Not to be too L.A.," I add, "but, let's hike soon?"

Marie writes back quickly. "Of course," she says.

Max gives me a tight little smile.

The next afternoon Max takes me downstairs to a car with no driver in it. I'm surprised by the absence—we've never been alone together outside of the apartment, and it feels unnatural somehow.

"This isn't a Rosanna outing," he says. "There's something I want to show you. A corpse flower. It blooms every ten years. And it's time any day now for it to open. I want us to be there together when it does."

It's strange to be alone in the car, unprotected by the silent presence of the driver. It's somehow more intimate than being together in the apartment. Such a small space. I find myself fighting the urge to reach over and take his hand, as though we are any two other people, fond of each other, on an excursion, driving through the city alone. Not a Rosanna excursion. So who is this for? For Max? For me? The radio hums quietly. I force myself to look away from him, to look at anything else, the cars outside, sepia and still in the heat, the crumbling purple of the mountains through the tinted glass of the window. I know without him saying it that this is not a place he has taken Rosanna. That this is somehow mine.

"It's the most amazing thing," he says, a little breathless.

It's good to hear him talk about something that's outside us both, which doesn't concern the project at all. It's almost as if what passes between is ordinary, a tenderness built on affection and mutual regard. Rather than, well, whatever it actually is. Are we coworkers? Friends? Something stranger, darker than that?

"What's it like?" I say, wanting to keep him speaking.

"Carnivorous. Huge. Taller than you, although, to be fair, you're not very tall. And the smell is the worst thing you can imagine! There's a reason they call it the corpse flower, you'll see, it's just awful."

"Sounds gross," I say. "Why do you want to see it, again? Can't we just go to the beach?"

Part of this is Rosanna, carrying out her friendly, teasing affect, and part of it is me. A strange thawing of the silent place inside where my old self lives. I feel uneasy, a little nauseated. But I don't know any other way to behave.

Max laughs. "It's not gross!" he says. "It's fascinating. A completely strange thing, totally unique. Almost impossible to find in the wild. One of a kind. A cultivated beauty. Like you."

"Oh," I say, "enormous and smelly. *Now* I understand. You really have a type, huh?"

He laughs, a real laugh, devoid of bitterness. He is the one to reach over and squeeze my hand.

"But really, though," I say, "what is it about this flower? Are you interested in flowers in general? Are you secretly some kind of botanist? There's so much I don't know about you."

I've never asked Max about himself before. It didn't feel right, to intrude into his past, when he never asked me about mine. This is probably because there is no mystery for him; he knows everything he needs to know. But still, it's the principle of the thing. I am surprised when he answers without hesitating.

"Nothing like that," he says. "I didn't go to college or anything. I'm a hobbyist, I guess. But I was kind of a weird kid. I spent a lot of time alone. We had this neighbor, though, Mrs. Nutting, who had the most incredible garden. When things were strained at home, I used to go over there and just spend hours with her, talking about flowers. She taught me everything she knew."

"Do you talk to her now?" I ask.

He slants his eyes away from me to look back at the road, suddenly uncomfortable, his shoulders inching closer to his ears. "Not really," he says. "I don't really talk to anyone. My life is different now. My work—I work a lot. I don't think there's anyone who would understand."

Max lets go of my hand and reaches over to turn up the volume on the radio. We drive in silence for the rest of the ride, each too embarrassed to speak. We are alike, the two of us. I understand, I think.

At the botanical garden we stand silent in front of the long furled leaf of the flower. He's right, it's as tall as I am in my bare feet, and beautiful. Otherworldly, with its strange pale center, the flower unfurling like a spinning dancer's skirt. No one takes my picture. They seem totally oblivious to my presence. Their focus is on the flower, sitting silent in the humid greenhouse, its leaves stubbornly shut, growing in dark and tender privacy. I had thought this would be a relief, no longer having to feel the pressure of so many strange eyes. Instead it's unsettling, like walking through a room of friends without being seen. The crowd around us presses close, their bodies warm in the warm air. My hand brushes against Max's, finger on finger, interlaced, and for a brief moment his hand opens up like the flower is supposed to and his fingers catch on tight to mine. We stand close, protected by the anonymity of the crowd, hand in hand, together, like any two other people, like strangers. For one brief moment, our bodies belong to us.

"Isn't it incredible?" Max says.

His voice is a revelation. Totally sincere. The greenhouse the flower blooms in is small and cramped and full of people, the smell of the flower compounded by the various smells of so many bodies, taking up space, pressing up against me skin to skin. But I do not feel overwhelmed. Max distracts me with his beauty, the naked wonder written on his face.

"It really is," I say.

11

*F*or the first time, Max leaves me at the curb. He pulls up in front of the house, and at first I don't know what to do. Does he really want me to go into the building by myself? How will I get into my room? The door, surely, is always locked, even when we're gone. But Max reaches across me and opens the car door, letting the cold night air rush in, pooling at my feet.

"Go on," he says, his voice surprisingly gentle, almost hard to hear over the low radio, classical again, like it was on my first night, our first night together.

"But how will I get in?" I ask.

Max smiles. "I trust you. The door's unlocked."

I nod, oddly numb. This should be a relief, Max trusts me now, Rosanna trusts me, the door is, will always be unlocked from now on. But I don't feel relieved. I feel nervous. He's abandoning me. The door will always be unlocked, and I will always be inside, vulnerable to whoever comes to find me.

"Well, okay then," I say. I feel an odd formality, a distance. A reminder that we are coworkers before anything else. "Good night, Max," I say. "Tell Rosanna I say hello."

I walk by myself up the narrow staircase. I open my own unlocked door. I hesitate in the doorway; there is a new unruly energy in the room, as though someone has been here while Max and I were away. The air feels unfamiliar. Unclean. Of course everything looks the same, the magazines still stacked in the same neat order on the windowsill, dishes piled dirty in the sink. The phone is the only valuable thing I own, and it's where I left it, sitting on the edge of the table, quiet as a coiled snake. Has Rosanna been here, looking around? The air seems to carry some faint floral perfume, as delicate as green hay. Maybe that's the perfume Rosanna wears now. I tell myself I am crazy to suspect her. No one has been here, no one even knows this room exists. Still, that night I push a chair in front of my unlockable door. *Just in case*, I tell myself. Just in case.

The next afternoon the phone buzzes. It's a text from an unfamiliar number, telling me to come downstairs. Max, I think, dispensing with the small intimacies that tie us to each other already. In the garden alone, there had been such tenderness between us. It makes sense that he would withdraw now, threatened. Trying to make the truth that is building between us disappear. Well, two can play that game. I can make him wait, too. I take my time getting dressed, putting on clothes he doesn't particularly like, a high-waisted skirt, a turtleneck in olive green that Max thinks washes us out. I go to the kitchen and remove the wad of bills hidden in a jar of kosher salt and tuck it in my purse. *Just in case*, I think again. It feels good to have another secret to keep, this one all my own.

I am strangely reluctant to move the chair from in front of the door. I know Max must have been the one to text me, but what if he wasn't? What if it's a stranger, waiting outside the door to catch me in the act of emerging into the world disguised as Rosanna, and I am discovered, ruined, worse? I've been living in a strange dream. Maybe somebody thinks it's time for me to wake up.

The day has a surreal quality to it. The light feels dense, thick with something building, gathering force. And when I open the door of the car, the back seat is empty. Everything else is normal, the air conditioner blowing cold, the quiet murmur of classical music, the outside sepia through tinted windows, the impassive silent back of the driver. But the back seat is empty. I am alone.

Don't panic, I think as the driver pulls away from the curb. I force myself to breathe. It is getting harder and harder. This must be a test, some sort of reflection of our closeness the day before, my new open-door privileges, to see if he can trust me to remain calm, greet him appropriately as I meet him wherever he is waiting for me. Max has never told me I'm not allowed to speak to the driver, and so now I do, trying to sound normal. *I am normal*, I think. I am Rosanna and I am normal and everything is fine.

"Where's Max?" I ask.

I light my phone up in my lap, but there is no word from Max, no sign. I text the unfamiliar number back. "Max, is this your number? Where are you?" I type.

Nothing.

The driver doesn't say anything, either. He clicks on his turn signal, eases us out onto the busy street at the bottom of the hill. It is as though I haven't said anything at all. For a moment, I wonder if I've actually spoken, did I imagine that, too? I don't know anything about this man. I don't know if I can trust him. I don't even know if he's been the same driver this whole time, I can't even remember ever looking at his face. The back of his head is anonymously well-groomed, with short hair, no distinguishing marks. He could be anyone. He could be taking me anywhere. My heart speeds up. I try again. "Is he meeting me wherever we're going?"

But there is only silence in response.

It isn't long before the car pulls up to the curb, packed with the usual crowd of shabby men with expensive cameras, waiting for someone like me to make an appearance. I can see them shift, so close to the windows, circling like a pack of wolves. And no Max. No sign of him at all. Seeming to sense our vulnerability, they move closer until we are hemmed in on all sides. I can hear my name, a murmur low through the glass like cruel laughter: *Rosanna*, they whisper to one another, like it's a secret I shouldn't be told. I am taking too long, I know. I bend over so my head is clamped between my knees and try to steady my breath, to think. How did they know I was coming? It must have been Max. He must know where I am. I try to be comforted by this, but their appearance feels random, like they're alive to my movements, sensing a shift in trajectory in the same way a flock of birds catches the wind. I think of the great black flocks of starlings settling into the trees outside my grandmother's house before she died, how in the evening when the sun started to set we would sit out on the porch waiting, scanning the clear sky for black specks, and there would be nothing, nothing until suddenly the air was full of birds, tiny and immense, a swooping parabola of wings, a shadow that widened and collapsed into itself, dipping down, down over the fields and circling the house in a whirl, a funnel, the rush of their chatter, the flap of their wings passing over us, spreading like ink spilled over the still blue page of the sky. Max knows I'm here. He must.

"Please," I say, "just tell me where Max is. Just tell me what he wants me to do now, and I'll do it, please."

He's supposed to protect me. He's supposed to keep me safe. That's the deal I've made with him, the promise we've made to each other, that I will do what he wants me to do and he will keep me safe. The driver still doesn't answer. The only sound is the low hum of the air conditioning. I am cold and scared and I can see the men outside the car adjusting their cameras around their necks, holding them up, their faces disappearing behind the machines until everything around me becomes flat black glare and reflection, until all I can see is Rosanna's face, over and over and over, staring back. I kick the back of the driver's seat just once, trying to get his attention, and then it feels so good that I kick it again and again. I can feel the weight of his back through the seat, and he must feel me, too. It must hurt. But he doesn't move. He can't. He is afraid to react in the same way I am afraid to react around Max, to let slip the mask of restrained pleasantness and bare my sharpened teeth.

And then I feel her. Just a slight whisper, a tingle in my fingertips, but she is there. She is in the back seat of this car with me, Rosanna, consistent, faithful Rosanna, protecting me when Max cannot. Inside me I feel a heaviness, the tingling weight of her arrival. Outside, the men with the cameras chatter and shift, preparing to ask their questions. Rosanna doesn't ask questions. She doesn't worry. She does what she wants to do. Her voice is close and tender in my ear, whispering these truths, our truths, so sweetly I feel my breath slow.

"Sorry," I say to the driver.

But I'm not sorry. It feels good. I take one deep breath. Another. I smooth down my hair. I fix my skirt. I step out of the car.

"Rosanna," they say, cameras clicking. "Rosanna."

"Good to see you, boys," we reply.

Every expensive store looks the same. I have never been to this one, but I know how to move naturally though spaces lined with overpriced consumable goods. Everything looks like something Rosanna, I, already own. I know how to nod to the salesgirl like we are old friends, how to not react when she pretends to keep doing whatever she had been doing when I came in, acting like she doesn't recognize me. Of course she does. Everyone does. I watch her in the mirrors of the open dressing rooms, how she sneaks glances through the curtain of her hair. She knows who I am. This centers me, being recognized, known. I know the script. I can do this without Max.

"Hey," I say, catching her eye in the reflection. "I love your top!"

Going for approachable today. Engaging. Rosanna when she wants to please, still newly reemerged, friendly to everyone, putting on her best public face.

The girl looks startled, as though one of the mannequins has turned its blank face toward her inquiringly.

"Thanks," she finally says, and then, braver, "Is there anything I can help you with today, Miss Feld?"

An uncertain smile here, a pause. She wants to make sure she's said the right thing, that I won't mind being recognized. It's a nice store, a nice neighborhood. She must be used to people like me. I feel a kinship toward her, for the way that we are both quietly keeping things running for people with more money and more power than we will ever have. She plays her role as I play mine.

"Please," I say, "Rosanna."

"Rosanna," she says.

I name myself not only for her, but so we both remember who I am. And her face lights up at this small intimacy, a gift, so easy for me to give.

"I'm looking for something special," I say. "A little present for myself."

I will give it to Max, I think, and he will give it to Rosanna. A sign that I have been out in the world without them. A token of my regard. So she'll know that I know she's with me now, so he'll know we're doing fine without him.

"Sure," the salesgirl says, "I can help you with that."

She takes a tray of jewelry from under the glass of the counter, some understated gold bangles, a line of rings nestled into a velvet case. Small, subtle, expensive-looking. Very Rosanna. I lean forward and pick up a bangle, slide it gracefully over my slim wrist. I feel like a dancer performing a familiar routine—fluid, easy, empty. Automatic. I imagine watching myself from a distance through the eyes of the men waiting outside, through Max's eyes as we watch the footage, later tonight. I hear the admiring tone of voice he uses as he points out the warmth of her expression, the precise way she moves. Again I feel the strange sliding feeling of being both here and not here. Both the observer and the observed. Both the tourist in the jeep, camera pressed tight in my sweating hands, and the lioness outside, licking her bloody claws.

"See," I hear Max say, his voice as strong in my ear as if he were really there beside me, "the way she touches the salesgirl's wrist? Establishing a moment of rapport. She'll remember that when she talks to the magazines later. It will make her speak kindly of Rosanna."

I reach out. I touch the salesgirl's wrist. "Beautiful," I say. "Thank you. Do you have a favorite piece?"

One necklace catches my eye. It's nothing Rosanna would wear, a small gold snake curled into a figure eight. It's wrong, not for her. But I want it. Not for Rosanna, for me. I can feel the weight of it in my hands, smooth, the gold warming in between my fingers, breathing itself into life. I want desperately for her to take it from the case, present it to me, mine. But she passes over it, picking up a thin chain of a bracelet.

"See," she says, "the subtle pressed gold design on the edges? If you hold it up to the light, it shines, it's so delicate, hand-engraved, you'll barely even know you're wearing it."

Rosanna is at the level of wealth where you want your money to disappear into the things you buy. To be totally inconspicuous. Whenever we briefly had money, growing up, we pumped it into things that looked expensive, shiny watches, purses with enormous logos glowering on the sides, things easy to sell once the money was gone. Rosanna's watch has a narrow face, a thin calfskin leather strap. It looks like nothing. It costs more than all my old clothes put together. Not hundreds, thousands. Not a single thousand, tens. The salesgirl slips the bangle around my wrist. She's right. I can scarcely feel its weight. If I hadn't been looking straight at it, I wouldn't know it was there at all. Beautiful, discreet. It's perfect for Rosanna.

"It's perfect," I say. "I'll take it."

From a distance, I watch Rosanna reach forward, pick up the bangle. I look down at my wrist and see her bones mirrored beneath mine. She is there now, hidden in her house, slipping the bangle on over her wrist, a small gift, a souvenir from the outside world. From me. And don't I deserve a little something, for being as thoughtful as all that?

"And this necklace as well," I hear myself say.

I get the bangle gift-wrapped, put it on one of Rosanna's heavy-metal cards. I wear the necklace out of the store, tucked hidden under my clothes. I pay for it with a few bills peeled from the roll of cash in my purse. What Max doesn't know won't hurt him.

Rosanna emerges into the afternoon light alone, a small white bag hung over one arm. The men waiting at the door open into a scattered cloud, buckshot, covering the most ground to do the most harm, shouting questions like thrown rocks.

"Rosanna, how's your boyfriend?"

"How does it feel being alone?"

"Rosanna, are you lonely? Take me with you! I'll be your man."

The pictures where I look miserable make the most money. So I smile. I keep smiling. I smile and smile and smile. Rosanna says nothing. Rosanna doesn't care. She smiles her famous smile with me, and together we climb into the back seat of the car.

That night in the apartment, the phone lights up again. Max. I let it ring twice before I answer, a small withholding that makes me feel a bright flash of power. I feel the shape of my new necklace against my skin under the soft cloth of Rosanna's nightgown, pulsing like a second heartbeat.

"Hello?" I say.

He knows that I know who it is. But it's fun to pretend. I like the thought of making Max just a little nervous. Making him worry about who else I thought might call.

"Did you miss me today?" he asks.

I've never heard him sound this way before, his voice soft and sleepy. On nights when he used to stay over, he would sit and watch me until I was unconscious. Now his voice is like the belly of a small dog, rolled over on its back and wiggling for approval. It's like he's not talking to me at all, lost in the memory of some other late-night conversation long ago.

"That depends," I say. "Did you miss me?"

"I was born missing you," he says. And then, after a pause, "You understand why I had to send you out alone, don't you?"

"Yes," I say. "I do."

"I wanted you to understand what it's like for her."

"I understand," I say.

Better than you do, I think.

"I wanted you to see that it's harder than you think it will be. It's important that you realize I won't always be there to protect you. I can't always be there for Rosanna, either. I needed you to understand that."

I feel a fierce wave of protectiveness for her, for us. I can be alone. I am never alone, I realize that now. I carry Rosanna in my bones. She doesn't have the same consolation. And she has already lost so much. More and more I realize I understand her in ways he cannot. Rosanna will always be outside of Max, above him. I have taken her inside me. We are the same. I feel her loneliness, heavy as glass, wrapped cold around my heart.

"I don't need you," I say. "Rosanna does. I don't mind going out on my own. I don't mind anything. But you need to stay with her, Max. Make her feel safe. That's why I'm here, right? So she never has to be alone. Promise me."

But there is only silence on the other end of the line.

"I bought her a present," I say. "Will you give it to her from me? Tell her that I'm thinking of her. I hope she likes it. I want her to know that I'm nice."

I lie back on the futon, phone pressed sweaty between my ear and shoulder, and listen to the silence. I feel like a teenager—well, a movie version of a teenager, anyway, maybe the kind of teenager Rosanna was, the kind with a quiet family and peaceful nights, with lots of friends to call. Max is still quiet. If I listen hard, I can almost hear him breathing. It is as though he is lying here beside me. For a long time, I am silent, too.

"So how did I do?" I ask finally.

I make my voice as small and soft as I can so he'll have to hold the phone close to hear me. He will have checked the gossip sites already, read what the salesgirl said to the paparazzi after I left. He has already analyzed the most minute of my movements, my gestures, each word I said. Wherever she goes, Rosanna disturbs the world around her, a rock rippling smooth water. Did she join Max in analyzing the evidence of my day? Is she watching me, the same way we're watching her? She's not with him now, I can tell. He's alone.

I try to picture Max's apartment. Messy, I think. When I moved in here there had been a thin layer of pale, sticky dust covering every horizontal surface. And that was my space, my life, which he is otherwise so meticulous about. I think of him sitting alone in a large room, expensive and anonymous, pre-furnished beige, no books on the shelves, no pictures on the walls. But no, he wouldn't be at home. Maybe he doesn't have a home at all. He has spent the day with Rosanna, taking care of her. She has had some kind of episode, so he had to leave me alone to take care of her. Now, finally, he has gotten her to sleep. He lies on that rough-textured gray couch in the office. He wouldn't be bold enough to go into the living room, the sitting room, the den, places she actually uses, places he still considers her property, lines too thick for him to cross. He is curled up there with his jacket folded under his head, close enough that if she wakes, she can call him and he will come to her. Not beside her bed, though. Not as close to her as he is to me. But still, it's good to know he's close to her. That if she wakes in the dark, she won't find herself alone.

"It was a good start," says Max. "You look good. You bought jewelry? Always a safe bet."

My voice on the phone must be different enough from hers that he can speak about us as two separate people. Out there, I am Rosanna. In here, alone, I am not. I remember the way my body felt, the sun hot on my face, the cool gold on my skin. *That* was *me*, I tell myself. I was there. He can't deny me that truth.

"You know, I'm really proud of you," says Max. "I knew you could handle it, but still it was a surprise that you did so well. Perfect, really. Not a hitch. Which is good, because we'll have to start sending you out on your own more and more now."

"Without you?" I ask.

I can feel Rosanna's energy shift inside me, prickle to attention. Without Max, I think. With me. On our own.

"Without me," he says. "We'll have to find you someone else to be out in the world with. I heard the questions the paparazzi asked, and they're right, it's starting to look odd. Loneliness is not aspirational."

Who is Max to talk about loneliness? Does he have friends? How can he? He spends so much time with me, and when he's not here, he's with Rosanna. I remember what Holly said to him—there's no way he could talk about this with anyone else, this hidden life we share. It's hard to speak about anything else while carrying the weight of so many secrets. You might say something wrong, you might start talking and be unable to stop, talk and talk until you had given yourself away. It was better to stay by yourself, not to say anything at all. That's what I had done. It's what Rosanna had done, too. And now Max, the three of us together, all alone. Loneliness compounding loneliness, clinging to our skin like a bad smell.

"I'm not lonely," I say. "I have you."

Max sighs. "In a way, yes, I know. But it looks bad. You must realize that. Soon we'll have to start introducing you to some of Rosanna's old friends. Not that Rosanna had a lot of friends. She didn't like most people."

It's disorienting, the way that he does this, switching from past to present like Rosanna is flickering into and out of existence depending on the time of day, his mood. At times, it is as if she is a story he is telling me. As if he had made her up.

"*Had?*" I say. "What about now? Does she have friends now?"

I want to make him say it. I want to make him tell me what she's like.

"Of course she does," he says. A pause. "But she doesn't get out much. So no, not really. Now she has me."

Max doesn't come for the next few days. When he's not with me, I sit as still as I can, thinking about Rosanna, looking out the window for the car. I try to feel her inside me. I walk back and forth across the room, measuring the length with my steps: ten to the door, ten to the window, five to cross from the futon to the wall. If the driver comes, I go wherever he takes me, shopping, to the movies, on walks, alone, in the park. It's exciting at first, the wide feeling of the whole world opening up around me, but I quickly get used to it. In the evenings, when the parrots come back to the garden, I try to teach them words to say back to me. I lean out the small window over the courtyard, speaking simple phrases for them as they circle and squabble, pecking at one another. I want to teach them to tell me I exist.

The more time I spend alone, the more I find that small parts of my old self come leaking back unbidden. The light on the popcorn ceiling in the basement, the fake orange smell of the fluid we used to clean the bathrooms in the group home. They are stones in my pockets, pulling me down, keeping me further from the truth. I say mantras, count cars passing, find shapes in the clouds, anything to stay distracted. When that doesn't work, I go into the kitchen and hold my hand over the hot plate. Nothing that will leave a mark, just a little jolt of pain to bring me back into my body, to remind me that I am only body, all body. That for now my body is enough.

At night, in bed, I work on erasing my memories. I have a very precise method. I let some image from my old life rise up to the surface—my father, say, picking me up and putting me on his shoulders, the way that his big hands catch hold of my small waist, the dizzy lift in the pit of my stomach, the giddy, nauseating joy of being so small and so fragile. Slowly, carefully, I transfer the memory to Rosanna. I picture the same strong arms, the same feeling of safety. Now the arms belong to Rosanna's father. And I am Rosanna. Night after night I focus on the same memory, making small changes, adding the way he laughs low in his throat when he visits her in the videos, the smell of the cigarettes he smokes clinging to the fabric of his jacket. Slowly my own father's shadow fades until there is nothing left of him. The memory that appears is now Rosanna's. I focus on that feeling until I fall asleep, slipping into dreams that are not my own. I wake up feeling a little lighter. I am cleaner and cleaner, more and more pure. When Max comes, he will speak to me like I am a person he knows. He will look into my eyes. Outside the window, the birds will call in a chorus: *hello*, they will say, *hello*. Whoever, whatever I had been before is disappearing. Soon there will be nothing left. Soon I will be gone.

Max comes by the apartment with a bottle of wine. I'm not sure what day of the week it is, what time. It is warm, late. I have been alone all day. I have been alone for a while, I can't remember how long. There is a fire, he tells me, somewhere in the hills, and the sky outside is flat and pink and troubled-looking, with the spongy texture of a battered stucco wall. The sun is a dim pulse in the sky. We are leaning on the edge of the open window, watching the world burn. There is nothing but us and the sun and the ash and the silence of the canyon. The streets are empty even of parked cars. I wonder if we're supposed to evacuate. I wonder if the neighbors are already gone. Max stands close beside me, his arm brushing against mine every time he lifts the glass to his lips. I watch the ash float down from the sky, some of it landing in my glass. When I drink, it clings to my lips, chalky. Like the ashes of some long-dead thing.

"We're ready to start booking you appearances," Max says. "Talk shows, first. Now that we've established your presence in the city, I want you to make your public debut. That's why you're here, after all, to help Rosanna further her brand. You've been doing so well with the paparazzi, I think you're ready for your first interview."

The interviews were the first part of Rosanna I knew, dimly back home, and then here, with the magazines, the tapes. I have practiced her lines on waiters and strangers and paparazzi and even Max, until my body moves the right way without my telling it what to do, my mouth forms the right words. I raise my eyebrows the way she does in moments of coyness, tipping her head. Everyone will see me. I will sit in front of them—Rosanna's fans, her public—and let them call me by her name. Inside everything is quiet and still and blank, white noise in a white room. Inside I am fine I am fine I am fine.

"Is that what Rosanna wants me to do?" I ask.

"Yes," Max says.

"And you're not convinced."

He shrugs.

"Well, you're out in the world now. Someone has to do it. We don't really have a choice."

"I'll do whatever you think is best for her," I say.

I notice that I've been clutching at my chest, where the necklace is hidden under my clothes. I let it go quickly, dropping my hand like I've burned the skin. Max doesn't seem to notice. I lean my head into his shoulder, smell the warm smell of him, soft, against my face. I think about Rosanna's father lifting her up. I think about biting him hard, puncturing the thin skin of his neck.

"Don't worry, I'm ready," I say.

Max books me on a daytime talk show to promote Rosanna's new handbag line. I'll be sitting down with a woman who has interviewed Rosanna a handful of times. Max says this is so we will have tapes to watch, specific conversations to refer back to, so I can see the way Rosanna conducts herself, how their conversational patterns play off each other, the tactics she will use to try to trap me into saying things I don't want to say. This seems like a dangerous game to me. She has met me before, she knows me. She may recognize that something isn't right. Max says this is silly, that I will do fine.

"She's like anyone else that you've met so far," he says. "The photographers, the women who work in the stores. She doesn't care about Rosanna. She doesn't even know her. She is familiar with Rosanna the brand, that's all, the same way everyone else is. She'll see what she's expecting to see."

Max starts coming over every night, bringing tapes, pictures of the handbags for me to study, sample swatches of leather dyed a muted rainbow of shades. I still go out during the day, but not as much, just a few small errands here and there, enough to be seen, enough that people remember me. Otherwise I stay inside, watching interview footage until the sun sets and Max comes by with take-out, suspiciously cheerful. I don't ask him what he's been doing all day, and he doesn't ask me. We sit on the couch, slowly working our way through a list of practice questions, strategizing together. Or, rather, he strategizes and I nod along, trying to pay attention to the videos of Rosanna playing on the screen, forming my own ideas of how she would behave.

"We're building a redemption narrative," says Max.

"Redemption?" I ask. "Does Rosanna need redeeming?"

"No," says Max, "and we want to make it clear that you're not asking for forgiveness. You haven't done anything that needs forgiving. You're asking for understanding, trying to reconnect to your fans, helping them sympathize with all you've gone through. Ideally we would have a cry break somewhere in the first third of the show so you can build an emotional arc: hope, the sadness of returning to a difficult past, then optimism, cut with a little charming anxiety about the future."

The emotional space I've occupied as Rosanna so far has mostly been confined to surface-level aspiration. Looking pretty and buying things, I can do. The rest is uncertain. More and more, I can feel her heaviness inside me, hear the quiet buzz of her truth, but I am not sure if that will be good enough. I don't think Rosanna's truth is anything close to what Max thinks it should be.

"That's a lot," I say.

"Don't worry," says Max. "Everyone will be rooting for you to succeed. We'll make sure you get the questions beforehand and that you have practice answering them. It will be easy."

"So what am I supposed to tell her about why it's been so long? I know, rehab, exhaustion, whatever, but I've seen the tapes—she's going to want more information."

Max gives me a brittle little smile. "We'll go over it," he says. "But nothing specific. It's important to protect Rosanna's privacy. Just hit the buzzwords. Addictive personality, enabling, needing a break. Push through until she gets bored asking. You'll be great. Everyone will love you. Everyone loves Rosanna."

"Max," I say, "what happens if this doesn't go well? What will happen if I fail?"

He looks at me for a long time. *"Don't,"* he finally says.

Our main problem is that it isn't enough for me to mirror the old Rosanna, to be perfect in every remembered detail. That had been what the paparazzi wanted, what we needed for marketable photographs, for brief appearances in the lives of people invested in the consistency of Rosanna's brand the same way Max is, clinging to a version of Rosanna that exists only in photographs. But the entire premise of the interview is that I have changed. I have been through a difficult time and come out a survivor, born again. Max doesn't seem to understand this. He doesn't want realism, he wants reproduction. Something he can control. When we run through the footage of the interviews, he wants my answers, my intonations, to be exactly the same as Rosanna's had been, suffused with the same false weight. He wants me to return as if I had never been gone. Like nothing has changed, and I can slip back into my old life uninterrupted, unpausing a film. He coaches me with an insistence on precision, having me mirror Rosanna's smallest movements, making me copy them over and over and over until my body starts to ache. *Again*, he keeps saying, *again*, putting his hands on my shoulders, turning me, pushing my head to one side. The weight of him is immense.

"And how is your relationship with your father?" the interviewer and Max say, leaning forward on the couch, a look of tender concern on their faces.

I have never met Rosanna's father. I haven't seen my own father in years. Rosanna herself didn't see her father much. He was married to a woman closer to her age than her mother's and had two young children to worry about. Rosanna was grown up. She didn't need him. His appearances on the tapes are sporadic and brief, pockmarked with awkward silences, father and daughter staring past each other out of frame. He never comes to her house, and she doesn't go to his. Most often they have breakfast, sitting across from each other, not saying much. I think of one of these tapes, Rosanna's father uncomfortable, twisting his coffee cup in his hands. She has just called off her engagement, although why she felt necessary to tell him this, I cannot say. She can't be deluded enough to expect he'll be a source of comfort. Surely not. He sighs when she tells him, not looking at her face.

"That's too bad, kiddo," he says."Another one bites the dust, eh?"

"Wow, Dad," says Rosanna. "Gee, a series of loveless relationships with emotionally withholding men whose approval I crave. I wonder where that pattern could have come from?"

Her dad raises his hands in a gesture of mock defeat. "Hey hey, maybe you could be a little less picky, that's all I'm saying. You're thirty, right?"

"Twenty-eight," she snaps.

Rosanna's father scans the room, seeming to hope he'll see someone he knows, someone who will rescue him from this person, his daughter, this strange woman he is failing to understand.

"I don't see my dad often," I say. "We're both busy people, but I will always love him and be there for him. And he for me. At the end of the day, I'm a daddy's girl."

As I speak, I picture the tension in their shoulders, sitting hunched together in that booth, their mirrored body language giving them away.

But Max frowns. "No," he says, "that's not the right tone. Not at all. Rosanna's father is someone people know. They're picturing his face as you talk about him. He has this great public presence, totally gregarious, warm. You need to confirm what they believe about him, about you."

I try again. "I don't see my dad often."

I pause, loading my voice with heavy, toffee-sticky regret.

"We're both busy people."

Nostalgia.

"But I will always love him and be there for him, and he for me."

Fondness. Solicitude.

"At the end of the day, I'm a daddy's girl!"

I land on a tight high note, a gymnast sticking the dismount with triumphantly raised arms.

"Better," says Max. "Try again."

Again. This time my voice hews exactly to the recorded Rosanna, the same inflections, pauses, breaths. I am the Rosanna that has always existed, the Rosanna who was interviewed before she and her father grew more and more distant, gradually becoming estranged. The Rosanna Max wants so badly to know. I wonder what she will think about my interpretation, hidden away in that vast and silent house, watching that old false vision of herself repeated back to her, always perfect, always the same, a flock of jabbering parrots, an infinitely repeating hallway lined with mirrors. Wasn't that Rosanna the version of herself that destroyed her? She had hated being zipped inside that too-tight skin.

It seems wrong to make her watch me repeat her mistakes. A small betrayal. So when Max leaves for the night, I rewatch the tapes he has left with me. I make edits, answering questions the way I know Rosanna wants them answered now. It feels better. It feels true. I can sense her somewhere close, moving inside me with purpose, filling me with a strange propulsive energy that keeps me up until the sun begins to rise. Max wants me to be the Rosanna he understands. But I know the truth. I am not that dead and troubled girl. I am Rosanna's only true ally, the real Rosanna, the living Rosanna, the Rosanna who waits for me in that silent house, longing to be set free. I will say the words she wants me to say. I will let her truths fall heavy from my lips. I will be newer and I will be better. I will do whatever it is I discover she wants me to do.

12

 I feel fine, excited even, until the moment we pull up to the sound-stage door. The car idles in the wide space between two buildings, their high arched roofs hunched against the low gray sky, the red recording light shining bloody on the stucco wall. At the gate, they had waved us through with no hesitation. "It's good to see you back, Ms. Feld," the guard said. We drove through a fake New York and a fake Old West, past a big fake pond that Max told me stood in for the Red Sea when they still made Bible movies, two plexiglass walls under the surface neatly slicing the water in half, a manufactured miracle. A woman taps on the window and the driver rolls it down. She's close to my old age, younger than Rosanna, thin, blond, her hair gathered into a messy ponytail. She looks tired.

 "Hi, all!" she says. "I can take Rosanna from here. Ms. Feld, if you'll follow me?"

 I look to Max. He wasn't expecting this, I can tell by the way he isn't looking at me, his back hunched tense over the light of his phone. He wants me to say something, insist he come with me, I can tell. But Rosanna is a professional. Being alone wouldn't bother her at all. I can't let it bother me, either. It's better for me to be alone with my intuition, feeling my way toward whatever it is Rosanna wants me to do here.

"See you later, Max," I say.

Max just nods, his lips set in a tight line.

The blond woman takes me to a room with my name on the door. It's cramped inside, smaller than my room, but not by much, with no windows, a large mirror to create the illusion of space. There's a plate strewn with slices of fruit, glinting like flesh in the reflected light. I walk past the woman and arrange myself on the couch. To my surprise, she sits down beside me with her clipboard on her lap, so close our knees almost touch. There's a strong smell of deodorant and drugstore perfume, synthetic and vanilla sweet, rising off her skin. It's nauseating. I feel the front of my head begin to pound. Rosanna is sensitive to artificial fragrances.

"I'm here to prep you for the show," the woman says. "I understand that your assistant handled our pre-interview phone call, which isn't super usual for us, so I hope you'll bear with me. I wanted to make sure you were up to speed with the topics we'll be discussing later."

"Max and I have gone over it," I say. "We'll be focusing on the handbag line, right? And I'd love for us to talk about how well they fit in with the rest of my leather goods brand."

The woman's perfume seems to be growing more and more intense, filling the room, a sweet miasma like the steam rising off a pot of caramel. She nods, makes a note on her clipboard. "Perfect," she says. "Our audience is all about female entrepreneurship and empowerment, so they'll be all over that. Next, she wants to ask what you've been up to since our last interview with you. I understand you have a few topics that are off-limits, but—"

"Whatever Max told you on the phone," I say.

I don't mean to be rude, but the smell is becoming overwhelming. I'm used to being around strangers by now, but the closeness of her is too intense. I'm losing focus, losing track of the quiet electrical hum Rosanna makes inside me, and if that happens, if I lose her, this interview will be a disaster. I try to sound calm, but even I can hear the tremor in my voice, every feeling in me pressing close to the surface, a bruise. The woman looks confused, setting her clipboard down. I can tell she's wondering if the rumors are true. If I'm damaged beyond repair.

"People often change their minds about what they feel comfortable discussing," she says, careful. "I just wanted to check with you in case you had any new thoughts."

"Thank you," I say.

Rosanna would be calm, so I am calm, forcing my fluttering heartbeat to slow, like I've heard monks can, meditating, controlling even the most intimate and automatic of their bodily functions with the strength of their faith. It's not my heartbeat. It's not my heart.

"I appreciate your checking in," I say. "But I think we're all set."

I stand up, offering her my hand. Although I'm calmer now, I need, very badly, to be alone. There's something about this woman that makes me nervous, with her smug efficiency, her lists. She has a plan, too. And it might not intersect with ours. I tell myself I will be fine. We will stick to the script Max has written for us. I will make Rosanna's corrections as I go.

"Of course," she says. But her manner has changed. She grips her clipboard with tight hands. At the door, she pauses, turns, with a guilty look, speaking softly. I have to lean closer to hear her, inhaling that awful perfume.

"I know I shouldn't say this, but it's not too late. If you don't want to do this, you don't have to. People back out more than you'd expect."

It's nice that she'd put her job on the line to tell me I can quit if I want to. But nobody is nice just to be nice here. If she's nice, it means she wants something from me. If she wants something from me, it means I have power. I feel the confidence returning, Rosanna growing stronger. I sit up straight on the soft cushions.

"You're sweet," I say. "But I'll be fine. Just pre-show nerves. I'll see you out there!"

She smiles again, looking almost disappointed.

"Sure thing," she says.

The door closes behind her.

I check my makeup in the mirror, look at my phone to make sure

I haven't gotten any texts from Max. There's nothing. He must be confident that I'll do fine without his help. That or he's angry, he wants me to feel abandoned, on my own. Either way, I don't care. I'm not alone. I'll be fine. In the mirror, I watch myself take a slice of pineapple from the plate, the slight, strange delay between when I put it into my mouth, the bright yellow disappearing between my perfect lips, and when I taste it, acid, sharp, eating away at the flesh of my tongue. A lag like a skipping record. In the mirror my reflection looks back. It is like watching an image of Rosanna. I eat another piece, painful, sweet. I look into my eyes. *I am beautiful*, I tell myself. We are beautiful. We are beautiful, and I will be fine. Another knock on the door, another woman younger than I look, older than I am. She tells me it's time to get ready for the show.

It's weirdly bright outside my dressing room, a phalanx of spotlights shining down like an artificial sun. And beyond the lights, nothing, the ceiling so far away it disappears into black. The set is supposed to resemble the hostess's apartment, wide windows overlooking green screen, an orange rug, a golden statuette of a dog. Beside the dog, a small blue porcelain lamp, switched on, its yellow light shining uselessly into the larger white light, which comes from high beyond the reach of the imagined ceiling. Outside the ring of lights, there are chairs for an audience, rising over me like the slow slope of a mountain, but no audience in them. I look for Max, but the lights are too bright to see beyond. I can't see him, but I tell myself he's there, picture his face in the back row, watching, ready to intervene if anything goes wrong, not close enough to tell me what to do.

My interviewer is here already. I won't say she's waiting for me— her back is turned as she speaks to a crowd of staffers, among whom I recognize the messy blond hair of the woman from my dressing room—but I see the way she stiffens when I approach, her shoulders moving back just slightly. She knows I'm here. I have learned to read the signs. She is making me wait for just a moment, just long enough for me to notice I'm waiting, before she turns, smiling, taking my hands in hers, pulling me close, kissing me on both cheeks. I can feel her every movement before it happens, so I am ready to react with graceful precision to her gestures, easy in her hands. Still, the smell of her is overwhelming. I'm still getting used to dealing with the realities of strangers' bodies, their deodorant, their body wash, that persistent undercurrent of sweat. The interviewer smells like her assistant did, a more expensive version of that sweet scent— heavier, more significant, a scent that clings to your clothes, claims space. I can feel it latching onto me, burrowing close against my skin, obscuring Rosanna's own smell. I smile, breathing through my mouth, trying to ignore my aching head.

"It's so nice to have you on the show again," she says, her voice warm but distant, glossily professional. I can feel the pressure of her gaze on me like a weight. "I'm looking forward to our little chat."

Before I can respond, she is sitting down beside me, her face smoothed into pleasant neutrality, straightening the hem of her skirt with a sharp gesture of her hand, the cameras rolling. I don't have time for reflection, nerves. It is beginning. It has begun. I look at the woman across from me. *Redemption,* I think. I smile my slight sad smile.

"I'm sitting down today with Rosanna Feld, a woman who has been in the public eye since the moment she was born. We'll be talking about her passion for design, her life in the limelight, and her decision to take some time alone to rediscover her truth. What was she looking for? What did she find? Stay tuned to find out."

Her voice is totally different now that the cameras are rolling. Before, there was something compressed about her, critical, pinched. Now she sounds warm, her voice modulated, sharp tones sanded down to amiable smoothness, like your best friend giving you advice.

"Rosanna, welcome to our show," she says. "We are all so pleased to have you."

"Thank you, Susan," I say. "I am so, so pleased to be here. This is so nerdy, but honestly I'm really excited to get a chance to talk about my new handbag line. I've been working so hard on it, and I'm really pleased to get the chance to share it with you guys."

"That's good to hear," she says. "I'm glad to hear it. We are so excited you have something you're interested in working on. I know your work has always been important in difficult times."

Here, she gives me a simperingly sympathetic look of concern. I remember what the assistant said, female empowerment and entre-preneurship. I can sell that. I nod.

"I think it's so important," I say. "Work. Having work you care about, as a woman. You can't practice good self-care if you're not spending your life doing work you care about!"

I am boring myself. Rosanna never talks so explicitly about the things she makes, never tries to sell to you. She is just so effervescent, so full of life that you want to get close to her any way you can, to buy anything that might remind you of her.

"So was it hard," the interviewer asks, "not working all that time you were gone?" She leans forward slightly in her chair, as if by bringing herself closer to me she will trick me into believing in her illusion of privacy, that it is just the two of us here, two friends sitting down for a chat.

"Not really," I say. "It was what I needed to do. I have such a wonderful team, the wheels were always in motion, even when I wasn't healthy enough to make the choices I needed to make. I knew I could trust them. And that's what's so great about running your own business. I love being empowered to make the decisions that are right for me without having to ask anyone's permission. I think giving yourself permission to be a little selfish sometimes is so important."

"*Selfish,*" she says. "That's an interesting word. Do you feel you've been selfish, Rosanna?"

"Not selfish," I say. "No, just prioritizing my own needs. I don't think there's anything wrong with that, do you?"

My hands are starting to sweat.

"So you feel you've placed your own needs first before the needs of the people around you? How has that impacted your personal life? Your relationships?"

"Well, of course I've had to make compromises," I say. "Of course there are things I would change. But I don't believe regret is a productive emotion."

"So you don't regret anything you've done?"

"Of course I feel awful for having caused pain to the people around me. For worrying my fans by staying away so long. But I can't take that back. I can't take any of it back."

"Don't you wish you could? If those people were here with us now, wouldn't you want to apologize for the pain you've caused?"

"I would," I say. "Of course I would. And I have privately made my amends."

My voice sounds like Rosanna's, the words that I am saying might plausibly flow from her lips. It is almost right. Almost. But I'm too self-conscious, too aware of forming my tone to match Rosanna's, of how intentional the process is. This should be natural. I should just be talking naturally. But I'm in it now, there's no looking back. What choice do I have but to keep talking and hope something good comes out?

"There's only so much work apologies can do," I say. "What really matters is change. We have to live the lives we are given. We have to learn from our mistakes. There's no starting over. There's just going on, carrying forward the lessons we've learned."

She furrows her brow. That same phony concerned look. "And what have you learned?" she asks. "Why are you here, Rosanna?"

I had been to so many social workers over the years. I had believed them at first, when I was young, when they said that talking about my life would change it. But it only seemed to change it for the worse. Whatever I told them would be echoed back to me later, painfully, my words stripped of their context, my honesty nothing more than evidence. I learned to tell things the right way, mirror back the world to them the way they wanted to see it. This woman is the same. She wants the same thing from Rosanna they had wanted from me. Redemption, neatly packaged, just like Max said. Gratitude, grace. A cry break a third of the way through.

"Well," I say.

I pause. I sigh. I look past her, past the camera for a long moment, long enough to make her nervous, make her think that I might stop talking. I can see by her face that she's thinking, unsure whether it is time for her to interrupt, try to force me to dig deeper for those high ratings.

Just when it seems she is about to speak, I continue, "It was time, I suppose. I needed to be alone for a while. For longer than I expected. I think some of your viewers know this already, but I've been in treatment. And it took some time and it was really hard, but I did the work on myself I needed to do. So I'm back. I'm back to thank my fans for standing by me. I can't tell you how much it meant to me knowing I had their love and support during that difficult time. Thank you. Thank you all. I could not have gotten well again without you."

I look straight at the camera, through it, through to the monitor, to the viewers, each of them, casting my voice into the future, to wherever Max is watching. So he will see. So they will all see. So they will know that I am here, really here, to stay. I reach across the small white table and take the interviewer's hand in mine.

"I know I've had your support, too," I say. "That's why I chose your show for my first interview. I can't thank you enough for how kind you've been. For having me come here to tell my own story. You do such good, important work, and I'm honored to be part of that."

My words float in the air, a black cloud, filling up the empty space above us, all around. I am slipping further and further into Max's version of Rosanna, all false sweetness, delay, an image mouthing along silently behind a speeding audio track. I pause, look down at my hands, contemplative, calm, up again, a quick, self-effacing smile. My face twitches unnaturally on the monitor's screen.

"Thank you, Rosanna," says the interviewer. "I appreciate it. But we're not here to talk about me. We're here to talk about you. With as much honesty and integrity as we can."

And that's it. Something catches inside me. I have reached the limit of what I've been trained to do. I need to go deeper. I think of my game, nights when I'm falling asleep, writing Rosanna's memories over my own. Shadows through a tracing paper, two images transformed into one. My memories of being here and my body's presence are overlaid like that now. Two universes are intersecting, a parrot dipping down to drink from the mirrored surface of my courtyard fountain, its body joined between air and water, meeting itself at the tender barrier of the liquid's skin. I look into the interviewer's eyes, remembering Rosanna's experience of this space. I let myself grow heavy, her flesh mapped over my own, the combined weight of our two bodies sinking deeper into the couch. I focus on remembering the physical sensations, the weight of material on my skin, the smell of her, of me, the herb sweetness of our shampoo, our old sweat sunk into the fabric of our clothes, the two of us sitting on all these couches, answering the same questions over and over and over, playing a role we have long since grown bored of, each time remembering all the other times, all the questions that have come before, the same answers over and over and over, the same gestures, our arms tired, the same sagging feeling of being scrutinized, observed, exhausted. I am sitting here, where she was. I am wearing her clothes. I am exhausted, too. I close my eyes just for a second, feeling her come into me, fill me up with light. The doubled warmth of two fast-beating hearts. I open them again. Here I am. I am here. The skin of my new body feels creamy tight, like the soft drape of a sheet mask. Not entirely natural. But comfortable enough, for now.

"Of course," I say. "And I want to be honest with you. Nothing is more important to me than sharing my truth with you all. My supporters. My fans. You. You all deserve to know whatever it is that will help you heal the way I have."

"Well then," my interviewer says. She leans even farther forward in her chair, her body at such an acute angle that I am almost afraid she will topple. "Let me ask you something, Rosanna. I know it's a difficult question. But I think we have to be present for each other, as fellow seekers of the truth."

As if there is any such thing as honesty. Honestly, I am so bored of the phoniness of it all, the fake concern. Could there be anything less original than all this? All she wants is for me to tell her something they can turn into a clip, break in half to sell more ad space. Her question the cliffhanger, my answer the drop into the abyss.

"Of course," I say. "Anything." I make sure to smile sweetly.

"Are you an addict, Rosanna?"

It's such a stupid question. These people, they'll ask anything, they have no shame. It's just like the photographers, that same base impulse, that same deep mining of other people's pain, only here it's all dressed up like we're friends. I remember last time, when she talked about her ex-husband and then I talked about mine, and then she cut out the part of the interview where she was talking so only my confession was left. Thinking about it makes my chest tight. I had tried to be honest with her. She hadn't wanted it. No one did. I'm so sick of sitting on all these couches. I'm so sick of being asked— no, being forced—to lie. So this time I won't lie. I let my eyes go soft with the false promise of tears. But it's not time. Not yet.

"Honestly," I say, "yes. Yes, I am."

She gets this sly little look on her face, like she's caught me. "And what are you addicted to?" she asks.

I shift in my chair, drawing it out. I remember the last time. She looks older than I remember, her skin dull beneath thick layers of concealer. You want your ratings, lady? Fine. So do I.

"*Love,*" I say. I draw the word out with a soft little sigh. "I'm addicted to love."

Saying it, I know it's true. She has the truth she wanted, in a way. Max, the boys on my phone, my father, my fans, my best friend—all I want is to be loved, to be loved so well, so strongly, that the weight of it will pin me to the earth. Make me real. My interviewer, watching, seems to glow. I can feel her want, her longing, floating toward me through the air like the tendrils of a climbing vine.

"Is it fair to say you've suffered from sex addiction?" she says.

She is trying to sound concerned, neutral, but her excitement is impossible to conceal. This is too easy. I shake my head.

"No," I say. "I know you've had problems with promiscuity in the past, and I sympathize, but for me it was always more about my heart than my body. I needed so much from the people around me. I asked for so much. Too much. I was like a vampire, draining all the energy and love I could from my friends, my fans, everyone. Trying to love me was like trying to fill a black hole. I destroyed everyone who came too close. I don't do that anymore. I know better now. I am better. I am better than I ever was before."

I look out again to the audience, all those rows of darkened seats, each seat standing in for a hundred women, a thousand, cloaked in the blue light of a hundred thousand screens, all of them beautiful, all of them loving, all of them watching me. I am not looking for Max, but I am sure I see his face smiling back at me from the crowd. Tenderness. I remember the things that I would ask him to do, how I spoke unkindly to him, made him wait for me for hours. Things will be different now.

"So substances weren't a problem?" she asks. "Drugs?"

She has kept that soft tone, kind, but I can tell she's annoyed.

"It wasn't ever about one particular substance or another. It was about the lack I was trying to fill. I needed so much. Everything I did, I was always just trying to replace whatever it was I was missing, to be overwhelmed by small pleasures. I used meaningless joy to distract myself from the lack of meaning in my life. Because true meaning comes from self-love. And I didn't like myself very much back then. I didn't know anyone who did. Do you?"

I already know the answer. To be fair, I don't like her very much, either. Finally she leans back. I have shocked her, slightly, out of her single-minded pursuit of dirt.

"I don't know," she says. "I suppose so. I try to practice good self-care."

"That's not what I asked," I say. "I asked if you hate yourself as much as I hated myself. And I really hated myself. I hated myself so much."

"I try," she says, and I cut her off, without seeming to, speaking in the pause she takes to consider.

"But isn't it hard?" I say. "It's so hard, feeling like everyone's always too busy for you. Like you're not important. In some ways, I think I've been fighting against that feeling my whole life. Not now. I know about your loneliness. I've read your books. I know things haven't always been easy for you."

She leans back, silent, until she is melting into the back of the chair, attempting to regain her lost momentum. "That's true," she says. "But I've come so far."

Her eyes are getting skittish, shifting away from me, up toward the rafters, the camera, anywhere but my face. I keep staring at her. I will make her look at me, no matter how hard she tries to avoid it. I will make her see me as I am.

"Before Mark left you for that PA, you must have known, must have sensed even then that you were alone in your relationship. Even when it looked so good to the outside world. That there was no one listening to you. And didn't that remind you of all those old fears? That you're useless? That no one will ever love you, because on some deep, fundamental level, you are not good enough to be loved?"

Still, she does not respond. We sit for a few moments in silence. Now I am the one to soften, move toward her, my voice even tenderer than her own.

"Tell me how you survived." I say.

I watch the tears streak her foundation—one, two—and then her face is striped with fading makeup, eyeliner dripping black from her eyes. My cry break, as promised. My redemption. I feel the studio lights burning hot on my neck. I feel heavy with power. Reborn.

Max is waiting in the car, idling outside the door to the studio.

"Maxie," I say, "that was a fiasco. You have to work harder on prepping me next time. That woman was totally unorganized, I practically had to do her job for her. From now on, we're prepping a list of anecdotes and laugh lines in advance, and I'm doing the pre-show interviews on my own. I obviously can't trust you to handle it."

I remember what I had said on the show earlier, and I feel bad for a moment. I do need to be kinder to him. I will be kinder to him. The poor boy works so hard.

"Still," I say, "it could have been worse. I'd better text Bruce."

I go to take my phone out of my purse, text my agent, like I normally do after these things. But there's something wrong. It's not the phone I remember, sleek and new. It's a battered thing with a cracked screen—my old phone, maybe, from years ago. Max is holding something in his hands. I look. It's my phone, the phone I remember, new, unblemished, that rose-gold back. I take it out of his hands. "Whoops," I say, "looks like we accidentally switched."

I type in the passcode, my father's birthday, once, twice. Nothing. On a whim, I try my own birthday, and the phone unlocks, opening on an unfamiliar screen.

"Did you change my password?" I say. "Honestly, Max, what's wrong with you?"

I can see his face, how white it is, how stiff. Good. He knows he's made a mistake. He pauses for a moment, his eyes darting back and forth between me and the driver. I can tell that there's something he wants to say to me that he can't say in front of this man.

"You'd better not text Bruce just yet," Max finally says.

"What are you talking about?" I say. "Of course I need to text him. I always do."

He lowers his voice even further. "Just wait," he says, practically whispering. "Until we're back at the house, okay?"

The car idles, the driver's eyes shifty in the rearview mirror. Max's face has gone totally white. He's looking at me with something almost like terror.

"Okay," he says, his voice returning to a normal volume, a high false cheer directed at the driver's back, "let's go back to Ms. Feld's building. We're done here."

The driver nods, steering us back toward the gate through the empty streets of fake New York. Max places his hand over the screen, something urgent in his gaze.

"Rosanna," he says, "just wait, okay? I'll explain when we get back to the apartment."

"The apartment building?" I say. "Is now really the time to visit that old thing? Can't we just go back to the house? I'm tired."

"I know you're tired," says Max, "I'm tired, too. But just wait. I'll explain when we get there, okay?"

He reaches forward to take the phone from my hand, and as I shift away from him, I feel the cold brush of something alien against my skin, under my dress, the brush of metal on skin—the snake, I remember, nothing I would buy. It doesn't belong to me. To who I think I am. Its ruby eyes flash bloody bright inside my head with a violence that feels like something breaking. I hear a noise, a click inside, a heavy door blown shut by wind, a rushing in my ears, a wrenching feeling, something deep inside me being torn out by the roots. I feel as though I have woken from sleep to find myself buried miles underground, the walls of my coffin close around me. And all at once I know that this is not my phone, this is not my necklace, this is not my neck, this is not my life. I am not who I think I am.

"Oh," I say.

Max is looking at me, wide-eyed. He looks as though he's seen a ghost.

"Of course," I say. "I'm sorry. I must be tired, the lights—I, I got confused for a minute."

I stop. There is a wetness on my face. Am I crying? I lift my hands to touch it and realize that my nose is bleeding, the enormous pressure in my head building until it broke and now there is blood, blood everywhere, and Max takes the phone from my lap, tilts my head back for me, pinches the bridge of my nose as the blood drips salty down my tongue. I do not move. I cannot breathe. Beside me, Max keeps staring. He looks at me like I'm someone he knows. They all do. But I'm not her. I'm not anyone at all.

Max stays with me that night, not saying much, sleeping close beside me, curled up on the floor. He stays until the interview airs, watching tapes of Rosanna, eating takeout, my normally strict diet lifted, a treat. I still feel shaky, unmoored from my body. Eating feels wrong, a grotesque imitation of life. Rosanna claims to love Chinese food, so Max orders it every night and we sit close, passing containers of dumplings, lo mein, orange chicken, white rice back and forth between us, our fingers shining with oil. I eat as much as I can, more than he does, so that he can see how effortless all this is, that I am a woman of endless ability, endless appetite. Whenever he steps out for a moment, I do burpees until I throw up.

· · ·

When the show airs Max watches it with me. He has taped it live or had someone else record it, and the process of sliding the disk into the player, the whirring pause, makes it feel like any other tape, amplifying the doubled strangeness of watching myself, Rosanna, me as Rosanna, a collapsing hall of mirrors.

I'm up there saying things I don't remember saying. ("We've sourced the leather from the most darling little tannery outside Marrakesh. I spent some time traveling in the region, climbing the Atlas Mountains to get a better sense of how my designs could reflect the landscape. It was an incredible experience.") And saying things I do. ("I needed so much.")

My memory stops about the time that the host starts crying. I watch myself lean toward her, gently put my hand on her knee. I watch myself murmur something reassuring. I watch myself go on with the interview as she collects herself. I watch myself do fine. I look natural, like Rosanna, like someone who belongs. I feel the glow of the world I briefly slipped into. I want to do it again. I want more.

When Max is around, I am more myself than ever, the version of myself that he has built, solicitous, careful, full of small tendernesses just for him. I make him tea, sit close beside him on the couch. I ask questions about Rosanna as if she is something outside of me, as if there is anything I could ask him about her that I don't already know. I am having a harder and harder time remembering what I was before he came, but for the purpose of this little playacting re-creation of my old self, it doesn't matter. That girl is dead. I create a new old self, someone mild and blank, the girl Max thought he was getting. The one he likes. I wonder whether Max remembers my old name. I won't remind him if he doesn't.

Each day I can feel myself getting sucked further and further into Rosanna's life, like being gently pulled by a riptide out into the water of a warm sea. Swimming against the current is impossible. I am far too far from shore. It's easier just to relax and wait for whatever is coming next, watching my old self recede into the hazy distance. Letting my new image rise from that water, as placid as Venus, floating foam on the waves.

Max watches me from the corner of his eye when he thinks I'm not looking, won't notice. Pretending to think myself unobserved, I do small imperfect things, things Rosanna would never do, wiping my nose on my sweater sleeve, biting my nails, clearing my throat. Reminding him of the grotesque spaces of my body. I can see him gradually begin to relax. He stops watching me so closely. Now it is my turn to watch him. I stare straight ahead toward the screen, recording everything he does from the edges of my unblinking vision.

Outside my new body, life goes on. Max sends me out again on my small errands, and the paparazzi ask about the interview.

"Welcome back, Rosanna," they say. "How does it feel?"

I smile into the halo flare of flashbulbs. I wave. A little girl asks me to sign her autograph book, so I do, my hand slipping easily into the swooping dashes of Rosanna's signature, making a joke with her, giving her a smile. Each moment in the outside world disappears impossibly fast, like sugar melting on the tongue. Time flows around me. Water over a stone.

"It feels good," I say.

Everything is different when I am alone. Something is growing inside me, white roots groping through dark earth. I close the room's curtains and sit in the half dark, breathing, just breathing, until I feel myself flowing out of my body's confines and making my way up toward the ceiling. Gone. That old filth, the old impurity of me, is lost now. Everything is eroding, slowly being washed away. I picture my old self like a black cloud, leaving my body with every exhalation. Opening a blank space for Rosanna to fill. I can feel her slipping into me, a hand into a glove. I sit there in the dark and I am sitting in the dark in my own room, the vastness of my house around me like an empty shell. Somewhere, in a small apartment down the hill, I can sense the presence of my body. She is breathing in and out. She is imagining me here, imagining her. She is waiting for me to arrive.

13

The phone has been sitting silent on the table since Max gave it to me. I put it in my purse when I leave the house, because that is what Rosanna would do, but it doesn't feel real. It's more of a totemic object, a symbol of something to come. I carry Rosanna's phone the way my grandmother hung the medals of saints from the mirror of her beat-up Mazda to help her find parking spots, even though she never went to church. It's a gesture, a reaching toward, some vague belief in a better life. I feel immediately guilty for thinking of this. Rosanna doesn't remember her grandmother.

Max and I sit silent across the table at yet another lunch. There has been a certain awkwardness between us since that strange exchange in the back of the car, each of us watching the other for clues about what is coming next. The ease that we earned over those long slow weeks and months seems to have evaporated. We are like strangers now, careful with each other, watching what we say. I am beginning to resent Max, whose stifling presence feels more and more like a barrier between Rosanna and me. We don't need him. He's scared of that, I think. How secondary he's becoming to all of this.

I'm eating another Caesar salad, using the crisp stems of the romaine to wipe up the oily dressing that pools at the edges of my plate. I'm so sick of Caesar salads. Max orders different meals every time. Surely there must be other foods, other things Rosanna enjoyed eating, or would enjoy now if she had the chance. I can feel the quiet murmur of what she really wants inside of me every time we look at a menu. *Millet bowl,* she says, *seared ahi.* But Max is comforted by the familiar, by routine, so I'm stuck having lunch in a series of identical expensively casual restaurants, eating the same meal over and over, like some kind of bizarrely bougie version of *Groundhog Day. What a problem to have,* I think. What a stupidly inconsequential problem. I smile across the table at Max, trying not to let any of this show on my face, struggling to look like I'm having a good time. In case anyone's watching. If there's one thing I've learned, it's that someone's always watching.

And then, in the bottom of my bag, I feel a buzz. My first thought, irrationally, is that some kind of animal has climbed into my purse and begun its attack, but I see Max's smile as he looks down at his phone, placed faceup on the table, and gives me a significant look. I take out the phone. I look at the name on the screen. Marie. She's seen the interview. She reminds me of our plans.

"Hike tomorrow?" she says.

Relief flashes through me. *Finally.* I want to learn about the Rosanna that this woman, her oldest, maybe only, friend knows. But isn't this taking it a little too far? They've known each other so long—won't Marie notice the small discrepancies between us? Or maybe she does know. Maybe this is Rosanna's version of quality control. She can't come see me herself, so she's sending someone she trusts. I can picture Marie so clearly, typing out that text. There she is, in her big house in the hills somewhere close to mine, sitting at her kitchen island, children huddled around her feet. Maybe she looks tired. She looks tired, I decide. I am prettier than she is, now.

"Sure thing!" I write. "Can't wait to see you, babe!"

Marie is imagining me here, too. And here I am, just like she pictures me. I try to confine my perceptions to the immediate perfection of my Rosanna body: my pink polished nails; the soft sleeves of my long white shirt; that amethyst banded ring glinting from the crook of my finger, her grandmother's, whom she doesn't remember, but at least she got this ring. My message lights up Max's phone, and he gives me a slight, hesitant nod.

"Wait," I say. "Did you want me to say no? Should I cancel on her?"

"Not at all," he says, smiling, pretending to smile. "I mean, I think if you'll have fun of course you should go, and it's great that she's the one to reach out. Puts us, you, in a position of power. So that's good."

Still, his voice is flat. I lower my own, lean closer to him, limp salad forgotten. "Max," I say, "if you think I'm not ready for this, you have to tell me. That's your job. I need you to let me know what you think I should do."

"That's not it," he says. "We both know you're ready if you want to be. You've worked hard. This had to happen sooner or later."

"It'll be fine," I say. "I'll do the same thing with her that I did at the interview."

He gives me a sharp look.

"Okay, not the same thing, I know I wasn't perfect, but the ratings were great, people are responding really positively! And I've watched—I've spent so much time with Marie. I'm comfortable with her. I know how this goes. Keep it superficial, right? I can do that. I have lots of practice with superficiality, let me tell you."

"It's just . . . ," says Max. He keeps his voice low. His eyes skate guiltily around the room. "I know that she can be . . . distracting for you. And I don't want you to get distracted. We've been working so hard, rebuilding your image with the public. You need to focus, and if you start spending too much time with Marie, that might be difficult. She has taken a lot of your energy in the past. So yes, go on your hike, have a lovely time, but remember this is work. Don't get carried away."

He falls silent as the waiter comes by with the bill. We put it on my credit card, her credit card, a business expense. Rosanna's signature flows easily from the pen, which is identical to every pen they give you in places like this, gold at both tips, embossed with the restaurant's name. I still notice these things. I can't help noticing, although I have long since ceased to be impressed.

"Don't worry," I say. "I couldn't forget I was working if I tried."

The night before the hike, when I sleep, I picture Marie on the other side of the canyon in her big white bed beside her husband, my image a hologram, a memory, floating right in front of her face, too far away to touch. Instead of projecting myself into Rosanna like I usually do, I work on bringing myself closer and closer to Marie. So she can see my new face. Acclimate. I want her to recognize me, to know me as a person she can trust.

Max wakes me up in the blue dark, pacing back and forth at the foot of my bed, his footsteps anxiously uneven. These days I sleep more and more, but usually, even when I wake up late in the afternoon, I am alone. Max no longer stays over. He is busy with other things. Now, listening, I lie still for a moment, tracking the quiet sounds he makes, allowing myself to feel reassured. To pretend that nothing between us has changed. The light through my eyelids grows purple, bruised. Slowly I open my eyes. Max stands there, looking down onto the street. His back is hunched, his suit rumpled. I wonder if he's slept. I make a small animal noise low in my throat to let him know I'm awake, I'm watching him, and he turns around, startled. He's holding a bottle of unappealingly bright green liquid, and he passes it to me, pretending to smile.

"Here," he says, "I got you a present."

I sit up.

"I don't want this," I say. "Where's my coffee?"

Rosanna is grumpy in the mornings, so I am grumpy, too. In my old life I practiced a kind of chipper unobtrusiveness learned from so many years of living in other people's houses. It has prepared me well for my new role, a new kind of exhaustion where niceness is not the only thing I have to pretend. This morning I feel fine. If anything, I'm happy, thinking about Marie waking up from dreams of me, imagining my face. I want to share my excitement with Max. But I can't, so I tell myself it's luxurious to be in a bad mood, to express some petty need and know it will be instantly, unquestioningly met. And as always with my meaningless requests, Max complies. There is a possibility of a whole new kind of tenderness hidden within my badness, if it is the right kind of badness, deployed at the right time. But tenderness is no longer the only thing I need from him. And I am so, so tired.

"Drink up," Max says, handing me a lukewarm to-go cup. Where does he even find a cappuccino at five in the morning? He is the master, I think, of insignificant miracles. "And then I need you to at least pretend to be interested in this juice. Marie loves the stuff. She says it's good for inflammation. That's her big thing right now, inflammation. Hopefully if she sees you drinking this, it'll start her talking. That's the main thing. Keep her talking. Don't let her ask too many questions."

As he talks, he looks just past me, his gaze drifting beside my ear. I wonder if I look more convincingly like her in his peripheral vision. If that's as much of me as he can stand.

"She'll ask me, though," I say. "She has to ask. I'm her best friend, and it's been such a long time. She's going to ask me a lot of questions, about where I've been, what I've been doing."

There is a meanness in this, sneaking around his justifications, not letting him mollify himself. This is hard. This is going to be hard, and I want to make him admit that. I want him to give me some credit. He twists his hands in his lap, and I slide the blunt rim of the bottle between my lips and drink. Everything feels exaggerated, the smooth bite of glass, the liquid it brings up into my mouth, bitter and sandy-textured with the ground-up grit of kale stems. I wonder if I am more nervous than I am allowing myself to believe.

Max stands and walks away from me to face the window again. He gazes down into the quiet street. I wonder what he sees outside. How does the view look to him, someone with so many other things to look at? Who can go out into that wide world any time he wants, who needs no permission but his own. Does he notice all the small details I cling to, the changing shapes of the clouds, the cracks in the street where the weeds poke through? Does he see what I see? I don't believe he does.

"Stay focused on your talking points," he says. "Keep the conversation light. Marie's not really the curious type, so it should be easy to misdirect her. And Rosanna never really opened up to Marie. She couldn't. Rosanna didn't trust Marie, and you shouldn't, either. There were very few people she trusted."

Here his voice goes softer, fond. He thinks that he was one of those people. I wonder if he's right. I think of Rosanna, lonely then, alone now. *Poor darling*, I think. *Poor thing*. Rosanna wanted Max to think she trusted him. So that's what I want him to think, too. *I trust you*, I think. At least I want to believe I can.

"Okay," I say, "I get it. I'm sorry, I guess I'm a little nervous, this is big. It's a big day."

I have talked myself into a corner. Now I really am starting to get nervous.

"It is a big day," Max says. "And I expect you to do well. If Marie is prying, just say something vague about wellness. Needing some time. Redirect the conversation to her life, her problems. It should be easy."

"But what if it isn't?" I ask.

Hearing the words float in the still air of the room, I realize the precariousness of my situation. I have gotten away with lying to strangers, the press, people who knew Rosanna vaguely from a distance or not at all. Of course, for them, I am close enough to the real thing. But this is different. This is Marie. She knows Rosanna as she really is, or as she had been before she disappeared. What if she notices something different about me? What if I'm not good enough for her? If she notices a change, she will go to Rosanna. And if she does that, everything is over for me. I feel something inside me skip, speed up.

"It will be," says Max. "Don't think about it too much."

I feel around for a response in the blank spaces of my brain, going over the flash cards, images of Marie, her husband, their mutual friends. None of this helps. I close my eyes. I make myself relax.

Somewhere deep down, quiet, I can feel the pull of her. Rosanna will guide me. She always has. *Just be natural*, I tell myself. Help her help you.

If Max can tell that I am frightened, he doesn't let on. Maybe he likes it. This is the one way in which I am not like Rosanna, will never be like her. Unlike Rosanna, I am afraid.

Marie is waiting for me at the trailhead. It is a shock seeing her standing there. Real. In some ways she is so familiar, the way she stands, her tense, distracted expression as she gazes down at her phone. But she looks older than I expected. More human. In the videos, she is perfect, all sleek, toned muscles and easy grace. Here she is just another woman, waiting, nervous, her skin fragile in the full light of the sun. I feel a tenderness toward her that is so intense, so painful, I can barely move. It almost feels like the real thing.

"Marie," I say. "Hello."

She looks up. Tiny flashes of emotion break across her face like clicked-through slides in an old projector—longing, confusion, rage—appearing and disappearing so quickly that I barely have a chance to register them. She settles somewhere neutral, her face smoothly expressionless. Somehow it makes me sad, that she has to pretend for me. She shouldn't have to do that. And I realize that she needs me to succeed as badly as he does. More, maybe. For her, I have to make this real. I need everything I say to her to be true. For Rosanna's sake, even more than my own.

"Hello," she finally says.

"Babe!" I say, plastering my face into the wide smile I use when Rosanna sees someone she knows. "So good to see you. It's been too, too long."

I hope this is the right expression. I've never smiled for someone Rosanna knows as well as Marie. On the tapes they are affectionate with each other, embracing, air-kissing, each telling the other how beautiful she is, how much she loves her. I'm ready for that kind of warmth, that closeness. I need it, even if it doesn't entirely belong to me. But Marie just stands there, looking at me with a strange open-faced curiosity. Finally she smiles. It is a tight smile, and it doesn't reach her eyes, but it is a smile nonetheless.

"Rosanna," Marie says. There is a question in her voice, a hesitation. I feel that she is staring right through my expensive clothes, past my perfect body, to the stretch marks on my thighs, my surgery scars. Even with all the creams Max buys me, the vitamin oils and mineral pastes and positively charged crystal waters, they still shine angry red against the pale surface of my skin.

"It's good to see you," I say. I spread my arms wide to embrace her, feeling the stiffness where they removed the fat from under my arms. I can only hope she won't notice. Marie hesitates. And then she comes to me slowly, a little awkward, but close enough to smell that I am wearing Rosanna's perfume, unwashed exercise clothes, close enough against my false surface to absorb the familiar presence of the woman she loves. Her friend. She relaxes, just a little, into my arms. I wrap them tight around her and give her a squeeze. A wash of emotion fills my throat, tears pressing hot against the base of my tongue. She loves Rosanna so much. Rosanna is so loved.

"You, too," she says.

Still, she shifts away from me after only a moment. I let her go, afraid that if I hold on too long, the heavy smell of my own body will seep through, betraying me.

"What are you even doing back here?" she says. "From the email you sent me I thought that you were giving up on L.A. for good."

"And you?" I say. "Never!"

There's a pause. *Maybe I was wrong*, I think. Maybe Rosanna has kept the truth from her. Maybe she doesn't know.

"Well, you look great," she finally says. "The time away must have agreed with you. Maybe I should try disappearing for a year. Apparently it does wonders for the skin."

A year. It has been a year since Marie has seen Rosanna.

"You seem to be doing well, too," I say. "The website, and all of the interviews and everything, I've been keeping up! And I have so many questions for you, I don't know how I'll ever find time to ask them all."

I speak in a steady, enthusiastic voice. I do not show any emotion

Rosanna wouldn't feel, Rosanna, whose decision this was. Rosanna who left. Marie looks away from me. I can tell that she is fighting hard to keep her expression neutral.

"Anyhow," she says, "it is nice to see you. It really is good to have you back."

"I know it's been a long time," I say. "I'm sorry. I promise I'll make it up to you eventually."

"I don't think it's a question of making anything up," says Marie. "You're living your life. I'm living mine. In a way, I guess it's normal."

I can understand Rosanna walking away from everything else, or wanting to. Marie is her friend, though, or thinks she is. What terrible mistake must she have made to earn this kind of treatment? And why aren't we talking about it now?

"It might be normal," I say. "But that doesn't mean I like it. At least I've managed to keep up with your blog!"

I shake the green juice in her general direction, the contents of the bottle sloshing muddy against the sides.

"So you're reforming?" she says, false cheer animating her voice. "I'll believe it when I see it."

"Well, I'm trying. As they say in therapy, it's a process."

"Ooh," says Marie, "therapy! What's next, self-awareness? Don't you go changing on me now."

And she smiles. This time her face seems to move more, her eyes wrinkling at the corners. A small smile, a mean smile, but a real smile nonetheless.

"Very funny," I say. "Now come on, let's walk."

The path up the mountain is narrow, dusty. At first, on the lower slopes, we pass a few other hikers, most of them women, most alone, some walking tiny dogs or big ones who pull the women down the mountain with their bulk. The women give us the looks I am used to, the sideways glance from the corner of their eyes that means they know who I am. I pretend not to notice, but in my head I count how many of them look at me first, how many at Marie. Every glance lands reassuringly on my skin, adding to my solidity, reaffirming my presence on the mountain, in the world. *I am here,* I tell myself. *I am really here.* Gradually I let myself relax. As the slope gets steeper, the crowd thins until it is just Marie and me, walking in silence. I sift through my brain for something useful to say. I remember what Max said, that I should get her talking about her lifestyle brand, her writing, her family. Let her do the work for me.

"Well, you're right about inflammation," I say. "This stuff really helps."

I take a sip of my drink, a big one, the gritty liquid sour on my tongue, and try very hard not to gag.

"Since when do you care about stuff like that?" Marie asks.

She is walking fast. Even with all the exercise I've been doing, I struggle to match her pace. I am unaccustomed to traversing any distance longer than the width of my room, and it tells, my toned body burning in new places, the air of the outside world strange in my lungs. I laugh a breathless little laugh.

"Since I turned thirty, I guess!" I say. "It had to happen sooner or later. And Max has got me hooked on these turmeric root shakes. He reads your blog, too. That's where he got the recipe. Honestly I've never felt better!"

Marie finally slows down so her pace matches mine. She looks at me sideways. "Wait," she says. "You're still in contact with Max?"

Even more air goes out of my lungs, a gasp I disguise as inhalation. I am glad now that I'm out of breath. It gives me a second to think about what to say, and I fall back just a step, trying to ignore the quick rush of panic that has grabbed me by the throat. What does Marie know about Max that I do not? What does Rosanna know? I want to ask her questions, to pump her for information, but no, I can't—Rosanna already knows how she feels about Max. She wouldn't have to go to Marie for confirmation, especially if she's changed her mind in the intervening year. Another woman passes us on her way up, walking two enormous Huskies on matching braided-leather leashes. Their hair is glossy from high protein diets and expensive shampoo, their teeth glinting in the clean light. I feel her look at me, the way her gaze lingers. Is she recognizing me on her own, or has Max asked her to keep an eye on me? We, he says sometimes, talking about the project. How many of us are there? There is no safety even here, with a woman who is supposed to be my best friend. Maybe I can trust her. Maybe I can't. But there is no guarantee that whatever I tell her will stay between us. What happened between Rosanna and Max is something I will have to discover on my own.

"Yes," I say finally, careful. "Of course I still talk to Max. He works for me, after all. And we're very close. Why wouldn't we be?"

This seems safe, vague enough that I could be asking Marie for her own interpretation rather than getting her to recall my own words.

"Well, the last time we talked . . . ," says Marie, "actually, more than once, you said that you thought his interest in you was a little . . . well, more than professional. Creepy."

She must see the look of panic that flashes across my face too quickly to control, so she interrupts herself. "But hey, now we know you weren't in a super stable place back then, right? Maybe you changed your mind?"

"Yeah." I wait a second to see if anything lights up in recognition. Am I speaking a truth Rosanna understands? But there is nothing. "I guess I did," I finally say.

It's hard to push the words out. I am no longer pretending. I really can't breathe. Marie stops beside me and puts her hand on my back, her face coated thick with a concern that looks genuine, but honestly who knows? I have lost my ability to distinguish between real emotion and pretend, the felt and the faked.

"You okay?" she asks.

"I'm fine," I say. "Just got a little dizzy. It's been a while since I've been outside, you know? At the wellness center . . ."

I let my voice trail off, look into the distance, feeling around inside me for that pulse of reality that lets me know that I'm on the right track, close to doing the right thing. But there is nothing. No sign of life inside. I let the real confusion and fright inside of me rise to the surface, let my eyes glaze over and go blurry.

"Hey," says Marie, "hey, it's fine. I get it. Whatever. You're allowed to change your mind."

"I mean, you're not wrong," I say. "That is something I . . . I said that. About Max. That is something I said. I guess he just annoyed me sometimes. He was always underfoot, you know? I really depend on him, though. Not all change is good. Max helps me. For all his flaws, he has always been helpful. So I decided to keep him. There were other changes that were more pressing."

"I see," Marie says finally. "Well, I'm glad to hear you're making changes."

"I am," I say. "I have been. I don't like to talk about it much, but if it weren't for Max, I wouldn't be here with you. He has always taken care of me. I pushed him away, yes, but he always came back. Max is the one person I can count on. For all his flaws."

Marie nods, her lips tight.

"Not that I can't count on you," I say. "I meant employees, you know that."

"Just drop it," she says. "It's fine. I'm sorry I asked. It's really none of my business, right? I mean, there's a reason you haven't seen me for so long."

"It's not just you," I say. "I haven't seen anyone."

"Except for Max," she says, "the alleged creep."

"Yeah, but that's different. He works for me."

"And I'm your oldest friend."

"Of course you are," I say. "I'm sorry. I just needed to be alone for a while. I don't know what else to say."

We have climbed higher now, the city spread out beige vague at our feet. I catch up to Marie. Some part of the old competitiveness must remain, because she smiles a little, seeing me sweat. I feel a quick little pulse of annoyance. Is that all this is? The same old pointless competition, repeated forever, on a horrible infinite loop? It's too dangerous to keep talking like this. I try to figure out what comes next.

"So the website's doing well, I take it?" I ask. "You always make the best things. I still have a little bit of that rose-hip-infused honey you gave me for Christmas a few years ago. The kitchen's under construction right now, so I'm living vicariously through your food photos!"

This is a lie we have come up with to keep Marie from inviting herself over to Rosanna's house. Marie can be a nuisance, Max says, always dropping by when she's not wanted. Rosanna doesn't want to see her now. It would be too painful, Max says. *But creepy,* I think. Maybe I should say something that will make Marie want to stop by the house. Maybe Rosanna really does need her more than I do. There must be some way we can explain our situation in language Marie will be able to understand.

"Well, you have that whole empty building down the hill," she says. "That's what, eight kitchens to eat honey in? Besides, do you really want to talk about my blog right now? Is that really the most pressing issue on your mind?"

"Yeah," I say, "you know what, I *do* want to talk about it. The normal stuff. The boring stuff. Real life, gossip, whatever. I missed you so much while I was away. I'm so sick of spending all this time in my head. I'm sick of talking about myself. Sometimes it feels like that's all I do, just talk and talk about all my dumb problems. I want to hear about you. So tell me, how's life? How are you? How's all the everyday stuff that bores you to tears?"

Marie looks at me for a long moment. And then suddenly, incredibly, she laughs. "You really are reforming," she says. "If you want to know, I'll tell you. But you have to at least pretend you're interested."

"I will," I say. "I am. Believe me, your domestic situation is fascinating to me. Preschool dramas. Bloody noses. Whatever, I want to hear about it all."

"Well, Edward is fine," she says. "They're all fine. To be honest, I don't want to talk about him or the children. It's all anyone asks you about when you're married. It's like you're not even a person anymore. It's exhausting."

"I know what you mean," I say. "I haven't felt like a person in months now. Years. Never, maybe. The more I think about it, the more I realize I've never been a person in my life."

Marie laughs. "Well, you're not a person, are you? You're . . ."— and she puts on an exaggeratedly dramatic voice to say this part— "the famous Rosanna Feld."

I look at her. Really look. At her hair, her hands, the perfect line of her profile against the sky—all the little fragments that make up this woman, my friend. I like this Marie much more than I do the version of her that exists on the tapes. Maybe I'm better than the Rosanna on the tapes, too. A feeling stirs to life inside of me. A real feeling. Mine. I picture us, Marie and me, alone on the couch, our bodies mirrors. We might not be so perfect out here, but I like her. I like us together. Friends.

We pause at the top of the hill and look out over the city. Wrapped up in our conversation, I haven't noticed how high we've climbed. My new body is stronger than I realized. I am stronger than I realized.

"Look," says Marie, "it's terrible. The smog is so thick you can't see the islands."

She points out past the ends of the boulevards, toward a blurrier part of the shining sea, buckling the horizon with reflected light.

"I wish we didn't have to live in this horrible place. I hate it, I really do. Remember when we said we'd leave?"

"Well," I say, "you live in Ojai now, right? At least part-time. So we're halfway there!"

She laughs. I was nervous that she might not laugh, but she laughs, she likes it, and I am grateful to her. I let my face relax into a mask of agreeable attentiveness, an expression I have practiced night after night in the mirror and now settle into without thinking, my face draping soft over the familiar framework of the expression. I feel myself begin to drift out of the tight space of my borrowed body, out over the blank expanse of the city, limitless. I breathe in the dusty air, the clear, clean light. It is all so easy. I look back at my body, at Marie and me standing so close to the edge of the cliff. We look perfect. Just like the real thing.

"But you haven't seen my house in Ojai," says Marie.

I come back into my body, heavy. I thought that we were done with this, that she had forgiven me. Of course it isn't that easy. I adjust my expression to be more thoughtful, somber.

"You haven't seen the kids in ages. Or me, for that matter. Everything is different than it was before. And you seem different, too."

There is a disease I read about once in my old life, where people become convinced that their loved ones have been replaced by an impostor. Someone who looks the same, shares their memories, says all the right things, but is a different person entirely, strange to them. No one else notices the change; no one else will believe them when they talk about it. A small difference isn't the end of the world. People change every day. Every second a new version of ourselves comes into being. Marie expects to see Rosanna. And here I am. She has no choice but to believe in me. The alternative is madness. I look her in the eyes, look right at her, and smile.

"Reformed, right?" I say. "I've got the glow of the chosen."

We stand there in silence for a moment and I think, *Now, now I will open the door a crack. I will let the light shine in.*

"It's funny, though," I say after a few minutes of silence. "Somehow I don't actually remember the last time I saw you. Where were we? Do you remember?"

I try to keep my voice light, dispassionate, like her answer doesn't matter. I reach out and take her hand. It's smaller than Max's, cold. This is something I had envied her and Rosanna, their closeness, their easy physicality. It's mine now. I can feel the rough edges of her nails. Does she bite them? The small imperfection comforts me.

"It doesn't really matter," I say. "I'm just curious. My memory seems so fuzzy lately."

Marie untangles her fingers from mine. I try to hide my disappointment.

"It was the dinner," she says. "You remember, at my house? The market dinner. You brought your new boyfriend. I was so happy that you were finally seeing someone nice instead of sneaking around with that married guy you were always so mysterious about. I still don't know what you were thinking. But there was some weird tension between you two. You were acting distant. Sad. You barely spoke to me at all that night. And after that, poof!"

She makes a little explosive gesture in the air. A boyfriend. Rosanna's boyfriend. And before that, another boyfriend, a boyfriend with a wife? I feel as though some larger picture is snapping into place, some rejection, some pain that has driven her away from the world. And why is Max withholding this information from me?

"I was sad that night," I say. "I remember. I just felt awful. I guess that was what made me realize how badly I needed a break. My whole body hurt, every part of me, just this vague horrible ache. Like I was slowly being crushed. Everything that had been happening, with the married guy and everything, it caught up to me. And I felt awful. I just felt like the most terrible person in the world."

Marie looks at me with such concern that I want to keep talking, to tell her the truth, not about who I am, of course, but about how I feel. How every day I'm slipping further and further into a darkness whose mysterious pull I do not understand. How I am eroding. Fading away. I keep my face tilted toward the blur of the city below. I am having trouble focusing.

"I'm sorry," Marie says. "You should have said something. I wish I had known."

"Yeah," I say, forcing myself to continue, "it was bad, especially since that guy was such an asshole. Even if he wasn't married, it was hardly an upgrade. We were totally fighting."

"No," says Marie slowly, considering, "not fighting. But it was weird. It seemed like you were avoiding him, like you were trying not to talk to him. Or me, for that matter. I worried that you were about to disappear into one of your misery phases. And when you stopped showing up after that, stopped responding to my texts, when a month passed, and another . . ."

"You worried," I say.

On the hill below us, blackened by wildfire, stands a copse of scrubby palm trees, pointing like accusing fingers toward the sky. I look at them and think, *They know*. I hold my breath and wait for Marie to accuse me of all the terrible things Rosanna has done. I deserve it. We both do. Instead, she sighs.

"Yeah," she says, "but I let you disappear. I haven't been a very good friend."

"Oh no," I say, "I don't—"

But she cuts me off. "Don't make excuses for me. I know how you must have felt. Hearing you say that just now, how badly you were suffering, you were right. I knew that. I knew you were in pain. And I should have tried harder to get in touch. But you didn't reach out to me, either. At least I have an excuse—I have Edward and the children. My whole life is about them now, about their needs. Not like in the old days, when it was just us two and we could do whatever we wanted. It's amazing to think we were ever so young. But we grew up. I grew up. And you were gone. One day we were having dinner, talking about the future, and the next, nothing. Canceled plans, a few texts, then silence. I didn't know what to think. I knew how bad it could get for you, of course I worried. You took two months—two months, Rosanna—to respond to an email I sent checking in. Rosanna, I thought you were dead. I understand trouble, of course. You've been in trouble before, we both have. But you didn't think to give me any warning. You didn't ask for help. I could have helped you if you had asked. The whole time you were gone, I thought you hated me. You must have."

"No," I say, "no, I could never. I couldn't hate you if I tried. I'm so sorry, Marie. Really I am. I didn't want to bother you. But I should have told you what I was going through. I should have known that you wanted to know. From now on, I'll always tell you, I promise. I'm different now. I'm a better person. I'm a different person, Marie."

She shakes her head, looking so sad I can hardly stand it. I am full of a sick rage, nauseated by my own selfishness. How could I do such a thing to her?

"I'm not going to ask you where you've been," she says. "I know you'd tell me if you could. But you can never disappear on me like that again. Never. I won't take you back next time you do. For both of our sakes. You can never worry me like that. Promise me, and we don't have to talk about it anymore. It will be like nothing ever happened. I just need to hear from your own lips that you're back for good, and staying. That you're okay."

"Of course I am," I say.

I am trying so hard not to cry, but it is no use. The tears are leaking hot from the corners of my eyes, and Marie wraps me up again in her arms. And now I am really crying, sobbing, my body shaking, gasping for breath, drowning in this new feeling, this real feeling crashing over me in powerful waves, pulling me down, and I crumple into her and she holds me, stroking my back lightly with her close-bitten nails. It has been so long since I was held like this, with a true and deep affection. Marie loves me. And I love her. It's as simple as that. I will never leave. I will never hurt her again. I will help Rosanna keep her best friend close.

"I promise," I say. "Marie, I promise."

In her arms, I feel so stupid and small, alive to the world around me, to the smell of smoke in the air, to the gentle press of her skin on my skin. So alive it's painful. Below us, the city spreads itself out, enormous and pale, the ocean glinting at its edges like a distant fire. Marie unwraps me from her arms. She places one hand, gentle, on my cheek.

"You know something?" she says. "I kind of hate you right now. But I missed you. Of course I did. I'm glad you're back."

"I missed you, too," I say.

At the bottom of the hill we embrace, and I climb into my car alone. I don't know where Max is, but he isn't here. And for now I don't care. For now it's good to be alone, just me, with the same back of the driver's head, the same landscape of scrubby brush and traffic. Everything the same, everything shining with a new light. The low hum of my background anxiety is gone. I am glad to be alone with my thoughts. I have a friend. Marie likes me! Talking to her made me feel as though a locked door inside me was opening up. Now I will be able to access new parts of Rosanna, aspects of her that even Max didn't know about. I am filling up the blank spaces of myself with her. We will be closer than ever now, joined by the medium of Marie, another triad, the three of us counterbalancing Max, me in the middle, Rosanna on both sides. I take my phone out of my pocket.

"It was so good seeing you!" I type. "Let's get together again soon."

I picture Marie, moving away in her car, growing farther and farther from me with each passing second, checking her phone in the back seat, or not yet, maybe. She still hasn't responded. Maybe it's because she's driving. Maybe Marie gets to drive her own car. Maybe someday I will, too. As the driver pulls up to the curb, I quickly delete the messages off the phone. They're harmless, of course, totally harmless, but still unsanctioned. I remember what Max said about not getting too close to Marie, not letting her take up too much of my time. I get the feeling he wouldn't approve.

Max is waiting for me in the living room. He doesn't turn around when he hears the door open. His shoulders are hunched tight.

"Have fun?" he says. "Did you have a nice time with your little friend?"

His voice is sarcastic and flat. I feel so excited about my progress, so full of buzzing energy, that I don't really mind. I know he's jealous, but this is a big deal. I will infect him with my happiness. It went so well, better than I imagined. Another hurdle successfully cleared. And more than that. I have a friend now. Someone who understands me. Someone who brings me as close to Rosanna as I can get.

"Max!" I say. "Yes! I had a wonderful time."

Still nothing. I thought he would be excited. He should be excited with . . . *for* me. I want him to acknowledge what a big deal this is. If he's in a bad mood, that's his responsibility, not mine.

"Seriously, Max, it went so well. We really didn't have to worry at all. Marie's great, and the hike went perfectly. You were right, she was easy to talk to, stiff at first, definitely angry with me, Rosanna, but then she opened up, and it was so great. I really understand her, and she gets me, you know? Rosanna will be pleased."

"So you liked her so much that you decided to go make your own plans. Even after I warned you. I told you this would happen."

I'm silent, scrambling for an excuse, but he continues before I can say a word.

"You thought I wouldn't see this text, maybe. Thought you two would sneak around behind my back, have a laugh at my expense? I told you she was bad for you. A distraction."

Of course he was keeping a close eye on things. He probably had his phone open the whole time I was gone, keeping tabs on me. How could I have been so stupid?

"No," I say, "it was for you, I thought . . . I thought it was what Rosanna would do. They do like to talk often, don't they? I thought it was a good idea. It's how she would behave."

"So why did you delete it?"

"Oh, did I?" I say. Shit. "I'm sorry, I'm still new to this smart-phone thing, I didn't realize. Should I resend it? Or will that look desperate?"

Max finally turns to look at me. He puts out his hand.

"Give me the phone," he says.

For a moment, I hesitate. *My escape route*, I think. *My way out. Gone.*

"Okay," I say.

He snatches it from my hand and moves closer to me. His voice is gentle now. Dangerous.

"Did I tell you to make plans?" he asks. "I did not. I said no such thing. You think you know how to do this better than I do? Better than Rosanna?"

I remember what Marie said before. What Rosanna said. Don't trust him. He should be happy for me. His job is to be happy. He isn't doing his job. I am doing my job. I am doing what Rosanna wants me to do. I straighten my spine and look him in the eye.

"Of course not," I say.

He needs to believe I trust him. For now, at least. While he still has the phone. While he still controls my access to the outside world. Until Rosanna comes, I need Max to love me. I wrap my arms around his back, the same pose I took with Marie. I feel his stiffness in my arms. But I convinced her. I can convince him, too.

"Of course I don't think I know better," I say. "I wouldn't even be here without you. This is all because of you, you know that. Everything I am is yours, Max. It's thanks to you it went so well today. We really get along, she likes me. She'll do whatever Rosanna needs her to do. That's all you, Max. That's all thanks to you."

He still won't look at me. His gaze hovers somewhere around the arch of the ceiling. His body, in my arms, remains stiff.

"You don't get it," he says. "You're no one to her. She doesn't like you."

I blink. "What are you talking about? Yes, she does. Of course she does. I'm her best friend, she was totally convinced, she likes me a lot."

"She doesn't like you. Nobody likes you. She likes Rosanna."

"But I am Rosanna," I say slowly, like he is a child I need to explain these things to. He's the one who doesn't get it. Who else would I be, out there? What else is left for me? "For her I am Rosanna, now."

Max pushes me away and begins to walk back and forth across the room, kneading his hands together, palm against palm, in a slow, repetitive motion. Counting. There is a look on his face I cannot bring myself to understand. I will not let myself be frightened of him. Rosanna has the power here, not Max, whatever he might think. He is temporary, a stopgap, a stumbling block.

"Max," I say, "look at it this way. She's my oldest friend. If I can convince her, I can convince anyone. I am so close, Max, and it's thanks to you. I want so badly to do well, and I am doing well, she likes me. She likes me because of you. Because I am the way you made me. And she's wonderful, Max. She really is. I can see why Rosanna likes her. I like her, too, very much."

He laughs, a tight, bitter little laugh. "Your oldest friend?"

"Well, Rosanna's."

"Rosanna's friend?"

"Yes."

"Not yours."

"No."

"Who is your friend?"

"No one," I say.

"Not no one," he says. "I'm your friend. You know that, don't you? That I'm your friend?"

And all at once I understand what's going on. He just wants to know he's safe. He wants to know I still belong to him, the way Rosanna never will. That he is the most important person in the world to me. I make my voice soft and small. I put my hand on his arm.

"Max," I say, "of course you're my friend. Truest and only. You're the one person who knows me as I really am. And I am so happy to be here with you, working together. Aren't you happy with me? Isn't Rosanna happy? Haven't I done everything you asked? Haven't I done a good job?"

He takes my hands in his, holding them softly, pressure in his fingertips. I try to memorize the way they feel, the smooth warmth of his palms, the little callus on the base of his ring finger, the bend in the knuckle of his pinkie. I want to know him even better than he knows me. For the future. Just in case.

"I'm trying my best," I say.

"I know you are," he says.

His grip begins tightening. "But you're making it harder for yourself when you send messages I haven't told you to send. You're making it harder for Rosanna. It's my job to look out for you both in this dangerous world. I'm your only friend. You need me to take care of you. Bad things will happen if you don't let me take care of you."

His voice is gentle, but his hands are wrapped tight around mine, my fingers starting to ache. Next time I will figure out some other way. Next time he won't find out.

"I only want what's best for you," he says. "For both of you. I hope you know that."

Around me, I can feel the quiet weight of the empty building, pressing itself in around us, as cold and silent as a tomb. There is nobody here to protect me. I lie into the empty air.

"I know," I say. "I know."

14

With each passing day there are more and more new articles. I pin them to the wall, adding them to the images of Rosanna so that over and over again we are "Just Like Us," "Stepping Out," the two of us side by side in a series of perfect outfits, little sister, big sister, twins, the wall an echoed mirror of our faces, her face. I feel increasingly detached from what's going on around me, the outings, the people Max has me meet, the beautiful things I buy, he buys, Rosanna buys for me. I am swimming underwater, everything languorous, heavy, and strange.

I spend my days floating through a world that feels increasingly unreal. I spend my nights with the tapes. Max leaves me boxes of the footage I'm already familiar with, the safe stuff, he thinks. He doesn't know that nothing is safe with me. I have started breaking the footage down more and more microscopically, looking for clues. I switch from scene to scene, arranged thematically, spending huge chunks of time with Rosanna angry, or sad, or reading magazines, or talking to her housekeeper in the kitchen, the camera angled down from a high shelf. I watch her float in her bright square pool, eyes closed, the Hollywood Sign glowering down from a hill across the canyon. It's disorienting watching her life broken into perfect little chunks like this. What would my life here look like, packed away in darkness for some stranger to discover?

I sit on the couch watching, drinking one Diet Coke after another, a metallic blood taste building at the back of my throat. *I used to hate this stuff,* I think. I'm not even sure if this is true. If I hated it before, I love it now. It has become the only thing I can stand putting into my body. Everything else feels heavy and violent and rotten. I really eat only when Max sends me out to lunch with someone or comes around for my dream-girl binges, when I pretend that I don't count calories, that food is nothing to me, as it is to Rosanna, with her army of nutritionists and personal trainers. The fridge is empty except for rows and rows of slim silver cans that clink softly against one another when I open the door at three in the morning, the fridge's light filling the apartment, a physical presence in the dark, quiet room.

I start with footage of Rosanna alone. There is more of it than I thought there would be. Hours. The camera switching on as I come into the empty rooms of my house in the hills, walking through the terra-cotta hallways, the lights coming on when the camera does so it looks like I'm carrying light with me, emitting it from my pores. I sit in the kitchen drinking tea or eating a small bowl of bright red sorbet with a narrow gold spoon. I talk to myself, my voice echoing as I memorize lines, practice for the next day's interview or press appearance. Humming under my breath. Singing. I wonder if I am happy. Once, my face tense, I cross through the corner of the frame in the darkened living room with a bundle of herbs burning in my hand, my pale feet floating on the dark floor, lights flickering on as I pass, off as I exit the video's frame. Behind me, the windows form a dark mirror, reflecting my rippling movement through the empty room, another Rosanna appearing and disappearing like a shadow. Does she know she is being watched? Does she know I am the one watching?

My favorite tapes are the conversations between Rosanna and

Marie, whom I haven't talked to since our hike. I want to. Every time Max makes me make plans with another casual stranger, I feel my heart sink. The only person I want to see is Marie. I keep taking my phone out of my pocket, clicking it on and off again, trying to gather the courage to ask Max if I can see her, chickening out. Watching her is almost as good. I feel us slowly growing closer across distance, across time. On the tapes we each mirror the lines of the other's body, folded, fetal, our bodies closed parentheses, my body in the same pose here on the outside, curled up on the couch. There is a sameness to us. It was hard to see when I had viewed our interactions one at a time, spaced out over weeks. I hadn't noticed it when I saw Marie in person, either; she was wholly outside me then. But our bodies are the same size, with the same taut, practiced grace of the expensively exercised. We speak in the same tones, make the same fluid gestures, laugh the same laugh—tinkling, artificial, charming—doubling and redoubling, the two of us, the same girl, mirrored, and here I am, watching, the same girl again, the three of us, the two, one. I have seen this before, girls disappearing into each other, slipping into one another's spaces, packs of girls roaming the hallways and malls of my small town like wild dogs, untouchable, a girl group wall of sound, gorgeous, crushing, floating in a cloud of vanilla-scented body spray. There is a power in this disappearance. It lit them up from the inside. I had never had power like that before. I have it now. I think of all the women who want to look like Rosanna. The women who buy her makeup line, wear clothes that look like her clothes. Little Rosannas all around the country. All over the world. In the grand scheme of things, I am nothing new.

Marie and I have the same conversations over and over, a woman addressing herself in the mirror. There is something dreamlike about it: two identical bodies slowly, gracefully aging, our clothes, our hair, gradually evolving in concert as the world shifts around us. In the early tapes, we sit close, our knees always touching, easy with each other. Over time we move inexorably farther and farther apart. It's like watching the slow drift of continents, an island disappearing over the horizon until there is nothing left but light and the water, an endless undifferentiated smear of blue where there used to be a world. What we talk about seems almost beside the point. We stick to the same territory, an empty space that can be circled and recircled, some deeper feeling lurking just beneath the surface, too precious to touch. If I watch carefully enough, maybe I will be able to remember what it was.

"How's your love life?" I ask Marie, Marie asks me. "How are the boys?"

We both speak in the same arch tone, performing for some invisible audience, we are, we think, too smart to worry about these things, even though here we are, worrying.

"Oh my god," we say. "It's pathetic," we say. "It's something to do, I guess," and it makes for good press, all of this endless seeing and being seen, but we would rather be here, alone, together. I pour Marie another glass of wine. She lifts it to her lips, my grace in her long pale arms. The mutual creation of a greater whole, a project beyond us both. And also nothing more than this. Two women sitting together on a couch, talking for long hours into the night.

But as the tapes go on, the tone of our conversations begins to change. Even though I know it's coming, the same thing, the same time every night, it's hard not to take it personally when the shift comes. Like it's my own failure I'm watching. Like I have somehow influenced them. *It would be better,* I think, *to stop watching earlier in the night, to end with us sitting close, looking into each other's eyes,* but I can't, I keep watching over and over, as though by watching I can exert some influence, keep them frozen, somehow, close. And if I can do that, Marie will remember me. And if she remembers me, she will call.

What happens is this. Marie falls in love. I keep talking about the boys, the bars, the clubs with that same disengaged interest. I want her to know she's still the center of everything for me. But she doesn't seem to notice. The gossip she shares takes on a bitter edge. She talks about the failures of bodies, who is having trouble getting pregnant or can't seem to shed the weight after they've done it, the poor things, the inadequate things. None of this, she is sure, will happen to her, to her husband, who almost seems as though he is taking up space in the room, sitting between us on that narrow couch. Her pity turns on me, too.

"I can't imagine what it must be like for you," she says, "still dating. I don't know how you do it. There's someone really special for you out there, I know it."

The Rosanna on the screen rolls her eyes, but in the living room, I always lean forward.

"Yes," I say, "I know it, too."

Maybe I've already found her, I think. *Maybe my special person is you.*

There is a shot, a beat after, when her gaze shifts toward the camera and she seems to see me. *Almost,* I think. I am so close. If only I could reach toward her, put my hand on her arm, let her know how important she is to me. But I can't. I just watch as she sits a little farther from Rosanna on the couch, over and over, every night. I think about how time spreads out, looped in on itself in a tangle like the silky lumps of an inexpertly folded fitted sheet. As I talk to Marie, I try to make my voice be an exact replica of Rosanna's, saying better words, the words she should have said.

"I'm sorry I'm withdrawing from you," I say. "I'm scared. I'm so afraid of losing you. Please, Marie, don't let it happen. Don't let me let you go this time."

If time slips somehow, becomes unmoored, my voice will drift into that room, seamless, to that other place, and hearing me, Rosanna will echo, the two of us speaking with one voice, my old self and my new, like a parent in the audience of a shy child's school play, mouthing along with her practiced lines, love flowing out from me so strong she can feel it, tenderness like a tidal pull. It doesn't work. It doesn't happen. Marie moves farther away, a baby on her lap, her husband's ghost filling her body, and she's speaking in his voice now, moving with his gestures, not mine. Rosanna and I finally sit silent. I can feel something growing inside me. Here I am, and there I am, too, on the other side of their screen. I am curled up in my dark room on my small couch, like a child, her child, in my womb. I wonder why I didn't tell Marie how much I needed her. Why I never even tried. I search and search my brain, but my memories seem fogged somehow. There are things I cannot remember, no matter how hard I try.

I always watch the same tape last. The tape tucked underneath the mattress. The tape I had hidden from Max. It's hard the first time. I'm not sure if it's right, if I should watch it without his permission, Rosanna's. I hold it in my hands for a long beat, turning it over. I should return it to him, slide it anonymously into the box. But I like that it is mine. Some part of Rosanna that belongs only to me. And when I watch it, I see I was right—it's different, somehow, from the others. The camera work is shakier, the quality less glossy, an experimental feeling to it, somehow, of someone working out the kinks. It is the only span of uninterrupted footage longer than twenty minutes, a full hour of Rosanna's life. It is the best and only thing I own.

The tape starts with Rosanna sleeping. A long shot of her face, brow crinkled a little in the center, reacting to some dream. I can see her breathing, her chest moving up and down, slow, even breaths. It is both peaceful and strange to see her so helpless, watched by whoever was holding the camera. Watched now by me. The camera leaves the bedroom, moving through the dark house, down the whitewashed stairwell, the dark wood creaking under someone's feet, out into the high-ceilinged spaces of the ground floor. It lingers here and there on a series of objects, a statuette of a greyhound, a closed door, the box that holds the doorbell, maybe, or some kind of alarm. Things Rosanna would see if she was the one holding the camera. It feels anthropological, scientific, investigating the marginal spaces of the life she's made for herself. Making some kind of inventory. I like to think that it's the first video, that she is younger, that the smooth openness of her face in the first section is some version of Rosanna that no longer exists. And someone is watching her. Someone is beginning to plan whatever enormous project I am a part of, whatever it is I can sense around me, looming up over the horizon, a mountain hidden by darkness.

Leaving the house, the camera goes into the garden. I can hear someone's footsteps on the gravel, the sliding crunch as they turn to film the large front door, panning up the exterior of the house, past the archway in front where an enormous yellow lamp hangs, watery bright, a small sun. The camera pans across the side of the house, down again as the door opens, a vague movement in the bottom of the frame, like a glitch, an error, and there is Rosanna, standing in the hallway, body loose against the doorframe, light streaming out around her.

"Come to bed," she says to the darkness. "I miss you."

There is such a tenderness in her voice. A softness absent from the other tapes. I like to pretend she's talking to me. She reaches forward. The yellow light from the lamp throws her face into sharp relief, so her beautiful face becomes a blunt-edged skull. The camera switches off. As my eyes close, I imagine Rosanna's face, rising toward me out of the night.

I can't sleep anymore. I hate to sleep. I hate the dreams that come from sleeping, the confused images that push themselves through to the surface of my mind no matter how many glasses of wine I drink, how many sleeping pills I take. My dreams stubbornly remain my own, a monstrous intrusion of my old self, little snatches of image, of the movie theater lobby, Scott, my mother's face, the faces of women I haven't spoken to in years appearing as their ghostly child selves, tight pigtails, smiling. I hate them all. I force myself to stay awake as long as I can. In the hour before the sun rises as I begin to succumb to exhaustion, I put a tape on mute and close my eyes. I lay with my hands floating in front of my face, two moths drifting toward the light of the screen, their fingers feelers, her face my moon. When I open my eyes, Rosanna's hands are always in the same position as mine. I am getting closer. I can tell. She is closer than ever to me. The day will come when there is nothing left for me to remember. And when it does, Rosanna will be ready to slip into the body I leave behind, like water into an empty glass.

. . .

The idea of seeing Rosanna begins to obsess me. Even more powerful is the idea of being seen by her. I no longer imagine her coming to me. Now I dream of the day when I will walk through the gold-lit archway of that hidden house, cross through to the bright white kitchen. Of Rosanna, waiting there for me in the sunlight. Smiling. Before, when I thought my work was for Max, I liked to imagine calling him into the room with me. How I would sit down facing him, our bodies close, my back to the television. How I would turn the sound off and speak her words for him, she my mirror, I something better, closer, real. In that moment, she would become my reflection. My shadow. Stuck inside the prison of the screen, when I am close enough to touch. But something stranger than that is happening. Something is starting to shift inside of me, a bulb in frozen soil. It feels impossibly fragile. I have to protect it from the pressure of his gaze. So when Max is watching I make sure to throw in a few errors. Small things, nothing big enough to make him angry. I want him to think that this is hard for me. That this is work. I stumble just a little over a long word, or speak a moment after Rosanna, a moment before. My hands are a little heavier as they move through the air, laden with her. I let myself feel the extra weight.

"I'm in talks with my agent about signing a new deal with the makeup people," we say together, our voices seamlessly holding the same pace. "The perfume . . . ," we say, and I pause a fraction of a second longer than she does before the next line: ". . . was such a hit."

You can tell that there are two people speaking, but speaking together in sync, their voices similar enough. You can tell I am pretending. One woman pretending to be another. Not two women becoming one. Max smiles and nods, reassured. He's seeing what he wants to see.

"They want to start selling it in drugstores," we say. "But isn't this supposed to be about aspiration? I don't quite think that sends the right message. There's nothing aspirational about fluorescent lighting."

"She can't tell me what to do, but—" says Rosanna.

"She can't tell me what to do, and——" I say.

"Of course I value her opinion."

"You slipped!" says Max. He sounds delighted, a small child catching an adult in a lie. I sigh, and he puts his hand, soothing, on the small of my back.

"I'm so stupid," I say. "I'm sorry, I promise I've been practicing."

"It's okay," he says. "You're getting better. Let's try again."

Max doesn't know. But I know. The time for practicing is over. I have done all I can. I am ready for a new kind of knowledge now.

The longer I spend in front of the television, the less certain I am about who exactly I am watching. The longer I watch, the more false her gestures seem, overly rehearsed, somehow, not quite right. Whatever it is that is most urgent about her presence, most real, has begun to seep through the screen, into my body. What is left there now is nothing more than a shadow. A ghost image, faded, like an overexposed Polaroid, film run through an X-ray machine at the end of a vacation, all those beautiful memories wiped clean. I don't pretend to understand the mechanism of it, how she is making it happen, but when I watch the tapes now, I can no longer find Rosanna. There is nothing there to find. She is here with me, on the outside. I have set her free. She is here with me, in the silent corners of our apartment, the shadows sliding up the wall, the drip in the kitchen sink like the drumming of fingers, Rosanna all around me, her presence a menace and a comfort both. I sit in the dark feeling her tingle in my fingertips. Slowly I stop watching the footage on my own. I am happy enough to do it when Max asks, when he comes over with those ridiculous bags full of food he thinks we will like. But we have transcended the vile demands of my body. We smile and thank him, sit close on the couch. We watch me on those tapes, my awkward movements, a stiff falseness that couldn't be anything but a copy, and who copied Rosanna better than I did, the old me, that strange, ungainly girl. Perhaps Max has found some way to film me practicing. He has inserted me, with all my glib, imperfect falseness, into the sacred spaces of Rosanna's life. But no. This is magic. Beyond him. Beyond us both. I let my eyes drift, unfocused, over the bright surfaces of the screen. It is better not to watch. It is better to stay here in the dark. It is better to sit with my eyes closed, pretending, running through perfect scenes in my head. We never make a false step. We are always self-possessed and certain. We light everyone up with our shine. The two of us, together, one.

"Again," Max says. "You were slow this time."

"Sorry!" we say. "I know."

15

*I*t's time for me to see Marie. Max won't like it, but he'll agree if I make him think it's his idea. I cover the coffee table, the floors, with spread-out images of Marie from the magazines. Rosanna and Marie at lunch, picking up her kids from day care, the reams and reams of best-friend photo shoots. They grew up together in the public eye, both the only children of famous parents, and people feel attached to their connection. Their friendship is highly marketable. I leave the bottle of sleeping pills and an almost empty glass of water on the floor beside the futon. I lay myself down and close my eyes.

Max rushes to me, knocking over the glass. Water seeps across the photos. I wait to see if he will stop paying attention to me and make sure Rosanna's image is saved, and he hesitates for a moment, a breath, not even that. I can feel him looking down. But he doesn't pick the photos. He picks me. He lifts me up, shaking me. "Wake up," he says, a note of panic in his voice. "Come on!" He's not calling anyone, I notice, not asking for help. Not letting anyone know what he thinks I have done. A long and breathless moment passes. Slowly I open my eyes.

"What's going on?" I say.

I let him watch me survey the chaos, allow the awareness of what has happened while I was sleeping to break sharp across my face.

"Oh my god," I say, "I'm so sorry, this looks totally crazy. I thought I would be able to clean up before you got back. I was just looking through some old magazines and fell asleep before I could take my pill. I'm so sorry, Maxie, you know I try to keep things clean, the way Rosanna likes."

He is holding me in his arms, still afraid to let go. He is shaking, just a bit, the afterburn of adrenaline coursing through his veins.

"It's okay," he says, "I thought . . ."

He stops speaking, just shakes his head, dispelling a bad dream. "I'm glad you're okay."

"Yeah," I say, "I'm cool." I pull myself slowly off the couch and start picking up magazines.

"Why are you looking at these?" asks Max.

"I know," I say. "It's stupid, right? But I've been worrying."

Max looks at me cautiously. "What are you worrying about?"

"It's nothing," I say. "It's probably nothing, but—"

I gesture at the magazines. "I've been wondering what we can do about the Marie problem."

"Problem?" Max says.

"She still hasn't called. And I'm starting to think it might look strange—normally we spend so much time together."

Max is quiet for a minute. "Well, you'll have to see her eventually," he says.

"Yes," I say, "I know."

I wait. I let the silence build between us.

"But more than occasionally, right?" I say. "I know how much she meant to Rosanna's public. All this." I gesture. "It'll look odd, won't it? If I don't reconcile with her. Or should we find someone else? A new friend? A new Marie?"

He looks at me strangely. I had imagined us together choosing some likely candidate from among Rosanna's acquaintances for her to get publicly closer to, holding auditions, coffee dates, seeing whose image got us the most pages in the tabloids. But now I see what he has heard me imagine, a replacement for Marie as I have replaced Rosanna. Another me. The look Max gives me is full of horror.

"I mean, she can't be her only friend, right?" I say quickly. "There must be someone else I can spend time with."

His face settles. "Of course there is," he says. "But still, people love Rosanna and Marie."

He scans the gleaming sprawl of images. There we are, laughing, arms around each other, gazing into the camera like it's the face of a third friend, welcoming the public in.

"It wouldn't be the same," Max finally says. "Rosanna wouldn't like it."

"I'm just nervous, I guess," I say. "It feels so awkward, reaching out."

"Here's what we'll do," says Max.

He takes my phone. As he scrolls through old texts, I try to figure out how long it's been since the hike. A little under a month—long, but not too long. I am getting used to socializing again. I am gaining my sea legs. Marie is kind to me, she'll understand that I had to make her wait. Max sifts through the pile to find a magazine that isn't water-damaged. He takes my phone and snaps a picture, the two of us looking impossibly young. In the picture, I sit next to Marie, side by side on a red leather banquette. It is late at night, and I lean my head against her shoulder. We both look exhausted. Happy. Totally natural together.

"Coffee?" he types. "The usual spot? Miss you, lady!"

She responds in less than a minute. "Of course!" she says. "I miss you, too."

Marie and I meet at the small café at the foot of the canyon in which my apartment and, presumably, Rosanna's house are hidden, an old building with amber-tinted windows obscured by waxy-leaved ivy, roots burrowing deep into the soft brick of the exterior. The menu is full of weird seventies relics like salads composed of ham and black olives and cottage cheese. It is not a particularly cool place. But it's quiet and nearly always empty, and the waitresses don't care who we are. In the old days we would meet there to nurse hangovers and talk about our problems unobserved. It's the perfect place to rekindle a lapsing friendship, recall fond memories. Twenty minutes, Max says. He waits in the car outside. From now on, I understand, Max will always wait in the car whenever I meet with Marie. Neither of us will acknowledge this. We will act as though it is mere coincidence that he happens to have the time to sit close to wherever we are and wait. I will pretend this is normal, something Rosanna wants. I will not allow myself to resent him.

Marie sits with her back toward me, reading the menu with what seems like unusual concentration. She smiles when she sees me but doesn't stand to give me a hug. I sit close to her on the same side of the booth, and after hesitating for a moment, Marie pours creamer into my coffee for me.

"I remember," she says. "Two of these nasty little powdered vegetable oil things, right, and lots of sugar."

"Hey," I say, "at least it's vegetables! And sugarcane is also a plant."

She takes the packet from me.

"Here," she says, "let me. You have to be careful of your nails. I'm sure you haven't been taking care of them. They're already brittle and you wear way too much nail polish. Have you been rubbing jojoba oil on your cuticles, like we talked about?"

I hold my hand up speculatively in front of the window. Against the glass, the vines creep, feeling their way toward us. My nails look fine to me. "I don't even know what a jojoba is," I say.

"Ha-ha," says Marie. "Sure you do. I can tell you've been using it, they look much better."

"See," I say, "I told you Max was reading your blog. I bet he picked some up for me and I didn't even notice."

Marie looks away when I say his name. I feel an odd dip of disappointment; it's important to me, I realize, that they like each other, or at least get along well enough so as not to get in my way.

"Anyway," Marie says, "how are the renovations going?"

"Oh god," I say, "don't ask. My contractor is refusing to put in the ridiculously expensive hand-painted Portuguese bathroom tile I ordered last month, which was, by the way, a nightmare to get through customs, and now he can't work with it, the backing's warped. It's always something with that man."

Marie laughs. "See," she says, "you should've let me come over and consult before you got started. I have a great eye, everybody says so. And I know all the best contractors. Remember how helpful I was with the renovations of that disastrously ugly apartment building you bought down the hill? We totally restored it to its former glory."

So Rosanna owns my apartment. The thought is reassuring—is it possible that she restored an entire building just for me?

"I remember," I say, and it's like I do. I can see Marie's hand in everything now that I consider it: the original wood flooring; the period-appropriate wavery glass, with the pockets of imperfect bubbles near the center of the top pane in the kitchen. "It's beautiful. You'll have to come over and see it some time. The place could use a little sprucing up."

The waitress comes over to refill our coffees, and it's not very good, thin and brown and vaguely burned-tasting, but we both nod yes and sit silent as she pours, out of habit, the old habit of feeling watched. When she leaves, Marie squeezes my knee under the table.

"I totally get it, though," she says. "How stressful renovations can be. I remember when we redid our kitchen, I swear I thought we were going to get a divorce. Edward has such a particular sense of how everything needs to look. He's all about minimalism, you know, to the point where nothing is functional, and he wanted this sleek 'James Bond villain bachelor pad' look and I swear I thought, *Well, that's it, he doesn't want to have children!* But we compromised, we made it through. You will, too."

I notice that she lifts her hand off my knee when she says her husband's name. He stops us from talking frankly when we are all together, and intercedes even when it is the two of us alone. His body fills the space that has grown between us.

"I know I will," I say. "I have to."

Marie takes a sip of coffee, makes a face, and smiles at me. It really is pretty bad.

"Still," she says, "why now? You've already got a lot on your plate. Wouldn't it be better to wait until things are more settled?"

I think of the dark house from the videos. Of the closed windows, the shut front door like a stopped mouth, like the castle in *Sleeping Beauty*, a place where plants never die and fruit never rots and dust never settles on the gleaming marble surfaces of the kitchen. A dollhouse, a snow globe. A dead place. As dead as the still white surface of a salt sea, paved with the bones of long-dead creatures, glowing white under the bright light of the moon.

"I don't really think I had a choice," I say. "It's too much like the old days, somehow, living there. I found myself falling into bad patterns even when I didn't want to. I didn't feel like I was living in it. I felt like I was haunting it. The only way for me to stay there and survive is to change everything about it. So it's a reflection of the person I am now, not whoever I used to be. I don't think either of us liked that person very much."

Marie takes my hand. "Don't say that," she says. "Of course I did."

"Really?" I say. "You did? And that's the reason we're finally hanging out regularly for the first time in a year, because I was such a delight?"

She laughs. "Okay, you got me there. We've had our rough patches. But I always cared about you."

Someday I will live in Rosanna's house. I will eat off her dishes. I will sleep in her bed. I will throw open the windows, let the outside in. The house will live again. Everything will be the same as it used to be.

"And now?" I say. "Do you like me now?"

Marie looks at me for a long time before she responds. And then she smiles again, and I can feel sensation rushing back into my numb fingertips. "I didn't think it was possible," she says. "But I like you even more."

"I like you, too," I say. "More than before. Because now I feel like I really know you."

Marie looks at me strangely. "What do you mean by that?" she asks.

I take a sip of my coffee, casual. I choose my words carefully.

"I don't know," I finally say. "I guess just that I'm trying really hard to know you. *You*. Not my old idea of who you were, what you could do for me. And I want you to know me, too. The real me. Not some old idea of who I was or should be."

I think of the dead house, Rosanna hidden away inside. The words press against my lips, heavy as a stone on my tongue. I have a strange and powerful urge to confirm what she must already suspect, to tell her my true name. I can hear traffic passing outside. It is slow here, except for tourists who stop and walk into the middle of the street to take pictures of themselves standing underneath the Hollywood Sign, open palms splayed empty toward the sky. People post warnings in the street higher up—STREET CLOSED, LOCALS ONLY, NO ACCESS—all lies. Down here no one honks. We understand what it feels like to have come so far. Close, so close, but not quite close enough. A place where everyone tells you you've arrived, but nothing is quite like you imagined it would be. We smile at them in their badly parked rental cars, and most of us, I think, wish them well.

"I do know you," says Marie.

"Of course you do," I say. "Better than anyone."

We stop for a beat outside the car and pose for the photographers, Marie wraps her arms around my shoulders, the two of us smiling into the camera's eye. "Stepping Out: BFFs Rosanna and Marie Spotted on a Catch-Up Coffee Date," they say. Max will be pleased, I know it. I can't quite guess how Rosanna will feel.

Soon we are together all the time. And more and more, I am with Max as well. I still have my time in public, of course, when I'm alone apart from the strangers watching me, putting my face out into the world. But Max seems to shadow me, his blurry image hovering in the background of every picture, the unspeaking third in the triad of Marie and me, my haunting, my unholy ghost. I tell myself it makes me feel safe, knowing he is watching, always close.

It is when I am with Marie that I feel the most aware of Rosanna's presence inside me. She isn't with me much when Max is around.

When I am in the apartment alone, I can feel her close, observing, her presence somewhere in the dark spot of my eyes, wherever it is I cannot see, but not part of me. With Marie, she is right there, warming up my empty spaces with her light, her heat, telling me what to say and how to say it, the two of us one. I can never explain this to Max, but I need Marie now. When I'm with her, I relax into the version of myself she knows. Marie loves us. I know this by the way she listens so closely, her hand on mine, the attentive softness of her. We get coffee and go on walks. We are photographed together in Rosanna's favorite stores. I buy her a little gold bracelet with dark resin beads strung along it like tiny eyes. It's very expensive.

"It's nothing," I say.

Everyone wants something from Rosanna. Not Marie. Marie just wants Rosanna for herself, the same way Max and I do. Shouldn't Max be pleased by this? I watch him go tense when the phone lights up, see the hesitating tightness in his hands. He wants to keep me for himself. He wants me in the meetings he sets up, making money for him; he wants me to launch products, do interviews, keep the complex machinery of Rosanna's empire humming smoothly while she rests. He does not want me to be a person like Rosanna was. He does not want me to be a person at all. I pretend that I have not realized this. To Max, it must appear that I think myself free, that I cannot see the bars of my gilded cage. He cannot know that secretly I am negotiating the space, each day giving myself just a little more room, just a little more freedom to breathe.

I go to dinner at Marie's, sitting at the kitchen table in a warm circle of light. Shadows creep close to the soles of our bare feet. Marie keeps a shoe-free house. The two of us talk back and forth, rapid-fire, reminiscing. Carried along by the familiar rhythms of our speech, I feel myself start to relax. I loosen my hold on rationality, let Rosanna take over.

"Oh my god," I say, "that apartment was such a shithole."

"Shithole is relative," says Marie, "when Daddy's paying the rent."

"Come on," says her husband, "no swearing in front of the kids."

"That's right," says Marie. "Stop swearing, Rosanna."

"Oh, I'll stop swearing," I say. "But remember who was paying your rent back then, Mommy."

Marie laughs. She must be remembering the days when she was nineteen years old and had a mother who wanted to show her fan base she believed in tough love. I let her live in my guesthouse until her career took off and she got a guesthouse of her own.

"That's not the same thing," she says. "And you know it."

Her husband interrupts. "Wait," he says, "who *was* paying your rent?"

"Well, not *paying* paying," says Marie. "But my mom was so withholding, you know that. Rosanna helped me out sometimes."

"That's a relief," says her husband. "I thought you had a secret sugar daddy."

"I do now," says Marie.

She winks at him. I pretend I am being sarcastic when I roll my eyes.

The nanny is waiting in the other room, and midway through dinner, after the children have finished all the beige things on their plates and abandoned their heirloom carrots with one polite bite, they are excused to go play with her, leaving the three of us alone.

"At last," says Marie, "Rosanna is allowed to swear."

"Not you, though," says her husband. "Keep it clean."

"Naturally," says Marie. "I'm a mother—I wouldn't dream of it. My darling children are always with me, in my heart."

She scoots closer to her husband, leans her body against his. I try to ignore the little ping of jealousy that goes off at the back of my skull. I have Max, I tell myself, who's just as finicky and controlling as Edward is. I can lean my head against his shoulder, too. It's the same thing.

"So how's the business, Edward?" I ask. "Any projects in the works?"

I know the answer already. Marie's husband is nominally some kind of carpenter. He has a sleekly designed website full of hand-carved benches, a studio in Boyle Heights staffed with recent graduates of lesser liberal arts colleges. All of this costs more money than it makes—a sensitive subject, I know, for them both. Normally I would be more discreet, but I have had a few glasses of the bio-dynamic orange wine I brought them (Marie avoids sulfites) and am feeling mean. Maybe Rosanna really does have a drinking problem.

Marie answers for him. "Business is business," she says. "Edward is working on a wonderful new line of benches for next season. And you know how busy things are in Ojai. We've starting growing okra this year, did I tell you?"

Edward just nods. "Always something," he says. "I don't suppose I could interest you in a bench?"

"One bench?" I say. "Please, I'll take three. I'm trying to return to my sugar daddy roots."

I see a little cloud of tension cross his eyes, but he smiles gamely. "In that case," he says, "I have a hell of a dining room table to sell you."

He's funny. Somehow I didn't remember that.

"Of course," I say. "I'll take all the tables you've got."

Marie leans forward and pours me another glass of wine. I can see Edward watching her, the small motions of her perfect body; there she is, the beautiful woman who belongs to him, his wife. It makes my heart ache, watching them. I feel like half a person, a shell. Her glass is empty, too, and I reach for the bottle, wanting to give her something, even something so small, to show them both that I know how to meet her needs.

"It's okay," says Edward, "I got it."

He fills her glass. His other arm is wrapped around her shoulders. He smiles at me across the table when I try to catch her eye. But she doesn't even notice. She's looking up at him.

"Thanks, babe," she says.

That night the apartment feels smaller than ever. I keep thinking of Marie and Edward's house, the expensively decorated empty rooms folding in around them like a nautilus shell, each room with its own decorator, its own color scheme: the dark greens and masculine grays of the pool room; the wide white space of the entranceway; the rainbow craft room, perfectly orderly, shelves full of immaculately dusted spools of yarn; Marie's closets, vast and white and pink. Here the colors are muted by dust. I can measure the space with countable steps. I feel pent up, a chick pressing against the hard sphere of its shell. I try to sit still and remember. Normally this is fine. I can spend hours curled up, staring into the darkness on the other side of my eyelids. If I look long enough, flashes of bruised color bloom like strange nocturnal flowers. Not tonight. Tonight I grope around in my dark spaces for some hint of Rosanna's presence. But she is gone. At last I am horribly, finally alone.

I think of Marie in bed with her husband, wrapped up in those confining arms. They will have spent the rest of the evening sitting in the garden they grew together, or at least together hired someone to grow. It's a beautiful night, the air dense with the smell of jasmine, hot asphalt, exhaust. The moon is high and silver, looming huge over the horizon, so close it looks like its belly will scrape the mountains' jagged edge. I can feel it pull me, stirring the hidden tides of my blood. I want to get out so badly for just a little while, to feel the air on my face. I need space. I need openness. I can't stand being locked up like this. I roam the apartment like a distracted animal, turning the taps on and off again, opening and closing the closet doors, every window, every cabinet, every drawer.

And then I remember. The front door is unlocked. Max had dropped me off at the curb. I was thinking about asking him up, seeing if he wanted to watch videos with me, but he sped off up into the hills, saying he needed to go see Rosanna. Typical, I had thought, the one night I want to spend time with him, he's too busy for me. I had pouted on my way through the dark hallways, preoccupied with thinking about how selfish he was, how inconsistent. How could Rosanna have chosen someone like him as an employee? I had opened the door myself. I had closed the door behind me. The door was and is unlocked.

Maybe Max knows the door is open. Maybe he wants me to be tempted to wander, so he can catch me in the act. Why else would he have left me alone? I feel him watching me. He must be. I am not alone now. I am never alone. But the walls of the room seem to be closing in. If I could just open the door, maybe go out into the hallway, breathe a little, would that be so bad? Rosanna owns the whole building. She has fixed it all up just for me. Don't I owe it to her to explore a little? This is what I will tell Max if he's waiting outside.

I put my hand back on the doorknob. My sweaty fingers slip and the knob starts to turn. I clutch the door shut. My head warps with swimming waves of light, and I sink back onto the floor, hands and knees on the wood, knots swelling up to meet my skin. I push an acid rush of vomit back down my throat. I close my eyes and think of the space around me, the empty building, the sleeping houses, the dark weight of the night air outside. Hands flat, still crouching on the floor, I push. The door swings silent into the silence. I heave my body through the doorframe, a movement like slinging a heavy sack of groceries into the trunk of a car. And then I am out. I stand up slowly. I take one breath. Another. A cautious first step forward. I leave the door open, just in case.

The hallway looks different in the moonlight. Dreamy. Vague. It looks perfect, like Rosanna's house. My hands are shaking; my whole body is shaking. To steady myself I run the tips of my fingers along both narrow walls, letting my eyes close, feeling my way across the sand-rough stucco, the smooth wood of my neighbors' doors, not allowing myself to pause for breath or think until I am through the cold vault of the entryway and out that second unlocked door and the heavy night air swallows me up.

My feet are cold. I have forgotten to wear shoes; they're somewhere in my apartment, empty as an abandoned cicada shell. The gravel walkway stretches out in front of me, impossibly long, to the dark lapping asphalt of the street. I am afraid of the sharp bite of rocks on my skin, afraid that a car will swoop around the corner and surprise me here, pinning me to the road like a butterfly splayed in a frame. But I can't go back. I hold my breath like a swimmer standing on a high dive, looking down into the cold water glinting below.

There was this thing I used to do when I was very small and needed to calm myself down. Noticing. I guess I thought if I could pay attention to every sound around me, name them all, they couldn't hurt me. I try it now. It is late, and mostly silent. The only sound is the distant rush of the freeway, constant, vague, like running water. I think of it as the breath of the city, flowing, smooth, an automatic process. A sign of life. It quiets the terror that has been building inside me. I close my eyes and step off the stairs. Airborne. Eyes still closed, I begin to walk up through the darkness toward the sky, as far as my legs will take me.

When I get back, I stand in front of the closed door of the building for a long time, looking up at the dark window of my room. Max is in there, waiting for me in the quiet dark. I know it. But when I come into the hallway, the door is still open. There is nothing, no one, waiting for me inside. I sit on the bed, watching the movement of dark palm fronds against the purple sky. My body hangs limp on my bones, aching with the strain of unaccustomed motion. The bottoms of my feet are sore and raw. I wait for what feels like a long time before I realize that he is not coming. He does not know I have been gone. I am unnoticed. I am alone. I lay myself down on the bed and weep. I sob until I am breathless. Until my body begins to shake. Soon I fall into a dreamless sleep.

In the morning I stretch my sore calves, crafting pads from gauze and Vaseline to protect my skin from the rub of my stiff leather shoes. I greet Max normally. I have an ordinary day. That night the door is unlocked. That night I walk again. Again the next night. And the next. I begin to feel safe passing through the darkness of the hills; I have never seen anyone else out walking, not once. Sometimes a car will pass, but I duck down a side road or crouch in someone's driveway until it's gone. I try not to let myself think about all those windows, my body reflected in them as I walk past, rippling, a darkened mirror. But even if there is someone watching, what will they see? A small figure moving quickly until she disappears from view. An anonymous woman. An insomniac who could be anyone, who is no one at all. Every night when I return to the apartment, I hope and fear that Max will have noticed. But I always come back to an empty room. The hollow shell I've left behind.

I develop a new ritual. Before, when I watched the tapes, I let my internal sense of Rosanna guide my movements, feeling the energetic whisper in my hovering palms. Now I move my body in the same way, tracing vaguely familiar paths through the hills, following a pull inside me that seems to grow stronger every night. I go up and down the same hills over and over, making my way through narrow staircases, winding streets. Sometimes I cross through an unlocked gate and sit hidden in a stranger's garden, staring up at the low belly of the sky. I stop and stand for long minutes in the shadows of overgrown bougainvillea vines, hidden, waiting to feel where I need to go next. I don't know where I am walking. But I know it is because of Rosanna. Someday soon she will let herself be found. Someday soon I will find a house with large arched windows, wood floors shining through them like pools of dark water, all lit up with bright golden light. And when I find her, when I come to her, she will be waiting for me to arrive. I am growing closer, I know, one step at a time.

16

The weeks slide by, a sunny blur. I increase the space I take up in the world by buying things, a pair of tight-fitting black pants, a little blue fish in a crystal bowl, an indigo-dyed table runner, three bouquets of flowers, a lamp. I eat six different salads in six different restaurants. Because of me, quantifiable amounts of carbon are displaced from the engines of trucks and cars, waiters are tipped, busboys earn their minimum wage. Capital flows through the world as loose and easy as water in a river. Max takes me to the park and I run along the paths wearing the worst-selling pieces from my new athletic line, leaf-print leggings and a sea-green top, the car idling beside me, driving slow, the engine drowning out the shouts of the photographers. I wave and smile. I smile and wave. The leggings sell out that afternoon.

For months I have been making tiny adjustments to the instructions Max gives me. At first I thought they were errors, but now I realize that what seemed like imprecision was really my way of moving closer to Rosanna. The real Rosanna. The living Rosanna. Max wants me to be like the statue of her in the Hollywood Wax Museum, perfect, frozen, wearing the same outfit for ten years straight. He wants to pump all resistant traces of life from me, leave me wide-eyed and pliant and dead. But Rosanna isn't pliant.

Rosanna isn't dead. The only way I can survive this is to become intentional about my corrections. I will become more like her than he can imagine.

When Max sends me out on my next see-and-be-seen solo shopping trip, I buy a leather jacket, close cut with a diagonal zipper. When I touch it, I feel a tingling in my fingertips. Rosanna wants it. So I buy it. It costs three thousand dollars. I put it on my card. I do not clear my purchase with Max. "Rosanna's New Look," the tabloids say. I can feel my offshore account filling up quietly while I sleep, the interest compounding, money piling on money, cozying itself up into vast new stores of wealth. And I love to spend Rosanna's money. My purse is full of loose bills. I start to tip better than she did, twenty instead of fifteen percent. I slip a fifty into the jar when Max and I stop off to pick up juice. The woman behind the counter smiles. I make sure Max doesn't see. I pet dogs now. Dogs are totally nonjudgmental. Rosanna would like them, even though they are probably the only ones who can smell my old smell. A tabloid takes a picture of me bent over a Pomeranian tied up outside a bar. "Rosanna's Puppy Love." It's relatable. It's cute. My wall is covered with new pictures. When people think of Rosanna now, remember her grocery shopping for sponsored products, sitting at a lunch meeting, walking the red carpet, it is my image, mine, that reverberates inside them. I trace Rosanna's face with my fingertips. Nothing hurts anymore. I am the woman they want to become.

Each night I go farther, guided by my internal hum. I start on the same path, left at the door, up the hill, past the chrome-faced mansions gleaming like pulled teeth, the glossy fence of the always locked garden with OZ spelled in tile shards on the gate, the narrow tower of the fake Victorian, the high stone walls of the Spanish Revival, the sign, half overgrown by bushes, depicting three golden pyramids, HOLLYWOOD OASIS written across the bottom in pixelated tile. On my early walks, I stayed close, afraid that I would get lost or that Max would come back and find me missing. But I have been walking for a long time. I am no longer afraid. I move with the slickness of a figure skater crossing a hard frozen pond, black asphalt like black ice, the spool of the hill's maze unraveling inside me, pulling me forward and then back again, home. Every night I walk a little farther. Every night I find new things. Up I go, and up.

Tonight the city is silent around me, except, of course, for the distant sound of the freeway. The air is thick with the smell of jasmine, gasoline, bruised jacaranda flowers, something heavy and sticky and bubblegum sweet. I am tense and electric, coiled up so tight I can hardly stand to close my eyes. I want to exhaust myself enough to feel at home in my body, to push myself forward until I am too tired to think. I want to be all body, no mind, with nothing to distract me. So I walk. My legs are starting to ache by the time I see the first unfamiliar thing, a white gate surrounded by high barbed-wire-topped fences, a sign saying HOLLYWOOD RESERVOIR. I look and there are no cameras, so I slide myself through a gap in the fence and keep walking.

It is quiet here. A narrow trail passing under scrubby pines, the shine of dark water below me and houses above, perched on the top of the hillside, all wide black windows, open to the night. I see a sugar-cube-white box of a house, shimmering patterns of blue drifting over its front. A pool. I desperately want to submerge myself, to soak up that pale blue light. That house and the houses surrounding it have darkened windows, quiet and still. It must be after three. The sky is low and brooding purple, empty. There is nothing—no passing cars, no helicopters—to disturb the perfect silence. If I am quick and quiet, no one will see me. No one will know I was here at all.

I clamber up the slippery hillside, dust sloughing soft over my white shoes, staining my hands, and there is the house in front of me, a kidney-shaped pool glowing at my feet, pulsing as though it is filtering blood, a working part of some larger living thing. I stand still for a long moment, look into the mirror of the windows. Nothing looks back. Slowly I unbutton my pajama top, take off my coat, my pants, kick off my dust-stained shoes, and slide, naked, into the water. It closes around me as I float. In the stillness, I can feel my heart slow. I look up at the bruised sky and something overwhelms me, an urge so strong that I have to sink down to the bottom of the pool before it escapes me, the sound waves exiting my body as bubbles, my body convulsing, and I push myself onto the rough stucco and I scream and scream and scream. I come to the surface slowly, airless, and float for just one more moment, listening to the stillness until it is broken finally by the distant whir of a helicopter, its searchlight sweeping the mountainside's scrub of manzanitas and wild sage. Searching for someone in the dark folds of the hills. I wonder if anyone is looking for me.

I climb out of the pool. I pull on my clothes, denim sticking to the damp surface of my legs. As quietly as I can, I pass through the narrow passageway beside the house and find myself on an unfamiliar street. I can't be far from the apartment. I know this logically. But the street is indistinguishable from a thousand other streets, white wooden gates with vines climbing over the top, desert plots of blooming cacti and creeping jellied leaves, the raked gravel of a Zen garden. A tunnel of pink bougainvillea closes me off from the sky. Something isn't working. My chest begins to grow tight. The interior pull seems confused, simultaneously urging me in two different directions, both uphill and down, a clamor that makes my skull ache. The houses seem huddled, their backs to the street, as if they are conspiring against me. I look hard at every little thing I pass—the window boxes, the parked cars, the single concrete lamppost—searching for something I can interpret as a sign. And then I round the corner and the two hums click into place, growing louder and louder until I have to suppress the urge to cover my ears, and there it is in front of me, the place I didn't even know I was looking for, that I have been looking for all along. I am standing in front of Rosanna's house.

The house is hidden from the street by a high iron gate swirled pliant into loops and counter loops, a meringue-topped cake, a frozen ocean. Every tape I have seen has been oriented from the inside, making it seem expansive, full of light. Out here, it looks like it's cowering in the darkness. Closed off. I press my face against the gate, peering through a gap in the scrolls down the driveway to the door, that distinctive hanging lamp. It's dark now, but I can picture it lit up so clearly—Rosanna, slumped in that doorway, washed in that yellow light. I notice the spill of leaves sprouting from the low trees planted on either side of the doorway, the bars on all the narrow windows, how the gutters have been molded into the shapes of grotesque faces, mouths open in a silent scream. I stand there for a long time, letting my memories click into place. There, on the side of the house, is the bird-of-paradise whose wide leaves I have glimpsed from the window of the kitchen as Rosanna makes salads, chopping carrots with that impossibly shiny knife. There is the window of her bedroom, the iron balcony she leans over, smoking a cigarette, her back to the camera, not saying a word. It is Rosanna's house, exactly the same as I hoped I'd find it. She has called me, and here I am. Just as I'd imagined, I have arrived.

It's late, I realize that. But Rosanna is a late-night person. I know her habits. Even now she may be roaming the dark halls of her dark house, thinking of me, wondering where I am. I press my body up against the gate, the iron scrolls cutting into my soft belly, and wait for a light to go on. *I'm here*, I think. *Notice me*. But there is nothing. I have climbed so many fences in my life. And this is a simple one, lots of empty spaces for foot- and handholds, nothing sharp at the top or waiting for me on the other side. I imagine lifting myself up, over, down onto the gravel of the driveway, the loud crunch my feet would make on the stones, how Rosanna would hear the sound and be afraid of the stranger at her gate. *No*, I think. *I can't do that to her.* The house remains still, silent as a mausoleum. The hum that has been inside of me for weeks, has propelled me through these hills toward her, is quiet now. I long for some small sign that she is looking back out at me, that she is pleased. I have come so far, am so close. Any moment now a light will come on. The door will crack and Rosanna will be standing there, her face hidden by darkness, her arms open to welcome me in. I will cross the threshold into her garden. She will take me into her arms. I picture us sitting close together on the couch, how she will run the tips of her fingers lightly over the ridges of our face. Neither of us speaking. A perfect understanding between us. Why would we have to say a thing?

Rosanna's clothes begin to dry, tightening around my form like a boa constrictor gently squeezing her prey. I think for the first time of the damage water can do, the bleaching effects of chlorine on my carefully balayaged hair. I should really go home and mitigate the impact of my night swim, my wandering. Wash the dirt from my jeans, set the white sneakers out on the windowsill to dry in the rising sun. The sky is beginning to go fuzzy at the edges, the first sign that it will soon grow pearly gray. *I should go*, I think, *I should go*. But I need to show Rosanna I was here. I need to leave some sign to let her know that I have been here, small enough that nobody passing by will notice but that she will understand. I kneel down in the gravel, careful to move slow, to not make a sound. I press the heel of my hand hard into a sharp protuberance of iron until the blood comes. It does not hurt to bleed. I reach through a gap in the gate, pressing myself as far in as I can. I carve a mark into the gravel, a swoop of red, the way, in stories my mother told me, the chosen people marked their doorways, a line Rosanna will have to cross. She will see it. And then she will know that I have found her, that I am coming. She will be waiting for me next time, I am sure.

I walk back down the hill to the apartment. I have no trouble finding my way. The hum is steady again, certain. It's close, less than a mile. I don't know how it is I haven't found the house before. Maybe it was because Rosanna didn't want me to. Maybe she was making me wait until I was ready. Well, I am ready now. The wound on my palm has stopped bleeding. In the bathroom I rub it with an organic salve from Rosanna's natural beauty line—shea butter, lavender, sage, faint ghosts of the sharp-smelling herbs that grow in the gardens in the hills. Rosanna must have a garden, too. Outside, the sun starts to rise, and I stand on the edge of my bathtub, hunched over, so I can lean out the small window, over the courtyard, straining my neck, searching for Rosanna's roof in the rows of tiered houses turning gray, then pink, a vibrant paint-box flare of houses standing silent in the growing light. As hard as I look, I can't manage to see a thing. She is lost to me again. But not for long.

17

*T*he apartment has shrunk. I hadn't noticed it the night before, preoccupied as I had been with sneaking silently up the stairs, carefully washing the dirt and grass stains from Rosanna's clothes, using a mixture of coconut oil and raw egg to try to make my hair pre-chlorine soft so I would be pristine by the time Max arrived. But it's daylight, and I notice it now. The light is high and uncompromising, and the room is filthy and small. Smaller than before. My exhaustion gives the day a shimmer of surreality, something shiny and opaque clouding the surface of my vision. I tell myself it's a trick of my mind, the light. I ignore the evidence my senses present me with, that the room is smaller. That somehow it has shrunk.

Max sits close beside me on the futon, his knees pointing toward mine.

"I'm so tired," I say. "I think I might lie down for a nap. I'll try it on after, I promise."

"You've been tired a lot lately," he says.

Careful, I think. But there is no sign of anger. His voice is calm.

"You're right," I say. "You're so observant, Maxie. I think I might have low iron."

"It's settled, then," he says, smiling. "You'll have your nap, then put on that nice dress you bought this afternoon and I'll take you to Musso's for a martini and a steak."

I think of all the wasted time of dinner, how much less time I'll have to explore the hills.

"Perfect!" I say. "Or two martinis? You know I love those things, that cute little carafe, the fussy waiters. Makes me feel like Hedy Lamarr."

Really, I don't drink much at all anymore. It makes it too hard to stay awake, nights when I should be walking. I will pretend to sip, and when Max goes to the bathroom I will down my water, pour the martini into the empty glass.

"All right," says Max, "but only if you eat some creamed spinach as well. We really can't have you being so exhausted. It isn't good for you. I worry. Besides, you'll need all your energy. Our hard work is paying off. We have a busy month coming up!"

Despite myself, I feel a bright little flash of pride. It lights up the back of my brain stem, waking me up. My hard work is paying off.

"Wonderful," I say. "Rosanna must be pleased."

Max is still looking away from me. "Yes," he says, "it's very good for her brand. Actually, we'll be booking her another appearance soon. A fashion segment. Critiquing red-carpet looks. They're sold on the novelty of you coming out of retirement swinging."

"No more interviews, though," I say, "for now?"

I thought my first sit-down would be the first of many. It got good ratings, lots of press. I am firmly back in the public eye. But Rosanna is hesitating. Max has made it clear that she wasn't happy with me. And if she isn't happy, he isn't, either.

"Not for now," says Max.

"We have to keep me in demand," I say, trying to think of a way in which this is a good thing, a sign that I am closer to success. "Overexposure was the problem last time, wasn't it?"

"Exactly," says Max. "That's exactly right."

"I remember," I say, and then quickly, when he gives me a strange look: "From the tapes. The quality of the coverage at the end was—"

"Lacking," says Max quickly, cutting me off.

"Yes," I say.

I don't think that's exactly the word for it. *Entirely absent* is more like it. A few erratic daytime interviews where it seems that Rosanna can't concentrate on the stories she's supposed to tell, her nervous eyes skittering toward the camera. And then nothing. Radio silence. But this time won't be like the last time. This must be why the apartment is starting to shrink. As I get better, it will get smaller, shrinking as I expand, a hermit crab's shell, a womb.

"Take your nap," says Max, standing, gathering his things. "Sweet dreams. I'll be back for you in a few hours."

"You sure you don't want to stay here?" I say, knowing there's no quicker way to get rid of Max than to make it seem like I want him around. "Maybe you could use a nap, too."

"That's sweet," says Max, "but I have errands to run. I should go see Rosanna, tell her what we have planned for tonight."

"No rest for the wicked," I say.

I wait until I can't hear his footsteps in the hallway anymore. A few hours, he said. It's a five-minute drive to Rosanna's house. How long will he really be gone? I pace back and forth, counting my steps, trying to measure the length of the room, keeping my feet as quiet as I can, in case there is someone listening. Every night, as I go farther, Max must make the room just a little bit smaller, a hairsbreadth, a microscopic fraction of an inch. The farther I walk, the smaller it gets. And now that I've gone as far as I can go, all the way to the house? What happens now? I sit down on the futon to think, closing my eyes, trying to calm the mad flutter in my chest. When I open my eyes, the room is beginning to go dark. I have slept for a few hours, I think. It is impossible to tell. I have no phone. There are no clocks. I get out of bed and begin to dress. I don't turn the lights on, not yet. I don't want to be reminded of the increasing smallness of my room. I do my makeup, minimal, natural, in the bathroom mirror. Max knocks on the door and I open it, smiling.

"You look beautiful," he says.

He means I look like her.

"Thank you," I say. "I try."

At the restaurant we sit across from each other in a slim two-seater booth. It is a Tuesday night, quiet, and the low-ceilinged room is deserted. Above us, topping a shiny span of dark wood paneling, hunting dogs cavort, a deer barely visible through the olive trees of a distant grove.

"I wanted to talk to you about something," says Max.

I take a deep breath. Of course he does. I picture him and Rosanna sitting together at the window last night, looking down at me, and I am filled with a terrible, overwhelming shame. But he's smiling. He's not angry. He takes my phone, Rosanna's phone, from his pocket.

"I'm returning your phone privileges to you," he says. There is no one seated at the tables around us, but still, he keeps his voice whisper soft. "You've been working really hard. You've earned my trust. Our trust."

He slides it across the dark glossy wood of our small table. "Here," he says. "Take a look. There's something I think you ought to see."

I turn the phone over, careful to keep my hands steady. There is a single notification on the screen, a text from Marie. "Farm dinner next week!" it says. "Not Ojai, all those fires, ugh, just our place in the hills. Sorry for the last-minute invite, I know your schedule fills up fast, but I wasn't sure if you'd want in. Say you'll be there?"

Yes, I think. *Oh please yes*.

"I don't know," I say. "What does Rosanna want me to do?"

I take a sip, a real sip, of my martini, the gin bracing on my tongue. I need it to cushion the blow I suspect is coming. But Max doesn't say no. He doesn't smile up at me or look me in the eye, but he gives a quick nod, cutting his steak with a sharp knife, scraping the plate with a sound that makes my jaw clench.

"You should go," he says. "You've been spending so much time with her anyway, this is the next logical step. It would look odd if you didn't. And it'll be an opportunity for you to meet the rest of Rosanna's circle all at once."

He slides a bloody lump of steak between his teeth. I feel my heartbeat quicken, a strange mixture of joy and disgust.

"I thought those people didn't eat," I say, down-to-earth, an outsider, the girl he expects. "Are we going to sit across the table from one another sipping one of Marie's juices out of our wineglasses?"

A vivid image of Rosanna flashes through my mind. She sits on a couch, legs carefully crossed. She throws her head back and laughs.

"Be serious," says Max, but he smiles. "This is a big deal. I need you to do your best, Rosanna."

I hide the joy climbing up into my throat. I'm going to see Marie again, and not only that, I will be her guest in her home, her best friend, sitting beside her at the table. Everyone will see us, everyone will know we belong together. And Max can't stay close at a party like that, with so many drivers, so many cars. For a few hours, at least, it will be as though Marie and I are alone, really alone. Like it was before. I smile at Max, a real smile this time.

"Of course I will," I say, "I always do."

"I know you do," he says. "We'll be picking you up that evening. You should go shopping in the morning, I'll send the driver. Buy yourself something nice. You'd like that, wouldn't you? I know you love to shop."

We, I think, and I know he probably means the driver, but what if this we is the real we, the ultimate we? What if Rosanna is waiting for me in the back seat of that car? It's all too much. I steady myself, pouring the rest of my martini from the carafe into my glass.

"Will you come shopping with me?" I say. "Maybe give me some suggestions on what I should wear? I don't like the idea of getting ready without you."

But I do. I love being out there alone. Having everyone look at me. Before I came here, I was a ghost. If you searched my old name, all that came up were articles about my father's trial. No images. You got the impression of a life half lived, someone slipping through the cracks on her way to disappearing entirely. It is different now. Now people look at me. Now I am seen.

"Of course," he says. "I'll make sure you look your best."

"Thank you, Max," I say. "I couldn't do it without you."

But I can. And I am. Rosanna always talks about living her best life. Well, my best life belongs to her. And here I am living it.

18

We spend the next week watching videos of Rosanna at dinner. Max sets up a place setting on the coffee table so I can practice how she holds a wineglass, a spoon, how she gestures with her fork when she wants to make a point. He serves food he imagines I might encounter at Marie's and watches me eat as Rosanna eats the same thing on the screen, both of us stacking empty oyster shells on the edge of our plate, twirling our spaghetti. We watch her talk to an endless variety of strangers and acquaintances, cycling through every possible mood.

We see her politely bored.

"So I," says the neighbor, an older man in a blue suit, as sleek and self-assured as a bull seal, "absolutely refused to pay higher taxes on the Palm Beach property."

"Oh, well done," says Rosanna. "That was very brave of you, wasn't it?"

She picks up a little clump of lettuce leaves and pops them into her mouth with practiced insouciance.

The neighbor sits up straighter, pleased. "I should think so," he says.

We see her enthralled.

"Oh nooo," she says, turning her entire body toward this other

neighbor, a stylist with a long cascade of fluffy red hair and a perfectly painted-on peach lipstick pout. "Honestly, they're getting
divorced? They literally just reconciled."

"*Reconciled* is a strong word," says Sabine, "considering she's been
sleeping with that DJ she met in Mykonos the whole time!"

Rosanna laughs into the palm of her hand.

I see how she reacts when her neighbor, an older, celebrated actor,
elbows soup into her lap.

"Yes, it's silk," she says, standing up, her head disappearing from
the frame. "But honestly it's no problem—this old thing, my god,
it's nothing. I'll buy a new one. No, I couldn't possibly send you the
bill."

In some shots, you can see a green blur at the edges. Leaves, I
imagine, or the petals of flowers. Rosanna looks up and over the
camera, unconscious of its presence, or pretending to be. A natural.

The day of the dinner, I go shopping for a dress. After a long period
of indecision, trying on what feels like every possible permutation of
fabric and cut and length, I settle on an elegant sheath. It looks like
a cross between something the old and new Rosannas would wear—
classically pretty, composed, restrained, but with a high slit, a bit
of a daring edge. Max comes by to pull a stack of flash cards from
the complete set, which he carefully divides into subgroups accord-
ing to the likelihood of each person's being at the dinner party. And
then he leaves. I know he is going to Rosanna's house, to spend the
afternoon with her, talk about the party, make plans for what will
happen in the future, my future, my next day, and my next. I picture
how her face might look tonight as she pulls up in the car with him.
Will she be more beautiful than I am? I try not to think about what
she might say. I spend the day alone. I review the cards.

Flipping through the stack quickly, I don't recognize a few people. I pick a card randomly from the stack, a man I remember from
the tapes, Leo, it says, producer, acquaintance, married to a woman

named Eleanor, good friend of Edward's, ask about his kids Olive and June. Another, a woman named Jennifer with whom she attended preschool, friendly, it says, but not close. Some of the cards have notes about the last time we had seen each other (Astrid was last spotted at Art Basel, where she and Rosanna fought over a Ruscha painting, expect mild tension, don't bring it up), or memories I can reference, places where we had good times, restaurants we ate at: the Spotted Duck, Red Medicine, El Conquistador. Most of them are just a picture, a brief bio, a name. I make quick work of memorizing the few I don't already know by heart. Of course none of these people really matter. Marie is the only person Rosanna wants to see. Everyone else is window dressing. I am sure Marie feels the same way. What else is a party but an excuse to be reminded of your own importance by surrounding yourself with extraneous people, soaking up their admiration while you stay close to the ones you actually care for?

I dress. I apply and reapply my lipstick—nude, at first; then mauve; and finally a slick, glossy red, the color of a cherry lollipop crushed on the sidewalk, violent in its brightness. This is my party. I want to look nice. So I make sure I look nice, I know how to do that now. I search for my old face beneath the new skin. But there is nothing looking back.

The car arrives. I go down the stairs slowly, walking with Rosanna's practiced grace, sure she will be waiting to wish me good luck. Max is driving the car. He gestures me into the front seat, and I smell a faint smell of cigarettes, something expensive and floral. Rosanna. Has she been here? Is she hiding in the back seat, silent, somewhere I can't see her? I swear that I can almost feel the pressure of her gaze. Just in case, I keep my eyes focused on the road. I have a feeling that if I turn around and look at her she will disappear, insubstantial, an emissary from the underworld.

They drop me off at the formal front entrance to the house. I came through the family entrance before, the back door, but Max and I have practiced, taping off the living room so I could rehearse navigating Marie's garden, my eyes blindfolded by one of Rosanna's silk scarves. I know before I see it how the driveway passes through a narrow causeway between two guesthouses, their blank white facades turned away from the street, how there are so many layers of protection before you get to the house itself, the iron fence, the high walls, a dark passage lit by solar-powered garden lamps. Reassured by this familiar newness, I hop out of the car without a goodbye, feeling their eyes on my back as I walk down the path to the front door.

I'm ready to get away from Max for a while. I'll be nice to him when I see him at the end of the night. I'll tell him everything that happened, make him feel included, complain a little so he knows I wasn't too happy without him. Poor Max. I really shouldn't be so hard on him. I am, Rosanna is, all he has. But as the car pulls away from the gate I feel a tremendous weight lift from my shoulders. For one night, at least, I am free.

I move through the maze of buildings with unconscious ease, pulled through by the tug of some invisibly fine internal thread. Everything around me feels uncannily familiar, impossibly strange. It is like something from a dream, the dark night and the high white walls, the purple light-polluted sky, a smell of something sweet in the air, jasmine, oleander, a fleshy white flower opening its petals in the dark. I round the corner into an open courtyard filled with the bright chemical light of a kidney-shaped swimming pool. At the bottom there is a mosaic depicting some kind of animal, lifted on its back by a bird's sharp talons, the lines of it shimmering with the shifting light and movement of the water, writhing with sinister purpose.

There is a narrow bridge spanning the water, and on the other side a door, Marie waiting, her face lit from below with shifting blue light, an echo of the full moon rising over the house—pale, judgmental, pristine. For a moment, I pause on my side of the water, almost afraid to cross over. I feel as if I will have a hard time coming back. Like I am looking into the portal to another world.

"Rosanna," she calls, beckoning, breaking the spell.

It's just Marie, I tell myself. *Just Marie's house, just Marie's pool, nothing to be afraid of.* I close my eyes and cross. When I reach the other side and slip a little on the flat damp of the paving stones, she catches my arm and, without letting go, leans close and kisses me, just once, on the cheek. Her glossed lips leave a mark on my powdered skin, a sticky track like the path of a snail. I do not raise my hand to wipe it away.

"Thank you," I say.

Marie smiles like she doesn't understand. "I'm so glad you could make it," she says. "And don't you look beautiful!"

There's something in her voice that makes me wonder if I'm overdressed. It's a little too kind, a little too careful not to give offense. Marie herself is dressed more simply than I expected, in dark pants and a white shirt, gold glinting at her wrists and throat. Her husband comes out and stands beside her. The overhead light casts shadowed circles under his eyes and shows how his face has been allowed to age naturally, even wrinkle a little. He wraps his arms around Marie's shoulders like he has to protect her from me.

'It's nice to see you again, Rosanna," he says. "That's a stunning gown."

"Rosanna is always the best-dressed girl at the party," says Marie, "famously."

But she sneaks a sidelong glance at him as she says it. There is something between them that is invisible to me. I feel like I can't breathe.

"Well, thanks," I say.

My voice sounds oddly cheerful, false. In the silence that follows, a woman comes forward from the doorway, her hands already stretching out to clasp mine. I run through her card: Louisa, married to a producer, two children, nominally designs clothes, ask her about her diet. She, too, is wearing jeans, a striped shirt, and red lipstick, although her jewelry is brighter and more dangly than Marie's, her heels stacked higher. So much for the shoe-free house. I smile and take my hands from hers, smooth the fabric of my new dress down over my thighs.

"Rosanna!" she says, "how wonderful to see you. It's been ages.

And look at you, such a glow, have you gotten a little work done?" She attempts to lift her eyebrows, but her face remains smooth.

"And you!" I say. "Amazing. What is it, no carbs? Are you still doing that raw diet, you brave thing?"

Marie disappears into the living room on her husband's arm, leaving me alone with Louisa. I have to force myself not to call out to her, not to look at her as she disappears. I tell myself she will come back to me. She always does.

"Please," says Louisa, "time marches on. And clean living can only take you so far! You'll really have to give me your doctor's name. It's hard to find someone who's enough of an artist to keep you looking like a better version of your old self, not a total stranger. All the microdermabrasion in the world isn't going to turn back time. We're all getting older, aren't we?"

She laughs, and this time I'm sure there's something unkind in it. In the bright light of the hallway, I can see the telltale stiffness at the corners of her eyes, the plastic smoothness of her undimpling cheeks. She puts one hand on mine, testing the elasticity of my skin. I wonder what's next. Is she planning on asking to bathe in my blood?

"Well, most of us are," she says, leaning in. "You seem to be getting younger and younger. Honestly, Rosanna, what's your secret?"

"A lady never tells!" I say, shaking my hair back and trying to lift my eyebrows in feigned amusement. Max has taken care of this as well. My forehead is as stiff as hers, glossy and supine, the paralyzed skin pulled tight on the frame of my skull. I see her notice it, the smug little look of satisfaction that flashes across her face. I've passed.

"Excuse me," I say. "There's someone I simply must say hello to."

I walk past Louisa into the open living room, carefully decorated in a manner simulating the accidental results of good taste, with beautiful little objects scattered everywhere, handblown glass bowls and wooden figurines, wildflowers in rough clay vases. One whole wall is lined with books, grouped so a ripple of shifting color runs along the room, useless for anyone who actually wants to read.

Through the large window I can see the lights of the city, a million unblinking eyes staring up toward the splendor of the hills. There is a small cluster of people sitting on the couches in front of me.

"Well, hello!" I say. "Good to see everyone."

I scan the group as quickly as I can, reminding myself of the names of their dogs (Antonio, Sandwiches, Goldie, Bea) and children (Olive, June, Plume, Francis, Eliza-Jane), the time when we last saw each other (meetings, mostly, a couple over lunch), the way that I addressed them on the tapes, each with their own diminution, a slip of a nickname to bring them under my power. For a moment, their faces are blank. They look at me as if they've never seen me before. And there are a few of them, it's true, whom I don't recognize from the cards. These must be Marie's friends, not mine. I will not let myself worry about them. Not yet.

"What's wrong?" I say. "You look like you've seen a ghost. Don't tell me you've forgotten your old friend Rosanna. Surely it hasn't been so long as all that!"

When I left the house, I felt beautiful. I had made a good decision, I thought, a long black dress with a slit up the side, tasteful, elegant, sexy but still restrained. But the women here are all dressed like Marie. I look woefully out of place, a poor person's idea of how a rich person dresses. One of the men takes pity on me.

"Rosanna," he says, standing up.

I recognize him from his card. Leo. An acquaintance, the man Rosanna had lunch with.

"Leo!" I say, filling my voice with enthusiasm, reaching toward him, my life raft, my thrown rope. "So good to see you. We haven't been in the same room since the Golden Globes, what was it, almost two years ago, now?"

He laughs a small laugh. "Don't remind me. I think I'm still hungover." Sitting back down, he motions to a place beside him on the couch. "And you're looking better than ever, of course." His voice is strangely tight, with this weird fake jokiness I don't quite understand.

I look around for Marie, but she is nowhere to be found. Around us, men and women lounge in small clusters of two and three, drinking bright red liquid out of tiny crystal glasses. Their casual air is the product of spending years cosseted by so much money and power that they never have to bother with the pursuit of perfection. Perfection is for the middle class, the striving women Marie and I sell our lifestyle brands to. You don't have to be perfect when your own flawlessness is contextually implied. Not sure what else to do, I sit down beside him and take a glass from the silver tray on the table, downing it faster than I should. I want to consume something, to feel grounded in this world of getting and taking and having. I smile at him, the closest I can get to a true, warm Rosanna smile.

"It's been too long!" I say. "I'll need a lot of catching up. What have you been doing with yourself the past few years? How is Eleanor? I have to say, I loved your last movie. What was it like for the two of you to work together?"

"Eleanor?" says Leo, sounding surprised. "She's fine." He lowers his voice. "But really, Rosanna," he says, "it is so nice to see you. I didn't know if I ever would again."

I smile with noncommittal warmth. That's what Rosanna would do with this presumptive attempt at intimacy. There must be something incredibly compelling about her that so many people, so many men, cling to her image as though they are drowning. She doesn't care about any of them. I look around for Marie in the kitchen, which would hold my entire apartment, its glossy blue open shelving crowded with bottles of olive oil and vinegar, a whole shelf devoted to different kinds of salt, all of it perfectly neat, lined up, unused. Someone else is making dinner. Maybe Marie is supervising them. I want to be with her, helping her, that intimacy of helping, of being the one asked behind the scenes, allowed access to the imperfections of preparation.

"Oh, you know me," I say, "always popping up in the most unexpected places! And speak of the devil!"

Leo's wife is standing beside the counter, talking to a tall man who has one sleeve of his pristine white shirt rolled up to reveal an armful of tattoos. I give her a little wave. Immediately she breaks off her conversation and makes a beeline for her husband and me.

"Rosanna!" she says, a little too loudly, I think, with a little too much false cheer.

What is it with these people, so insistent on this phony intimacy that they've built up between us? I hope she isn't as bad as her husband is proving himself to be.

"Eleanor!" I say, sounding equally cheerful. "Leo and I were just talking about you. And here you are, looking better than ever."

"How nice," she says. "And what a lovely dress that is! Leo, don't you think Rosanna's dress is lovely?"

"Hmm," says Leo, "I hadn't noticed. Yes, it is nice. It's a very nice dress."

"I thought you'd like it," says Eleanor, her tone barbed. "It looks like a dress you'd like."

"Well, you look lovely, too," I say, hoping this will stop them talking. "You've always had such a wonderfully restrained style."

I remember the card.

"And how are the children?"

"The children?" says Eleanor, "How kind of you to ask. I didn't know Rosanna cared about the children, did you, Leo?"

Her voice is as loaded with fake sweetness as a sugar-syrup-soaked baklava. I am growing increasingly annoyed at these people, this obnoxiously vast room, the domestic set dressing, whatever impulse led Marie to invite me here and leave me stranded, listening to strangers try to involve me in their domestic squabbles. I don't care about any of this. All I want to do is find Marie. And then there she is, sitting beside the husband of the woman who greeted me at the door, a little too close, I think, suggestive of an intimacy that should be exclusive to me, to us. Her husband is nowhere in sight. I'm glad, at least, for this small mercy. I have to go see her, remind her that she should be focusing on me.

"Sorry," I say, "I really should see if Marie needs anything. These parties make her so anxious, I can't help but feel it's my job to pitch in. I'll be right back."

It's out of character, I know, helping, but maybe I've changed in my time away. Maybe I'm helpful now. Sure enough, Eleanor looks at me strangely.

"Oh," she says, "I didn't know you two were still so close. I had thought when you left—well, you have a hard time with women, don't you? I didn't think female friendship was really your thing."

She reaches over and takes Leo's hand firmly in her own. *She must be drunk*, I think. This strange woman, overly personal, acting like she's better than me, and her husband practically crawling into my lap.

"Really," I say, giving her an extra bright smile, "I don't know where you got that idea. Of course Marie and I are still close. Closer than ever, actually." I remember my line from the talk show. "You know I'm all about women supporting women. Female entrepreneurship is a core value of my practice! Anyway, I'm sorry, but I really have to go."

Marie doesn't even look up when I approach her. She is listening to whatever that stupid man is telling her, and for a moment it is almost as though she does not recognize me. I look at her blank upturned face, and I know with absolute certainty that she does not want me here. I am filled with rage at these people, so smug and cosseted by their money, at myself, once so poor and stupid and now what? Nothing, worse than nothing, a cheap copy, a knock-off. I want to disappear. But I am here now. And there is nothing I can do about that. This was her idea, not mine. Her fault. I am determined to show her I fit in. That I belong.

"Marie," I say, "darling, I just had to tell you that you look magnificent, the house looks magnificent. You absolutely must give me the name of your decorator. You know, for my renovations. There are so many changes I want to make."

She looks at me with pity. It's too much. She must be able to hear my voice shaking, the falseness in it, how strangely overdone and arch I sound. I am doing so badly, I am trying so hard.

"Thanks, Rosanna," she says, ever gracious. "That's nice of you to say."

She smiles at me and gives me her hand, as small as a child's, the fingers light, her hollow bird bones. I can smell her, roses, and something else, earthy, animal, musk. I want to unwrap her fingers from mine one by one, bending them back until they break.

. . .

Dinner is held on the terrace, a long open-walled room a famous design magazine had described as an indoor-outdoor space, a term like *bespoke* or *xeriscape* that I had never used before I came here but now slips off my tongue easy as breath. The air feels thick, a physical presence. It seems to grow worse and worse every day, pressing up closer to my borrowed clothes, my borrowed skin. Some days, hot days, when I wake up too late and open the window, it is as though I have forgotten how to breathe. But it will rain soon. I can feel it. Something is growing, gathering force. There is a storm about to break. It's strange to think of water pouring down on this thin-spread city, the wide lonesome streets, the hollows of the canyons, everything filling up with water, clear and blue and clean. The ocean taking over places we have ruined for ourselves.

The place settings alternate man, woman, man, woman—the awkward arrangement of a singles mixer, a debutante ball. It's strange, after so many months of talking only to Max, to be so close to the bodies of other men. They have the faces of strangers, but they smell like he does, that same cold leather scent of expensive cologne. I keep my face on when I look at them, neutral but friendly, a slight upturning at the corners of my mouth that could be interpreted as a smile if a smile is what they need from me. To one side of me is a handsome stranger, and to the other sits Leo, whom I had hoped I was rid of for good. I tense my face up into a gracious little smile.

"We meet again," I say.

Before he can answer, I turn to the man on my other side. His face is new to me, not familiar from the cards. He's a little too handsome, almost showy, with his glossy tanned skin and hair combed into a mussed wave, falling in a perfect slope across his forehead. Like me, he is overdressed. An outsider. His suit is so new that the fabric seems to shine, expensive looking but not quite right somehow, a little long in the cuffs, the lapels cut slightly too wide. I find this comforting, that there is at least one other person here working as hard as I am.

"Hello!" I say brightly. "I don't believe we've met."

"No," he says, his already overwide smile widening even further when he sees who I am. "No, Miss Feld, I don't believe we have. Of course I'm a big admirer of your work."

"How sweet of you to say so!" I say.

What work? This man knows Rosanna's name, her face, and not much more. I'm sure to him I'm just a projection of some adolescent fantasy, but I'm glad that I at least have that. When we talk, he'll be trying to impress me. This will make things easier.

"It's always so nice to meet a fan," I say. "And you'll have to tell me all about your work as well!"

He beams, pleased to be accepted, "Just Like Us." On his other side is Marie, sitting a little too close, I think. But I'm sure she's seated him here because he's a nonentity who can be counted on to listen while she and I get to our true business of concentrating on each other. Finally things are settling into a pattern I recognize. Her husband is on the other side of her, talking to a neighbor, his hand clasped proprietarily over Marie's clenched fist on the table. But she's not looking at him now. Her attention is focused on me. A waiter sets down the amuse-bouche, a single quail egg crowned with one leaf—perfect, delicate, totally uninteresting.

"Marie," I say, leaning over the man between us, "this is so nice. Thank you again for having me."

She gives me a warm smile. "Of course," she says. "I'm glad you could make it."

But I keep her attention for only a moment. She turns to the man between us, asking him about the sitcom adaptation of *Waiting for Godot* he's workshopping for HBO, how he performed it in college (how long ago was that, I wonder), and isn't it a fascinating play, really speaks to the present moment, and Marie just smiles and nods. Maybe I was wrong. Maybe I'm the extraneous one here. I try again.

"It's so nice to see Edward," I say. "I'm sure he's proud to have all his hard work at the farm end up on such a beautiful table."

"You're lucky you caught him!" Marie says. "He spends most of his time down in Ojai, don't you, darling?"

Edward breaks off his conversation for a moment. "I love it," he says, "All that good clean country air."

He winks broadly. Marie smiles again, and turns back to the man between us.

"Rosanna," Leo says.

I notice he has not touched his food, the egg sitting in front of him intact. He is drinking, though, and pours himself another glass of wine, a few drops falling and staining the white weave of the tablecloth. I have to force myself not to reach forward and wipe it away: *not my problem*, I think, *not my fault*. I give him a polite little smile and turn back to Marie.

"I really must come visit," I say.

"Yes!" says Marie. She turns to the blond man. "You know," she says, "you should come visit sometime, too. It really is lovely out there, and it's always good to get out of L.A."

It is as if I haven't spoken at all. The blond man is talking again, expounding on the areas of his expertise, audience expectations and casting, the respective tax situations in Atlanta, Toronto, Oregon. This was a notable feature of conversations I'd had with people Rosanna knew, especially the men. They didn't expect me to contribute anything. As long as I keep nodding occasionally and remember my vague, receptive smile, I can let myself relax, slide out of my body. Normally it's kind of nice, almost meditative. An abnegation of the self. But here it rankles. To have to fall silent and nod obligingly at this nobody, this stranger, who should have been my ally but is instead so sure of his perfect right to take up space, command the attention that should be going to me, is infuriating.

"Don't talk to me about Toronto!" I say. "Marie, remember when I flew up to visit you on a shoot and just totally forgot to bring my passport? Thank god they're so lax about checking documents on private planes!"

Marie laughs and turns back to the blond man. "But things must have changed a great deal in the past few years, haven't they? I'm sure it's much harder to get around customs."

He nods and continues his monologue. I don't know what I had expected. Marie certainly wouldn't be able to replicate the intimacy of our conversation on the mountaintop here, or even the less intense closeness of our coffee dates. But I thought she would give me some minimal acknowledgment. It hurts to be totally ignored, to have to listen to some stranger bore us with the minutiae of his career, which I am sure will stall out as soon as he loses his good looks and stops being interesting to women like Marie. I watch her listen. I watch us both, the artificial movements of my face as I laugh Rosanna's laugh, cocking my head slightly to the right, the way she does to show she's fascinated and paying close attention, nodding her empathetic nods. My body is full of her. My mind is blank.

Leo leans toward me. I'm certain now that he has been drinking too much. His gaze floats to one side of my face, an unfocused drift. Under the table, his leg presses against mine, whether on purpose or through the accidental intimacy created by bench seating, I cannot tell. Eleanor, sitting close beside him, looks at me with equally avid curiosity. *At least* someone *here is interested in me*, I think. Fine. These people want to talk to me. So I'll talk to them.

"So," says Leo, "when are you going to tell us where you've been hiding?" He is speaking loudly enough that the couple across the table perk up and pretend they aren't listening.

"Come on," says Eleanor, "Leo, be polite. Now is not the time."

He shifts tactics, his tone becoming appeasing. "It's no big deal," he says to his wife, "I'm just asking," and to me, "I know I'm not supposed to bring it up, but, Rosanna, come on, you know how fond of you I—well, both of us—are. We were friends, good friends once. And you must feel you owe me some sort of an explanation."

As far as I know they are marginal acquaintances at best, people from my old, bad days of wildness I don't see very often. So either they're confused about Rosanna's feelings or there is something bigger here I'm not supposed to know about. Maybe talking to them will be worthwhile, after all. I knew that everything that had been part of Rosanna's life would eventually come to me. All I had to do was wait. And here it is now, arriving.

"Leo," says Eleanor, "please. You're making Rosanna uncomfortable. And frankly, you're making me uncomfortable as well."

I turn my focus on her, my sympathetic expression. "Thank

you, Eleanor," I say. "It's all right. But, Leo, you know I can't talk about it." I load my voice with regret. "Not here. Not in front of everyone. Maybe not ever, frankly. Honestly, I have a hard time even remembering anything that didn't happen a few months ago. It's been a difficult time. Everything still feels so close to the surface. All that pain."

Under the table, Leo puts his hand on my thigh. I look back at him, right in the eyes, unflinching. It feels like an intrusion. A violence. He shouldn't be touching me without asking. Only Max can do that. Something inside me thrums. I focus on Eleanor, making my voice low and sweet.

"I can't tell you how often I've thought of you," I say.

I look right into her eyes, my own eyes wide, so sincere I can see her flinch. She has to force herself to not look away. With his other hand, Eleanor's husband pours me another glass of wine. It tastes expensive. I know what expensive wine tastes like now, the fullness of it, something strange and broken and rough, the opposite of the sweet pink wine my mother drank in the summertime, bottle frosty from the fridge on those hot afternoons when we sat close, sweaty, on the plastic-covered couch in my grandmother's house, waiting for the phone to ring. But this is a dangerous game. I will not allow myself to think about my mother. The hand on my thigh moves up slowly, troubling the smooth sheen of the silk. I stay still. I will not let myself mind. If he's doing this, it's because Rosanna lets him. I need to discover why, what power he thinks he has over us.

"Anyway," I say, "I'm back now. I'm here. Isn't that the only thing that matters?"

"We've thought of you, too," says Leo, his voice hoarse.

There is a pause. He seems to be gathering himself. Marie's laughter presses up against my ear, a distant train pulling away into darkness. The waiters approach with the second course, flank steak on a bed of arugula and heirloom tomatoes, brushed with a balsamic quince paste glaze, everything, of course, allegedly from the Ojai garden. I use the interruption as an excuse to turn back toward the blond man and Marie. Marie sitting close to him. Marie laughing.

Marie liking him best. Leo fills my glass again. I drain it in one long gulp.

"Thanks," I say, without looking at him.

The blond man looks like the men Rosanna texts late at night. I picture his image on her phone, shiftlessly brooding. He is the kind of man who leases an expensive car and rents a house in the hills he cannot afford, who dates women like Marie until their husbands find out. We are not unalike. Both of us are valuable for our bodies, what those bodies can provide to women older than us, more powerful. I feel a strange kinship with him. He stares at Marie with wide eyes, as flat and blank as the eyes of a shark.

"Marie," I say again, and this time the look she gives me is distinctly annoyed. I feel a bright little pop of anger burst inside me. Why did she even invite me? Why am I here? She is leaning the full weight of her body toward the blond man. But he isn't looking back at her. His body is turned toward mine. I'm a better target, I realize. Single, getting a lot of press, more likely to be willing to publicize our relationship. She wants his attention, and he wants mine. I'll get to her through him.

"So," I say, "I thought I was going to get a chance to hear about your work."

I twist my body toward his, my knee wresting itself from Leo's grasp. Another problem that can wait, will have to wait until I am ready for it.

"I'm sure," I say, "that as an artist you find inspiration in your own life."

"Oh yes," he says, and I can see him brightening, "I do, but you know, you must remember, Miss Feld—"

"Rosanna," I say, "please. My friends call me by my first name. And we are friends now, aren't we?"

He practically blushes. "It's hard," he says. "I was just telling Marie, it's hard being under so much pressure, especially at first, and my agent and everyone . . . they just want me to make choices that are so commercial. That's not who I am."

"You're an artist."

"I'm an artist, and they need to understand that, but maybe I should start doing more commercials, because my parents keep telling me I need to come back to Gold River and my ex-girlfriend has practically moved in with them—"

"And they don't understand you."

"Not me or the business. These things take time, don't they?"

"Of course," I say, and I nod and look concerned and I drink and keep drinking, and soon it doesn't matter what he's saying, only the low thrum of his voice, the way he looks at me like I know all the secrets there are to know. Marie keeps making small, kind interjections, but we both know I hold the power now. I am prettier than her, unmarried, more famous. If I like him enough, I can give him anything he wants. And I do like him, sort of. I like the way he restores the balance between us, gets Marie to look brightly at me as I speak. And then Leo's hand comes down again on my knee. It is all I can do not to stab it with my steak knife.

"Rosanna," he says to the back of my head, "really, we need to talk."

I turn reluctantly. Eleanor is looking at me with a strange intensity. My annoyance is drowning out my curiosity. I find them so overbearing that even though I know they hold, or think they hold, some secret knowledge of Rosanna's life, I am reluctant to give them the attention they are clearly so desperate for.

"Some other time," I say, smiling.

My face is starting to feel a little loose.

"I'm having so much fun, aren't you? And all I do is talk. Talk and talk. I'm sick of talking. Sick to death. I think talking's incredibly overrated."

I put my arm around the blond man's shoulders, letting Leo see me do it, staring him right in the eyes. It is my body. I am the only one who gets to decide what I do with it.

"Darling," I say to the blond man, "I hope you'll take my advice. Talking's on its way out. Silent films are coming back any day now. No subtitles, either. All image. Image first, that's my motto. What else matters?"

He laughs uncertainly. He has no idea what I'm talking about. Neither do I, to be fair, but he has to pretend it makes sense. He has so much to prove. And I can help him prove it. My fingertips crackle with the static in the air, with power, my power, surging through my body, heady like the rush of love, Rosanna inside me, all the way through. Eleanor leans forward, taking her husband's other hand in her own, subtly trying to pull him away. But it doesn't work. He keeps staring at me. His hand stays on my knee.

"Come to Malibu," he says, quieter now—this is between us. "I know you've got a lot going on right now. But come with us after dinner. It'll be fun, I promise, and we can talk there."

"I've already told you how I feel about talking," I say.

But inside me, a little spark. Here's an idea. Here's something. I don't particularly feel like having it out with these strangers here, in front of everyone. But Malibu—Malibu sounds promising. A chance for me to finally see the ocean, after all this time living so close I can practically hear it in the whisper of the freeway. A chance for me to discover their secrets, to evade them as they try to dig for mine. Leo leans even closer.

"Seriously," he says, "come to Malibu. You're right, we can't talk here. It was absurd of me to suggest it. But we do need to talk. We have that wonderful little place down by the ocean, and we can sit up late, the three of us. It'll be fun. Like old times. After dinner we'll slip off. Marie won't mind."

His eyes seem to drift over the surface of my face, never quite settling down, his pupils black and vast. I wonder if he's been drinking as much as I have. Everything inside me feels slurred and easy. *I am still in control*, I tell myself, still in command of everything going on around me. Eleanor leans closer to her husband, a concerned look on her face. She smells good. Like Marie.

"I still have our old coke dealer's number," says Leo. "Come on, let's indulge, let's stay up together. We can go surfing in the sunrise. It'll be beautiful. Like old times."

Curiosity prickles the back of my spine. I want this part of her, too, the wild part, the old Rosanna, the Rosanna who made spontaneous choices, went places she wasn't supposed to go, did things that got her in trouble. I want to wear her freedom the way I wear her gestures, her habits, her expensive clothes. And isn't this the best way to do it? Discreetly, with people who at least feel that they are trustworthy, her friends? I can sense Max's presence somewhere down the hill, the engine of my expensive car idling, the way he sits silent in the front seat, his phone bathing his face in dead blue light. But I can convince him. Rosanna did. I can convince him, and I can go. I feel her blood in my veins, a prickle of energy. *Yes*, I think. *Yes, this is right*. Max will be as curious as I am. He will want to know Rosanna's secrets as much as I do, maybe more. And I can help him. I can make him say yes.

"Okay," I say, "I'll think about it. Be right back."

In the bathroom (white subway tile, gold fixtures, black glass candle filling the air with a heavy rose scent), I turn the tap on high and call Max. He answers on the first ring. I imagine him holding the phone tight in his hands, waiting, nervous. As the candle flickers, I watch my face shift in and out of being in the dark mirror.

"What is it?" Max asks. "What happened? Did something happen?"

"Hey," I say, "it's okay. I'm okay. Nothing happened. It's just some things have come up that we didn't cover. Was Rosanna sleeping with anyone here? A man called Leo?"

There is a long silence. "No," he says finally. But he sounds uncertain. "That's impossible. She would have told me. I . . . we . . . She would have said."

"Maybe so, Max," I say. "I'm sure she wanted to. But what if she couldn't? I think there's something going on here. Something beyond either of us. Something only Rosanna knows. Can you ask her? I know it's unorthodox, but just text her, ask her about Leo. For me?"

But he won't text her, I know. He's too curious, and she will almost certainly lie if he asks her directly, tell him to tell me to leave it alone. All I need to do is push just the right amount, delicate, careful, making sure Max thinks it's his idea. Again, there is silence on the other end of the line.

"This wasn't on the cards, Max," I say.

I keep my voice as gentle as I can. We're in this together, his leg as firmly clamped in Leo's sweaty palm as mine.

"Leo has a card, but there was nothing about their relationship. Just his name, the fact that he's married to Eleanor. His only appearance on the tape is that one lunch where they're drinking martinis together, and I thought she was acting sort of familiar, but I never expected anything like this. She's lying to you, Max. She's lying to us both."

"I remember that lunch," says Max. "From the footage. It was one time. Business. Nothing like . . . nothing like what you're saying."

"Max," I say, "I know you don't want to hear this from me, but you have to. She's keeping secrets from you, from us both. And now they want me to go with them to Malibu. I think you're right, we shouldn't tell Rosanna. I don't want to worry her. But I need to find out what it is he thinks he knows. So we can protect her from him."

"No," Max says again, "you're wrong."

It's as though he's talking to himself, as though I haven't said anything at all.

"She would have told me," he says. "There wasn't anyone else. There wasn't anyone."

His voice sounds fragile, strange. I imagine his stricken face in the faint glow of the streetlights shining through tinted glass.

"Well, there must be some reason he keeps putting his hand on my thigh," I say.

I pause so he can picture it. The body he sculpted with his elaborate diets, his exercise regime, the slinky dress he bought me with her money, another man's hand on her thigh.

"She wouldn't," he says even softer.

"She would," I say, "and she did. I need to go, Max. I need to understand what's happening."

"It's you," he says. "It isn't her. It's you. Flirting with him. I don't know what, encouraging him. That's you. If you need me to remove you from the situation, if you are unable to act responsibly, I will."

But I can hear the way his voice shakes. He isn't certain of the truth of what he says. He doesn't know any more about this than I do.

"It's not me," I say. "I promise. I wish it was. But we both know it's not me he wants. He wants Rosanna. And he wouldn't dare touch her if he didn't think she'd like it. They were sleeping together before she had that breakdown. They must have been. In fact, maybe it's his fault. Maybe it was his breaking up with her that pushed her over the edge. I need to find out what he knows. I need to protect you. And Rosanna, too. Who else is looking out for her but us? Who else does she have?"

Silence, still. I can hear the heavy intake of his breath. I picture him, his eyes closed, so scared, darkness all around him. Who else does Max have? Not Rosanna. No one but me.

"I'm going, Max," I say. "I have to. I'll take the phone with me. I'll let you know what happens. I'll make sure you're close. But I'm going. I need to find out what he knows."

Finally he speaks. His voice sounds strangely far away. Like he is calling up to me from the bottom of a well. "I'm coming to pick you up," he says. "At least let me drive. I'll stay close, just in case."

And I shake my head. As though he can see me. As though he is right there.

"No."

I had never said no to him before. Not ever. Not like this, so direct. No obfuscation, no softening the blow. Just no. The word feels strange in my mouth, as clear as a bell, as heavy as a stone. It feels so good to say it that I say it again.

"No, I can't leave, Maxie. I know it's dangerous. I know you're scared. But they know something. We need to protect Rosanna. You can pick me up in Malibu. I have the phone, I know my location is shared with you. Drive behind us, follow us there, don't let yourself be seen. Stay close. I'll call you if I need you, I promise."

I can feel the ache inside me throbbing to life. I am propelled by the strength of her wanting. There is a long silence on the other end of the line. Maybe Max thinks if he says nothing, if he doesn't make a choice, whatever comes next won't be his fault. I can hear his breathing, gentle white noise. He is watching the ribboned lights of the freeway below, a glowing stream. He is picturing my profile in every passing car. He is trying to remember my old name. Because there is nothing he can say to Rosanna. But it won't work. I want all of it, all of her, every part, even the parts of her Max doesn't like. The parts he doesn't know. And if Max remembers my name, I will not recognize it. It no longer belongs to me.

"Okay," he finally says. His voice is impossibly small. "Be careful. Find out what you can."

"Of course," I say. "Of course I will. I promise I'll be safe. Follow me. You wouldn't leave me alone, would you? You'll follow me, Max."

A pause. A silence. And then: "Yes," he says, "I will."

At the table, Eleanor, Leo, and the blond man are waiting for me. Marie is talking to her husband, but I can see how her eyes shift, tracking my progress back into the room. I give her a real, tender smile. *Dear Marie*, I think. *Sweet Marie*. I wonder what she knows. What knowledge has Rosanna been protecting her from?

I suffer through dessert, a quince tarte Tatin with crème anglaise, espressos, chocolates, endless chat, vibrating in my seat like a bow pulled taut. I'm ready. When the others begin to stand, gather their things, I turn to Eleanor and Leo.

"Come on," I say. "Let's go. I want to see the ocean."

The blond man wraps his arm around my legs. He's as drunk as Leo is. I try to give Eleanor a sympathetic look, but she avoids my gaze. "Can I come?" he says.

"Yes!" I say. "Darling, of course you can come. Don't be silly."

A witness, I think. Perfect. He'll protect me. He'll do whatever I want. They can't dig too deeply with him around.

"I'm bringing a date," I say.

I bend over and kiss Marie on the top of her head.

"Bye, Edward!" I say. "Thanks for reminding her to invite me. What a great party, sweets! I'll see you around."

Marie stands to kiss me on my cheek. Her gaze is heavy with some powerful emotion, anger or fear or concern? Right now it doesn't matter. I have other business to attend to, other deeper mysteries to solve. Inside, I feel that satiating hum. Rosanna is with me now.

19

The house looks exactly like I expect it to, big and clean and empty, looking out toward the ocean across a narrow swath of raked smooth sand. The ocean makes me nervous. I am nauseated by the heaving bulk of it, the vastness, water shaking like breath, in, out. It seems to whisper, words so soft I can't quite make them out, a troubling pressure building in the back of my head. But Rosanna has seen the ocean before. Rosanna is not scared. The moon hangs over us, low and round, tinted orange like the bloody insides of an egg held close in front of a flashlight, pulsing with thwarted life. Beside me on the couch, the blond man shifts his body closer to mine. I still haven't asked him what his name is. At this point I don't care. I try to read the pressure of skin on skin as acquiescence rather than aggression, a sign that he is giving in to me. Not the other way around.

In the kitchen Eleanor hospitably digs for a vial of cocaine hidden at the back of the spice rack. They hadn't needed to call anyone. This was probably for the best, that we keep it cozy, just the four of us, my situation is already complicated enough as it is, but it's odd that Leo pretended there was a need. In the bright light of the large white room, I can see a dullness matting Eleanor's skin. Thin lines at the corners of her eyes, hollows underneath. She looks haunted. Am I the responsible ghost? I think of her husband's hand on my thigh. What is there between us? And what does she know?

She taps out a line on the coffee table, pressing her face close to inhale, motioning us over, the blond man and me. Leo comes in from the patio, where he has been standing and smoking a cigarette, letting a cold burst of air puncture the stillness of the room. He's the only person I've met here who smokes other than Rosanna. Maybe he hoped I'd come outside with him, that we'd have some time alone.

Eleanor and Leo seem freed from pretense here and no longer sit close or even talk. They are focused on me. I can feel the warmth of their attention like two beams of light, and I am glad that I've brought along the blond man as insulation. They can't ask me anything too personal with him here, at least not without implicating themselves. I put my hand on his knee and give it a grateful little squeeze, his body sloping softly into mine, and I tell myself again that I am in charge.

"Your turn," Eleanor says.

I sit on the floor close beside her, trying to look casual, game. I hadn't done drugs in my old life. I was too afraid of getting caught, getting used to a habit too expensive to maintain without some loss of autonomy or personal control. I guess I don't have to worry about that now. I copy Eleanor's movements, a finger over the nostril, lean close, breathe deep, throw my head back, laughing. It burns, a strange medicinal taste in the back of my throat, like baking powder, salt water, acrid. I wonder if I've done something wrong. I hope I looked the way Rosanna did when she did it. I feel a new steadiness come over me, my heartbeat firmer, a new, more certain, assonance. My body hums. Rosanna had been at home here. So am I. I slip my arm around Eleanor's waist.

"Wow," I say, "it's been a minute."

I smile at Leo, giving him the slanted glance Rosanna uses when she asks for a cigarette or orders something with red meat—look how bad I am, it says, look how fun it is to be bad, to be me. His face stays still. Maybe he doesn't like his wife doing drugs. Maybe he's jealous I'm paying more attention to her than to him, jealous that

I brought along a human shield. It's not my problem. These people aren't my problem. I am theirs. I am overwhelmed with longing for Max. I don't know what I was thinking, coming here without him. My brain feels like it's bouncing around inside my head. All bloody liquid inside. But I'm here to work. I'm here to learn. For Rosanna's sake, I have to at least try to discover whatever it is I came here to find.

"So how have you all been?" I say. "I mean, really. I want to know everything. Tell me about what you've been doing! It's been so long, hasn't it, since we all spent time together."

This is good, I think. Casual. Vague enough to give them space to tell me whatever it is I need to know. Normally this is where I would describe a memory, bring up an inside joke, something we all know about, to make them comfortable. But Max hasn't prepped me, so I have nothing to say. I thought my understanding of Rosanna was bone-deep, instinctive, but without my flash cards and memorized facts I am helpless. I am as bad as Max, both of us knowing so much less than we think we do. The blond man stirs beside me, restless. I try not to look out toward the night, where the palm fronds froth, cracking whiplike against the glass.

"And whose fault is that?" says Leo, his voice light. He wants us to think he's joking. He's not. I am surprised that he has shifted so quickly to aggression, but then again, here I am in his house, another man's hand on my knee. It must hurt. I smile up at him from the floor. *So let it hurt,* I think. Is he Rosanna's married man?

"Come on," Eleanor says, "give her a break. We have all night to catch up."

She cuts me another line and I do it, my face floating up toward me through the dark glass. My phone nestles silent against my thigh. It feels heavier than it really is, dense. I wonder where Max is now. Is he close? Is he looking at my picture, blue in the shadows on the side of the highway? Is he trying still to remember my name? Or maybe he is calling Rosanna, letting her know what I have done. I lean forward and put my hand on the blond man's thigh, touching him the same way that Leo earlier had touched me. I do not ask for permission. Across the room, Leo's eyes lock on mine, flat and open, like a deer on a dark road surprised by headlights. I wonder if he's scared of me. I hope he is.

"So what was it," I ask, "that you wanted to talk about?"

"I thought you wanted to know how we were," says Leo. "Keep it casual, right? The only thing we want to know is where you've been, but apparently we're not allowed to talk about that."

Outside the wind picks up, the palm trees leaning together in a huddle, a sharp sound of snapping fronds. I thought that this would be more interesting. That Rosanna's secrets would be less mundane. But here we are, four lonely people, sitting too close together in a blank white room, so clean it feels inhuman, the violence of the outside world pressing close around us. There is something almost squalid about it. I think of Marie, smiling at her husband in the candlelight, and know I was wrong. She will never smile that way for me. There is nothing I can do, nothing I can learn, that will change the way she feels. Of course this isn't a new discovery. Rosanna already knows about the hidden imbalance at the heart of their relationship. Maybe that's why she's keeping secrets—she knows there are things that Marie isn't ready to hear.

"I don't want to know," says Eleanor.

"What?" says Leo.

"Just for the record. I don't really care where she was. I mean, Rosanna, you're great, but we didn't even know each other that well before you went wherever you disappeared to. I don't know why Leo is being so pushy. It's nice to see you, welcome back. But whatever you've been up to just doesn't feel like my business. Or his, to be honest."

Leo raises his hands, an abrupt motion. "I don't know what you want from me, Eleanor, Jesus. I'm just being friendly. Is that the end of the world? Showing concern for an old friend?"

An old friend, I think. *Sure. I bet you two were really close.* "It's fine," I say. "Please, I appreciate your concern. But I agree with Eleanor, I don't really want to get into it. Let's just hang out, okay? Have a fun night, old friends and new."

I force myself to stop clenching my jaw and give them all what I hope reads as a warm, easy smile.

The blond man joins in, eager to please. "Yeah," he says. "Thanks for bringing me, Rosanna. So nice meeting you guys."

It sounds like he wants to leave, thinks I'll take him with me when I go. My body feels electric, on fire with a slick, chemical rush, the back of my throat burning, all of me lit up. I wrap my arms around the blond man's neck, feel the warmth of him, the blood beating so close to the surface of his skin. I want to bite down until the blood comes bitter into my mouth. I feel my own power coursing through my veins. Marie or no Marie, I am the one with the power now.

But Leo is still looking at me. "Speaking of which," he says, "no offense, but why the hell is this guy here?"

The blond man seems to stop breathing. For one irrational instant I think I have killed him. Strangely, this idea is not particularly upsetting.

"Hey, man," he says, "I'm just trying to hang. You're the one that invited me."

"Leo!" says Eleanor. "Come on. It's not his fault. Be nice."

"Actually, Rosanna invited you," says Leo, "for some reason. I didn't. My wife's right. It's nothing personal, but honestly, Rosanna, why did you insist on bringing this stranger home with us? I thought you wanted to talk. What exactly is it that you think is going to happen here?"

I think that you are going to tell me everything I want to know. I think that you are going to tell me the secrets of myself. I try to focus on that feeling from before, that power. This should be easy. I shrug. "I wanted him here," I say. "So he's here. That's how it works."

"No," says Leo.

Now he's not trying to sound nice at all. He's given in to himself and he's just mean, just mean, self-serving Leo, and I'm supposed to be surprised by this? I'm supposed to be hurt? *I know you better than that*, I think. *And I don't know you at all.*

"That's not how this works," Leo says. He is standing now, pacing back and forth like a caged animal. "We haven't seen you in so long. It's been over a year? We saw each other every day, and then you disappear without saying a word."

"Wait," says Eleanor. "Every day? We barely knew—"

"Nothing," says Leo, cutting her off. "Just gone. Christ, Rosanna, I thought you were dead. And now you're back. But things aren't the same anymore. You've walked back into a different world."

"I thought you wanted to let things go?" I say. "I'm here, I'm fine, you're fine, let's just have fun together. If that's not how you feel, why don't you try being honest for once in your life. Tell your wife. Tell her why you're so angry at me."

Eleanor casts a look at her husband, silencing him. She looks at me with such sadness, recognition dawning in her eyes, and I think, *Who is this woman? What does she think she knows about me?*

"I don't need him to tell me anything," she says. "And I don't need you to tell me anything, either, not in my own house, not with my children sleeping upstairs. Having you come back with us was a mistake. It doesn't matter where you were or why you left, not really. We've grown up a lot in the past few years. I hoped you had, too."

Leo looks at her with tenderness. *He loves her*, I think. In his own way. He might have been fucking me, might be jealous and possessive and controlling, but he certainly wasn't planning on leaving. Rosanna never had a chance. I can still feel the pressure of his hand on my thigh and am filled with a powerful rage at his hypocrisy, theirs, the two of them so smug, like I'm the only person here who is pretending. As if any of us were in a position to judge. I'm leaving, I'll leave, but I want to make sure they know I'm on to them. I see what they are. I want to stand up for Rosanna. I'm the only one who will.

"Have things changed?" I say, standing up. "Have they, really? Are we all so incredibly grown up now? Because it looks to me like it's close to midnight on a weekday, and here we are sitting in your living room doing drugs while your children sleep upstairs, and that's not very responsible, is it? It was the best thing I ever did, leaving. Cutting off toxic people like you. I wish I had stayed away."

Eleanor stands up, too, directly across from me, the coffee table pressing sharp against both our shins. She is trying to look detached, I think, calm, but I can see how upset she is. I'm almost disappointed at her lack of control. She's as bad as her husband. In a way, they deserve each other.

"Rosanna," she says, her voice shaking, just slightly, no tears yet, "I'm glad, at least, that you're alive. It was interesting seeing you. But I think you should go now."

I take out my phone to text Max, holding it up to check the service, thinking of how I will wait alone on the beach. I will watch the waves until their motion feels natural to me. I will wade into the warm water, the moon's light soft on my clean white neck.

"I wish I could say the same of you," I say. "Don't worry, I'm going. I won't be bothering you again."

But as I move toward the door, Leo moves, too, stepping forward, blocking my path. He grabs me hard by the wrist, too hard, like Max, and no one is allowed to touch me like that but Max, and I raise my other hand to strike him, but just before I can, I see his face. Blank. So empty and clean that it scares me. And then, like watching a glass of water smash on the kitchen floor, a rush of emotion, confusion, rage, shock, all in the space of a breath. He lifts my hand up toward the light like I'm the winner in a boxing match and stares at it, looking for what, track marks, a mole, a scar? I try to pull my hand away, but he's holding on tight. I'm not as strong as I thought I was.

"Wait," he says.

He looks deep down into my eyes. *Rosanna slept with this man,* I think. She looks at him and sees a body she desires, a body she can control. I want him, too. I want to push him down on the couch, tear off his perfect clothes, scratch his skin, ruin him, all of this in front of his wife. He loves her, but he wants me. My power is undeniable. My body is a force more powerful than them both. He looks at me with that wild intensity, and I understand exactly what all this is about. He's so transparent, hopeless, really. I give him a seductive little smile.

"You're not Rosanna," Leo says.

There is a long silence. Leo holds tight to my wrist. He looks down into my eyes, down to where I keep myself hidden, and I can feel him dragging me up into the harsh and burning light. And suddenly I am back in the living room of my parents' house, the one we lived in toward the end, with filthy fluffy white carpeting throughout, all those closets, all those mirrors. My father is out for the night, business, he says, and this means that we probably won't see him till late the next afternoon. This is what my mother has been waiting for. There are suitcases hidden under her pile of fur coats, and when she wakes me, late, the sky blue-black, the neighborhood quiet, we pull them out and creep downstairs. I barely recognize the mousy woman standing at the foot of my bed, her combed-back hair, black jeans and top, her puffy, makeup-less face. She is a stranger to me. But she smells like my mother, she has my mother's voice, and so I, trusting, my tiny legs dangling above the dirty carpet, quietly put on my shoes and follow her through the darkened house. My mother does not have friends we can go to. My mother cannot drive a car. But what my mother does have is willpower and smarts and a handbag full of rolled-up dollar bills and the number of a taxi company. We will drive to a new town, take a bus, take another, paying in cash. We will disappear into the vastness of a country where nobody will be able to find us, the dogs on our tail losing the scent, panting, their tongues dry in the empty air. We will have each other. We will be fine. And then the door swings open. My father is standing there, rain blowing in around him, soaking the carpet at his feet. I turn to run upstairs, to hide, but he rushes forward, catches me by the wrist, and looks so deep into my eyes I think he will scoop me hollow, and then my mother is on him, screaming, and he hurls me so hard against the staircase that my head cracks, pain washing over me in a wave. Everything goes dark. I wake up to an open door, my father gone, my mother lying still beside me. The carpet is wet with rain, yes, but a deeper wet, too, a wet that is red and sticky and sweet, melted sugar, a dropped bottle of molasses seeping across the kitchen floor. I close my eyes again, willing it all to disappear. For the rain to come through the open door and wash it all away. Leo is still holding hard to my wrist. Still, he stares down into my eyes. Outside, the storm has picked up, wind beating hard against the windows, the sea growing louder and louder until it seems to shout, and Leo looks down at me the way my father did, and I wait for the moment of fracture, for him to throw me down on the hard edge of the table, for the sky to open up, for all of this to end like it was always going to—in violence, in darkness, in pain. But the storm does not break. It does not rain. That's the only thing I can think of, looking from Leo to Eleanor to the man I've brought to their house, all of them silent, all of them looking at me. Why isn't it raining? There is nothing but silence and the whisper-crack rush of wind outside. Whatever happens next, I hope it rains one last time. I want to see this dirty city clean.

In the stillness, I find my breath. I clear my throat. My lips move. "What the hell are you talking about?" I say.

My voice is shaky and filled with outrage. I try to remind myself of what being Rosanna feels like. Of what being a person feels like. *This is a normal reaction*, I tell myself. I am reacting normally. What Leo is saying is so strange. My heart beats so loud I can hear it, my wrist throbbing and aching in his grasp. Still, no one speaks. I shake my head, pretending I've misheard him.

"Leo, are you okay? What are you talking about?"

There is nothing that I have seen that helps me imagine how Rosanna might feel about being accused of impersonating herself. All I know is how I feel—confusion, nausea, rage. I have worked so hard, how dare he? How dare he suggest such a thing? This man who knows nothing about the real Rosanna, nothing about me. I try to fill my voice with that uncertainty. What Leo has said is an obviously crazy thing, surely we can all see that, a bizarre and delusional accusation. They, we, have no reason to believe him. But I have to move carefully. There is no room for sloppiness now. If Leo has caught me, there must be some tell, some sign he has picked up on. Like my father picked up on my mother's signs, knew to wait in the car out front until the lights came on, exposing us. There is always the moment of failure before the end, the slip that you don't catch, the error that passes silently and ruins everything you've worked so hard to build. The wrist, I think, yes, where he was looking, but more than that. I have made some fatal, invisible error that made him think to check.

Eleanor comes closer and gently puts her arm around Leo, shielding him—from what, from me? I have to make her believe she is shielding her husband from himself. That we are in this together. *Worry*, I think, *tenderness*. We both love him in our own way. We are joined in our concern for him in this moment, poor Leo, so confused, saying such strange things.

"Is he okay?" I ask.

"Don't talk to her," says Leo. "Babe," he says, turning to Eleanor, still holding tight to my wrist, and now he's shielding her, trying to force her to look into his eyes as she gazes past him, looking at me with confusion and alarm. "Listen to me. She's been acting so strange all night, I could tell something was wrong, and now I know for sure. Eleanor, believe me. Look at her wrist! It's not her! I know what I'm talking about, look."

Eleanor doesn't listen. Her eyes are clamped tight on my face, searching. I look just like Rosanna, I remind myself. My body is her body, my face her face. When Eleanor looks at me, it is Rosanna she sees.

"Honey," she says to him, small-voiced, "let go of her arm."

He lets go, maneuvering his body to stand between us, like I am something dangerous, a bomb about to explode. I massage my aching wrist, look at him with as much compassion as I can summon up. Somehow I am sorry not to touch him anymore. There is another long and painful silence. But the silence is good. Silence means that they are uncertain, that he is uncertain, that it is in my power to keep them here, in this uncertain space. I run through the night, my mind clicking along like I'm flipping through my flash cards: every gesture, every word, shifting landscapes of dark and dark and light. But there is nothing there to help me. There is only this silence. Nothing matters but this long silent moment, the four of us together in the gathering storm.

"This is so fucking weird," the blond man mutters.

He's talking to himself, I know, but I decide his words are mine. They're meant for me. That's the reason he's here, so I can have an ally. He's finally doing his job.

"Shut up!" says Leo. "Who are you, anyway? You don't know us, and you don't know her. You're useless. Nobody wants you here."

He's getting angrier and angrier. Good. This undermines his credibility. The first person to show his emotion, to flinch, is the one you don't believe. He is unraveling before us all.

"Stop!" says Eleanor. "Leo, why are you so angry? Will someone tell me what the hell is going on?

I give her a sympathetic look. What Leo is saying is insane. But there's still a chance that Eleanor, his wife, the person who loves him most, who is the most familiar with the contours of his mind, will believe him. It's easier for her to believe him than to accept the obvious conclusion that her husband is having some kind of breakdown right in the middle of their overpriced beachfront property. I need to balance the scales, make sure the blond man, at least, is on my side. It becomes easier and easier to believe a lie the more people already believe it. If I can convince him, I can convince Eleanor. And she can make Leo feel like he's going crazy.

"I know," I say, ignoring Leo. "I'm so sorry. I promise you he's never been like this before. Maybe I shouldn't have brought you here. It was inappropriate, I see that now. But I had no idea that things were so bad with Leo. I'm sorry you have to see him like this. Please don't judge him by his behavior tonight. He is a really good guy, I promise, and brilliant—well, you're an artist yourself, you understand. You know what artists are like. I just hope this hasn't been too upsetting for you."

I look into his dull blue eyes, full of gentleness, my voice even and low and sad.

"It's not your fault," he says.

I feel the tears welling up in my eyes, poor Rosanna. And he's right—poor Leo, he's sick, this isn't my fault. Eleanor looks from Leo to the two of us, her eyes slick with doubt. I can feel the power in the room begin to shift.

"Thank you," I say. "I appreciate that."

"She's lying," says Leo. "Don't listen to her."

I don't bother responding. Let him talk to himself, it only makes him look crazier. I turn to Eleanor. Direct gaze, tight mouth, raised eyebrows, you poor thing. I walk to the bar and pour us all glasses of whiskey so I can turn away from them for a moment, compose myself, make sure my hands aren't shaking too badly. They aren't. Good. I bring the tray of drinks back to the others so they can see the steady liquid, my unshaking grip, my graceful Rosanna walk.

"Here," I say, "I think we could all use a little calming down."

The blond man takes his drink. After a brief pause, so does Eleanor. Leo leaves his on the tray.

"Don't drink those," he says. "Since when did Rosanna get anyone else a drink? Since when did Rosanna offer to help? Something is very, very wrong. This isn't Rosanna. I promise you. I don't know who it is, but it's not her."

He is still standing as far from me as he can get, one hand tight on Eleanor's arm. I have been so patient. Now it's time for my patience to come to an end. I drink my whiskey in one gulp, clang the glass down on the table. They all jump.

"Jesus Christ," I say, "Leo, I'm sorry, I really am trying to be understanding, I know that it's been a while. Maybe you're stressed, you're drunk, whatever—I don't know what's going on with you—but you're really scaring us, especially Eleanor. Pull yourself together! Look at me, Leo. It's me! It's just me. You know me. You know who I am."

"You are not Rosanna," he says, slow but firm. Certain. Like he is talking to a child. "I don't know who you are. I don't know where she is. All I know is that you are not her." He turns to the others. "She's not Rosanna. She's manipulating you, don't listen to anything she says. I don't know who she is, but from the second she sat down with us I knew there was something off about her. Not quite right. And now I know for sure. Look at her wrist, Eleanor. Her birthmark is missing."

I hold my wrist in the loop of my fingers. I can feel the thin skin, blood pulsing quick in my blue veins. Max. He's marked me. The way mothers do with twins, dressing one in blue, another in pink, the way surgeons mark the diseased limb to make sure they don't incise the healthy half. This isn't Rosanna's doing, not her fault. She would never set me up to fail like Max has. Eleanor looks at me. There is something in her eyes, not doubt, not quite. A willingness to doubt. But I feel calmer than ever. I close my eyes. I sigh. I have him now. He's told me the one thing I didn't already know.

"Okay," I say, "okay. I didn't want to talk about that. But if it will make you feel better, help shatter whatever delusion has you in its grip, I guess I have to."

I pause. Everything is still again. Leo is listening. Even the blond man sits rapt on the edge of the couch, waiting for whatever is coming next.

"I can't really talk about what happened before I left. About what happened when I was gone. I can't, and I don't want to. But things were bad at the end. Things were really bad for a while. I didn't want to see anyone, do anything. I didn't want to be alive anymore. So . . ."

I turn my wrists over, angling them to my chest.

"There was scar tissue," I say. "But they lasered it off. Anything is possible now. I didn't think of replacing the birthmark. I thought it might be a sign that I had changed. I just hoped . . . I don't know. I was so ashamed. I didn't want anyone to know."

I let my voice grow heavy with intimated tears. Eleanor rests her hand gently on my lower back.

"It's okay," she says. "It's okay. You don't have to talk about it. We shouldn't have asked."

"That's bullshit," says Leo. "That's bullshit and you know it. Rosanna would never do something like that."

"I didn't think so, either," I say. "But then . . ." I pause. I hold back tears. I let my shoulders shake. "I did."

Eleanor looks between us, back and forth. She loves him. She wants to believe him. But she hasn't seen what he saw. She probably can't even picture the birthmark. Leo knows me better than she does. He knows my body so well. And right now she can't let herself think about that. I give her the same look I had given the actor—look at us, the sane ones, having to deal with this poor deluded person— but for her I fill it with compassion. *Good for you*, I think, *you poor thing*. She looks away. Guilty. She's still angry, but she believes me. The alternative is too outrageous. She has no other choice.

"Leo," she says, "honey, do you need to lie down?"

He finally looks away from me, lets go of Eleanor's arm. Now he's angry at her. Good. He comes closer to me, his body language aggressive. But I am not afraid of him. If he knew what was good for him, he'd be afraid of me. For a fraction of a second, I look right back at him so he can see I'm not scared, and then I flinch away so that the others will see I am. Eleanor springs forward to hold him back.

"Rosanna," she says, "I'm so sorry, he's harmless, I swear."

"Of course," I say, "I know that, it's fine, he doesn't know what he's saying."

"No," says Leo, "I know exactly what I'm saying, and I don't need to lie down. Nothing's wrong with me, I'm fine, but it's not her! I tell you, it's not her!"

"Okay, sweetheart," she says, "I know it seems that way to you right now. But you must realize how strange this sounds. It's so late, and we're all tired, and maybe the coke was a bad idea. I'm sorry. Rosanna, I'll call a car for you and your friend. This is all my fault. I'm so sorry about all this."

She looks like she is going to cry. And I feel so sorry for her, I really do, poor Eleanor, who is aging so expensively in her outdated house, whose husband is delusional and sleeping with god knows how many women. I cross the room and stand beside her. It seems important, somehow, to move as much as I can, to let them see me from every angle, prove there are no hidden flaws that need concealing, no bad side I'm trying to shield. Leo tracks my movements with his eyes. A trapped animal. I stroke Eleanor's back, ignore the way she flinches from my touch.

"Eleanor," I say, "please. You have nothing to apologize for. I should have thought about the effect that seeing me again would have, after such a long time apart. It's all just too much, isn't it? Not just for poor Leo. For all of us."

I fill my voice with as much gentle solicitude as I can manage. Slowly her hands stop shaking. Slowly she lets herself go limp. I pull her body toward my own, soft, eternally soft.

"Do you have anyone we can call? A doctor? Does he have a psychologist he works with? It's nothing to be ashamed of. We all need help sometimes."

She looks at me, her eyes filling up with tears, and shakes her head. "I don't know," she says. "I don't know what to do."

Behind her, Leo starts to pace back and forth across the room. I smooth Eleanor's hair back from her forehead. I look deeply into her eyes. I know that we can't actually call anyone in. Leo might talk, and as crazy as his story is, there is a chance, a vanishingly slim but dangerous chance, that someone might believe him. I have to appeal to her sense of shame.

"Of course," I say, "I don't want us to be too hasty, if you think we can handle this on our own. Maybe the best thing is to have him go to bed, see how he feels in the clear light of day. You can call me in the morning if you need to. If he wants to talk all this over. I know what it's like, being in the public eye. What a strain it can be, having everyone airing your dirty laundry. I can't imagine how difficult that would be for your children."

She lets go of my hands now, nervous, fluttering, adjusting her hair.

"Oh no," she says. "No, it's fine. He's fine. He's never been like this before, you know that. That coke must have been cut with something, and you know, we don't really do it anymore, we're not used to it, it's been so long. We're all tired, aren't we? It's been a long night. It's that, and the stress, just stress. He takes on so much, poor Leo, he always has, he works too hard. Please don't call anyone. Nobody needs to know."

Her voice fades. She is looking away now, not to me or her husband, but out the window, toward the sea. The wind beats against the glass, pressing stronger and stronger, trying to come inside. How did her life become this way? How did she become the woman reflected in the dark glass against the storm, no longer young, no longer perfect, no longer anybody's golden girl? I can tell she is trying not to cry. Good. I run my fingers gently through her hair. Rosanna probably wouldn't have been so nice. But Eleanor didn't really know Rosanna. And she is past the point of noticing, anyway. Leo isn't. He looks at me with those hard, flat eyes. I look right back at him.

"Stop talking about me like I'm not here," he says. He's trying to sound calm, but his voice grows tight, climbing high into his chest. He is determined to appear reasonable, sane. But it's too late. I can feel the relief, the triumph of it climbing hot into my throat. It is all I can do not to shout out loud.

"Don't worry," I tell Eleanor. "Please don't worry. Let's just calm him down, get him to bed. I won't tell anyone. This stays between us. It will all be over soon."

"I'm not crazy," says Leo. "I'm your husband, Eleanor, don't you trust me? I know what I'm talking about."

"Stop talking," she says, suddenly loud, full of unexpected certainty. "Just stop. How did you know about her wrist? How do you know about her body? Every day, Leo? Every day? I thought I had done something wrong, I thought it was my fault when you started pulling away, acting so distant. But it wasn't my fault, it was you. It was you, Leo. You love her, don't you? You pulled away from me because she left. You were mourning a breakup, and you made me think it was my fault. So shut the fuck up, you hypocrite. I don't care about your insane delusions. I don't want to hear you say a thing. Because no, I don't trust you. I don't trust you at all. You haven't earned anything from me. Not this. Not anything at all."

"Babe," he says, and he stops. There is nothing left for him to say. I look into his eyes. He doesn't believe me. He probably never will. But he will be too ashamed to say anything about it ever again. He knows now how it sounds. He knows he is a stranger in the world that will never acknowledge what he knows indisputably to be true. He moves across the room and stands silently behind Eleanor, not touching her, not saying anything at all. Together, they look out to where the moon peeks from the clouds, silent, over the sea.

In the car outside, Max is waiting, his eyes scooped hollow by the light of the phone. He has called a car for the blond man, who has disappeared into the darkness of the driveway, waiting. The wind has died down. He will be comfortable until it arrives.

"You were right," I say. "What a waste of time. And they don't know a thing about Rosanna that we don't. Not a thing."

Beside the empty highway, the moon continues its slow set over the sea. I look away so I won't have to see the vulnerability of relief breaking on his face. Inside me, still, that powerful thrum, that urge to touch someone the way Rosanna touched Leo. I am so lonesome in my new body. It has been so long since I was touched.

"I do need to tell you something, though," I say. "She was definitely sleeping with him. Not just once, either. She had been sleeping with him for a long, long time. You should tell her he's angry, if that's something you think she'd want to know. You should tell her he probably still loves her. Just in case she's wondering. Just in case she loves him, too."

We drive in silence to the hills, to the apartment. I know I should feel panicked. The worst has happened, and worse, perhaps, is to come. Leo could still tell everyone. He could convince Eleanor. The blond man could sell a tell-all, "My Strange Night with the Stars," earn a little money, boost his notoriety enough to get a part in a daytime soap. But I am strangely calm. I have his number, can buy time by leading him on until the evidence of our time together has faded and no one believes him, either.

I am as tense as a clenched fist, vibrating with desire. When the car pulls up to the curb, I reach out and hold Max's hand in mine. Soft. Warm. The close tenderness of him. I want to wipe that blank sadness off his face.

"Will you tell her?" I ask, more for the sake of distraction than anything else. "We don't know how she feels about him. Maybe she's still waiting for Leo. Maybe, for some reason, she loves him, too."

Max nods. He nods again, again, not saying a word, and then his whole body is shaking and he is sobbing silently, folded over the wheel in a posture of hopeless defeat. I lean over and pull him into my arms. That same strange feeling. *More*, I think, *more*. I don't understand why he's crying. But I can still try to fix it, still make him feel better. Like Rosanna would.

"Come upstairs," I say. "Just for a second. Let me take care of you."

He nods again, a gesture that could be agreement or just another shuddering sob. I walk to his side of the car and open the door. I help him out, his body a wet bag of sand holding back a flood, heavy and limp, an object in my arms.

In my room, I lay him down on the futon. He remains curled up, and I lie beside him, hold him in my arms. His whole body is shaking. He feels small, smaller than me, impossibly tender and little and young. *I love him*, I think. I was wrong. I don't resent him, I love him. I love him so much I can hardly stand it, I love him so much that it lives inside of me like a hurt, an ache, an urgent and parasitic desire. That's all. I lean in close and bring my lips to his cheek, the skin hot. I lick away one tear, another, the salty, bitter taste, bringing him into me, his body mine, my body ours, and he tilts his face up slightly and his lips are on my lips, his tongue on my tongue, that same burned, bitter taste of cigarettes and must, that same impossible tenderness, that urgency, his hands, calloused thumbs and fleshy palms pawing at the slit of Rosanna's dress, clumsy with desire. In the faint light from the street his face has a nakedness I've never seen before, totally open, utterly strange, his eyes clamped tight against my seeing. I must feel so familiar. I must feel just like her. "Rosanna," he says, so quiet, as if there were no one here, whispering into the silence of the room, like I am not a person, in that moment, not myself or her entirely, but no one, an emptiness, my body a stranger to us both. In the silence, the darkness, the three of us are one. "Yes," I say. "Yes, please, yes."

It's still dark when I wake up. The streetlight shines in through the window, casting violent shadows across my white sheets. I can see the low-slung belly of the sky, vulnerable and close, pale with the creeping fingers of dawn. The bed beside me is empty. Max is long gone. I hold my arm up into the light. I consider the empty space. My wrist throbs painful where my birthmark should be.

20

When I was a child, I wanted to be a nun. It wasn't from any particular abundance of faith; my family rarely went to church when I was young, and later, after my mother died, none of my foster parents were especially convincing in their attempts to save my soul. But I had a feeling that I was responsible for the evils of the world. That I was at fault when things went wrong. My mom would be crying or my dad would be angry or I would see something about a tornado on the news. *My fault*, I would think. *My fault*. Maybe if I removed myself from the world I could save it. I liked the idea of life in a convent, of sisterhood. I thought about how I would spend all day working in the garden or copying Bibles or doing whatever it was they did, lost in my duties, thinking only of the women around me, putting their needs first so I could forget my own. I want to be that way for Rosanna now. To devote myself. To disappear entirely. To offer up as proof, stigmata, the dark marks beneath my palm. I am so close to disappearing. I am so close to being saved. I sit in the window turning my wrist over in my lap, looking at it. My emptiness, my blank space, my lack. I had been caught because Leo had noticed the birthmark was missing. This was literally, substantively true. But he had noticed because he was looking. He had been looking because I hadn't been as good as I needed to be. I hadn't been flawless. I had been pretending. The cracks had showed. My fault again, my fault. If I have been caught once, I can be caught again. I will be caught again. It isn't good enough for me to pretend. I have to become. To think her thoughts. To carry her inside me. To let myself slip away until I am safe and I am clean and I am gone, and her freedom is my freedom, and she belongs to me as much as I belong to her. More.

I go through my library, carefully examining every image in the bright light of the kitchenette, looking for a picture where I can see the inside of Rosanna's arm. There are close-up shots of almost every other part of her body. Her stomach ("Rosanna's Baby Joy!"), her thighs ("Best and Worst Beach Bodies"), her biceps ("How Rosanna Got Stronger Than Ever"). Someone has even taken a grainy zoomed-in photograph of her shoulder from the night she got matching tattoos with a boyfriend, another after she got it lasered off, alone. And then finally I find something. Rosanna at the Met Gala a few years back, body draped in a low-backed silver dress, hair in a tight, sleek bun. She looks out at the camera, her gaze frank and inviting. And in a close-zoomed inset, there is a picture of the bracelet she's wearing, a diamond-and-platinum cuff, Art Deco, worth fifty thousand dollars, the caption says, on loan from Cartier. And beneath the bracelet, of course, a wrist. Rosanna's wrist, bony, birdlike, fine. On one side, a blurred shadow, exposed to the light where the diamonds hang down. The birthmark. Her birthmark. Mine. It's smaller than I imagined it would be. No bigger than a tiny drop of milk, tension domed and quivering on the rim of a glass, the blot of blood when a needle slides out, gentle against your skin. It's distinctive, though, an oval with unsteady edges, another, smaller, dot beside it. I understand why Leo remembered it, this tiny secret thing, an imperfection that belonged only to him. It won't be his anymore.

I rifle through the rack of Rosanna's purses until I find a ballpoint pen and a beat-up old hotel sewing kit, *Villa des Orangers, Marrakesh*, embossed in gold on the front. I close my eyes and picture it, those Moorish arches, the fragrant orangerie, the cool black-and-white marble of the high-domed lobby. I remember it well. I remember it all. There is a bottle of rubbing alcohol in the bathroom cabinet, and I pour some onto the cleanest washcloth I can find. I light the stove with a match, and when it sputters to life, take the small gold safety pin from the kit and hold it in the flame until the tip starts to glow. I snap the pen in two, watch the blank ink pool viscous in a chipped saucer, dip the hot tip of the safety pin, and, before I get a chance to reconsider, stab my wrist, just slightly off center, next to the place where I can see the tendon tense, the dark blue fork of vein. The skin puffs red where the needle goes in. I swear I can smell something burning. Again and again I dip the needle, and the mark begins to take shape, dark ink blooming rough-edged, cancerous, beneath the skin. It feels like I'm pulling it up from inside myself, black dark blood. I am aware of the closeness of my own pulse, the way my muscles pull and shift, the choking tangle of veins and guts and tender nerves, all of it held in place by sheer inertia. The enormous tidal monstrosity of me, wrapped in such thin skin. I make a second dot next to the first, this one perfectly round, a moon orbiting some strange dark planet. I hold my arm up to the window to examine my work. The darkness is as much a part of me now as it is a part of her. Whatever happens next, I promise myself one thing. I won't get caught. I won't ever get caught again.

I sit silent in the window, looking down on the empty street. Is it morning or afternoon? The same day of my disaster and salvation or the next? How long had I been sleeping? When did I wake? It is impossible to tell. My wrist throbs painful in my lap. I can barely stand to move it, wincing as I turn the pages of the magazine I read, or remember reading, gazing blindly down at the blurry words. Good. The pain tethers me to my body. I hope it keeps hurting. I hope I hurt forever. The pain will keep me strong. It will distract me from the hunger that will come as I wait. And Max will keep me waiting, of that I am certain. This time I am ready. I have been saving scraps in the back of the freezer, sneaking scoops of the powders and seeds and dried fruits he brings over in the mornings and stashing them in the silverware drawer. But I am not waiting for Max.

I am waiting for Rosanna. Soon something will happen. Leo will call. She will know, and she will come to me. The two of us alone, together forever. We will be stronger without him, without Max, growing in power, in purity. We will leave these four small walls, the filthy glass panes of my view. Together we will walk hand in hand through the hills, the city spread out begging at our feet.

And then a sound outside. The car. It hasn't even been a day. I am almost disappointed in Max. Rosanna deserves better. I can see his hunch as he gets out of the car, read the fragility in his body. He has even brought me coffee, late in the afternoon or evening as it is. His arms are full of flowers. I think, *Poor Max. Poor, lonely Max.* I take Rosanna's favorite foundation, mother of pearl, and daub it onto my wrist, blowing as it dries. Poor Max. Poor thing. He doesn't need to know that everything is different now. It's my job to protect him, just as it's his job to protect Rosanna. It's what she wants, I know. I unroll the long sleeves of my cashmere sweater, the fabric soft over my swollen skin. What Max doesn't know won't hurt him. Let him think he can tell the difference between us. Let him learn to miss me when I'm gone.

"Oh, hello, Maxie," I say when the door opens. "Where have you been hiding yourself? You know I get lonesome without you."

"Hi," he says.

Just that. But there is a new tenderness in his voice. He hands me the coffee, looking right into my eyes, still smiling as I put it down without even pretending to take a sip. The bouquet he's holding looks awkward in his arms, the drooping buds of the pink roses uncannily like flesh. These aren't flowers Rosanna would buy.

"I missed you, too," he says.

Without warning, he leans forward and kisses me on the mouth, still beaming, so his lips are stretched hard against his teeth and his teeth knock against mine. I don't know how to react. I thought last night was a slip, a lapse, a strange lapping over into another reality that we would both understand we could never speak about again.

And here he is kissing me, like it's the most ordinary thing in the world.

"Well, thanks for the coffee," I say.

"Anything for you," he says. "Anything."

He sits beside me, stroking my hair. His hand catches on a snarl and he pulls, just slightly too hard. I lean my head toward him with an animal gesture of submission, pain, letting him think it hurts. I'm waiting, biding my time. I want to find out what it is he thinks he knows.

"Your hair's getting a little long," he says. "We'll need to cut it."

"You're right," I say. "Thanks for noticing."

"I'm always watching out for you," he says. "You're my girl."

And for now, I suppose, he's right. I am. I smile as warmly as I can.

"Guess we'd better call Holly," I say.

"Actually," says Max, "I've been thinking. Maybe it's too risky having people come over here. I don't want anyone to interrupt our privacy, do you? Maybe I'd better cut your hair myself."

I picture him cutting my hair, collecting it, saving it. Bags and bags of the cast-off parts of me, his forever.

"Okay," I say. "That sounds nice."

I turn another page of the magazine. Any excuse to look away from his impossibly eager gaze. My wrist aches, but I do not flinch. I look down at the image, at my Rosanna wide glossy expanse of lip, my ten tips for a perfect summer, and our smile for a moment seems to waver. But I'm not scared. I'm not alone. I'm with Rosanna, now and always, and together we will conspire against him to save ourselves.

"Look at her," says Max. "Look how beautiful she looks."

He stares down, rapt, at the photograph. He thinks it's Rosanna. He's sure of it. I pick up another magazine, testing him.

"How do you think she looks here?" I ask.

There I am a few weeks ago in my leaf-print leggings, jogging along that beach. Even though it seems so distant from me now, a memory from another life, I know that Max was beside me, sitting silent in the back seat of the car, watching me run.

"Beautiful," he says. "She always looks so beautiful."

He can no longer tell which pictures are me and which are her. Which of us has her face and which my own. But is it possible he's right? That I am the one making a mistake, writing myself too efficiently onto Rosanna's memories? For a moment, I am uncertain. Reality seems to wobble and shift, with the brilliance of oil floating on dirty water. I pick up another magazine, flip through the images of me, Rosanna, us. Is that really my beautiful face, my dress? I check my wrist to make sure. In this shot, my arms are held behind my back. Some part of me must have known that something was missing, even if I didn't know what it was.

"Max," I say gently, as gently as I can manage, "that isn't her. It's me."

He laughs a gentle little laugh, pushes the hair from in front of my eyes. "Out there, you're her," he says. "In here, you belong to me. You're mine. You're not Rosanna when we're alone."

"Who am I, then?" I ask.

He smiles. "You're my girl."

I look over his head at an image of Rosanna on the wall, walking away from the cameras, smiling. Max can tell I'm not focusing. His grip tightens. He pulls me closer. His body is so near to mine that it is almost as though we are embracing. I look right back at him. I look and look. He thinks he can control me. He thinks that he can rob me of the last thing I own, the name he has given to me. He thinks he can call me by my old name. He doesn't know that name isn't mine anymore. That I am Rosanna or nothing at all, something somehow more and less than human, a creature existing beyond the bounds of time and logic, entirely beyond his understanding. He is trying so hard to appear fierce, protective, but there is a faltering at the edges of his eyes. He needs me now, more than I need him.

"I've been thinking," he says, "after last night. Maybe you should stay inside from now on. I don't like the idea of you, vulnerable, without me. I don't think you should go out anymore. It's not safe for you out there. And it's my job to protect you. I need to keep you close. I can't make the same mistakes I made last time, let people hurt you."

"Max," I say, "I don't think that's a very good idea. You need me out there, don't you? Rosanna needs me. She can't disappear again. Remember why I'm here—so that she can be safe. You're right, we need to keep her from the world. We need to protect her. But that's why I'm here."

I push past the tenseness of his arms and lean my head into his chest so he can smell me. I smell like her. I feel like her. This similarity protects me, breaks me into a reflecting hall of mirrors. Poor Max doesn't know where to look. He doesn't know whether he's addressing the reflection or the real thing.

"I know that it's hard for you," I say. "I know, I know. It's hard for me, too. And I'm sorry about last night. I'm sorry I told you about Leo. It should have been Rosanna's secret to tell, I know that now. But it was so nice afterward, wasn't it? Being together. Isn't that the way that it should be? Rosanna outside, and in here, me, yours?"

His grip loosens a little. I can breathe. I breathe in deep and reach up, wrap my arms around his neck. I look into his eyes, my whole body aching.

"Let me keep living as Rosanna," I say. "Let me live. I'll die if you keep me in here, Max. It'll ruin everything we've worked so hard for."

"Shh," he says, "it's okay. Of course it was nice. It was perfect. You're perfect. Don't get so worked up. You're good enough that you can stop. Finally. Isn't that what you always wanted? To be a real person? To have your own life? To stop pretending?"

His voice is low and soft and kind. So loving it makes me clench my teeth. Inside me, everything is still. Like *he* always wanted. This has nothing to do with me. It has nothing to do with Rosanna, either.

"I can't stop now," I say. "It's too late. I can't stop now. She needs me. It would ruin her, ruin everything if I disappeared, too."

"I'm sorry," he says, still holding me tight. "I really am. But it's just too dangerous. It's over. It's all over now. I need you here with me. Where it's safe. All that's left is one more excursion. You need to meet up with Marie and tell her you can't see her anymore. Tell her it's over. And we'll stay here, you and me together. We'll never be apart again. I promise you, sweetheart."

And I know it's done. I'm finished. Everything I've worked for, all my time and effort and work, it has all been for nothing. Worse than nothing—it has all been for Max. Max is the reason I'm here, he's the reason I'm doing the work I'm doing. I notice his hair is just a little longer than it needs to be, his clothes rumpled, skin pale and waxy looking. I am so used to seeing Max that my mind has filled in the gaps that are there now, made his blank spaces whole. There is something in him that is unraveling. I wonder if I am the one pulling the string. If he will collapse if I turn my back on him and walk away.

And then I realize I can't say no. I can't go home. I can't go back to my old life. I can't go forward, either. There is no future for me, not the way I imagined. My account full of money has a name on it that only Max knows. My passport, my new identity, the future he promised me, all of it is tied up in him. In his letting me go. I see myself again in my apartment with that view of the Eiffel Tower, but Max is behind me, his arms wrapped tight around my waist. There is no future there. There is nothing but this room, and whatever Max has planned waiting for me on the other side of it. Maybe there never was a future. Maybe he never planned on letting me go, the account a fiction, my beautiful strange new self an impossible lie. I know too much now. There is nowhere in the world I will be safe from what I know, and no one who will believe me if I try to tell. I look like Rosanna. I have her face, her name. There are people all over Los Angeles who would swear that I am who I say I am, a host of waiters, stylists, paparazzi who would tell you that it's happened again, Rosanna's cracked, disappeared, leaving Max, I am sure, to be her sole protector and legal guardian. Even Marie would believe it. Our new friendship is precarious, she has no real faith in me. I have no proof of who I used to be. That girl, that anonymous girl, died a quiet death a long time ago. There is no one left who remembers her name.

"Okay," I say. "I understand."

I'll tell Marie, I think. One last desperate gambit. I'll tell her everything. It's the only hope I have of getting out. I'll make Max think I agree with him, I'll meet her alone, and I'll tell her every-thing. She will help me escape. Surely I can manage to convince her, no matter how crazy all this sounds. She knows Rosanna so well, knows what she is and isn't like. She will have to believe me. I have to try. I know now that I have no other chance. I finally look into Max's eyes. I smile a wide, false smile.

"And if you think it's really what's best for Rosanna, I'm glad," I say, taking his hands in mine. "I'm glad that it'll be just you and me. I really am. You're right. It's what we want. It's all I've wanted all along. I love you, Max. I can't wait for my real life to start. The two of us together always. Alone."

Marie and I meet in our favorite café. Max texts her from Rosanna's phone, which he has taken back from me, and within the hour he is dropping me outside the familiar brick building and I am walking toward her as she sits in a booth, our booth, twisting her engage-ment ring around on her finger. She seems distracted somehow. Like she doesn't want to be here. I wonder what Max told her.

"Hey," I say, "thank you for coming. It's good to see you."

"It's good to see you, too," she says. "What's up? You said that we needed to talk?"

She's looking at me with such trust that I can't help but picture her expression once I tell her who I really am, the disappointment that will break across her face. She wants to help Rosanna, not me. She'll hate me for being here, for keeping Rosanna from her. *Not yet*, I think. *I'll start slow.*

"I wanted to apologize for the other night," I say. "For my behav-ior. I shouldn't have been drinking. I thought that I could just have one glass of wine, but I'm an addict, it doesn't work like that. I should have known better, and I'm sorry."

Marie gives me a strange look. "Really?" She says, "I thought you were fine. I mean, it was sort of odd that you left with Leo and Elea-nor, I'll give you that, I didn't even know you guys were friends, but otherwise you were in peak form. Beau was totally charmed by you, by the way. He's been texting me all morning about how he wants to cast you in that cockamamie *Waiting for Godot* project he's been workshopping. God knows where he's getting the funding."

"So you didn't think I was behaving strangely?"

"Not really," she says. "Is that what this is about? Honestly, Rosanna, those parties are so exhausting that I don't think I'd notice if Edward started making out with Beau. I'm so sorry you feel badly about your drinking. You know I support your sobriety. You'll let me know if there's anything I can do to help, right? Like we have some really nice sparkling waters in the fridge, you should have asked for one. But as far as I'm concerned, it was fine, honestly. You were fine. We're good."

So Marie hadn't noticed. Marie, who is supposed to know Rosanna better than anyone else in the world, who is supposed to be attuned to her every quirk and minor shift in personality, her confidante, her best friend, the woman who has known her nearly as long as she's been alive, hadn't noticed a thing. Hadn't even noticed that her birthmark was missing.

"Oh," I say. "Okay, that's good. I'm glad."

My voice is thin and shaky. Marie looks at me with concern. "Is that all you wanted to know?" she asks. "Is everything okay?"

I remember Eleanor's face when she looked at Leo. How easy it was to persuade everyone he was crazy. Because what he was saying was impossible. What he was saying could never be true. And I realize what I've done. What can I say to Marie in this moment? That I am not the woman whose face I wear? The woman who knows everything about her? Whose eyes she looks into with recognition, love? No, what I have to tell her is impossible. The only way is for her to guess. She'll never believe the truth if she hears it from my lying mouth.

"Do you ever feel like you're not yourself?" I ask.

My throat is so tight I can barely squeeze the words out, like eking the last bits of toothpaste from an empty tube. Everything within me slows. Marie looks into my eyes with such compassionate understanding, and I think it's over. Thank god, it's over. She will recognize me. I will no longer be alone. She will share my burden or she will destroy me. At least I will no longer be under Max's control. There she is, so close, so ordinary looking, the end of my life, arrived. She looks into my eyes. I into hers. I prepare to confess all the horrible things I've done, the lies I've told. The hurt I've caused Rosanna.

"I know the feeling," she says.

She looks out the window to the street, where a family of tourists stands in the middle of the road, smiling at someone we cannot see. I feel a tremendous heaviness inside me, my heart bruised and aching, as tender as an overripe peach. I can feel Rosanna weighing down my body, my blood heavy with her blood, twice as warm. I am not alone. I have never been alone, not this whole time. That's what Max has forgotten.

"Sometimes it's hard being Rosanna Feld," I say.

Marie looks at me with a quickness that is almost like flinching, an emotion I cannot read flickering as quickly as a passing shadow across her face. I want her to see me. I want her to take my hands in hers, to tell me she understands. She knows exactly how hard it is. She's here to help me survive.

"That's exactly it," she says, "the whole charade. You're never allowed to just be another person, to live. To just be Rosanna, a woman with her own wants and needs and hurts. I felt that way at my party, too. Everyone looking at me like I was this perfect hostess with no needs of my own. And it's, like, maybe I don't care about your stupid sitcom. Maybe I don't care about your feelings. I could go weeks without a single person asking me a question—well, nobody but my therapist, and I pay her. Even my family seems to see me as an imperfect reflection of my persona, this endlessly selfless earth mama, but I have needs, too, you know. You're the only person who ever asks me questions like that. Who thinks about the way I might be hurting, too. I'm so glad you're back. Sometimes I think you're the only person who really understands me."

Inside me, something cracks. And I know I can't tell her. "I'm glad you feel that way," I say, my voice pressed tight with tears. "I do understand you. I always have."

Marie, misunderstanding, takes my hands in hers and smiles.

She is doing the best she can, I know that, but still, a quick little jolt of anger passes through me. I had thought . . . what? That this could all be over? That she would look at me and know? That Marie somehow, self-involved and still a little angry at her more successful friend for leaving her alone for so long, could save me from the trap I have wandered into, willingly, with open eyes? No. She can't. It is not, it has never been, as simple as that.

Suddenly my body feels so light, so insubstantial that I think I might float away. Marie sits silent beside me. Just another woman. Another person chained to the real world who won't believe a word I say. I realize in that moment how hopelessly alone Rosanna must feel. Marie doesn't really know her. Max is too self-involved to be counted on. I am all she has. And she is all I have, too. The only person who can save me is Rosanna. She is the only person with enough power to save us both. Outside, the tourists have finished taking their picture. They walk back toward us, toward the curb, where my car, with Max inside it, waits, engine idling in the twilight, to take me home.

21

*M*ax leaves me alone in the apartment.

"I won't be gone long, darling," he says. "I promise. There are a few loose ends I need to tie up, some things I need to get for us. And then I'll be back to stay. We'll never be apart again."

"Don't take long," I say. "I miss you every second you're gone."

He likes this. He pulls me close and kisses me, just once, on the forehead.

"I'll come back as soon as I can," he says. "Don't worry. And then you and I will sit down and talk about what comes next."

He kisses me once more before he leaves. His lips are soft and warm, his body yielding. I think for a moment that he trusts me, that maybe he'll leave the door unlocked. But when he closes it, the lock clicks with a pronounced certainty, the bolt sliding tight.

I sit by the window for a long time. Everything in my body is buzzing, weighed down by panic. I can hear a little voice whispering at the back of my brain telling me to get up, pack a bag, make plans. But even the smallest movement seems exhausting. I remember reading once about how difficult it is to build machines that move like humans do. There are so many infinities of choice in our every gesture, in the way we straighten and bend our muscles in a particular sequence, adjusting our balance, our gait. The complexity of each motion is paralyzing when we become conscious of it. I feel it now. I am aware of every small movement. Of the impossibility of motion. I am trapped in the body they have created for me, this beautiful, terrible machine. There is nothing I can do. No one is coming for me, not tonight. Not ever. Slowly the panic fades, a terrible numbness settling over me like snow.

I turn to the magazines, searching again for clues. Rosanna has always stood by me there. Maybe she will come through for me again now. But the words seem to slide, shifting and blurring, making me seasick. I cannot bring myself to look at Rosanna's face directly. There is something uncanny about her expression; it is impossible to tell if she is laughing or screaming. Her red lips are always so wide that it is as if she is about to swallow me up. I force myself to focus on her hands, shift my own to mirror them, feeling the heat of an invisible coffee cup, clinching tight the handle of a heavy purse, her hands, my hands, ours. The idea of our two bodies calms me. Just as long as I don't have to look at her face, the imperfect mirroring, like catching an unexpected glimpse of yourself in a darkened window, that minute lag. Something that looks like you, is almost you, almost, but not quite.

And then I realize something terrible. It isn't her face at all. It's me. It's all me. I flip through the stack to make sure, scrutinizing every image. Every photo is an image of a day that I have lived, of my body in places I have gone with Max or at Max's prompting—all me, all mine, my own, my movements, my decisions, my flaws. The world is empty of Rosanna. She has left no sign of herself behind. It is my face, my own face, that nauseates me. It is my own face I am unable to bring myself to see. I think of that dark, abandoned-looking house. Maybe there was no breakdown. Maybe Max has done to her what he wants to do to me. Maybe she's trapped there, lonely, scared. And I helped him do it. I stand up too quickly, knocking the magazines to the floor. How has no one noticed? How is it possible that no one has noticed my disgusting imperfections, my flaws? No one but Leo. And everyone thinks that Leo is crazy. I want to step on the magazines, to destroy them, to tear through their cheap bright pages with my lips and teeth, I want, what I want is to consume them, to take them into myself, absorb them, my image, her face.

I get down on my knees, close to the floor. I pick up each magazine carefully, lifting with the tips of my fingers, gentle. It's important that I do not damage any part of her but that false face. I fan them out in a protective circle, sitting at the center, feeling the energy coming off them in steady waves, a powerful undertow. On the table above me is a sharp little paring knife. I had been using it, a moment before, to slice a small red pear onto a small blue plate. Now I open each magazine to the pages where Rosanna's face should be. Gently, meticulously, I slice out the faces with perfect jabbing cuts, removing them from her body. I want to leave the faces empty so there will be a space for her when she comes back into the world with me. When the time comes for her to be reborn and my flawed face becomes her own. I sit still for a long time, the faces held tight in my clenched hands. I can feel the paper softening, the ink starting to bleed, the edges of the images melting into my skin. Then slowly, deliberately, I put them into my mouth.

At first it is difficult. The paper is stiff and refuses to buckle, coating my tongue with something thick and toxic tasting. But it gets easier. The edges of the faces begin to soften and collapse into bitter paste. I can slide each one in between my lips tenderly, like communion, like a kiss, until finally I hold them all in my mouth, sanding their sharp edges down with my tongue, blanketing them in the nauseating rise and swell of spit, some of which trickles from the corners of my lips, black, I see, when I use the back of my hand to wipe it away. I chew and chew until they collapse into liquid, something like melted plastic, bile. I want desperately to spit them out. But I don't. I close my eyes. I force myself to swallow. The ink drips sticky down my throat. With it comes a new lightness. I wonder if Rosanna, wherever she is, can feel it, too. I picture her alone, sitting in the big white kitchen of that big white house, so close to where I sit, flipping through the same stack of magazines, considering the imperfect lines of my face. As she watches, it shifts, just a little, and transforms into her own. She sees herself restored. Whole again. I think of all the women across the country, in kitchens and bathrooms and waiting rooms, on airplanes and in the back rows of classrooms, at a stoplight behind the wheels of their cars, in line at the grocery store, reading these magazines. I think of all of them experiencing the same quick moment of transition, my face melting into Rosanna's. Isn't she beautiful, they will say to themselves. Isn't she just the most perfect thing?

I stand. I stretch. I am no longer dizzy. I feel a new solidity, an assurance that I haven't felt in a long time. I am tied to this body. No power on earth can erase me. I gather the magazines into a neat stack. I place them on the table, my hands steady. I check my teeth, lightly streaked with black ink, in the reflection in the window. I run my tongue across them until they shine clean. I look down the canyon in the direction of Rosanna's house. If I stand on the roof of my building, I might be able to see all the way to her garden, the broken mirror glint of her swimming pool. If she looks up, she will see me, too, her shadow, her reflection, close enough to touch. I feel something quiet click into place. Rosanna is with me now. I know what it is I have to do.

I take three of my sleeping pills and crush them to powder with the flat back of a spoon. I mix them with a splash of water until they dissolve into runny paste. I take a Diet Coke from the fridge and keep it ready on the windowsill, next to the glass. I pick up one of the faceless magazines, pretend to read. I sit back down. I wait for Max.

Loneliness presses tight around me, a confining embrace. The sun sets, the parrots settling, chattering to one another, rustling their wings. No cars pass up the hill. And even if one did, if I ran down into the street, if I got one to stop for me, somehow, what would I say? Below me, the city's grid switches on, all those lights down all those boulevards going bright at the exact same instant, everything coordinated, serene. In the stagnant little reflecting pool at the courtyard's center, the moon is rising, creeping, wide and flat and white, a tooth in a smiling, faceless mouth. Rosanna is in her house, in her bed, so close, the thrum of her growing stronger inside me. She needs me as much as I need her. More. She is out there, as alone as I am. I cannot give her up. That is the only thing I know, that I am all Rosanna has in the world, and she is all I have. We are, to each other, the only thing. I can feel her clamoring to speak, clawing at my throat. I open my mouth so her words can come out. *What?* I think. *What is it that you want to tell me?* And then a sound. The bolt turning. A light knock on the door. He has never knocked before. I open the can of soda, pour it into the glass. A little stir is enough to lift the powder up and distribute it farther, the bubbles agitating it into a finer and more invisible stream, the bitterness of artificial sweetener masking that deeper bitter taste. I take a drop on my own tongue just to make sure, but it tastes the same it always does, chemical, too sweet.

"Come in, darling," I say. "I'm so glad you're back."

The door opens. Max comes in. He is carrying another bouquet of flowers, large red roses drooping heavy on their stems. I've left the old flowers in a pile on the kitchen counter, and their scent, the light green of new rot, mixes with the freshness of the new flowers. The room smells like that botanical garden we visited together long ago. I notice as I take them from him that they have been stripped of thorns. Is this for Max's protection or my own?

"I'm sorry it took so long," he says.

"No no," I say, "it's fine. We have so much time for each other now, what's a few hours? Here, come sit. Have a drink with me."

My voice is soft, Rosanna sweet. I raise my own glass toward him. I take his hand in mine. I think of that day in the garden, when we were, for once, just two people trying their best. I am sorry it can't be that way forever. If I had her name, really had it, had her money and her power, maybe he could belong to me as much as he wants me to belong to him. But not like this. Never like this.

Max, trusting, lifts his glass. "What are we drinking to?" he asks.

"The future," I say. "Everything. Forever."

He smiles at me. He drinks.

It doesn't take long for the pills to kick in. Max starts to droop, his head nodding as heavy as the flowers, and I lie down beside him as he drops off into a sleep so deep he barely seems to breathe. I pull the blankets up over him, tuck him in tight. The way he used to when he drugged me. I kiss him on his forehead.

"Sweet dreams," I say.

I lace Rosanna's shoes with shaking hands. I walk through the unlocked door. I stand out front for a moment, waiting, the desert air cold against my skin. I can feel the pulse of the house inside me, Rosanna reaching toward me down the hill. I close my eyes. I step into the street. I walk.

The house is where I left it. I know I shouldn't be surprised by this—it's a house, just an ordinary house, it can't get up and move—but I am. There was some part of me that was sure it would be gone, the way the enchanted castle in fairy tales disappears with the dawn. Of course it's still nighttime; maybe that is the secret to finding my way. It's still nighttime, and the house is still there. On the gravel in front of me, a dark brown line. Blood, my blood. The sign I left. No one has opened the gate since then. No one has come in or out. Rosanna hasn't gone anywhere. She is inside, waiting for me.

The metal feels warmer than I remember, pliant. Alive. I hold myself against it, leaning on it with my weight, and then I step into the dip of a wrought-iron curl, lifting my weight up and over the top. A long moment in the air, landing with a soft crunch on the other side. I kick the gravel with my feet to cover up the line of blood. I feel the coiled snake of my necklace burning against my throat. I take it in my hand and pull until the chain breaks. With the tips of my fingers I scratch a deep hollow into the soil, dropping in the broken chain, covering it with blood-spattered gravel. Someone has been taking care of the garden. It looks like it does in the footage, the lawn cut close, the flower beds trimmed, an elegantly tangled swatch of color, snapdragons, daylily, milkweed. Even the gravel driveway is perfectly raked. No signs of tire tracks or feet.

Nothing messy. Nothing alive. I try to walk soft across it, leave the stones undisturbed, but it's impossible. My feet sink deep, the gravel making loud noises, a crack like breaking bones. The night leans close to hear, silent around me.

At the door, I hesitate. The porch light is off, and the shadows, gathering close on the unlit porch, pull my heart into my throat. I try the knob. It turns in my hand, easy. The door is unlocked. I wonder if I should wait to be found, if I am intrusive, rude. No. There should be no barriers between us. I am not a guest here. She has left the door unlocked for me. I am coming home. I hold my breath. I push. I watch the door swing open, away from me into the deeper darkness of the hall.

Inside, everything is coated in a thick layer of dust. I remember the way my apartment was when I found it, how Rosanna had let the filth of passing time slowly gather there, too, how I had to clean, how I will clean here, help her, the two of us, taking care of our house. I take small steps, silent, the click of my hard shoes muffled by the carpet of filth covering the hardwood floors. I feel so loose in my body that this added lack of stimulus, this disappearance into total sensory invisibility, unnerves me. I turn in the darkness. "Hello?" I say, mostly just to make a sound, to shatter the dead perfection of that silent place. But there is only silence in response. If anyone is waiting for me, they will wait a little longer. Tree branches press close against the windows. Bony fingers on bony hands. The house holds its breath. I walk quiet, the sharp light of the full moon painful on my skin.

The rooms are all where I think they will be. Everything is the same but strange somehow, the proportions wrong, spaces arranged in ways I don't expect, narrow corners, strange turns in the hallways, curves in the walls, unexpected steps leading up and down, all of it silent, empty, dead. A familiar place remembered in a dream. In the kitchen, a fruit bowl is stacked with oranges so old they have collapsed in on themselves. I pick one up and turn it over in my hand, feel the powdery crunch of mold as it turns to dust. In the living room the couches are covered in sheets. A book lying flat on the coffee table, its title erased by dust, the same mix of soot, pollen, dirt, dead skin, Rosanna's skin, her hair, everywhere. Dead flowers in a vase. Relics in an abandoned shrine.

In the backyard the pristine pool where Rosanna floated, floats, shines murky and green, an emerald, a boulder crusted with moss, the water scummed thick and opaque in the vague light of the moon. Dark shapes swim beneath the still surface. The fruit trees reach their heavy branches toward the ground, aching with citrus, oranges and lemons and limes like swollen boils, rotting on the branches, heavy with alien life. The grass here is overgrown. I kneel down and rustle my hands though it to make sure nothing is hiding there. I want to lie down and be still, still, until it grows up over me and swallows me up and I am absorbed by the roots, the land, a part of Rosanna's garden. But she is somewhere inside, waiting for me. I know it. The thrum grows stronger and stronger. Now there is nowhere left to go but up.

At the bottom of the stairs I wait, listening. Nothing. Nothing, still. The only movement comes from the neighbors' houses, bright across the canyon with their automatic backyard lights, looking at me, winking on as I climb, as though they can sense my movements through the narrow yellow windows of the turret. The gutter spouts outside are shouting, there is someone here who does not belong. The moon shines bright like water on water, the empty reflection of the pool. Closing my eyes, I feel my way up the stairs. My palms tingle against the air as if I am parting it with my body, making my way through some invisible amniotic fluid. If Rosanna is waiting, I will drop my hands and show myself to her suddenly, a mirror rising from the darkness. But it is quiet at the top, even more quiet than it was downstairs, because down there all I could hear was nothing and here it is something again, breath, heart, the creak of footsteps and bones, my body reasserting itself. *It will all be over soon*, I think. Soon Rosanna will know the truth.

I try every door along the hallway.

Every door is locked.

And then I come to the end.

Rosanna's room.

. . .

I wait at the door. I wait at the door for a long time, unwilling to go forward without some indication, some sign. There is a sense of holiness here, transgression. My hand rests softly on the wood. I am feeling for a pulse. I am feeling my way toward her, trying to sense what she is doing there, waiting, as she must be waiting, as I know she is waiting for me, in the darkness on the other side. But everything is still. I take one deep breath. Another. On the other side of the door, I can see Rosanna standing from the full white pillows of her full white bed, rising to embrace me. Her arms are open. There is a smile on her face, full of such profound love, such heartbreaking gentleness. Home. The doorknob warms, pulses as though someone is turning it from the other side, pulling on my hand so that without my making a choice, without any volition of my own, the knob turns and the door swings open and I see what is waiting for me inside.

The lamp on the bedside table is switched on, the light soft and golden. Warm. This is the warmth I was feeling my way toward. Rosanna has stepped out for a moment. She has left the light on for me. I wonder why I couldn't see it from the street and realize that this is the back of the house, not the front, that I had it all wrong. But it's okay now. I'll learn. Rosanna will teach me. There is a hairbrush on the vanity table with a few strands of hair in it, glinting in the light of the lamp. There is a carafe of water on the bedside table, two little yellow pills in a little white dish, one of the clothbound books of poems Max is so fond of buying her, a remote. Rosanna's nightgown is spread out on the bed—white, silk, soft. Light is spilling from everything in the room, the room itself alive, beating with a living pulse. I can't bring my old things with me here. I must enter a supplicant, naked, pure. I understand now why Max insisted on taking my old clothes away. I strip off my muddy shoes, the thick skin of my damp jeans. I throw them as far from my body as I can, so they are hidden by the darkness of the hall. I cross into the warm light of Rosanna's room. I sit at the vanity and brush my hair smooth, my face shimmering into life in the glass,

Rosanna's face looking back at me. I look into my eyes and know that I am perfect. There is no other place in the world for me. It has been a long night. It is good to be home. The nightgown is smooth against my bare skin, cold, like stepping into the icy water of the swimming pool outside. I take my pills. I get into my bed, pull the clammy sheets tight against my skin. On the wall in front of the bed there is a television. A little black box in front of it, lit up. I pick up the remote. I press play.

At first the tape seems ordinary. Like any of the other videos. For a moment I am not sure that I haven't seen it before, Rosanna getting dressed, the camera in the same place it always is, hidden in the darkness behind the mirror, her image clouded a little, dreamlike with the intervention of two-way glass, Rosanna's focused expression as she puts on her makeup swimming in and out of view. But on this tape, the room is empty, her station at the vanity abandoned. There is a long shot of the curtain, closed in front of the window, shifting slightly in what must be, judging from the quality of light, a night breeze. There are no sounds from the world outside. Not the wind. Not a car, passing on its way up the hill from the highway. No night bird's cry. After a long time, Rosanna switches on the light.

She walks to the window. Pulls back the curtain. If darkness can flood, then the room is flooded with darkness. I see the silhouette of her, hair ruffling in the breeze, as though she is fraying, slowly coming apart. I think of the way Max looked earlier, of their two bodies fading at the edges, the separation between them melting away. I feel something almost like hope. On the screen, there is the quiet click of a lighter, flame, lingering as she stands there looking out at nothing. She turns back into the room and begins walking, back and forth, back and forth, measuring the space they have built to hold her. I feel a little pop of recognition. I have walked like that. I have felt that way. At the mirror she grinds the cigarette out on the glass surface of the table. There are people hired to clean up after her. She is not afraid to make a mess. She looks into her own eyes, fierce, searching. She touches her face, pulls at her slack skin as though it is a mask she is unable to take off. She leans forward. She looks closer. She reaches out her two strong arms and wrenches the mirror off its base, dropping it to the cream carpet, where it lands with a muted thump, and suddenly she is holding the camera in her hands. Holding me. She looks at me with blank wonder, as if I am an object from another world. It is so close to the way I imagined it that tears well up and wash hot down my face. She is looking right into my eyes. The image twists and shakes as she turns the camera over, clicking off a switch, the world before me going black.

When it switches on again, some time has passed. Rosanna sits in front of me in her makeup chair, her hair combed, her makeup painted on. She looks younger. More alive.

"So this is interesting," she says. "This is an interesting discovery. Somebody has been watching me. And I know who it is. I think we should see what he has to say for himself, don't you?"

Down the narrow stairs again, the round eye of the foyer, out into the kitchen, where a man sits with his back to the camera. I can see the Hollywood Sign through the wall of windows, all lit up with spotlights, pale and blank against the tangle of the hill. The sound of helicopters drifts through the open frame, seeming to bounce against the low-hanging matte painting of the sky, bruised that pale Los Angeles nighttime purple, light from the traffic or a wildfire somewhere bouncing back at us, trapped reverberating beneath the clouds.

"Hello, Max," Rosanna says.

Max turns slowly. He looks at the camera for a long time. He looks through the camera at me. He looks tired. More tired even than he has looked of late. Circles under his eyes, hollow. Wrinkled, somehow, wilted, as though he has been drained of himself, tapped like the sap of a sweet-sapped tree. His face is a closed door. It is the first time I have seen him on tape. He is always around me, seems to know everything there is to know, and yet Rosanna never refers to him at all. It is as if, for her, he doesn't exist. Now he comes into being, and I see him as she sees him. Fragile. Helpless. Small. A person she does not take seriously. Someone to be pitied, rather than feared.

"Someone has done a very bad thing," says Rosanna. "And, Maxie, I'm sorry to say I think it was you."

Her voice sounds strange. Slurred. My body is beginning to feel loose, bendy rubber at the joints, the images in front of me taking on a haloed blur, as if filmed through a scrim of Vaseline. I wonder if Rosanna, too, has taken her pills. On-screen Max shakes his head.

"I wouldn't," he says.

He is pleading. It is almost embarrassing, how vulnerable he is. The raw need in his voice. I am watching something deeply private, something he would never want me to see. But hasn't he done the same thing to me? Now it's my turn to watch. My turn to know.

"I wouldn't do anything wrong," he says. "You know that. I would never do anything without thinking of you, Rosanna. Your needs. Everything I do is for you."

I can see the way he is looking at, trying not to look at, the camera, edgy. He stands, and standing up, he is taller than her. She is so small. As small as me. Somehow this is a shock.

"I don't believe you," she says. "You can't fool me anymore into thinking you're selfless. That you're good, sweet, nice old Max who thinks only of my happiness because he just loves me so much. You do love me, don't you? Or you think that you do."

"I love you," he says. "I promise."

He steps forward, reaching for her. She moves back, evading him. Still, she does not seem frightened. I would be frightened, if I were her. But all she knows is her own power over him. She still thinks he can't hurt her. I envy her this certainty.

"No you don't," she says. "You don't even know me. It's just that you don't have anyone else. No friends, as far as I can tell, no family. You've spent years silently in front of me, all those holidays sitting in cars outside parties waiting for me to be ready to go home, those days off when you answered the phone on its first ring. You were always there. You practically lived here, on that sad little cot in the guesthouse, and when I kept having all those nightmares, you came inside and slept at the foot of my bed like a dog. You never asked me for a thing. I thought it was because I was so great. That there was some goodness inside me you could see. Something worth protecting. Maybe everyone else was wrong. Maybe there was something in me worth loving, after all. But now I realize that I was a hobby. Some strange obsession. Something to take up your time. Because you don't have anything else."

"No," he says, his voice urgent, "I'm sorry I filmed you, but I did it because I care for you so much. I really do. You are the only thing in the world to me. Please, Rosanna, you have to believe me."

She shakes her head. "You did it because you wanted to solve me. To figure out everything I didn't want you to know. So congratulations are in order, I suppose. You did it. You cracked the code. You know everything there is to know. Of course you don't love me. Nobody does. And I don't blame you. I don't love you, either. I don't care about you at all. I don't care about anyone. I need you. *Needed* you. That's it. But I don't care about you. I'm a monster. We both know that."

He keeps his distance this time, looking smaller and smaller until there is nothing left but clothes, a child trying on his father's suit. He finally looks away from her, through the glass toward the cold white blur of the sign across the canyon.

"You're not a monster," says Max. "You're wonderful. You're Rosanna. No one has ever been as wonderful as you."

The helicopter chop grows louder. Rosanna is the one to move toward him now. Max is the one to move away.

"That's what you want to think," she says. "You've been working so hard to believe it. What other choice do you have? And now this."

She holds the camera toward him, an offering.

"This camera. This hidden camera you've been filming me with. My most private moments, everything. I think there must be more of them. I think there must be cameras all over this house. I know you, Max. You're thorough. I need you to show me where they are. And then I need you to leave. Forever."

He looks back at her again. His eyes are deep and wet and angry.

"I just wanted to know you," he says. "That's all. I don't think there's any harm in that."

She sighs. She puts the camera down on the edge of the counter, and I can see the muscles moving under her tight dress, her body articulating itself into parts as she gets closer to him, moving with terrible slowness, like something stalking, hiding in the high grass.

"Everyone wants to know me," she says. "But you haven't come closer than anyone else. You just have more raw data. That doesn't mean a thing. You're not special. There's nothing special about you. The only thing different about you, Max, is that you have no life to distract you from this pitiful mission of yours—to collect me, to discover the truth. But you've failed. Because the truth is this: there isn't anything to know. There is no great hidden secret for you to discover. Just a sad, shallow woman who hates you. Almost as much as she hates herself."

"Please," he says, "Rosanna."

"No," she says. "It's all been a mistake. I realize that now. Show me where the cameras are. Show me all the footage. And leave. I never want to see you again. You can have it all back when I'm dead. You can have everything. Maybe you can make something worthwhile out of it all. I certainly can't."

There is a long silence. Outside, the sound of helicopter seems to build, gathering like a storm, searchlights sweeping through the burned-out hollows of the hillside, looking, looking.

"I'll miss you," says Max.

"Oh, Maxie," says Rosanna, "I know. Of course you will. I won't miss you at all."

The camera goes dark.

Rosanna lies still in her bed at the center of the room. I recognize Max's gait now, in the way the footage moves, the measured rhythm of his steps as he crosses the threshold. If only he had filmed her with a handheld camera all along. I would have known the whole time.

"I'm sorry," he says. "I know I shouldn't come have come back here, I know you said not to, but I wanted to give you this last—"

And he breaks off, seeing her lie there impossibly still, seeing what I saw before him, what he didn't want to see, the bright orange pile of empty prescription bottles, the tipped-over bottle of white wine. I recognize the label, one of Rosanna's favorites, a flinty chenin blanc. I can taste it in my mouth, the flatness, wet stone and something more bitter, a chemical ache burning my throat, nothing but the best, and I know what he doesn't as he leans forward and shakes her, knew it, I think, from the moment I walked into this room and saw the faint ghost of the stain on the carpet beside the bed. Even through the screen, I can feel the dead heaviness of the air in that room, how it is thoroughly, utterly still. The way the air is still now. Nothing left alive. Rosanna no longer lives in that body. That body no longer controls her career, her decisions, her relationships, her bank account, Max. This body does. This body with her face.

"Rosanna?" Max says.

Silence. And then he is screaming and screaming and screaming, and he drops the camera onto the bed and I hear a sound like choking, he is trying to breathe life back into her, but it is too late, too late, even as he rushes to the window, trying to pull the night air into her body, carrying her body like it is something precious, her bones of a little bird, her hair spilling like water dark down over his arms. His body bulk darkens the window, which, as he stands there, holding her, weeping, this monster, my monster, cradling her like a baby, floods briefly with the light from a passing helicopter, dark shadows running off both their bodies. *A halo*, I think, *a portal, opening to carry her to the world beyond.* There is gentleness in the way he moves now, as he reaches toward her, touches her face, and she doesn't flinch for once, I think, I can feel him thinking, for once she lets him touch her, gentleness as they stand together and the camera is knocked onto the floor, and all I can see is their feet poised close like they are about to begin a waltz, and then she is gone, gone, lifted up, her feet rising out of frame like she is flying, a sound like a gasp, a sigh, a rush of his breath leaving her body. The frame is bright again, a beat, and silence, the dark silence of an empty room. I can see the shadows of Max's feet alone.

The camera clicks back on. Now it is close to the grass, a blur of living green. Rosanna's lawn, clipped close here, neat, a velvet expanse beyond the pool, sloping into the infinite distance. The sky is pink. The sun is rising. I can see a man walking away from me toward the house. I can see the slope of his shoulders, the hesitation in his walk. The door swings shut behind him. He is inside for a long time. The light on the blank white face of the house goes from gray to pink to the pale bleached yellow of bad teeth. The door opens. The man comes out. He is not alone. He is carrying a woman over his shoulder. I can see the clean white bottoms of her feet, shining in the rising sun. She is dressed beautifully, all in white, a long silk shift like the one I am wearing now, warming against my living skin. The water in the pool is dark and still. A black eye, looking up. He walks to the edge of the water. He shifts her body over his shoulder so he is holding her in his arms now, like a baby, a bride, looking into her face with something like conviction, a man performing a baptism, a miracle. Tears stream silent down his face. The world is silent around him. He descends, the fabric of his pants turning dark as the water, clean still, clear, eats him up. He walks until it reaches his waist, his arms where he carries her, and she begins to float. There is a hesitation, a beat when he cannot bring himself to let her go, and then his arms open. She stays suspended on the water, until slowly it seeps heavy into her hair, her dress, and she begins to sink down below the surface, the water rippling around her, gentle, and then still. Closing around her body. Amniotic. The man stands in the dark water, looking right out at me, so still, his eye on the eye of the camera, mine. I feel something coming into me. New life. The screen blinks black. And then downstairs, I hear a splash. Something is emerging from the green scabbed pool. One of those dark shapes is finding the light. I hear a creak. A door is opening. Something, someone is coming. Rosanna doesn't need her old body anymore. She needs this body. She needs me. For months and months, I have been preparing. I am ready for her to come. I pull the white sheets up over my face like a shroud, look out into the soft white nothing. I close my eyes. I wait.

. . .

When you open your eyes, you find yourself alone. You are never alone, but you are alone now, and you watch yourself as you rise from the water and stand in the middle of the grass, overgrown, silver and black in the light of the full moon like the surface of some strange planet. You stand there for a long time, light prickling your skin, your skin prickling with water, and you can feel your neighbors watching at the windows, waiting, some distant force like a physical pressure, a push, and, you smile and smile and smile up at the distant hillside, and there is always someone watching, and you are never alone, and *Here I am*, you think, "Here I am," you say, out loud, "I'm here," your own voice unfamiliar somehow. It has been a while. It has been a very long time since you spoke. The crabgrass pricks the bottoms of your feet. Your feet are soft from swimming. You have spent a long time in the water. At the bottom of the garden, behind you, you can see the mirror of the swimming pool wrinkling, small whispers where you came out of the water and you are both here and not here, in your body and out of your body, looking up at the purple night and down, down, at yourself standing in the distance, so tiny, small, and fragile that looking at yourself you are filled with an unbearable tenderness—there you are, all of you, every inch perfect, newborn. You can hear the small noises the water makes rippling itself closed. Soon it will be perfectly flat. There will be no sign you were ever there at all.

The house is dark around you, but you know where to go, the familiar steps smooth in the warm worn wood, and you're not afraid of splinters, of knocking against things in the dark. You don't have a body to harm. Your body is waiting for you upstairs, silent and still in that golden room, waiting for you to draw your first breath. You know this house and this house knows you, no one loves you like this house does, do they, the empty dark that has grown and grown to hold you safe, a den, a womb, the insides of a tortoise's shell, and you run your hand down the smooth vine of the banister, wood sleek slippery, the back of a snake sliding through dark water, rising to meet your hand, to guide you, through the hallway now, the light thick and blue and dense close-pressed against you, so cool, deeply cold, a silent nook at the bottom of a dark sea, to the lit open door at the end, where you find yourself waiting in your bed. You have been there all along. You slide inside yourself and pull the sheets around you, close. You fall into a deep, dreamless sleep.

I listen to the footsteps coming up the stairs. I listen to the pause at the door, the slow steps into the room, scared. But there is nothing to be afraid of. Someone pulls the sheet off my face. His own face, leaning over, so close to mine, is wet and vulnerable, the face of a child who has fallen, who keeps falling, who is waiting for help, bravely deciding he will not cry. I know this though my eyes are closed. He turns my left arm over, his fingers lingering on the wrist, and I hear him gasp at the warmth of me. Somewhere deep inside, I feel a fist unclenching. Whatever it is holding, I let go. There is something half remembered there, some other name, the contours of a profile glimpsed in a dark mirror, a bad dream disappearing back into the muddy depths of sleep. I feel the memory lighten, fuzz, fade. Disappear. I open my eyes. I breathe in. The air is brand-new in my lungs.

"Darling," I say, and he crumbles. I open my arms. The weight of him is familiar, strange.

"Rosanna," he says, his voice breaking in the middle. "Rosanna," he tries again, a sob, a promise, a prayer. "Rosanna," he says. "Rosanna."

Acknowledgments

It's impossible for me to convey how grateful I am to the incomparable Jennifer Jackson, my editor, for her boundless enthusiasm, her thorough and thoughtful notes, and talking me out of paying forty dollars to go to the Trolls Experience. And none of this would even be happening without Molly Atlas, the amazing, the steadfast, who believed in this weird little book and this weird little gal from day one, thank you. I owe a tremendous debt of gratitude to my teachers, Karen Russell, David Gates, T. Geronimo Johnson, Doug Dorst, Susan Morrison, Rebecca Bell Metereau, Tom Grimes, Lauren Elkin, Martin Reichart, and Eugene Osatachevski. To Ivy Pochoda, my mentor, my friend, for showing me how to be the most amazing and supportive member of a literary community, and Jennifer duBois, for being the most amazing and insightful reader, advisor, and Uzbek lunch companion. To Maria Bustillos, for hosting the best dinner parties and writing a million letters of recommendation. Thank you to all the attendees of the BAE Systems reading series, for reminding me of the joy of creativity and looking so damn good in my dresses, especially Clare Murray and the chickens, Louisa, Hildegarde, and our beloved Sandwiches. To my friends and readers, Marilyse Figueroa, Jeff Karr, Eddie Mathis, for your love and letters. To Maytal Eyal and Cleo Elfonte, for letting me be their human audiobook. To Erin Salada, commute companion, empty house dance party kween, and Molly Moltzen, president and founder of the Adventure Club. Vlad Beronja and Ellicott Pacheco, for the day trips. To Megan Forbes and Roja Chamankar, for the beautiful translations we worked on together. To Robert Meador, for introducing me to the fine art of American masculinity via cage fighting and being my friend. To Caroline Compton, for taking me in and introducing me to the fine art of the soap opera. To Patricia and Eva Munoz, for keeping me in groceries while I wrote the early drafts of this book; Jessi Cape, editrix extraordinaire, for always supporting and believing in me; and Brandon Watson, for taking a chance on a stranger who emailed you her column idea. To the Casablancas family, Juliet, Julian, Cal, and Zephyr, for your enthusiasm and love and (in Zephyr's case) napping so I could edit. To the Babitz sisters, Eve and Mirandy, for being my first models of life as a bohemian creative lady. Most of all, to my family, my parents, Kent and Nancy, for your constant love and support; my siblings, Lauren and Jackson, for making up stories with me on long road trips; Kate and Michael and Sophie, Lauren and Adam and Daniel, Carolyn and David, Nanaw and L-Dog, Grandma Mary, and especially, my grandfather Joseph Beyda, for believing in me, always, unconditionally, and letting me write in all your houses. Most of all, to Hari, love of my life, light of my soul, for being the best listener and best reader and best roommate and the best person I know. My life is so much better with you in it.